C000134802

# The WARS of MATT TOWER – BOOK 1

## The Story of Augusta's Fighter Ace

# PALADIN

## ENGLAND 1944–45

A historical romance novel by

# CHARLES W. BOWEN

PALADIN
The Story of Augusta's Fighter Ace—The WARS of MATT TOWER – Book 1

Copyright © 2022 by Charles W. Bowen

All rights reserved. No part of this publication or e-publication may be reproduced, distributed or transmitted in any form by any means including photocopying, recording or other electronic or mechanical methods without prior written permission from the author, except in the case of brief quotations embodied in reviews and certain other non-commercial uses permitted by copyright law. For permission requests, please contact the author.

Editing and project management by David Stacks
Stacks Editing
Augusta, Georgia USA
https://stacksediting.com

Cover design and interior design by Steven Plummer
SP Book Design
Fort Myers, Florida USA
https://spbookdesign.com

Published 2022

ISBN (paperback): 979-8-9860336-9-3
ISBN (hardback): 979-8-9860336-0-0
ISBN (ebook): 979-8-9860336-1-7

For information, contact:
Charles W. Bowen
860 Point Comfort Road
Augusta, GA 30907-9521 USA

Visit the author's website at charlesbowenbooks.com.

# Dedication

It's good to have the coals of one's inspiration fanned when needed. My precious helpmate did just that. Barbara Pruitt took charge of me on a beautiful October Saturday in 1958. With blessed patience she encouraged me and tolerated many interruptions. My heartbreak is that she passed from this life before this book's final period was put in place. This is for you, Sweetheart!

# Contents

# Introduction

*Paladin: The Story of Augusta's Fighter Ace—The Wars of Matt Tower Book 1 i*s based on actual events and people in England, where our story begins, and in Augusta, Georgia USA. The author created this work as a historical romance novel. Thus, the names of certain people, events and institutions have been altered. Literary license has been taken when appropriate.

# Acknowledgements

**E**NGLAND: I AM grateful to many who were active or influential during the World War II era addressed in this novel, and who patiently endured my interviews, some on more than one occasion. Particularly Colonel Glenn E. Duncan, commanding officer of the 353rd Fighter Group; Lieutenant Robert C. "Bob" Strobell, pilot, who tested German jets after World War II; Lieutenant George Donald "Don" Kammer, pilot; Captain Hoyt B. Duke, medical officer; Lieutenant Marie Murray, Army Nurse Corps; Lieutenant Elizabeth C. Grant, Army Nurse Corps; Dr. Graham E. Cross, 353rd Fighter Group historian; Commander Leslie Helms, Royal Navy; Colonel John C. Hurden, British Army; and Vida Hargreaves Davis, First Officer, Women's Royal Naval Service, a lovely South Wales transplant to Augusta.

**353rd Fighter Group**: Several historical works include the 353rd, but its most complete history is in the work of Dr. Graham E. Cross of Suffolk, England. Cross' two tomes—*Jonah's Feet Are Dry: The Experience of the 353rd Fighter Group During World War II* (2001) and *Slybirds: A Photographic Odyssey of the 353rd Fighter Group During the Second World War* (2017)—cover virtually every detail of the 353rd's beginning and combat record with coverage of noted pilots and missions flown. It was this author's pleasure to share information with Graham and contribute material to his work.

**Family**: I'm much indebted to my family, whose love and support proved invaluable as I researched and wrote these books. My wife Barbara, daughter Debbie, and son Greg, as well as other family members, provided special encouragement.

**Editing & Publication:** My sincere appreciation to David Stacks and Gloria Gill, whose editing gifts and talents were wonderfully applied to this work. They straightened up this novel and made me appear quite good in the process. Their investments of time and suggestions regularly fanned my inspiration. Thanks, guys! And Peggy Cheney, who test drove the story line from time to time and kept me thinking, thank you!

# CHAPTER 1

# Coming on Board

THE EAST ANGLIAN Express made good time after turning off the Colchester-Ipswich rail line. Since late 1942 it had faithfully kept the appointed rounds delivering American pilots to England's eastern air bases. Young men, as yet untried, were drawn into a global conflict the consequences of which they could scarcely grasp. By early 1944, the pace had picked up considerably as did the number of airmen.

Early in the war this black, shorter, six-wheeled engine, like so many others, was drafted from a switching terminal for general service, leaving the eight-wheeled heavies for military and industrial work. While slightly slower, this machine had no difficulty tugging along its six coaches. The cushioned brown-leather seating and long glass picture windows offered prewar travel comfort. Their normally dark-cream roofs had been changed to flat black as camouflage at the height of England's blitz. But it took nothing away from the dark-green enamel sides and crisp black trim of these coaches.

Near the end of its run now, the train carried but three of those flyers who, at the Hadleigh junction, bid farewell to comrades in arms destined for other bases in quaint country towns with names the tourist ponders. Wattisham, Martlesham Heath and Leiston, among others, would gain their moment in history, then slip again into quiet anonymity.

Conversation had played out, leaving the three second-lieutenant passengers at leisure as befit their several natures. Gerald Mattlowe "Matt" Tower Jr. propped against the coach window looking through his reflection at the green, quilted countryside and tiny hamlets slipping by. Lately it seemed he was always leaving some-place. His birthday came and went a week earlier with little razzing from his fellow flyers. Back home in Augusta, Georgia, there would have been his mother Eleanor's yellow lemon cake with white icing. She might try to send him one. Anything would be welcome since the mail was still chasing him. There were letters, often on his father's industrial-supply company letterhead when the content was a bit sensitive for his wife.

Matt had come straight out of college to war. Having partici-pated in swimming and baseball at the University of Georgia, he looked the athlete. An inch under six feet, his stature was firm but not bulky. Bright hazel eyes and dark-brown hair with a hint of wave accented a lightly tanned and firm but pleasant face with a contagious smile.

He contemplated his company, two guys he met in basic training at Souther Field near Americus, Georgia. All three were then assigned to advanced fighter training in Florida with Curtiss P-40 Warhawks. Roger Baker, five-eight with the build of a weightlifter, had long since surrendered to Morpheus with his long, green duffle bag as pillow. This farm boy from Phenix City, Alabama, had two faults: unruly black hair that required frequent trimming and an easily disturbed personality. Softer on the inside, though, he would give you the shirt off his back if there was need. At the end of his sophomore year at the University of Alabama, he took a leave to join the Army Air Force with the intention of earning a law degree when discharged.

Then there was Charles "Chuck" Shilling, the six-foot blond intently perusing a dated London newspaper. Casual but smart, and it was written on his face. His dry wit could deliver laughter when least expected. From Decatur, Georgia, he had the intention of joining his father's banking interest after earning a business degree from University of North Carolina at Chapel Hill. He just made it before enlisting in the Air Force. This paradox of personalities had molded into a friendship, encouraged no doubt by Southern regional bonds.

The United States, deeply committed to the war in Europe, launched her sorties from an England still taking it on the chin. In transit along the outskirts of London, the three Americans were treated to an unholy spectacle. Late in the night the city was aglow against a charcoal sky where explosions flashed as anti-aircraft shells traced the path of faintly visible German bombers. It was a sobering introduction for the three who, up until then, had only read about it.

Matt Tower had hardly considered another branch of military service. From his first ride at the county fair as a 10-year-old, there was a growing love affair with the airplane. He soloed in his senior year of high school.

The rail conductor closed the coach door behind him and stood for a moment as though inventorying his wards. At the end of a chain an exquisite gold watch filled his hand, complementing the bright buttons on a navy-blue uniform that could stand some pressing. This war had passed him by, but his gray temples and bearing suggested he was a veteran of an earlier conflict.

"Ladies and gentlemen, we will be arriving at Raydon Wood station in five minutes. Please locate your grips and personals."

"*Ladies?*" Matt mused to himself, for there was but one in the coach. The others, assorted males of various dress and class, were dotted sparsely about the remaining seats. He was, by nature, a student of character, and the female passenger was everything he ever perceived a proper English lady to be. Light-brown hair with but a touch of gray, rolled just so with hat neatly in place and dainty white gloves folded on the seat. Her hands were busy with needles and yarn, though their progress had yet to suggest the intended garment. A well-tailored light brown jacket left ample room for the patch of lace at the collar of her white blouse. While not Hollywood beautiful, she was attractive, with a pleasant gracious face that would most certainly turn a gentleman's head. Twice she glanced in the direction of the Americans, the second time with the trace of a smile, a warm smile, with no element of proposition. At least twenty years separated their ages, and it dawned on Matt that she might well have a loved one in this same fateful adventure.

As the train slowed, muffled blasts from the whistle signaled the station ahead. Matt stretched against the back of the seat and ran his fingers through his slightly disheveled hair. This was their stop, home of the 353$^{rd}$ Fighter Group, the Slybirds, U.S. Mighty 8$^{th}$ Air Force.

As they rounded a bend, Chuck Shilling crossed the aisle to get a better look. "Hey, guys, the sky's full of Jugs!"

Republic P-47 Thunderbolt fighters circled in landing pattern, dropping in turn to the airfield hidden beyond thick hedge rows. *"Like yellow jackets diving in a nest,"* Matt reflected. Many were the summers spent on Grandpa Musgrove's farm where he learned to find the jacket nests, neutralize them with a railroad fusee, and extract the larva. The bream and crappie would beg for his line to hit the water.

There were no more training fields now that the flyers had reached the front line. Anticipation saw some men quiet and withdrawn while others numbed themselves with the anesthesia of bottled spirits and lusty pilgrimages to the bawdyhouses. And there were those warriors by nature who set the pace and drew out of the others their moments of heroics and endurance. Matt was in that latter group: ready to fly and fight for his country, and to do it well.

The English lady sat patiently working the needles as the three Americans passed her row. Spontaneously, her hand rested on Matt's arm as her eyes searched the faces of the three flyers. "God go with you, lieutenants," her smiling lips prayed.

Just as quickly she returned to her needles and yarn. Matt was certain that she waited for someone special in the war. He had found that the English women were, for the most part, cordial and the men simply polite. No doubt it was a bitter sweetness for them that their colonial cousins must join in the fray.

The sigh and hiss of the resting engine replaced the roar of Pratt & Whitney radials as the last of the yellow jackets landed. The air was brisk and clean, worthy of a deep breath. All around, the land—some areas flat and some with a gentle roll—the geography reminded Matt of his grandfather's sprawling acreage. Quite evidently good farmland, but Matt had yet to peg the crops.

With a firm grip on his bags, Roger scanned the horizon. "Where the Sam Hill is everything?"

"Come on, Baker," Chuck laughed. "This is rural England."

"Well, I had my fill of rural. Twelve years in Podunk staring at a mule's butt!"

"Look at it this way, Roge', you're standing in the middle of history," Chuck teased. "The Normans and Romans were here. Old castles and ruins abound!"

"You city slickers give me a pain in the...."

"Come on, you two!" Matt interrupted quickly. "Don't start that crap out here."

They could hear the welcoming committee's engines before the two jeeps popped into view and slid to a stop beside the platform. A neatly uniformed master sergeant stepped briskly toward the flyers, every seam crisply pressed, buckle and brass mirror bright, cap precisely at the correct angle. The broad face sported a black mustache curled between rosy Scottish cheeks that formed a rather ludicrous fixed grin. "I'm Sergeant McDuff, lieutenants," he announced with a smartly executed salute. "I'm to meet Baker, Shilling, and Tower."

Matt returned the salute, struggling to stifle a chuckle, and pointed to each in his party. "Baker, Shilling, and Tower."

"Thank you, sir. I hope you weren't waiting long. I usually time the train whistle."

"You did well, sergeant," Chuck reassured. "Are we all you're getting?"

"Yes, sir. Five arrived yesterday and you round out the eight we were expecting. If you are ready, sir, I'd like to get you to the base." A born goldbricker, this affable master sergeant, Edward "Eddie" McDuff, proved over time to be a well-known and reliable base accommodator.

"Carry on, Sergeant."

McDuff's assistant, a slender private first class loosely clad in dark army green, double-timed over and began loading the bags. To Matt the kid couldn't have been over 17 and his curiosity welled. "How old are you, Private?"

The single striper struggled to look at ease. "I'm… I'm 20, sir," he stammered in a voice that could have sung tenor in the church choir.

As "20" hurried away to his duties, Sergeant McDuff glanced knowingly at Matt. "I don't think he is either, sir. But he's here and I try to look out for him."

With a short blast on the whistle, the train eased away from the platform, and Matt's eyes turned to the middle window of the coach. She was still patiently working the needles but never looked up.

As soon as the pilots contacted their seats, Sergeant McDuff was off at a rapid clip, with the white-knuckled private laboring to keep up. Unabashedly a collector of brownie points, McDuff would play tour guide, though most area landmarks were humble. "Here on the left, lieutenants, is Woodlands Farm," he bellowed over the jeep engine. "She makes pies for the base. On your right a marvel of the area, the famous Great Wood Forest of Raydon."

Matt, sucking wind on several turns at the hands of the speedy sergeant, was ready to bust McDuff's rank just as the base came into view. From the tone of activity this was indeed no training field. Hangars, support buildings, and blocks of barracks, all sporting the U.S. Army's favorite olive drab, would be home for the duration.

The jeeps came to rest at Operations where McDuff, ever accommodating, stood by with instructions. Base personnel on various missions came and went, nodding and sizing up the newcomers.

"Sergeant?" Roger drawled with evident irritation. "Where'd you learn to drive?"

Faking flustered concern, the sergeant came to attention. How could the newcomers know his reputation as the Scottish Express? The longer the trip, the more preoccupied he became and the faster he drove. There were many less charitable who suspected he received a certain sadistic kick when it happened.

Processing lasted well past mess call. A grateful trio piled flight gear and paperwork on the private's already burdened jeep while McDuff eagerly took the wheel of the other. Roger stood, refusing to board until he caught the sergeant's eye. McDuff grinned and nodded. The jeep's wheels would remain on the ground for now.

"Talk about basic housing!" Chuck snapped as they stopped at the end barrack and lugged gear and personals through the door of the half-cylindrical Quonset hut. "Who knows?" he added. "Vaulted ceilings are the coming thing. Wallpaper, a chandelier, oriental rug.... It could be home."

"Ha," Baker grumbled. "Like living in a giant sewer pipe!" He observed the long block of like buildings. "Better not come back drunk. You'll pick the wrong one!"

On a table by the door a folder displayed "Captain S. Herrington" at the top. McDuff addressed the newcomers' curiosity.

The three flyers paused, wanting to get the story on their immediate superior. "Captain Herrington?" McDuff nodded. "He's a good pilot. Five kills in the air and who knows how many on the deck. And hot on strafing, from what I hear."

"Okay, but what's he like personally?" Matt probed.

"He's direct. You won't have any trouble understanding him. He's a fair, straight shooter. I never knew a pilot who didn't want to fly with him."

"Where is he now?" Matt asked as he turned back to his bunk area.

"About now, debriefing. The squadron just returned from withdrawal support."

"Look here," Roger broke in. "My belly needs support. Does this country club have a bar and grill?"

"If I drop you at the officers' mess, they'll come up with something for you before new-pilot briefing. That's at 1600 in the ready room," McDuff reminded.

The private, having finished his duties, drove away. McDuff and his three charges made for the mess. Then, as the three flyers climbed out, McDuff offered his snap salute and wheeled the jeep around, an ill-timed negotiation since Roger was standing at the rear and dirt spewed straight across his shoes.

"Hey!" the stocky flyer exclaimed, jumping back. "Did you see that.... did you see that!" Roger's red face puffed in rage as he pulled a handkerchief from his pocket and went for his shoes. "I'll punch that jackass' lights out!"

*I wonder if he'll even make it through this tour,* Matt thought, shaking his head.

Time proved that Chuck was never a panacea when Roger was set upon in such instances. Their friendship rested in a love-hate relationship, and mutual provocation was simply irresistible. So he defended the villain. "I don't think he meant to do that, Roge'," Chuck injected with sober sincerity.

"The devil, you say! He's tried to kill us ever since we got off the train. He knew what he was doing. He's at the top of my list!"

"You guys need a referee?" a raspy, good-natured voice inquired. Three heads turned to see a slightly plump first lieutenant with a grin whose flight gear suggested a recent mission. His twinkling brown eyes surveyed Roger's antics with mild amusement. "It's nice to see a soldier who cares about his appearance for a change. I'm John Smaragdis," he added, extending a hand.

Introductions went around, and Roger was forced to bottle his rage in the presence of company. But the scent was still in the air, so Smaragdis sought to lighten the mood. "Join me for lunch, gentlemen, and I'll show you another amazing specimen of the base, one Willard, a pioneer in molecular gastronomy and our culinary magician"

Smaragdis draped an arm around Roger's shoulder and headed the three for the mess hall. "Come on, you'll do better with a full belly."

When they reached the counter, Smaragdis pointed a finger at the grinning mess sergeant. "*Voila*, Willard!" he announced joyfully.

"Crazy first name," Roger chirped sarcastically from the corner of his mouth.

Chuck looked at his fellow flyer for a moment and slowly shook his head. "You need more sleep, Baker?"

With impatience born of hunger, Smaragdis broke in. "You guys want to trust me or you want to flirt with the menu?"

"You've had the right answers so far," Matt replied, glancing at the others for approval. "Set us up."

"Willard, four lemonades and four number-one Dagwoods," he ordered, motioning his guests to a table. Smaragdis' good-natured, easily-met personality let him fit right in. But time would show he could mean business when pressed. His back against the wall and legs stretched along the bench, he probed further. "What fighter squadron are you guys assigned to?"

"350th," Matt replied.

"Now, tell me you're in Captain Herrington's command and we're fraternity brothers," Smaragdis said. Matt confirmed the connection.

The sandwiches were ready by then, and the four made a lemonade toast to the 350th Squadron. Roger, never out of character, lunged into the food, but Matt and Chuck began a round of 20 questions with Smaragdis. He had moved over from Metfield with the 353rd Fighter Group and had 15 missions under his belt. There were three swastikas on his fighter, compliments of a couple of Heinkel He 111 German bombers. "I caught those twin-engine devils in an unlikely area. From the way they acted I think they were training pilots. But they did shoot back. I've dusted some fighters, a couple real good, but I couldn't tell if any went down. We've been doing a lot of bomb and strafing missions, getting into tight little places our bombers usually miss."

The 353rd Fighter Group was no laggard among its contemporaries. At the time, Colonel Glenn E. Duncan, group commander, held the highest score, making him a quadruple ace with at least 20 kills. Captain Wayne Blickenstaff—later promoted to major and then lieutenant colonel—would start his run to 10 destroyed in November. Major Walter C. Beckham would have been in the top mix with 10 destroyed were he not lost in action on February 22, 1944. Except for recent arrivals, most of the group sported swastikas on their aircraft. There were a few group awards posted on the walls of Auger Inn, the officers' lounge and bar.

As Smaragdis lifted his sandwich, he noticed Matt sitting with head lowered and assumed that the odd beefy mixture of his sandwich had him spooked. The first lieutenant was about to offer reassurance when Chuck broke in. "It's all right," he injected between smacks. "He's kind of religious."

There's nothing wrong with that," Smaragdis replied as he took his first bite. "If you ain't got it when you get here, you'll probably have it after the first few missions."

They ate in silence for a time, with Smaragdis nodding occasionally at passing officers. As hunger was quenched, the mood grew more affable and the natural questions of home and family came around.

Smaragdis explained he went to war from his family's restaurant business in Maryland. He dreamed of a chain of Greek restaurants across the country one day. He had not convinced his father and uncle, who felt their hands were full with their present three.

Chuck Shilling lived in Decatur, Georgia. His father was senior vice president of a bank conglomerate headquartered in Atlanta. He had graduated from the University of North Carolina when Air Force service delayed a master's degree in economics. Roger Baker was from a crossroads community west of Phenix City, Alabama. His father, a second-generation farmer, had weathered the Great Depression and was working the family holdings with their first real success. Roger had labored and saved to attend college with the goal of a law degree one day.

Matt Tower's father was owner of a fair-sized mill and industrial supply company in Augusta, Georgia. Matt began his undergraduate studies out of state but soon transferred to the University of Georgia to earn a BBA degree in management. He had been with the family business only a few months when America entered the war.

Augusta, Matt's hometown, was founded by British General James E. Oglethorpe, who established the city as a trading post and fort halfway up the Savannah where the rapids ended river travel. Becoming a major inland crossroad of commerce and Indian trade, it later played an important role during the Revolutionary War and the War of Northern Aggression. When Mr. Whitney invented a practical cotton gin, the commodity became a cash crop and Augusta added textile manufacturing to its economic base.

Location, transportation by roads, rail and river all pointed to a bright future. But many generations watched and waited in what became a prolonged siesta. To young men like Matt Tower—traveled, back from school and eager to see things moving—questions abounded. But those lingering problems would one day test his metal as profoundly as the war. One bright spot was the emerging Masters Tournament founded by golfer Bobby Jones. Now, even that had been suspended for the duration of the war.

And so it was that this assortment of young men would join millions of others to push back the Axis powers. Roger had never seen a German in his life, but from everything he heard and read, a real distaste had developed. This redneck hated a bully worse than anything and he figured Hitler to be one. In time, it became an obsession that drove him over the thin line of recklessness.

"You shot down any Germans yet?" Roger questioned Smaragdis.

"I had the two in the air and a couple on the ground before I took off this morning," Smaragdis replied as he leaned back from the table. "Think I missed a fourth today. It was hard to tell. We picked up some B-17s coming out just west of Hanover. Some of them were really shot up. There was a straggler a mile or so back with an engine out. Four Messerschmitt 109s were sizing him up for an easy kill. So we slipped in on the up-sun side and I picked one out. Surprised the dickens out of him! There were strikes all over his left wing and some smoke, but he broke off and left with his buddies. Nobody saw him go down."

Smaragdis' audience was on the edge of their seats. It was the stuff they had trained for. Only one question remained. "Why didn't you run the son of a gun down and finish him off?" Matt argued.

"Well, on another mission you might. But the job then was to keep the German fighters away from the bombers. We could see some more of them off to the side. They were just waiting for us to go after that first bunch. One thing you learn out there is that you fight as a unit. You back each other up."

The three newcomers sat in pensive silence, their imaginations propelled for the moment to Smaragdis' embattled skies across the English Channel. What they would give for the comfort of his experience. But the mood was short-lived when they were joined by several of Smaragdis' friends—squadron members from other flights attracted to the new faces. They too were older members of the 350th Fighter Squadron, and after introductions went around, the whole party was lost in hangar talk much to the delight of the newcomers.

Sixteen hundred hours came around, pulling Matt and his flying partners away from the camaraderie at the officers' mess. Making their way to the briefing building, a huge reproduction of the barracks, they mingled with other replacement pilots waiting to meet the top brass. Flight jackets and officer pinks were the order of the day. Shaded lamps hung from the ceiling, illuminating the platform and large wall maps at one end of the room.

Sergeant McDuff, all spit and polish, had opened the building and secured the area. He knew the routine of these things.

Roger stood for a second longer than the others, a scowl distorting his face as he sized up McDuff. "I got him cornered now," he muttered to his two friends as he sat down.

Matt and Chuck shook their heads, waving him to silence. "Tenshut!" McDuff bellowed over the room. All rose amid the rustle of leather jackets and sliding chairs as the brass filed in. Led by a slender handsome bird colonel, they made their way to the platform. He was hatless, exposing a head of thick, dark, wavy hair. His gait and manner were relaxed and easy in a way that emitted a cool, genuine confidence. Milton Caniff easily could have slipped him into a Steve Canyon comic stip.

"As you were, men," he began in a smooth resonant voice. "I'm Colonel Glenn Duncan, commander of the 353rd Fighter Group, and in that capacity, it is my pleasure to welcome you as our newest members. You'll have a special welcome at the officers' club tonight as well."

Enthusiastic murmurs of approval rippled through the group of flyers as grins spread and elbows nudged. Colonel Duncan flashed a responsive smile and continued his address.

"Our mission is twofold. Bomber support, which all groups are engaged in, and 353$^{rd}$'s specialty with strafing and bombing. During the next few days, we'll sharpen your skills in the last two categories and get you familiar with the countryside. Your flight leader will decide when you're ready for combat."

Duncan took a couple of paces and folded his arms. He studied the floor for a moment then turned back to his audience.

"This is the payoff day for all the discipline and procedure that was drilled into you over the past months. You are members of a group that has an excellent reputation, and I expect you to contribute to it, not tarnish it. I hope I don't have to remind you that we are on a noble mission in this war. Every piece of Hitler's war machinery you destroy, every Nazi soldier you stop, shortens the road to peace."

Word of Colonel Duncan's personal accomplishments had spread among these replacement pilots and they heard him out with due respect. Here was a commander who flew at the front of the group's missions, whose instructions and advice were honed on the emery board of experience. So he talked on about the history of the 353$^{rd}$, what the missions would be like, and what he expected from his pilots.

"When you are dismissed, find your way to your flight leader, who will take over from here. Pilots assigned to 350 Squadron, see Captain Herrington to my left. Members of 351 Squadron see Captain Compton, and 352 Squadron see Captain Waggoner to my right. Before you are dismissed, I want to extend a hand of welcome and visit with you briefly."

Colonel Duncan stepped from the platform and began greeting the flyers at the front. Matt's eyes went to Herrington, who was standing in casual repose with the other flight leaders. Square jawed and slightly balding, he drew contentedly on a thin-stemmed pipe. Though not the poet's measure of a fighter pilot, his solid, medium build was indeed that of the classic warrior. Matt could picture him in a Roman chariot, the turret of a Sherman tank, or the bridge of a destroyer. But he had chosen the cockpit of a fighter plane that made him a double ace plus two in-air kills to date.

"Lieutenant Tower?"

The words spun Matt's head and he found himself eyeball to eyeball with Colonel Duncan, who by then had reached the last cluster of pilots.

"Sir!" was the best the daydreamer could manage.

The colonel's handshake was comfortably firm, his eyes clear and steady as they met Matt's. The young lieutenant studied them for a second, wishing he could envision what they had seen. The missions, the view through the gun sight, for that arena of the unknown with its paradox of exhilaration and anxiety, were increasingly on his mind.

"Your friends here tell me you're from Georgia," the colonel said.

"Yes, sir. Augusta."

"Well, I'm a Texan. If we keep going like this, we'll have a Confederate squadron."

There were good-natured chuckles, and after the usual pleasantries Duncan made his way back to the front, which triggered another "ten-shut!"

"Godspeed, gentlemen, and you're dismissed."

By the time they had finished the initial briefing with Captain Herrington, the sun had set and they were feeling the results of a long day. Each of the newcomers had been assigned a fighter, and the morning would find them hard into practice. After dinner Matt was drawn to the dispersal pads beyond the cluster of barracks. He zipped his flight jacket against the chill. England was like that. The weather could change within an hour.

Base security was forming up for the night shift, with MPs dotted about the field. Matt returned a few salutes as he reached the first group of fighters. The numbers were right and his fighter should be there. He smiled at some of the pet names on their cowlings as he squinted through the enclosing darkness: *Arkansas Traveler, Fran, Prudence V, Natalie Ann II,* and then there he was: *Sweet Pea.*

*"Sweet Pea?"* he mumbled, rolling the name around for effect.

But *Sweet Pea* it was, the little baby troublemaker of comic strip fame, emblazoned on the olive cowling of the plane and riding a bolt of lightning with blazing pistols in each hand. Matt circled the fighter, drinking her in, squatting to check the underside. The metal skin was ice-cube cold, but he ran his hand along the edge of the wing, wanting to know every inch of this special P-47 that he would entrust his life to.

That was when he met his crew chief, Milton Foxx, a tall, lanky Tennessee technical sergeant. "Milt-the-Stilt" was folded up in the cockpit for some last-minute checkout when Matt mounted the wing and put his head in for a look. Neither knowing the other was about, Milt came up as Matt leaned in. Their startled yelps split the night air. Matt was left hanging by one arm trying to claw himself back to a standing position.

MPs arrived at double time to find the crew chief frantically groping to haul the bewildered lieutenant upright again. When calm returned, Matt moved away from the plane with the MPs, assuring them no harm was done in the innocent encounter. He received a puzzling reply.

"I wouldn't bet on it, Lieutenant," the senior MP responded. "If I was a waging man, I'd say the Stilt set you up, sir."

*"How comforting,"* Matt concluded under his breath. The most important person on base to this pilot was an incorrigible jokester.

# CHAPTER 2

# Breaking In

RAYDON AIR BASE had been operating for months, but the 353<sup>rd</sup> Fighter Group had only arrived from Metfield within the last few weeks. It appeared in some quarters that the transition was still in progress. The cinema wasn't operating yet because the new equipment was British, and no one seemed to have the formula. A task force from technical was taking a go at it with promising results.

Matt and his fellow flyers didn't have to worry about spare time, though, since Herrington was giving their indoctrination top priority. The flight leader was everything McDuff had described but a bit more personable than they had expected.

In short order, the three newcomers were in the air twice a day, beating up the field and the established ranges in the area to refine their strafing tactics. After the third day Captain Tanner, an accomplished pilot trainer known as "Wild Bill," showed his first signs of approval.

"Method is fine," he said after their last session. "All you lack is some flak and the business end of a Messerschmitt to round your edges. You stack up!"

That was reassuring to men who had yet to taste combat. One eventually gained the confidence to streak across the field at 350 miles an hour, 100 feet off the ground, zigzagging at contrived targets. But at Raydon, they were reminded no one was objecting. Continental Europe would be another matter.

"Baker, when you close on a stand of trees you've a habit of delaying your climb out," Herrington schooled as they arrived at the officers' club. "That can take you out if she slips on you."

"Huh, that's the way I learned to fly, Captain, jumping trees."

"Jumping trees?"

"My uncle's in the crop-dusting business and he'd take me up with him. It wasn't long before I was flying the blooming thing."

A reflective grin spread over Roger's face as he rested his elbows on the table.

"Man, that plane was smooth. Just touch the stick and she'd do anything you asked. You know what I did? One day I cut school...."

"One day?" Chuck interrupted.

Roger paused long enough to glower at his antagonist.

"Uncle Robert was in town that day, and I slipped out there and took off. Man, I thought I was something, a 17-year-old jerk kid. I got bored after a while and the devil took the stick right out of my hands. There's a little town west of Phenix City with a long park in front of the courthouse. Big statue of some general right in the middle. I bombed the thing! Coated the whole park in white dust."

Roger's husky laughter melted with that of his audience while he paused to dry an eye. "Man, it was like kicking an ant bed," he said between guffaws. "Folks came out from everywhere!"

Matt regained his composure with some effort, for he loved a good story. He wanted to add one of his own though it wasn't as spectacular. "Well, I can't beat that," he began. "This friend and I took a Cub up a couple of times and bombed some coal trains. Those cars strung out a mile or so on the track. We would chase 'em down, shallow dive and drop peanut bags of flour on them. It was beautiful! Great white puffs of smoke on that black coal."

Herrington naturally glanced in Chuck's direction expecting yet another tall story, but he just shook his head and grinned.

"I just learned to fly by the book, Captain."

"Good!" Herrington exclaimed. "It's encouraging to have one sane aviator in the section."

For a while the talk was light, with the flight leader touching on the points he wanted improved. Then the long anticipated happened as Herrington leaned forward on his elbows. "As far as I'm concerned, you guys are as ready as we can make you. Your names are on the mission list. Tomorrow, Captain Newhart will lead the squadron on an early morning run at specified bridge targets. We're loaning Smaragdis to lead Green Section, so it will be you three and me in Red."

Numbing excitement raced through Matt as he heard the words. To have the brakes off at last was worth every pulsating tingle in his body. When Herrington tired of their questions he adjourned the meeting. The rest must wait for 0500 hours in the ready room.

During that first week at the base there had been little free time. Except for bicycle runs to Wenham Queen near the base or the little pub in Raydon village, it had been flying and study. Now they were dismissed until mission time the next morning, and Matt needed something to occupy his mind. Anything, that is, except another trip to the pub, since Roger was showing every indication of sponging up some brown ale. That was always a bad scene and Matt wasn't in the mood to caretake a drunk. A better thing awaited him as he arrived at the barracks. Someone had picked up the mail and a small bundle lay on his bunk.

He stirred the coals in the heater stove and added a few, knowing the value of an early start on an English night. A front window caught the remaining light of day, so he sat there to sort his mail. A large, brown envelope, carefully wrapped, had weathered the month-long trip. It was bulky but soft, and curiosity required he open it first. He knew by the handwriting it was from his family, for Eleanor Tower's penmanship was of the old school. Her talents as an artist underscored all that the hands attempted. Born to a prominent family in Burke County, Georgia, she had been educated at Agnes Scott College in the arts and social graces. But this lovely petite lady bore her heritage with a winsome unpretentiousness that endeared her to a legion of friends.

Matt peeled away the side of the envelope and reached for its contents. A handsomely tailored, pastel-blue silk scarf, still neatly folded, slipped into his hand. He clasped it for a moment as though sensing the pressure of the dainty fingers that had folded it just so, and suddenly it was difficult to swallow. Then slowly, blurry hazel eyes gave way to a smile and he leaned back, relishing the moment.

"*I know, Mom*" he mumbled under his breath, "*wear it when it's cold.*"

His father was capable of extraordinary business letters, for Matt had read many of them. But he insisted on handwritten personal correspondence, which unfortunately bordered on the illegible. It was almost a game, like reading one of Dr. Preston Agee's hurried prescriptions.

*"Dear Son,"* That part was usually easy. *"You are missed. From your last letter we suspect you will be in England by the time this arrives. Well, Augusta is really caught up in the war effort with scrap iron and paper drives all around. In the evening we can hear machine guns being tested at Augusta Arsenal. The echo bounces around the whole Hill area. Yesterday two large tanks wound their way up Kings Way to the Arsenal for whatever they do to them. Must involve*

*armament of some kind. You wouldn't recognize Daniel Field with its sandbagged anti-aircraft guns, but the assortment of military aircraft would likely take your interest. Wrightsboro Road between Highland and Buena Vista is closed off as part of the airport. Two or three times a week, bombers make practice runs over the city at night. It's something to see the search lights light up their bellies. Mother is leaning over my shoulder right now telling me to stop writing about such things. None of it sits well with her, as you might expect. So on a lighter and brighter note, the company will have its most successful second quarter in history. Lord, that it was due to something other than war! Now Pearl's in here and wants to convey her love. She gets all choked up when she cleans your room and she hasn't cooked decent pancakes since you left. A man can't even write his own letter! I see your mother busy at one and I'm sure it will be more informative on the important things. Please remember to write her. Every morning after her devotional time she goes to the window by the door and straightens and presses the little flag with its lone blue star. God bless you, son! Love, Dad."*

His mother's letters were always long, giving every piece of information possible on things important from the female perspective. But he treasured them. *The Augusta Chronicle* and *Augusta Herald* would hold a poor second to her coverage of community happenings. And as always, she closed with a verse from the Holy Bible that would marvelously capture the thoughts of her heart and prayers for him. Sleep would come slowly this night, for the mission was much on his mind. He marveled at the timing of the letters because later, as he lay in the lonely darkness, they alone possessed the wherewith to distract his mind. It was the thoughts of those he loved that finally lulled him to sleep.

Hours later, from his cozy cocoon, Matt grew increasingly aware of light and sound. Someone tugged at his leg, and he could feel the covers sliding down his chest. The sudden chill sent a quiver through his body and he instinctively chased the fleeting blanket. "What... what the devil?" he stammered at his attacker.

Chuck's face came into focus. "Duty calls, oh great warrior! It's 0400."

Having won the tug of war, Matt wrapped himself in the blanket and sat on the side of his bunk. His first thought was to con someone into swapping bunks with him because his was certainly not the warmest spot in the hut. Straining to keep the cool air from seeping under his wrap, he shuffled to the nearest of two sources of heat. There, a recent spade full of coke was finally taking effect.

Smaragdis and the others were in various states of dress as each worked his way into flight gear. Herrington left earlier for Operations and would meet them at the briefing hut. As Matt struggled to reenter the world of the quick, he shuffled nearer the stove. In a rather pathetic gesture, he held his clothing to the heat piece by piece. Roger, watching out of the corner of his eye, turned to Matt. "You'll never toughen up that way, old buddy. They say Hitler takes a cold enema every morning."

Smaragdis, halfway into his flight pants, burst into laughter, which shook him off balance and sprawled him across his bunk. They all were roaring then, except Chuck, who battled to keep a straight face. "Where you get that stuff, Baker? Tell you what, you go first!"

But it was what they needed, the merciful release of laughter to quell the latent anxiety of these first timers. Spirits were still high as they joined other pilots of the squadron assembling in the dark for the truck run to briefing. Matt had taken the ride often that week but never in the dark. It was a new sensation and he appreciated the company and conversation of the seasoned flyers that made it seem old hat. They arrived to find captains Newhart and Herrington stringing mission lines on the war maps at the front of the room. Newhart turned to the mingling pilots, and a hush fell over the room.

"I'm delighted you could all be here," he grinned broadly.

As the ripple of nervous laughter subsided, Newhart got down to business.

"It's a Chattanooga, gentlemen. We will be after two specific rail bridges just west of Rouen," he began as the pointer ran across the English Channel to France.

"Red and White Sections will carry bombs and rockets while Green Section flies cover. On the way back we'll do what we can with targets of opportunity."

Matt chuckled to himself as he glanced around the room. It was a cinch to spot his own kind, the new guys, earnestly compiling their notes. The squadron leader was thorough and decisive in his presentation, which included clear, direct answers to pilot queries about the mission. A good leader never had a question in his eyes or a waver in his voice but set the plan and exhibited the confidence that carried others along with him. That was how the briefing went until the last detail was in place.

"If there are no further questions," Newhart concluded, "you're dismissed to the ready room for breakfast."

The aroma of freshly brewed coffee and bacon was never as good as just then. But Matt ate modestly, his appetite the victim of excitement. Besides, Smaragdis had cautioned about overloading on coffee because these missions took a few hours. Conversation among the clusters of men was light, trivial, and optimistic as each sought the reassurance and comradeship compelled by the hour. They had 10 minutes left before leaving for the planes, and most of the pilots excused themselves to make the most of it.

Why all military vehicles squealed when they stopped perplexed Matt. But there it was again, that high-pitched concert as the trucks rocked to a halt on the dispersal pads. He zipped and buttoned his suit against the determined chill as they unloaded. Two tiny diamonds lingered in the heavens, a rare canopy for an English morning and a signal that the weather was holding. Except for scattered voices giving directions, there was little talk as the men moved away to the planes. Matt had exchanged thumbs up and slaps on the back with his two friends, for they would all be loners in a crowd in the coming hours.

As always, Milt-the-Stilt was there, clothed against the cold, coffee mug in one hand and ever-present dirty rag in the other. Matt had speculated on its purpose either as his trademark security blanket or that it had simply grown to his hand.

"You're gonna do jes fine, Lieutenant," he intoned in his Tennessee drawl. "*Sweet Pea*'ll do right by ya. Besides, you got something in this little baby ain't nobody else got," he concluded, patting the side of the fighter.

Matt looked back at the tall, narrow face curled into a grin, a face only a mother and pilots could love. He didn't have the foggiest idea what Milt was talking about nor the time to pursue it, so he settled quickly into the cockpit, fingers running nervously over the controls as he readied the fighter for ignition. The still of the night was already broken by revving engines down the line. Matt glanced over his left wing to take the start signal from the crewman. Four great blades began their lazy rotation to the accompanying whine of 2,300 horsepower rousing from a cold night's sleep. Thick clouds of exhaust belched from the ports as the big fighter shook itself to life.

The little diamonds were fading slowly from the sky now against the first hint of dawn.

"*How like the duck hunt in early morning,*" Matt thought to himself, when one must look straight up to catch the silhouette of flying birds.

Herrington's voice crackled into the earphones. "Red One to Red Section, do you read me?"

Matt followed in turn with radio check-in as he circled his fighter onto the taxiway. Ahead, he could see the engine exhaust flashes, like so many fireflies weaving across the darkened field. Twelve of Seldom Squadron's Thunderbolts turned into place. He reached up and fluffed the blue scarf about his throat then slid the cockpit canopy shut. From the tower he saw the green flair streak into the sky, and Herrington barked the order to his pilots. "Red Section, go!"

Captain Newhart had paused with the flyers for a moment of prayer just before they climbed into the trucks, and Matt breathed another privately now as he shoved the throttle.

*"Yea, though I fly through the shadow of death, Thou art with me,"* he paraphrased the Twenty-Third Psalm. Flying speed came slowly to the heavily armed craft, and Matt's eyes darted from runway to speed indicator and back. At last he felt the tail coming up and shortly the familiar sway as tons of metal defied gravity. Red Two was airborne.

They turned east to the channel, then south along the coast at 1,200 feet. The two heavenly diamonds were gone now, and the first grayish glow of the eastern horizon lit Matt's cockpit. He had a strong urge to gab with his fellow pilots, to see how they were making it strung out in the early dawn sky. But radio silence was imperative at this stage of a mission. With their Fatherland under Allied bombs, Hitler's pickets had grown sensitive to anything with wings. So for this side of the English Channel came Captain Newhart's last verbal order. "All right children, let's bob for apples!"

It was the signal for the squadron to drop to 300 feet as they turned out over the water to avoid radar as long as possible. There they would race the sun to reach the French coast before the bright of day.

The channel was a relatively short hop, but playing follow-the-leader in limited light dragged it out for the first timers. For a while Matt could glimpse the swells of gray sea, but as they neared the French coast, fog was developing. Captain Newhart eased the squadron higher as the mist thickened to keep the fighters just at the top of it. They would have to risk detection, which was the lesser of two evils. From a distance the Germans would have difficulty seeing them, but when the ground fog ran out Newhart didn't want to be over a flak tower.

Matt never saw the coast, for they had raced miles inland before the fog broke. When it did, they reached for altitude. The sun was up and France spread out beneath them, its green and tan square plots not unlike England's from the air. As billows of white passed just below them, Newhart signaled for more altitude. That mattered if they encountered enemy aircraft.

"Light flak!" he injected for the benefit of the first timers.

They were just under 10,000 feet now. Below, Matt could make out the silver thread of a river winding its way toward the sea. Their target was near, a few miles to the east.

"Arm your bombs, Red and White," Newhart's voice called calmly.

Green Section banked away and dropped down to test the defenses at the rail bridge, where it appeared widening was in progress to accommodate vehicles. Red and White Sections circled to gain an up-sun position.

"Green One to Seldom Leader, we've got two flak towers down here and some truck-mounted guns."

Matt could hear Green One's wing guns, and he looked down to see the flight strafing the bridge area. The four fighters had ganged up first on one tower, then the other.

"Seldom Leader, we've taken out the flak towers, but the truck guns are in the trees. You'll do best on a north-to-south run," the Green Leader reported.

"Roger, Green One. Make room for us down there," Newhart replied as he led White Section into a shallow, circling dive.

Red Section circled to follow. Four thousand feet and dropping, 250 miles per hour. The Thunderbolt could do 435 if it needed to. Matt's brow felt sticky and little beads of sweat slid down his temples, but he held true to the training manual, wing over to keep target in sight. Green Section had made their last pass at the trucks in the trees and were climbing away to give top cover.

White Section was loaded with experience, and their dive was executed smartly. The bombs spread along the tracks and produced two direct hits on the rail bridge.

"All right, Red," Herrington's voice broke in. "Let's get you baptized nice and easy. Line your pipper and lead the target."

Matt counted the seconds, then banked in behind Red One. He was committed now, racing head-on to the target. Herrington had released and pulled up, his bombs opening a gap in the bridge. White Section made a short pass back at the truck guns then pulled up and reached for altitude.

The target swayed slightly from side to side as Matt stared through the gunsight. Thirty-five hundred feet, 3,000 feet, the altimeter was spinning down, 2,000.... nose up slightly, bombs away! He pulled back on the stick and strained against the Gs as *Sweet Pea* whined out of its run. He heard nothing but the roar of the engine. No boom. Had he missed entirely?

"Good shot, Red Two!" Herrington blurted into the radio.

As Matt banked away, he got a look at the results. His bombs struck the bridge where it joined the bank, leaving another gaping hole. He was ecstatic, his first shot of combat and it wasn't wasted. The emotional reaction was sudden. His legs quivered as he pushed the rudder pedals. A tingling sensation played through his fingers, but he was grinning. Chuck and Roger had little to aim at, but their bombs smashed into the riverbank, further undermining the foundations of the bridge. Seldom Squadron had done itself proud.

"Huddle up, Seldom!" Newhart ordered. "Let's move it!"

The squadron resumed formation and took a due-west heading to bypass Dieppe, known for its heavy flak. They were free to seek targets of opportunity, and Newhart had some in mind. Within minutes they were over the main rail lines leading to La Havre. If they were lucky, they would find a train or ordnance depot. Green Section had climbed to 12,000 feet and resumed its role as top cover.

"Jerry knows we're here," the squadron leader warned. "Let's twist those necks and roll those eyes!"

For Matt, the bridge attack had momentarily overshadowed the prospect of enemy reprisal. Newhart's words put rubber in this first-timer's neck, and he became all eyes. They were only a few minutes from the sea and if the hunt didn't pay off soon, they would have to climb to avoid the coastal guns.

"Red Section, what do you see to the side of the tracks at one o'clock?" Herrington questioned his pilots.

Matt scanned the countryside intently, but the only thing out of place to him was the thin stream of mist leading into the forest. He called it to Herrington's attention.

"Jackpot, Tower! Now, what could that mean?"

They all knew full well what it could mean. Newhart had watched it for the last mile but waited to see if his students would pick up on it. He led the squadron into a shallow dive until they were at treetop then circled out and around the forest.

"What's it look like up there, Green Leader?" he called to the top cover.

"It's clear from where we sit. You've got a fat target at three miles and *four zero* degrees," Smaragdis replied.

"Arm your rockets," Newhart ordered as he poured on the speed.

They could see the smoke from the engine now, thick and black, rising above the trees. The captain had timed it well, for the train was halfway out of the forest as they lined up the strafing run.

"What the blazes is he doing out this late in the morning?" Herrington questioned the squadron leader.

"I don't know, but it's his problem now! Running through the trees blocked his view."

Matt counted 10 cars, three carrying covered vehicles. In front of the engine and at the rear of the train were open cars with the unmistakable profile of mounted guns. White Section was set to make the first pass, and they hugged the earth like nothing the newcomers had seen before. Newhart concentrated on the front gun car and the engine. It was hardly a contest because the Germans had a devil of a time leveling their guns at the low-flying targets. The engineer chose full throttle as his defense, which tested the aiming skills of the pilots, and the first two rockets raced past the lead car. Not so with the next ones, which found their mark. One hit the first boxcar, taking the front of the roof off, while the second destroyed the engine cab.

The runaway train was an awesome spectacle spewing steam, smoke, and fire across the countryside. Two of the soldiers from the gun car were attempting to climb back to the engine, evidently bent on bringing the monster under control. Matt could see tracers following White Section as it pulled up, but there appeared to be no hits. Red Section, starting its run, dropped so low Matt couldn't get a reading on his altimeter.

"Take the cars in the middle," Herrington barked into the radio. "After you fire, find a clean hole and jump the train, then get back down fast until you see me pull up."

They had banked in just ahead of the train so the pass would not leave them near the guns of the trailing car. Red One's rockets were away, and the thin white streams streaked out for the target. One broadsided the second boxcar, which erupted into a crimson mushroom loading the sky with debris. They had lucked upon an ammunitions car and it was better than the Fourth of July. Matt was so taken by the violent display, he lost track of his first target, but recovered in time to line his sight on the cargo of the flatcar. It was a small target compared to boxcars, but he had called it for his own and pressed the trigger. His first rocket zipped between the cars, but the second caught the covered vehicle on its front end.

The explosion rolled it into the trailing car, separating it from the train and spilling the remains of a tank across the ground. Matt had nailed his first German Panzer.

"Green Leader to Seldom Leader," Smaragdis broke in. "We've got company. Bogeys at *one eight zero*, maybe 10,000 feet."

"What's it look like, Green One?"

"They're fighters, maybe a dozen, and they're heading our way."

"The devil!" Newhart shot back. "A man can't get his work done for the interruptions!"

The squadron leader had led White Section around for another pass and was determined to finish the job. "Red One, see what you can do with those gun cars. Make a pass, then take 'em up."

This would be the last chance to get their money's worth from the rockets because all must be jettisoned in case the enemy aircraft engaged. In the distance, Matt could see German troops dropping over the side of the open cars and diving for cover behind the rail bed. He and Herrington would take the lead gun car, leaving the rear one to Chuck and Roger.

Herrington began firing his guns to keep the troops pinned down. They had automatic small arms, and that kind of concentrated firepower could cause problems at close range. His rockets caught the car broadside, leaving nothing in range then but the damaged engine. Matt wasn't about to waste the opportunity or drop his rockets in a field, so he emptied the rack at the smoldering machine. Rockets four and five made solid strikes while the other two missed.

Matt wasn't displeased with his performance. His composure and responsiveness in this first combat action were a source of immense satisfaction to him. It was a steadier hand that held the stick as he climbed to join the squadron.

Matt had yet to see the enemy aircraft, but he listened intently to the chatter between Smaragdis and Newhart. His section would be hard-pressed to reach 10,000 feet before they were intercepted.

"Looks like Messerschmitt 109s. I count eight," Green Leader said. "They're circling up-sun, sizing us up."

"You see anything else in the area?"

"Negative."

"Then let's let 'em know we're willing!" Seldom Leader ordered.

The squadron fanned out in combat formation, and Matt instinctively flipped the safety switch, anticipating Herrington's command.

"Clear your guns!"

*Sweet Pea* shivered slightly at the bark of his eight 50-calibers, but the weapons were working perfectly. Better to know than suffer surprise in the thick of battle. The situation had Matt's undivided attention, his fingers itching again with that inevitable tingle as his mind rehearsed the combat manual.

Red and White Sections had reached 7,000 feet as the Messerschmitts began their dive. The Germans evidently missed Smaragdis' section, hidden 5,000 feet up into the sun, for their attack was single-mindedly at those responsible for the damage below, and they bore down with the confidence of superior numbers and altitude. Newhart positioned White Section in the lead, line abreast, slightly above, giving the first timers a look at how it was done.

Matt saw it as a game of chicken with two teams head on, each daring the other to break. He had seen that once in his high school years as two fools squared off their hotrods down the white line of Walton Way Extension. The only advantage he saw now were the options of *up* or *down*. At 500 yards Matt could see the orange flashes from the enemy wings. They opened fire early, hoping to scatter the Americans, but that didn't happen. White Section flew no neophytes that morning and quickly returned the fire. It was then the Huns learned of Green Section's presence as Smaragdis joined the engagement from above. An abrupt tactical adjustment was required of the enemy, and they chose to dive with the pursuers hot on their tails.

"Catch 'em, Red!" Newhart bellowed over the radio. "Get 'em as they go under!"

The Messerschmitts had closed to less than 300 yards when Green Section got their attention, and they dived in close under Red Section's Thunderbolts. Matt pushed his fighter's nose down, saw a gray blur barreling below, and fired a long burst, but the pass was far too swift to get a strike. The sky became a maze of banking wings as White and Green Sections turned to give chase.

"I'm hit! Crap, I'm hit!" Andy Johnson called from White Three.

The landing gear on the right side of the redheaded Midwesterner's fighter was hanging half down and a thin stream of vapor trailed from beneath the wing.

"Red Leader, stay with him and take a *three two zero* heading until you get in the channel. We'll catch up shortly," Newhart said as his fighter dropped to join the chase.

"I'd like to get in on that, dang it," Roger grumbled into his mike.

"You can relax, Baker. They won't stay around. That was designed to burn up our fuel so we'd go home," Herrington answered.

True to the prediction, Matt could see the German fighters streaking for the deck in the direction of Paris. Seldom's pursuit was more symbolic than effective as they tried to send a little lead home on the enemy's tail. The pressing problem was White Three's wounds. Herrington positioned his fighter under the cripple to assess the damage.

"You didn't get that from the 109s, Andy," he reported. "You picked up some flak back there, either at the bridge or the train. How's your hydraulic pressure?"

"Dropping."

"All right, let's try to get you home."

White Three labored to reach 5,000 feet as the Thunderbolts

headed for the channel. No pilot relished the prospect of crashing, especially behind enemy lines. Matt shook his head in concern as he saw the right landing gear begin to protrude beneath Andy's fighter.

"Getting hard to hold her nose up, Red Leader."

Damage was more extensive than Herrington let on. The metal skin of the plane was ripped from its right wing forward to the cowling. He feared more than the hydraulic lines were involved but wanted to keep Andy's spirits up until something else showed.

"Work the hand pump," he suggested calmly.

Herrington was excellent, chatting with the distressed pilot and pouring on the encouragement as seconds dragged into minutes. All eyes searched the horizon for the big fishbowl that separated them from England and safety.

The three first timers were hard-pressed to offer anything original, but their joint cheer bombarded the airways as the coast came into view, a welcome sight that refueled the hope recently drained by Andy's steady decline in altitude. The altimeters registered 6,000 feet when they left the shores of France behind.

"Captain, I can't hold this thing much longer!" Andy broke in.

"Oh, yes you can!" Herrington shot back. "Wrap one of those lanky bowlegs around the stick."

That "something else" Herrington had feared was showing up now and it didn't look good, A stream of dark vapor was trailing from the wounded fighter. They were down to 5,000 feet and dropping faster.

"I've got to ditch this thing. It's shaking to pieces!" Andy bellowed.

The flight leader knew better. Bellying into water carried multiple risks. "Don't ditch! If you can't hold it, roll her over and bail out."

There was nothing anyone could do as Andy forced the canopy back. For the newcomers, such scenes would take a lot of getting used to in the coming months. Then, in a final act of obedience, the grand old jug of a fighter nosed up slightly and turned on its side as Andy positioned to jump.

"Tell 'em to keep my supper warm, Captain!"

It was his last transmission as he climbed out and fell away from the plane. They had parted company at just under 3,000 feet, floating together for a second, before the Thunderbolt nosed down in a spin. It sank within minutes after impact, vanishing in a great swell of the hungry gray sea.

Andy's parachute had opened, and Red Section circled the area while Herrington radioed the downed flyer's position. Anxious seconds ticked away after he hit the water, for the chute could drown him in the wind and currents. But he played it by the book, freeing himself and inflating the small yellow raft.

When Herrington twice confirmed acceptance of his transmission, they had done all possible for the downed flyer. Only when fuel reached the critical level was the section willing to break away, dipping their wings in supportive salute at the bobbing raft.

It was a quiet and reflective three first timers who touched down at Raydon, caught in the paradox of anxiety for one of their own and the blessed release from an arduous mission.

# CHAPTER 3

# The Biscuit Maker's Helper

IT WASN'T ENOUGH that the newcomers had experienced the stress of their first mission, compounded by the downing of Andy Johnson. The grind extended through a rigorous debriefing. Matt would notice in the following weeks the Intelligence Division's preoccupation with all missions involving areas in and around Normandy.

Free now from the duties of the day the bedraggled flyers sought refuge at the officers' club, affectionately dubbed Auger Inn. It was early evening and the congregation was assembling. In one corner where a jovial party of flyers toyed with the radio, the music was American and sweet. Matt stretched his weary body in a chair nearby. At intermission, the British announcer greeted his Air Force audience.

*"We wish to welcome lieutenants R. Baker, C. Shilling and G. Tower to the 353$^{rd}$ Fighter Group. We understand their first mission*

*was today and they lost members of their squadron. You know, lieutenants, that's the way it will be. Pity you've been taken so far away from home and loved ones to die in a lost cause that really is none of your business."*

Matt pulled himself forward in the chair, astounded to hear his name on the wireless. He poked Chuck across the table to be sure he was listening.

The mocking voice continued. *"Yes, that's right. We know all about you and we like to prepare especially warm greetings for newcomers like yourselves when you cross the channel again."*

"Who the Sam Hill is that guy?" Roger demanded.

One of the listeners looked back from the radio, a wide grin spreading across his face. "That's Lord Haw Haw broadcasting from Germany. Stick around. It gets better as he goes along."

The British traitor kept up his insidious dialogue for a while, putting Newhart down as incompetent, guilty of attacking a fake target, and reminding all that they had something special waiting for them also.

Matt leaned over to one of the seasoned flyers. "How does that guy know about us? Where did he get our names?"

"No telling. Where have you been the last few days?"

"Nowhere much. They've been flying the daylights out of us. Maybe a pub or two," Matt replied.

"That's all it takes, old buddy!"

They had been warned about travel and idle talk off base. But it was hard for Matt to imagine Englishmen as Nazi sympathizers stalking the haunts of their American allies, especially considering all their country had suffered. But a Fifth Column was alive and well in Britain. Germany's *Abwehr*, the military's intelligence service, was well entrenched throughout its occupied territories and those nations rising against them. Britain and the United States had not been left out.

The British traitor continued his harangue, bringing in other units and pilots much to the amusement of those circling the radio. But the newcomers weren't accustomed to this sport of the airways. *"Is there nothing holy?"* Matt muttered to himself.

By the time Captain Herrington arrived, the airways were filled with the lively strains of Harry James' rendition of *Ciribiribin*. The captain twirled a chair around and joined Matt's table. "Just wanted to be seen with the famous," he chuckled. "I caught some of the broadcast at Operations."

"It's unnerving as the devil when the enemy seems to know more than we do," Chuck replied.

Herrington stretched and leaned his elbows on the table. "The guys wouldn't miss Haw Haw's broadcast. He's the highlight of the day. Sometimes we get old Axis Sally on our case. Don't let 'em rattle your cage. Most of their stuff comes right off the box top."

They could tell from the gleam in his eyes that the section leader was satisfied about something. "Andy beat the odds," he began. "Rescue pulled him out of the channel about an hour ago."

That's all Roger needed to hear: a legitimate excuse to order a round of drinks to toast the good fortune. Drinking was not the popular sport with Matt that it was with Roger. But the news was so welcome, the Georgia boy extended a glass in the spirit of the moment. The downed pilot apparently was powder blue from exposure when they got him but warming up nicely in the hospital.

They rehashed the mission around the table and rattled on in small talk until the flyers, one by one, turned to other interests. Herrington, sitting next to Matt, drew contentedly on his pipe. "Well, Tower, how does it feel to have your first mission behind you?"

"I know I did it, Captain, but it's kind of like I dreamed it."

Herrington pulled the pipe from his mouth and leaned toward Matt. "I watched you pretty close today. You held position well, stuck to my wing"

That was what Matt wanted to hear. He didn't want to be an "also flew." When opportunity presented itself, he would be available, and it was about to present itself in more ways than he imagined. "Well, sir, you told us all we needed was some flak and the business end of a Messerschmitt to round the edges. I saw both today."

Herrington nursed the pipe with long easy draws until it seemed his head was literally in the clouds. The young lieutenant grew a bit uneasy under the section leader's steady gaze, but he refused to let it show. It was the captain's way of reading people and Matt felt he was being read, so he sipped his beverage coolly and waited it out.

"Tower, when the group was at Metfield I took a little R&R in Colchester one weekend and met this RAF lieutenant named Cobbs. The guy caught 20mm shrapnel in the leg and was on temporary training assignment. He's stationed at Ipswich airfield where the English have a bomber defense school of some kind. Anyway, they've got a Messerschmitt over there and he flies it against the trainees."

Suddenly Matt wasn't nearly as sleepy as he had thought. He prayed under his breath for what he felt might be coming. Herrington paused long enough to pack the pipe and consider the reception he was getting from his audience of one.

"Anyway, I made a deal with him," the section leader continued, "and we met a few times over the countryside. Had some hellacious dogfights! Didn't know how the brass would take it, so neither of us mentioned it. But I used some of what I learned on the section, and Colonel Duncan noticed the difference after a couple of missions. I got my nerve up and broke the news to him."

Herrington's pause to fire up the pipe taxed Matt's patience to the limit. Perhaps a verbal nudge would move the captain along. "What did he say?"

"He said, 'Work on it.' So I prevailed on McDuff, and he came up with a dozen pairs of nylons and a couple bottles of Scotch whiskey. Obliging chaps, the British."

Matt propped his elbows on the table, giving Herrington his undivided attention. "If the chance comes, I want in!"

Herrington leaned back from the table, balancing his chair on the rear legs. "The first time you run into a gaggle of those things and they want to fight, it's the devil of an experience. That bunch today didn't want to engage. They just wanted to break up the fun and waste our gas. We'll see what tomorrow brings."

A restless night was Matt's reward for his first sortie over Europe, mixed with concern lest some orderly come in and shake him awake. He didn't fear another mission, only that he would miss a turn with the German fighter at Ipswich.

The next morning, much to his relief, the mission roster was still bare. The continent was under clouds, putting everything on hold. Matt hung around the ready room, throwing darts and keeping his fingers crossed. His patience paid off. "It's on," Herrington announced. "Operations is in a holding pattern for the next few hours. We need to get you and your two buddies out of here now. Three jugs at the maintenance hangar need check flights. They're your ticket."

It disappointed Matt that *Sweet Pea* would remain at Raydon, but the fighter was battle ready and must be available to another pilot. Their mounts were waiting as Herrington promised, sporting fresh paint over the mended combat damage. Colorful yellow-and-black checkerboard cowlings cut a smart profile against the pale sky, and Matt drew on all his patience to walk ground check with the crew chief.

In the air at last, a patchwork of fields and forest slipped beneath them like a film in slow motion, serene and peaceful as though unaware of war. How different from France, where every cluster of trees was suspect for anti-aircraft. On the horizon, the broad waters of the River Orwell laced the ancient inland port of Ipswich to Orwell Estuary. It was their landmark, and Matt called the tower.

Within minutes the chunky Thunderbolts landed and followed the pilot truck to their hard stands near sleek Spitfires. Two RAF officers approached as the Americans deplaned. The young Britisher saluted smartly, "Good morning, lieutenants. Pilot Officer Sutter here."

Matt introduced his company and asked where they might find Flight Lieutenant William Cobbs. The RAF officer pointed to a group of flyers gathered around a fighter some distance away. "He's over there completing a class. Shouldn't be long now."

The Americans made their way to the gathering and stood behind the circle of students. Cobbs was quite convincing as the three waited patiently, enjoying every minute of the clear, practical instruction. Only when the British officer stepped down from the wooden carton was his slightness of stature apparent. Matt estimated five six or so, but his body was strong and hard. There was nothing skinny about him. Dark reddish-brown hair curling from beneath the aviator's helmet matched his trim mustache. Still favoring a slight limp, he had remained the eternal soldier, all Englishman in a small, wiry package. When the class was dismissed Cobbs singled out the Americans and made his way to them. "I say now, who have we here?"

He returned their salute and extended a hand in greeting as introductions went around. "So you are Stan Herrington's Slybirds. Fine officer, fine pilot."

"How's the leg, sir?" Matt inquired.

"Coming along nicely; nothing to it. You should see Douglas Bader. Doesn't have a bloody thing below the knee. Makes it around on metal legs, mind you. Probably shot down as many Huns as anybody in the RAF."

"Captain Herrington spoke very highly of you, sir," Matt said. "And how much the sessions with your Messerschmitt have meant to his squadron."

"*Sessions* is it, now?" The flight lieutenant chuckled as he tapped a cigarette from a crumpled package. "Would you like a look at the bloody little kite?"

From a distance one might have mistaken the Messerschmitt

for a Spitfire. They had left it in native gray and black, but with prominent RAF markings. The evident differences centered around exhaust ports and spinner. Cobbs allowed it had been a problem early on, and the RAF devised bright trim for the aircraft's tail and cowling to help distinguish it.

With the enthusiasm of a devoted pilot, he began pointing out the better qualities of the German fighter. "This is a Messerschmitt 109-G, quite the hotter of Jerry's flock. Its tail assembly was damaged by our coastal guns and the pilot was forced to nose it in on the beach. Took our boys the better of two months to patch it up."

Matt moved slowly around the nimble fighter, running his hands over its metal skin. This was a cousin of the gray blurs that streaked beneath him over France. She sported a 15mm cannon and two 7.9mm machine guns, points that conjured increasing respect for the business end of the legendary aircraft. Cobbs delighted in showing off the 109 and would have spent another hour divulging its secrets had Roger not begun his inevitable starvation act.

"Forgive me, gentlemen," the Britisher apologized. "I quite forgot the hour. We can continue after lunch. I'll just drop these charts at headquarters and have you as my guests."

They piled into the Humber staff car, which Cobbs commandeered as impetuously as he talked flying. True to his word, he was but a moment at headquarters then resumed his position behind the wheel.

"I hope the weather holds," Cobbs said, peering up through the windshield. "It's rather thick to the east."

"All right chaps, it's your choice. The stuffy old officers' club or NAAFI." Not knowing one from the other, the Americans left it to their host, who instinctively chose the NAAFI canteen. (NAAFI is short for Navy, Army and Air Force Institutes, the British military's equivalent of the American PX, or Post Exchange.)

The canteen was a hodgepodge of PX, short orders, and amusements, a welcome contrast to the chilly gray outside. The RAF types were making full use as Matt's party paused at the door to take it all in. Chuck responded quickly to the crack of billiard balls across the room, for that was his game. They had found a home away from home.

The printed menu could as easily have been in Greek, for most items were in the British vernacular, much to everyone's amusement. Matt wrestled with it for a time, finally giving in to the safe way. "What are you going to have, Will?" he inquired of the flight lieutenant.

"I think a toad-in-the-hole with side greens would do nicely," he replied.

Matt let that soak in slowly, pretending not to be puzzled, but Cobbs wasn't fooled. He let the American stew for a moment before he could hold a chuckle back no longer. "It's a sausage baked in batter, Yank, with a type of salad."

"I'd go for that," Roger injected quickly. "How big are they?"

"In your case, I'd order two."

The food and drink were excellent, and Matt felt much revived. The time had been profitable as well in getting to know the British officer, whose rank would be *captain* in the American Air Force. Cobbs had entered service near the end of the intense period of the Battle of Britain and there were harrowing chapters to his personal history. His wound came during a strafing rhubarb along the Dutch coast. Fragments from an explosive shell ripped his leg, and he was forced to fly home with one hand twisting a belt around his thigh.

As they were finishing the meal, two of Cobbs' trainees stopped by and tactfully invited themselves to the table: Peter Browne, a dark-haired, clean-cut youngster; and Lloyd Sanson, whose oval face and pink cheeks personified the classic English lad. They had been attracted by the American uniforms. Evidently awed by the flight lieutenant's guests, the young Britishers—in neophyte exuberance—assumed them to be seasoned flyers. This enthusiastic rush had the Americans struggling to conceal their amusement.

"Have you made any kills as yet?" the classic Sanson inquired eagerly. The three Americans glanced at each other, none wanting to confess their one-mission careers. Matt smiled and passed the floor to the quick-witted Shilling.

Chuck stared thoughtfully at his clasped hands resting on the table and sighed. "I really hate to think about it sometimes. You see, we were deep in France when the bogeys were spotted that morning well below our squadron. Being up-sun, our leader led the attack and caught the gaggle of Messerschmitts completely by surprise. By the time they saw us and broke, we were set for perfect deflection shots."

The pilot officers were eating it up while Cobbs sat silently with his hand clasped over his mouth. "How many did you get?" Browne asked excitedly.

"Oh, the Lord alone knows," Chuck replied soberly. "There were Messerschmitt parts spinning all over the sky." The American paused as though struggling for composure before his eyes rolled up to the trainees. "The only reason we didn't do better is that our windshields were so thick with blood and oil we were forced to go on instruments."

For a moment, utter silence prevailed. The trainees stared at Chuck, their enthusiastic smiles fading away slowly. Had Cobbs not been sitting to the side, he would have given the ruse away, for his face was crimson with suppressed laughter.

"You bloody rotter!" Browne exclaimed as a grin crept across his face. "Putting us through all that rag."

It was a good laugh among the six men and a quick ice breaker, for now they could converse candidly as fellow members of the profession. But it wasn't long before Cobbs broke up the session as he reminded the Americans that time was short for their turn at the German fighter.

"Let's cap it off with a bit of sweets," he suggested to the Americans. "I'll introduce you to Mrs. Pearson's sweet biscuits."

The four made their way to the confection booth, where a long glass case shielded a variety of pastry delights. Behind the counter a plump little English lady busily packaged an order. With her bright smile and silvery-laced hair rolled in place, she epitomized the mothers of England. As they neared the counter, she saw Cobbs and turned in his direction, her hands on padded hips.

"Well, Cobbs, what's the likes of you doing here at this hour?" she scolded playfully, her lilting voice bathed in heavy accent.

The flight lieutenant relaxed against the counter and grinned up at her. "A special treat for my American friends, Mrs. Pearson. We'd like some of your delightful sweet biscuits."

"Oh, luv, you know there's not a crumb by this hour. I'm sorry," she responded dejectedly. Cobbs patted the counter restlessly, then turned to his three charges. "Well, I've buggered it up, gentlemen. Sorry I made such a thing of it, whetting your appetite like that for the dessert of angels."

The left-handed compliment brought a smile, and she lowered her head to hide it as much as possible. "Now don't you start your grizzling, Will Cobbs," she admonished with a chuckle.

Matt was amused by this ploy with the charming little lady. He liked her right off, especially the spunky way she held her own with the RAF officer. But he sensed that Cobbs was working up to something and he decided to play along. "Yes, ma'am," Matt injected. "We came all the way from Raydon at his suggestion."

"Oh, be off with ye'!" she replied, cocking her head doubtfully. "Ma'am, is it now? Well, aren't we the polite one! More than I can say for some people," she added, nodding in Cobbs' direction. "What are your names, lads?" Matt introduced his fellow flyers and Mrs. Pearson smiled at each in turn. "Dear me," she said. "They're still sending children to fight the war."

"Don't mind her," Cobbs broke in. "She'd mother the whole base if they'd let her."

"I've a cousin in the States, you know," she went on. "Virginia, that's where she lives. Have you been to Virginia, Lieutenant Tower?"

"Yes, ma'am. My mom has relatives in Richmond."

"Your mother saw to your rearing, that's plain to see," she added, placing a chubby hand over an ample bosom. "You're so like my Freddie. He's got your eyes for certain."

"He's your son?" Matt questioned.

"Yes, my only."

"Where is he?"

"He's somewhere in Italy," she replied, her chest rising and falling in a deep sigh. "This family's fought the Germans in two wars. His father before him." Her lower lip quivered ever so slightly. "I haven't heard a word in over a month," she added, moving a finger to the corner of her eye.

An awkward moment ensued for the four pilots who, like so many others, barreled off to war intent on the noble cause, never grasping in full the trepidation of loved ones left behind. She rested a hand on the counter as composure slowly returned, and Matt reached over to gently cover it with his own. "Look, I don't think there's a safer place he could be." She looked questioningly into his eyes, trusting them for encouragement. "You know what they say about the Italians. They'd rather make love than war."

She patted Matt's hand and turned to Cobbs. "I like your friends, Will. Gentlemen for a change!"

Chuck and Roger had wandered off during the small talk, intrigued by the activity at the billiard tables. If the two could agree on anything, it was to team up for a hustle, be it poker, pool or what have you. Matt was ready to give his goodbyes to Mrs. Pearson as she returned from another sale.

"Dearies, wait a moment. I want you to have something." She retrieved a small bag from under the counter and called to her assistant in the pantry. "Vivie, would you bring me that white box on the bottom shelf, dear?"

Leaning back on the counter, Matt folded his arms to wait while Cobbs rubbed his hands in anticipation. "I think we've outfoxed her," he whispered.

Matt heard the box slide onto the counter and turned with eyes ready to feast on the tasty sweets. But the hands that served him were not those of Mrs. Pearson. These were slender with well-kept nails. His eyes slowly traced the shapely arms to their shoulders where perky twists of light golden-brown hair rested. Dark blue eyes returned his gaze as a hesitant smile parted ample, slightly pursed lips.

The lights from above cast a sheen around her head which, in this moment of encounter, created an angelic image. For a moment Matt was suspended in time, unaware of breath or heartbeat. Since arriving in England there had been little time or opportunity to consider the ladies. There were girls back in the States, some more serious than others, but none quite like this one. *Prim* was the word that came to his mind, refreshingly feminine. But she was a bit more guarded in manner than he had experienced before. Almost mysteriously so.

Such an encounter certainly required one of his articulate openers. But his mind, still recovering, would only perceive; it could not produce. From his best effort emerged a trite, "thank you."

Too quickly she moved away dutifully returning to her chores. His eyes, on auto pilot, never left her. Cobbs enjoyed somewhat the same sensations, but his were directed at the sweet biscuits.

"Now, don't you say a word," Mrs. Pearson coached. "Commander Potts ordered these, but he'll not miss a few."

The two flyers lifted several of the treasures from the box as Cobbs looked up at the little English lady. "This won't leave you holding the can, will it, Mrs. P?"

"Heavens, no!" she laughed. "He doesn't need them anyway." She lowered her voice to secrecy level. "He takes after his name a bit, you know. Potts," she repeated, patting her abdomen softly.

"Well, they are delicious," Cobbs said. "But no sweeter than the hands that made them."

A little blush tinted Mrs. Pearson's cheeks, and her chubby hands flew to her face. "Aye, you're a cute one, ducky!" she chuckled merrily.

Matt had grown oblivious by now to the inane chatter around him. As his gaze turned to the young lady, he was surprised to see her looking intently in his direction. When their eyes met, she turned quickly back to the work at hand. Her movements allowed him a glimpse of legs and ankles, causing the biscuit to pause at his lips. As she moved back down the counter she noticed his hesitation. "Do you like them, Lieutenant?" she inquired.

Matt's eyes rolled off the dainty gams. "They're wonderful!" he nodded.

She missed the implications of his response and continued stocking the show case. Matt eased his coffee cup down his side and poured most of it into an ash can. "Could I have a refill?" he asked as nonchalantly as possible. It was the only thing he could think of that might keep her nearby.

Her movements were precise, smooth, as though she had thought them out beforehand. She raised the kettle and searched the counter top. "Where's your cup, Lieutenant?"

He had been caught with his cup down, so to speak, and brought it up casually, struggling to conceal the little scheme as best he could. Now he had time to appreciate the way she wore the light-blue turtleneck sweater and navy jumper skirt. If he worked it right, the encounter might be prolonged with conversation. "How long have you been working at the base?" he began.

"It's my first time here," she replied as she filled the cup. "But I've volunteered with NAAFI the better of a year or so."

"Another airfield?" Matt kept trying.

"I think not," she replied without looking up. "I came because Mrs. Pearson was in such a strait. Her assistant is ill."

"Something against the Air Force?" he questioned playfully.

He paused, waiting, but she continued with her work, almost as though she had not heard. Her lips had narrowed a bit, and Matt began to fear that he may have pressed too hard. Perhaps a different approach. "That's a pretty name, Vivie. What's it short for?"

She glanced up briefly while her hands remained busy. "I'm afraid, Lieutenant, that you have the advantage of me."

She was indeed different from those he had known in the past. Taken back a bit by her assessment of his manners, he was inexplicably pleased because of it. Unintentionally, he had painted himself into a corner and wanted desperately to escape.

He leaned back from the counter and straightened his flight jacket. "Look, I'm sorry. That wasn't very polite of me, was it?" he offered, shaking his head. "I'm Matt Tower, US 8th Air Force out of Raydon."

The apology must have been written all over his face, for when she glanced his way there was the trace of a smile. "And I'm Vivian Davis, NAAFI volunteer out of Ipswich," she mimicked.

From the noise across the room, the billiard hustle must have been in full swing. Even Cobbs had been drawn to the table as he heard the wild boasts and heavy betting. It was UK against US in a fateful playoff and the money was passing freely. With her customers occupied across the room, Mrs. Pearson sought the company of the one flyer remaining at the counter.

"And just what are you three doing at an RAF base?" Mrs. Pearson inquired of Matt.

He was happy to have the conversational pressure shared by a third party because he had been doing an excellent job of putting his foot in his mouth. "We're getting some firsthand experience with a German fighter," he replied. "They have a Messerschmitt on the base."

He was talking to Mrs. Pearson but he was watching Vivie, and while she appeared to be unaware of his interest, the biscuit maker wasn't. Had Matt been less preoccupied he might have detected the knowing twinkle in her eyes. They talked for a while then, friendly small chatter, though Vivie contributed little to the conversation. But she did remain nearby, which pleased him immensely.

The vibration was slight, but Matt instinctively recognized the mounting rumble of fighter engines. As the conversation lulled, the rumble grew, echoing across the field. While it was music to his ears, Mrs. Pearson acknowledged it passively, long experienced with such sounds. But Vivie's lips tightened, the nimble fingers moving briskly as though searching for occupation.

This seemed to concern Mrs. Pearson greatly and she moved to the younger woman, "Vivie?" The noise passed quickly, fading to a distant hum. Vivie brushed the hair from her forehead. "I'm fine," she whispered. "On second thought, perhaps a little break would help."

Things were happening too fast for Matt. First with the little drama at the counter and now Cobbs signaling that it was time to leave. Vivie had moved to the doorway of the storage room, canceling a crucial moment of rapport for the American flyer. There was little he could do at the time but bid them good morning. "I guess that was the bell for my first class," he sighed, patting the countertop.

He placed the cup on the counter and found himself doing those fidgety things one does when there's no easy exit. Vivie had flashed a parting smile before disappearing through the doorway, leaving him with the base mother. Mrs. Pearson, still reflecting concern, sought to ease the tension by offering him a few extra biscuits to carry along. "Do be careful, Lieutenant," she cautioned with a smile. "Fly safely."

He turned back, gliding his fingers through his wavy brown hair, searching for an innocent excuse to return later. "Why don't you hold those for me, Mrs. Pearson, and I'll have them when we get back."

The twinkle was back in her eyes then as she lifted a biscuit to her lips and watched the handsome young American move away.

# CHAPTER 4

# Advanced Training, Air and Ground

THE ROWDY GROUP was leaving the canteen as Matt caught up. He drew in a deep breath of the still cool noonday air to clear his head. Chuck and Roger were bickering as usual though both held a wad of currency in their hands.

"Dang your timing, Baker. Don't you ever do that again!" Chuck spouted angrily.

"What?"

"Double or nothing our bet on a shot like that. That could have ruined us, man!"

Roger roared with laughter at his partner's testiness and waved the money in his face. "I got faith in you, buddy. The ball dropped. We got the smackers right here!"

Matt could see that something extraordinary had taken place

and, being a fair pool shot himself, he tried to show proper interest. "What the heck happened?"

Chuck paused in their walk to set up the shot with his hands. "We're high ball, okay, with the 12 left on the table. I got a long shot between their two and four to catch the 12 with enough spin to sink it in the corner pocket. If that ain't enough, this fool blurts out, 'double or nothing!'"

"And that fool made it!" Roger injected, roaring with laughter again. "He thought he was gonna leave two month's pay on the table!"

When they reached the ready room, they expected to find Cobbs, since that had been his instructions, but they found only Pilot Officer Sutter, who rose from the table to greet them.

"Have you seen Lieutenant Cobbs?" Matt inquired.

"Indeed I have, chaps. And he left a message for you." Sutter directed them to a large wall map and placed his pointer just east of Ipswich. "He wants you to climb to 5,000 feet, about here, just north of the Orwell, and proceed to the coast on a heading of *eight zero* degrees."

"And then what?" Roger inquired, shifting his feet impatiently.

The pilot officer clasped his hands behind his back, drew himself up, and rocked on his heels in his smug British manner. "I do believe he intends to shoot you down before you reach the channel."

*"English sport!"* Matt thought to himself. Well, fine. It was the kind of challenge he liked, and it did an excellent job of taking his mind off the sweet shop. At least for the time being. He had the gnawing feeling that he had left something more than his biscuits back there.

With the challenge on, the Americans wasted no time getting airborne. Somewhere ahead in the hazy sky, the English flyer lay in wait, an old hand at scaring the pants off new pilots.

Neither side would tune to the other's radio frequency until interception was made. While the Americans were not that experienced,

Matt had every intention of making it difficult for Cobbs to get a clean bounce. "All right, Red Section, let's rubber neck it good! We'll make him work for it."

He led the section in a lazy weave to give maximum view to their flanks and stern. They had been flying for just over five minutes and it appeared the ceiling had dropped a bit. Squinting across the horizon, Matt thought he glimpsed the fine line of the coast. He smiled to himself, feeling a little satisfaction that they just might be giving Cobbs more of a run than he expected.

"Maybe we should stop weaving and give him a chance to hit us," Chuck broke in. "We'll be over the beach in a minute."

In that same instant their earphones were shattered with the loud imitation of machine gun fire. They had been bounced royally. Responding to the stinging reality, Matt yelled, "Break!" and instinctively banked his fighter defensively.

Roger's angry voice boomed over the radio. "Where the devil is he?"

The flight lieutenant's reply crackled into the radio. "Right below you, old chap, eating your bloody belly out!"

The Britisher had held out on them, for as they caught sight of him rising in their rear mirrors, another enemy dived in from their starboard side. The silhouette of a second Messerschmitt 109 singled out Chuck's Thunderbolt. Roger took advantage of his relative freedom to roll above his attacker and quickly filled the headphones with his own machine gun fire.

Matt's hands were full with Cobbs on his tail, but by now surprise had turned to indignation, and he determined to get away from his pursuer. Cobbs was good, and conventional tactics weren't going to shake him. In the excitement, Matt pushed the throttle full forward, forgetting the point of emergency power. The unexpected boost pinned his head and shoulders to the back rest as water injection drove the engine to its limits.

Fighting surprise, he recovered quickly and held his speed while rocking the ship defensively. It wasn't long before Cobbs' "machine guns" stopped. Matt scanned the rear; no Messerschmitt. He counted to five, then pulled into a banking climb and kicked the left rudder to send the fighter back at the enemy.

"Good show, Tower!" Cobbs boomed into the radio. "Now, let's see if you can do me in!"

By the time Matt had lined up his fighter, the Messerschmitt was completing an evasive turn in the distance. Cobbs let him catch up just to the point that a hit could be made, then rolled the German fighter on its side and dropped out of the American's sights. Roger had lost the second German fighter by then. There couldn't have been another three flyers more ticked or ready to learn than the pilots of Red Section.

"All right, Slybirds. Form up your section and we'll have a go at it," Cobbs instructed.

The friendly enemies chased across the darkening sky, attacking, evading and counterattacking as the Americans had their turn with the German fighters. Five men who would rather fly than eat passed the afternoon in the thrill of mock combat. Only when the rain became so bad as to cloud their vision were they inclined to a cease fire.

The ceiling was dropping fast as the combat party headed for Ipswich, and Matt struggled with a rising wind to hold formation. He blinked against the brilliant sheet lightning that whited out his cockpit every few seconds. Their mania for the war games had allowed the storm to enclose them, and the voices that had chattered boldly minutes before were now tense with concern as the flyers struggled to reach the field.

Matt had landed in overcast and fog, but never in a storm like the one building around him. He offered a silent prayer of thanks that they had not been far from the field. Cobbs called for a straight-in landing as they approached at 400 feet to keep the field in view. To Matt, the natural elements were more distracting than the flak over France, where he at least could maneuver out of it. It took all his skill to fly the fighter down onto the runway and hold it on the rollout. Only when all lift was lost and the tail wheel hit the pavement did he allow himself a sigh of relief.

As the fighters splashed across the dispersal area, ground crews stood by with sheets of canvas, but the flyers got a good drenching anyway as they scrambled out of the cramped cockpits. With shouts of relief, they burst into the ready room and shook themselves like so many hairy dogs.

"I'd say that settles it for the day," Cobbs laughed as he searched his pockets for a dry cigarette. "Bye the bye, lieutenants, meet Flight Lieutenant Hale here. He flew the other Messerschmitt." It had been a total surprise for the Americans, but they appreciated the lesson on the unexpected.

The three students complimented their British peers on a splendid exercise as they huddled around the fireplace warming and drying themselves. They were still on a high, full of questions, absorbing all the experience they could from these two bright eagles of the RAF.

With the storm growing in intensity, operations had come to a standstill, leaving Cobbs and his guests in sole possession of the building. Sharp thunderclaps sent a quiver through the frame structure, rattling aged windows originally constructed by a flying club long before the war. Cobbs responded by searching the ceiling as though anticipating its imminent collapse. "I say, lieutenants, if this keeps up you may just be our guests for the night."

Chuck moved away from the window where he had been monitoring the storm, seated himself at the table, and began shuffling a deck of cards. "What have you got to offer?" he inquired of their host. "Anything but those lumpy English mattresses?"

"Oh, we've some spares in the officers' quarters that would do rather well," Cobbs replied reassuringly. "As well, there's quite a do tonight. Headquarters is throwing a bash at the club for our new wing commander. Excellent band from Colchester, I hear."

"I'm certain we'd steal the show," Matt chuckled as he brushed his hands over his wrinkled flight suit.

"Well, if you decide to attend, we'll freshen you up a bit," Cobbs replied.

Chuck finished shuffling the cards and spread the deck across the table. "Count me in if we stay over. In the meantime, why don't we dry out with a hand of poker and some coffee?"

"How about a spot of tea?" Hale injected as he moved to the small service counter. "It's about that time, you know." He felt the pot, shook it, then pushed it to one side. "What bloody luck! It's cold as a herring."

"Tea? Coffee?" Roger sighed. "A man would wither away to nothing in this outfit. What we need is serious food and drink."

"Well, we'll have both!" Hale replied. "One of us will slip over to the club. Or NAAFI; that's a bit closer."

Matt had been halfheartedly positioning the chairs around the table. He enjoyed a game of cards as much as the rest, but the mention of NAAFI sealed a decision he had been toying with. "I say, Tower, we can't lumber our guests like that," Cobbs replied as he closed the doors of the bare cabinet. "It's really our do, you know."

Matt tactfully faced down the opposition and hurriedly donned his flight jacket. "No, no, I insist. You four cool it. I know the way. It's our thanks for your hospitality."

Cobbs could see that the American was set on going, and if he was that insistent, the Britisher would not argue the point. He had been flying with dozens of RAF students that week, considerably beyond his doctor-imposed limit, and though he hid it well his leg was throbbing. "All right, Tower, have at it, then. You might take the staff car out there in case the rain increases again."

Matt quickly took their orders, retrieved the keys, and hurried to the staff car. Precipitation was minimal now, but he switched the headlights on as a precaution. He knew the general direction of the canteen and was rather satisfied with himself, making only one wrong turn. After all, he was driving from the right seat for the first time.

The base was like a ghost town with operations shut down. But there was light from the canteen, and business appeared brisk as its clients dashed in and out beneath their floppy English parkas. Matt had wasted no time getting to the canteen, but once inside he slowed down considerably in the event either of the ladies at the sweet shop was looking in his direction.

He saw only Mrs. Pearson, and she appeared to be closing for the day. A paradox of thoughts rushed through his mind. Should he wait to see if Vivie returned or venture on over? Perhaps it was better to go over now, certainly not as obvious. *"She doesn't know me from Adam's house cat,"* he muttered under his breath. *"If I just had more time!"*

There was something about this woman that held Matt's interest, something far beyond the attractiveness that first caught his eye. *Genuine* best expressed it. No pretention. She would be honest and expect you to be. Perceiving these qualities gave him an unexpected warmth in her presence. He wanted to know her better than "Adam's house cat."

Matt brushed what neatness he could into the flight suit and smoothed the locks of his hair as he crossed the room. Mrs. Pearson, leaning with both hands on the counter, beamed as she saw him approaching. "Well, if it isn't me Yank! You're a man of your word, Lieutenant. Biscuits for dessert, wasn't it?"

"Indeed, as you Britishers say."

The baked goods were as delicious as he had expected and there followed the homey small talk of the lovely little lady who made them. She would, in a minute, mother any young man who came her way as Cobbs had warned. But in Matt's case, it seemed she displayed an extra fondness.

Mrs. Pearson babbled on like a brook. He knew he was hanging around longer than he should, but it would be difficult to leave without resolving the question in his mind. When Mrs. Pearson moved away to serve another customer, Matt deliberated over his options. He could simply say something in such a way that Vivie's name would come up or, and his fingers tingled at the thought, he could flat out ask where she was.

Thus engrossed, he was hardly aware when Mrs. Pearson returned to his end of the counter. She stood for a moment, arms folded under the ample bosom, and surveyed the lingering American flyer. Her head tilted a bit as though in question, and the trace of a smile touched her lips ever so slightly. "Why don't you give it another minute or so, dearie?"

A little puzzled, he leaned back from the counter and sought to collect his thoughts. "Give what a minute?" he inquired.

"Vivie!" she said. "She'll be off break in a moment or so."

Matt could feel the flush creeping up his neck as he stood with hands in pocket attempting the most unassuming pose. "What makes you say that?"

"Come now, Lieutenant," she drew the words out, mocking gently. "I had my eye on you this morning, and I'm thinking you had your eye on my little helper."

He stood for a moment, the perfect penitent, but unable to restrain the smile that crept across his face. "Man! Was I that evident?"

The perky English matron chuckled merrily, completely at home in these waters. "The last time I saw a look like that, Commander Potts was selecting his pastries."

If she was that aware, then Matt would risk confiding in her. He prayed she would not be of the mind to discourage his attentions. "I'd really like to know her better," he confessed.

"And perhaps you shall. She's offered to assist me here for a day or so," Mrs. Pearson replied. But the consolation did not produce the expected response and she rubbed her chin thoughtfully. "Now, that is what you'd like, isn't it, Lieutenant?"

"That would be great!" he replied. "But even if we have to stay overnight, we'd be flying out when the weather breaks in the morning."

"Pity," she moaned.

They were interrupted briefly as two airmen sought to make purchases and Mrs. Pearson moved away to serve them. Matt drummed his fingers, impatiently waiting for the transaction to be completed, for he needed her advice on another question. "What do you think my chances would be if I asked her to stay for a party tonight?"

It wasn't a question Mrs. Pearson relished, and she bided her time by reaching for a cloth to wipe the counter. "Well, I'd say your chances of asking her are quite good," she sighed. "But of her accepting, now that's another thing."

The pessimism didn't go down well with Matt, and true to his nature, he pressed on. "Does she have something against Yanks?" he joked. "Or maybe there's another guy?"

The little lady glanced up from her chore and smiled at the question. "I doubt that, Lieutenant. I don't agree with her, mind you, but that's Vivie's business. Oh, she's had a bloke or two leaning over the counter, but they were a crude lot for the most. I've known Vivie since she was a wee thing and she's not a common girl."

Matt had perceived as much and it added to the mystique that surrounded her. So, good soldier that he was, he waited and endured. His reward came in the measured click of heels from the hallway. Vivie breezed through the door carrying a shopping bag. "Nearly forgot this," she said. As yet unaware of the American flyer, she placed the bag at the end of the counter and folded her sweater beside it.

Mrs. Pearson glanced at Matt with a merry twinkle in her eyes. "Dear, would you give this old woman a break just now?"

"Of course, Mary; you just beetle off. I'll be right here," came the cheery reply.

The sweet shop manager made a hasty exit, but she didn't go far. Guardian instinct and a matron's curiosity reined her up in a hall chair where she disguised her surveillance with a magazine. Vivie, having her things in order, returned to the counter to find the lone American sentinel.

"Oh!" she exclaimed in mild surprise. "I didn't see you, Lieutenant." She studied his face for a moment then flashed a winsome little smile. "You were here this morning, weren't you?"

"Yes, I was," he replied. "These pastries are downright addictive!"

"Mrs. Pearson is a marvelous cook. I do so envy her. Is there anything I can get for you, Lieutenant?"

"She was saving some of the biscuits for me. Do you see them back there anywhere?"

Vivie appeared more at ease than when they had met earlier. Remembering that experience, Matt determined to avoid any personal questions and stick to small talk. "You know, it's a great thing Mrs. Pearson does."

"All this cooking?" Vivie inquired as she passed his box of pastries over the counter.

"Well, that too. But I really mean her taking the time to serve these airmen, to be out here talking to them the way she does. Some of them are a long way from home. In my case, for the first time. I hear her talking about her family and, I don't know, I guess it makes the world a little smaller."

Vivie paused for a moment, showing her first real attention to Matt. "Do you have brothers or sisters, Lieutenant?"

"I have a sister. She's a little older than me. She had a baby, a girl. They named her Susan," Matt paused reflectively, his eyes staring into the past. "Susan Anna Carter. Would you believe I'm an uncle?"

That was the first time he heard her laugh. A short one, granted, but with a merry lilt. It fit her well. One would expect her to laugh just that way. "You know, I never got to see that baby. I was on base in New Jersey readying to ship out when I got the message."

Vivie frowned sympathetically, her eyes searching Matt's. "You miss them, don't you? Your family?"

Matt, his hands on the counter, stared into the display case. "Sometimes you miss them so hard...."

Neither spoke for a time, allowing the din of canteen activity to fill the conversational void. Vivie sighed softly and returned to her chores of closing the shop. "Yes, one does, one does indeed," she whispered.

There was so much he wanted to know about her, but he suppressed the urge lest he touch a sensitive cord. While he cherished this time alone with Vivie, it was somewhat of a relief when Mrs. Pearson rejoined them. There was much mystery yet surrounding Miss Davis of the NAAFI volunteers, and perhaps the little biscuit maker would be a good conversational barometer to keep him out of trouble.

Matt felt pressure on his shoulder and turned instinctively to learn its source. Chuck stood with arm extended, a questioning scowl distorting his face. "What the heck's taking you so long, Tower? You realize there's four starving men back there in that soggy little dump?"

Matt's eyes went to his watch. He had been gone nearly an hour, the original mission completely forgotten. This was a heck of a comeuppance to endure before the lady he sought to impress, but he knew he deserved it. "Look," he began as casually as possible. "Something came up."

"Something came up?" Chuck questioned indignantly.

"Yeah, something came up," Matt repeated as he led his angry friend to one side. He pulled the short-order list from his pocket and pressed it into Chuck's hand. "I'll explain about it later, but I've got to ask you a favor."

Chuck stared blankly at his fidgety fellow flyer. "Matt, do you understand that we are hungry and mad? Not necessarily in that order, either. I came over here to prevent a lynching, and you're setting me up for a favor?"

"Okay, Okay! I'm a little late. I'll owe you one. I'll owe all of you one, okay? Would you please just take that list and get the orders for me? Here, here's the money." Matt pulled the British currency from his pocket and pressed it into Chuck's other hand. "I'll be there in a minute. I'll come help you when it's ready."

The angered flyer just stood there, uncertain whether he was more put-out or amused with his friend's eccentric behavior. Then, as he saw Matt gazing back at the pastry counter, it all began coming together for him. "Great czars!" Chuck exclaimed, shaking his head.

"Well, will you help me out or not?" Matt pressed eagerly.

"What's next?" Chuck murmured as he turned away and headed for the short-order bar.

On the way back to the pastry counter, Matt plotted how he might overcome the interruption gracefully. Vivie had moved to the end of the counter, but Mrs. Pearson seemed interested in his problem. "The responsibility of command," he lied. "You'd think grown men could take care of themselves."

The insensitive hands of time were cheating him, what with the ladies trying to close for the day and Chuck likely to call any minute. Whatever trump cards he held must be played now, so he chose his words carefully. "Ladies," he began with sufficient volume to reach Vivie's ears. "It's a miserable night. The weather officer says it'll be another couple of hours before this front moves through."

"Dear!" Mrs. Pearson responded. "I don't relish the trip into town. It's quite enough to drive it in the dark."

Vivie did not respond well to the prospect either, her quickening work pace reflecting her anxiety. "Would you take some advice from a perfect stranger, then?" Matt said.

"Meaning yourself?" Mrs. Pearson inquired as she reached over and patted his hand. "You're a bit more than a stranger, Lieutenant."

"Well, there's a party at the officers' club for some new brass, and Will says the band is really going to be something. Now, I don't have anybody to take, so I'm wondering if you two ladies would be my guests."

He glanced from one to the other hoping for a favorable indication, but the invitation was getting mixed reviews. Mrs. Pearson finally broke the silence. She was clearly moved by his thought. "And what would you want with an old woman at such a do?" she asked playfully.

Though Mrs. Pearson seemed to be considering the offer seriously, Vivie had retreated a step or two, her face drawn in serious thought. The biscuit maker turned to the younger woman, her hands extended palms-up in question. "What do you think, dear? It would be a change."

Only the faint rumble of voices across the room dented the silence. It was an agonizing pause for Matt, making it all too evident that Vivie was groping for an excuse. "It would be an imposition on Mum, I fear. I would be rather late getting in."

"Of course," Mrs. Pearson said. "I'd have to let my Harry know. But as far as Etta's concerned, dear, I don't think she would mind under the circumstances. We can give them a tinkle and see."

Vivie never changed her pace as she worked her way nearer and nearer the storeroom door. The biscuit maker and the flyer waited patiently for her response, though his heart began to sink. "Thank you," came the polite but sober reply. "But I think not."

As Vivie disappeared through the door Mrs. Pearson turned to Matt, her narrow shoulders rising and falling in a helpless shrug. "I'm sorry, Lieutenant."

Matt's heart sank in disappointment. "Uhhh," he moaned. "If I just had more time."

But there was no more time, for Chuck was signaling frantically from across the room. Matt retrieved the box of biscuits and smiled at Mrs. Pearson. "Thanks for your help. If things change and you can come to the party, I'll be there and the invitation still holds."

She watched the forlorn American flyer walk away. There was little more she could do in the face of her assistant's response, so she busied herself with the few remaining chores before they closed the shop. Vivie leaned against the door casing, her hands covering her pretty face. The base mother reached out and touched the younger woman's shoulder in concern. "He meant no harm, dear. I think he simply liked you. There's no way he could understand your feelings."

But she was not consoled easily. "I knew if I came here all the wrong things would happen. Hearing those planes roaring about the field, the flyers, the talk." Her arms folded across her body, her dainty hands clutching for her shoulders. "I've tried, Mary. Oh how I've tried!" she cried as tears painted glistening streams on her soft white cheeks.

As Vivie fought to control her sobs, Mrs. Pearson took her hand. "Come, dear, I'll close the counter and we'll sit for a while. Good heavens, we've missed tea as it is. I'll get a cup for the two of us."

Leaving Vivie seated in the hallway she placed the closed sign on the counter, poured two cups of England's standard, and returned to the younger woman. Clasping her cup in both hands, Vivie closed her eyes and sipped the hot brew, drawing comfort from its penetrating warmth.

"Better?" Mrs. Pearson inquired as she settled herself in the opposite chair.

"A little." Vivie's damp eyes blinked open and met the gaze of her senior friend. "I'm so sorry, Mary. I behaved like a perfect twit, didn't I?"

Mrs. Pearson smiled approvingly at Vivie's recovery. "No, no, dear.

You've done far better than I dared hope. I know it was difficult for you to come with me today, but you'll be so much the better for it."

"I'm certain that American flyer thinks I'm simply awful." She put the cup down to tend to her hair and dry her pink eyes. "He seemed to press so, and with everything else...."

"I know, dear, but he had little choice, what with the time and all. He doesn't seem like a bad sort. Quite the gentleman and rather handsome if you ask me."

"Oh, he appeared pleasant enough," she agreed with the flicker of a smile. "But I'm not certain I'm ready for all that just yet. Besides, I've had enough of our own men mucking about as it is."

Mrs. Pearson leaned over and rested her hand on Vivie's arm. "Don't feel ready or won't feel ready?" she probed.

Vivie lowered her head in silence, a nimble finger tracing the design on the napkin in her lap. They sat quietly with only an occasional clink of spoon and cup until Mrs. Pearson, sensing an impasse, leaned forward in her chair. "So," she said, pushing herself up. "I'll see that he gets the word. It might have been a delightful evening."

# CHAPTER 5

# You Can Get Hurt Doing This

**B**Y MORNING ONLY a thin trace of fog lay over the British base as the Bedford truck, with its cargo of American flyers, came to a stop near the waiting Thunderbolts. Matt had not rested well. When it was evident his invited guests were not coming, he left the party early and put himself to bed. Even now there were still unsettled feelings and he was ready to leave, to return to Raydon and lose himself in the demands of duty. Once in the air, his head would clear, for flight was sweet, occupying, predictable.

Student pilots dotted the dispersal waiting their turns at the German fighters in the cold morning sky. Matt could pretty much tell which ones had closed the party last night. What a surprise they had coming. Will Cobbs broke off his briefing and walked over to the Americans. "Good morning, gentlemen. You look none the worse for your nocturnal fling," he jested.

"You come over to Raydon next time and we'll get even," Chuck grinned.

"I'd love nothing better, chaps. Be certain I get an invitation!"

Matt pulled himself onto the P-47's broad wing and slipped into the cockpit. The huge propeller began rotating with the familiar clank and whine that never ceased to make his adrenaline surge. He looked back for a final salute to his host, only to see Cobbs running toward the plane waving his hand. "Hold it, Tower!" he bellowed over the engine.

The American throttled back and leaned out of the cockpit. "What's up?"

Cobbs stretched up to push a white envelope into Matt's hand. "I forgot this. It was left in my postal tray for you," he yelled, then double-timed it across the pad to rejoin his students.

The Thunderbolts roared into the English sky, leaving their onlookers as shrinking dots on the field below. Matt turned the section out over the broad river and set a heading for Raydon. With the fighters on course and trimmed out, he removed a glove and settled back, eager to learn the contents of the envelope.

The single sheet of paper unfolded to reveal a short note in distinctively feminine script. *"My Dear Lieutenant Tower,"* it began. *"I'm so sorry we were unable to accept your invitation to the party. It must have been delightful. Under different circumstances perhaps it would have been possible. As a consolation for your evident disappointment, I make this suggestion. Should you have occasion to visit Ipswich for R&R, you may find Falcon's Rest suitable lodging. By coincidence, Vivie's parents own the inn and she lives there. May God fly with you always. Sincerely, Mary Pearson."*

Matt sat for a time, shaking his head in wonder. *"And may God bless you, dear lady,"* he whispered.

Curiosity was eating at Chuck as he watched Matt's pantomime through the cockpit window. "Hey, great leader, what are you reading over there, the newspaper?"

But Matt wasn't ready to share the matter. "Oh, just some

directions and instructions, old buddy," came the reply as he folded the paper away.

Roger caught that much of the exchange and thought he had missed something important. "Instructions on what?"

Matt's retort was rift with devilish laughter. "On how to make this thing rolllllll!" he cried, suddenly banking the fighter into a series of great widening spirals to the utter amazement of his fellow flyers.

"Tower, you've been weird since we landed at that Limey base. What the heck's the matter with you?" Roger demanded. When there was no reply, he pressed Chuck. "Do you know what's going on, Shilling?"

The questioned pilot gently rocked his wings. *"It is my lady, O' it is my love! O' that she knew she were!"*

"What?" Roger demanded in dismay.

*"Romeo and Juliet,"* came the yawning reply. "Act Two, Scene Two."

Roger throttled back, putting some distance between his two companions and himself. "You're both nuts!" he spouted. "I'm dropping back a couple hundred feet before I get killed!"

His act was more a put down of the two pilots than of anxiety, for in no time Matt had them in a landing pattern ready to touch down at Raydon. They hit the runway smartly, taxied the fighters to the maintenance hangar and signed off their reports on the performance of the aircraft.

Chuck hitched a ride for them with two military policemen going in the direction of their barracks. Roger was none too pleased about that, either, as they huddled in the back of the brightly marked jeep. "It'll be all over the base now," he lamented, "Roger Baker, picked up by MPs! I appreciate the devil out of this, Shilling," he added, pulling up his collar so that only his nose and forehead were showing.

As they entered the barracks, Captain Herrington was pecking away at the typewriter with all the enthusiasm of one digging his own grave. He was a fighter pilot, not a secretary, and he hated the periodic reports, so much so that under the burden, no smoke swirled from the pear-shaped pipe. The only ejection appeared to be dead ashes that popped out with each jab at the writing machine. He paused and glanced at the intruders. "So the prodigal sons return. Well, tell me about it. Did you get your money's worth?"

They agreed enthusiastically that they had and seemed more than ready to lay the whole event on Herrington in one sitting. He knew all the right questions, giving them a superb debriefing in light of his own substantial experience. A smile of approval crossed his face as he leaned back in the chair and fired up the pipe. "Well, let's trust that the investment pays a dividend for the squadron, gentlemen, because next week you three will be mother hen to some of the replacement pilots coming in."

Matt raised a questioning eyebrow. "Do we have enough experience for that, Captain?"

"I think you will by then. The weather is looking a lot better, and we'll be flying at squadron strength for the next few days," Herrington replied.

The rest of the day was spent catching up on inevitable briefings about survival at sea and evasion tactics if downed in enemy territory. Matt could never decide if the meetings were designed to comfort him or to fan the flames of terror in him so he would fly better. As far as he was concerned, and from what he observed in the rank and file, the latter seemed to be the case.

He was glad to see the day end, to put it behind him. His weariness was more from boredom than anything else, but before turning in he would check the mission roster for Saturday. Herrington's prediction was correct. Right under "22 April 1944," all of Red Section was penciled in. Indeed, it appeared to be a full group participation. *"Now we're getting somewhere!"* Matt muttered under his breath.

Try as he might, sleep would not keep its appointment. At first, he blamed the lumpy mattress, figuring he had been spoiled by his English bed the night before. It was soon evident, though, that Vivie was the culprit, hiding in the recesses of his mind. *"Falcon's Rest,"* he whispered in the dark. "I wonder if Operations has any information on Ipswich. Got to check that tomorrow."

Though sleep was long in coming he had no difficulty leaving the bed at sunup due to an exuberance nurtured, no doubt, by the Ipswich matter and the day's pending mission. Briefing was at 1500 hours, giving him ample time to check on the quaint English town with the perplexing name. But that proved to be a disappointing pursuit, turning up only an aerial photograph and book matches from a fancy pub. He would have to let it go for the time being.

Forty-nine pilots lent an ear as Lieutenant Colonel Ben Rimerman outlined the mission. The stocky, balding officer was popular with the group, an instinctive leader, always on the cutting edge of the action. Slybird would escort 3$^{rd}$ Division B-17 bombers to a target in the Dusseldorf area of northwest Germany where oil and industrial targets still abounded. This would be Matt's first mission over the enemy's homeland. His eyes followed with sober discernment the lengthy line on the map from Raydon well into Hitler's bailiwick.

The sight of Milt-the-Stilt perched on *Sweet Pea's* wing was reassuring to Matt. If anything was wrong, the lanky crew chief would be puttering around the fighter and stalling for time. Only the armorers remained at work with last minute checks on the eight 50-calibers in its wings. An oversized tank clung to the chunky fighter's belly, extending its range a good 250 miles. This would be a long mission.

"How's she doing?" Matt greeted the sergeant.

"This old jug's raring to go, Lieutenant." He ambled over to *Sweet Pea's* pilot and began the check walk with him. "Sir, y'all a be right over them Nazis this time. Would you do me a favor?"

The inquiry took Matt's mind off his tingling fingers, which always seemed to be directly connected in some way with the butterflies in his stomach. "Now what could that be, Sergeant?"

"Bust the devil out of one of 'em for me."

Matt paused to consider the logic of such an evident request. "That's the whole idea, Sarge."

"No sir, it's that me and *Sweet Pea's* got a kind of a score to settle." Milt folded his arms over his chest and stared out across the field at the fighters being readied for takeoff. "Just before you got to Raydon, Lieutenant, I was crew chief for Lieutenant Perkins. Nebraska boy, going out on his fourth mission. He never come back. Me and the boys sat out here 'til dark that day." The sergeant slipped his hands into bulky coverall pockets and began walking again. "Very next day, message come through the Red Cross he'd had a son."

Neither man spoke as they finished the check walk, but Milt could tell from Matt's expression that he shared the sense of tragedy. The sergeant patted the side of the Thunderbolt as the flyer prepared to mount the wing. "This here would have been his plane when he got back. He was due for one of them new D's."

Matt settled into the cockpit and looked back at the sober crew chief. "*Sweet Pea* will do right by you," came the familiar assurance.

Fifty Slybirds faced each other along the main east-west runway as the takeoff signal came from the tower. For Matt, experiencing his first full group mission, it was a spectacular sight. The earth vibrated from the roar of thousands of horsepower pulling the big fighters into position, and the exhilaration he shared with the others was almost overwhelming. One felt a sense of invincibility in so large a formation, and the comradery of passing pilots offering the thumbs-up salute.

Colonel Rimerman, as mission leader, would fly with Matt's Seldom Squadron, followed by the 351st Lawyer Squadron and the 352nd Jockey Squadron. Matt was again flying wing for Herrington as Red Section took its turn down the runway. The group formed up and headed out over the North Sea, gray as dishwater beneath the afternoon sky. As the coast of Europe came into view, the group climbed to 20,000 feet and turned on a heading to intercept the bombers.

Slybird made landfall near Vlissingen, Netherlands, and began a sweep to locate the bombers. After 25 minutes of hunting and precious fuel consumed, Rimerman called in for a coded fix on their location. As was often the case, they were several miles off the rendezvous, this time near Gent, Belgium, and Slybird headed south.

Old eagle-eye Smaragdis was first to spot them. "Big Friends at 11 o'clock, Colonel!"

Matt picked out the vapor trails that streamed like white ribbons for miles behind the bombers. There must have been 300 of them in staggered boxes across the sky.

"Keep your distance, Slybird, until they know who we are," Rimerman warned.

After several tries, he got through to the wing leader, who was more than pleased to have the company. The group positioned itself around the bombers with Seldom strung along the left flank, Lawyer at top cover, and Jockey at right flank. Matt was close enough now to see the silhouettes of the men behind the bristling guns of the nearest bomber. From his angle the tall-tail 17's stretched beyond the horizon into infinity, a spectacle that history would share with relatively few men.

Just south of Antwerp the bombers changed altitude and position for the bombing run. That's when the flak started. At first, there were isolated puffs of black. Then, as the Germans found the range, they paved the sky with explosions. With the target only minutes away the bombers held their course, though Matt knew some must be taking at least minor damage. The fighters could do nothing to help in this situation but only maneuver for their own preservation. "When the flak stops the Luftwaffe comes," Rimerman reminded matter-of-factly.

They would choose that time between the anti-aircraft positions to dive in for attack, hoping to disrupt the bomb run and destroy as many planes as possible. Below and to his right Matt saw a bomber, evidently hit and streaming smoke from an engine. He expected to see it abort, but it held position, steady on course, its captain simply reporting the condition. Then, almost as abruptly, the flak stopped, dwindling down to inaccurate spotted puffs.

"Bogeys! Nine o'clock! Bogeys! One o'clock!" Old eagle eye was at it again.

"Drop your tanks!" Rimerman ordered.

Matt spotted the nine o'clock gaggle within a second of Smaragdis' warning, and he felt some satisfaction that his eye was getting better. The Messerschmitts circled to the front of the bombers, positioning for a head-on attack. Lawyer anticipated this and began their dive to intercept the Germans.

"They'll come straight through on the first pass," Herrington called to his section. "The bombers can't fire that way without hitting each other. We're going after them when they come out. Stay with me!"

Matt's mouth was so dry he couldn't swallow. Beads of sweat soaked his helmet, and he checked the gun safety switch a half-dozen times to be sure it was off. He watched as the bombers held steady, boring in head-on with the enemy fighters. Lawyer was waiting for them, which disrupted the charge, but half of the 109s slipped through. "Take 'em when they come out. But stay away from the bombers. They'll shoot your butt down!" Herrington reminded.

Within seconds the German fighters had passed through the bombers and fanned out like quail breaking cover. Red Section had its work cut out for it.

"Coming at you, Red One!" Smaragdis called from his rear position.

Herrington had seen the two 109s coming out of the bomber formation to his right and was already banking in pursuit. "Heads up, Tower! We're going in!"

Matt scanned the sky dutifully, then matched his section leader's turn. The Messerschmitts were determined to make another pass at the bombers and rolled back in their direction. It wasn't the smartest move on their part, for Herrington dropped in behind the element leader like a hawk.

Rimerman's White Section had engaged the German foursome that first attacked the bombers, and it was evident from radio chatter that Jockey Squadron was now busy on the left flank. Matt had no time to keep up with it all as he and Herrington closed on their own bogeys. He glanced in the rear mirror to clear his stern and saw Chuck and Roger diving at an unknown target. At 300 yards, Herrington opened up with his 50s, and strike marks flashed on the German's left wing.

The Messerschmitts broke almost instantly and Herrington followed the leader, firing intermittently as the Hun crossed his sights. "Clear the rear, Tower!" he bellowed. "Go get the other one!"

Matt was an instant from following the order, but instinct froze his arm. It was good that it did, for the second 109 rolled over the top of Herrington and fell in behind. Matt could see the puffs from its guns, and Red Leader was forced to break off. "Oh, crap!" the captain yelled into the radio. The first Messerschmitt limped off to the side, a perfect potential deflection shot, but Matt could not leave Herrington. "Where are you, Tower?"

There was no time for Matt to reply because the 109 behind Herrington was boring in for the kill. The section leader did a fair job of staying out of the German's sights, but that strategy would soon have them on the deck—not the place they wanted to be this deep in enemy territory.

The German fighter was above Matt, well out in front, anything but a textbook shot. His first burst of fire accomplished nothing. Not only was the German at maximum range, but his movements were too unpredictable. Matt felt the birth of panic that he was letting Herrington down, but he reigned in his emotions quickly. They had trained for this moment. *"Think, fool!"* he scolded himself. Will Cobbs' lessons flashed through his mind: *"Don't watch the enemy; watch the guy he's chasing."*

Having closed some of the distance between the 109 and himself, Matt centered his attention on Herrington's movements. When the section leader pulled to the left, he did the same, and the German drifted right through his sights. Again *Sweet Pea's* 50-calibers rattled the Thunderbolt's frame, but this time there were strikes in the enemy's tail section. It was enough to break the German off, and he rolled into a dive to evade his attacker. Matt's heart pounded as he followed the sleek gray and black Messerschmitt, anticipation of a first destroyed driving him on.

"Break, Red!" someone thundered over the radio. Matt instinctively banked his fighter away. Then, searching the sky, he grew painfully aware the warning was not for him. His response had cost a possible first victory. As he leveled off, the sight that greeted him was anything but the invincible force of aircraft with which he had climbed into the English sky. He was below and behind the bombers, around which dot-sized fighters raced in erratic patterns. He knew his fellow flyers were up there because of the frantic radio transmissions, but who was who?

"Return to your positions, Red Section," Herrington's voice crackled over the confusion.

It was a hard order to follow with so many available targets, but to do otherwise would leave the bombers at the mercy of another wave of Luftwaffe. Matt nosed up the fighter and headed for the left flank of the bombers, which were catching the full brunt of a last-minute German effort. The B-17 with the smoking engine was still in formation, but the Big Friends faced a new threat on the right flank. Twin-engine Messerschmitts approached from up sun, releasing a volley of rockets and heavy cannon fire with devastating effect.

One 17 took a direct hit in the tail section, completely separating the bomber from its rear member. Another, hit in its starboard wing, lost an engine. It was a rude initiation for Matt, this first sight of friendly aircraft under attack and the death spirals of the mortally damaged. With grim helplessness he watched the severed bomber, and like every airman in the sky that day, he prayed for the sight of 10 blossoming parachutes. But none came. All the way down, until he lost sight of the bomber, there were no chutes.

Jockey Squadron was quick to respond to the twin-engine fighters. Matt could see one of them nosing up, smoke pouring from an engine. When it exploded moments later in an orange flash, he was certain he had willed it, so furious were his thoughts, The other three dived for home with Jockey in hot pursuit. The stick quivered under his shaky hand, and he reached up with the other to rough his flight helmet in an attempt to calm himself.

The bombers were on final approach to the target as evidenced by renewed heavy flak and the sudden scarcity of the Luftwaffe. They were on their own now. Slybird pulled back to watch the Big Friends boring over the roadway of black bursts to deliver their packages to the Third Reich.

Of the 300 participants, nine would not return. Five because of flak and four the compliments of Messerschmitts. The fighters would lick their wounds as well. Lieutenant Doris of Jockey Squadron would not return from pursuit of the twin-engine fighters, and two of Seldom's White Section Thunderbolts were limping and unfit for combat. While Herrington's jug was fightable, strike damage scarred both wings and the rear fuselage.

As Slybird Group turned for home, it left a sky smudged in black, with smoke and vapor trails where celestial enemies had etched their determinations on that great canvas sky. As the group began reforming, the squadron leaders took stock of their numbers. Jockey was short an entire section, and a fighter was missing from

Lawyer. Having been separated from the group in the heat of battle, all but Lieutenant Doris would return to Raydon by various routes. But Slybird was far from being skunked. There were 12 confirmed enemy destroyed and several probables. Others would carry lead home in their tails.

Withdrawal support fighters from England would have the job of picking up the bombers as they left the target area. But Rimerman was not prone to return to base with ammunition to spare. Soon he divided the group into one flight with fight left in it and one that needed to retire early. Matt would be in the first flight as it dived to make strafing sweeps on the way home as fuel would allow.

They leveled off at 5,000 feet on a general course for the coast. Matt was still gripping the stick like a turkey leg at Thanksgiving. He pried his fingers away and reached up to pull the oxygen mask aside. Closing his eyes for a second, he massaged the tension from his face. The tingle had left his fingers, but his chest still rose and fell with the ebbing excitement of the hour.

Predictably, Roger's impatient voice broke the momentary silence. "Where'd the Krauts go, Captain?"

"They're not chicken, Baker," Herrington replied. "They're saving it up for the bombers. Pray withdrawal support finds them in time."

"Let's get down on the deck, Slybird, and see what we can find," Rimerman broke in.

They skirted Antwerp to avoid the anti-aircraft and followed the big river to the Dutch border. In one of its coves, the Germans had erected docks and tucked them under camouflage netting. But Slybird, true to its name, caught a tug attempting to dock a string of barges. This was Rimerman's meat. He and Duncan were naturals when it came to strafing, and in minutes, the mission leader had 20 Thunderbolts strung out for attack.

The constant paradox of peace and war played on a soldier's emotions. Matt was no exception. From the turbulent skies over

Germany, the group now raced across lush countryside dotted with farms and hamlets where men and women carried on despite the war. The fighters were at treetop level as they turned for the river, a maneuver which placed them parallel to a winding valley. It was late afternoon, and the shadows of the taller trees crept out to take their rest on grassy meadows and tilled fields. As a rickety horse-drawn cart rushed into view, its aged driver sprang to his feet and shot his arms up in a victory salute. He held that pose, turning with the Americans until they could see him no longer.

It was a piece of drama, one of many that Matt's mind would replay again and again in the years to come. The old man, forced to submit to the invasion of his homeland, could not restrain himself and freely exercised the only act of defiance at his disposal. For a moment, these were his fighters. If there was anything to shoot at, Matt determined to put a few rounds in it for the old Dutchman.

They were hedgehopping now, trying to keep the trees between them and the opposite riverbank. Rimerman gave the signal, and the fighters rose like kites in the wind, then dropped over the leafy groves and fanned out for attack across the swollen waters.

The makeshift port was well hidden in the cove. Had it not been for the barges in tow, the Germans would have been home free. Rimerman led the first wave at the tug, his burst of fire spewing a path of frothy geysers straight into the hapless ship. Matt could see the seamen jumping ship fore and aft as debris flew into the air from its deck and bridge.

Herrington led the second wave at the dock area, and as the shoreline grew larger, white tracer streaks arched out in greeting. The Thunderbolts made poor targets for the lighter guns as they zipped along inches above the river, their prop wash fanning a wake on its surface. But being over the target was another matter, where they would be eye level with the flak towers.

"Green Leader," Herrington directed their sister section, "work over the left end of the dock. We've got the right."

Matt watched his tracers streak in random patterns across the docking area. Camouflage obscured the results, but he knew his 50s were chewing up whatever they came across. The fighters were closing on the target so quickly he had but seconds to choose a final shot. Lining up on the bulky right end of the docks, he squeezed off a long burst. To his surprise, the dark silhouette came alive with tiny white flashes. He strained for a look as *Sweet Pea* sailed over at full throttle, but the subject of his fire remained a mystery.

For a second, Matt thought he had scraped the trees. It felt and sounded like branches slapping the side of his fighter. As he banked away from the target, it happened again. This time the impact was just below his left knee, with a simultaneous crack and clatter of torn metal. *"Anti-aircraft!"* his mind screamed. When he pulled up from the strafing run, the flak tower had been indiscernible in the fading light, and the gunners caught him going away. He kept the fighter as low as visibility allowed and swung back out over the river. The tug was on fire, and Rimerman's flight continued to rip up the barges.

From the relative safety of mid-river, Matt could now appraise his pass at the docks. Thick black smoke boiled off the crimson inferno that covered his target area. By chance, he had fired on a fuel cache waiting to be loaded, and now the whole area was cast in the eerie glow of fire and sunset.

"Who got the fuel dump?" Rimerman asked, his voice crisp with excitement. Matt started to reply, but Herrington beat him to it. "One of my boys, Ben. My wingman, Red Two!"

"Heck of a job, Tower! I'll shake your hand when we get back," the colonel said. "All right, Slybird, let's get out of here while there's light and fuel."

Matt was still recovering from the strafing run as the flight formed up. The group leader's unexpected recognition was a well-timed balm for his spirits. Just as he began to bask a little, the mounting stench of fuel reached his nostrils and he was aware of air blowing against his leg. Cocking his head for a better look, he saw two holes the size of his fist in the cockpit wall.

Herrington noticed his wingman's uneven flight. "How's it going over there, Tower?"

"Couple of holes blown in the cabin, Captain. Lot of fumes coming in from somewhere," Matt replied. "I'm trying to get this canopy cracked open."

"Might make it worse, Red Two. Try your oxygen mask first."

Random puffs of coastal flak chased the Thunderbolts out over the North Sea, where Matt would find himself locked in a bitter test of endurance. Desperate for relief from the fumes, he removed his gloves and crammed them into the gaping holes. Helpful, but not a cure. How good the coast of England would look just now, but that would be a while. The urge for air was overwhelming, and Matt decided to try opening the canopy anyway. As long as he leaned near the instrument panel, it was almost bearable, though his flying was impaired. Thus he began the labored schedule of leaning into the canopy opening, then sitting up with the oxygen mask to steady the ship, yet never completely free of the noxious fumes.

The other flyers tried to keep up a running dialogue of encouragement with the stricken pilot, but to do so interfered with his breathing. If that weren't enough, Matt was becoming aware of discomfort in his left leg. It was stinging smartly on the back between his ankle and knee. But what really concerned him was the soggy warmth in his boot. Anxious questions filled his mind: How badly was he bleeding? Would he pass out before he could land?

He hated to use the mike because of the fumes, but he could become a danger to the flight and wanted to make his condition known. "Red Two to Red Leader," he called, his voice tense but controlled. "Captain, I've been hit in the leg. I don't know how bad it is. I might get a little clumsy over here."

"Okay, Tower," Herrington replied. There was no urgency in his voice, nothing to alarm the troubled flyer, for he had handled many a similar case. "Let's move out to the right and talk this thing over."

The two Thunderbolts eased over a few hundred yards from the rest of the flight while the captain kept up his old-hat routine. "Now, I'm going to stick with you, Tower. You just fly off my wing, okay? Not that much farther to go!"

There was little sun left. It peeked timidly over the horizon, barely illuminating the miles of gray swells as though ashamed of the predicament it was leaving the young flyer in. His mind was no help either, for it kept picturing him bobbing about in the drink, struggling to free himself from his parachute. But he determined to hold on in the face of stinging eyes, burning nose, and soggy boot, preferring to take his chances in some English beet field or the deep below if need be.

"Land ho!" Roger Baker's voice boomed over the radio. "Matt, baby, we're home. A few more minutes. You can do it!"

Matt heard the words and he understood, but the battle had opened on another front with growing waves of wooziness. He really wanted to just let the stick go and roll out of the plane. In the background he heard Rimerman talking to the homing trailer. "Boyhood homer, this is Slybird. Can you give us a vector?"

The welcome voice of the controller gave a radar position and coordinates for approach.

"Boyhood, we've a wounded and a possible crash landing."

Matt was coughing every few breaths, laboriously striving to maintain his breathing routine. They were down to 1,000 feet, and Rimerman requested a straight-in approach for the troubled pilot and Herrington, who stuck like glue to his wounded wingman. "Okay, Red Two, there are the lights. Get the canopy all the way open."

Stinging eyes sent streams of tears down Matt's face. He could not distinguish the landing lights. They were a thin white blur. Little beyond Herrington's fighter was clear anymore, and he was totally dependent on the section leader's maneuvers. "Red Two, throttle back with me.... That's it.... Now ease it into half flaps. Watch your nose."

They were on final approach now, and for the first time Matt could make out the two rows of landing lights. "You're hot!" Herrington cautioned. "Back off.... Level her up! Level her up!"

The two Thunderbolts zigzagged their way down to the runway with Herrington in the lead. Matt was beyond thinking and had resigned himself to simply duplicate the moves of his leader. Rimerman's flares drifted slowly over the base, signaling to the world a wounded flyer's distress. Crash trucks and ambulance were already crossing the field. On the third bounce, *Sweet Pea* veered to the right and finished its rollout in the grass, tail rising then dropping back to earth.

Matt's hands shook so badly he could hardly get out of the seat harness. Between coughs and gags, he rolled himself out of the cockpit and literally slid down the wing, his exhausted body crumpling to the ground. By the time rescue arrived, he was on his knees, hands clutching a blade of the prop, throwing his guts up. He slumped back into the arms of the first medic to reach him. "My leg," he moaned hoarsely. "Check my leg."

When things came back into focus, Matt was in the hospital, flat on his back, staring into the genial, reassuring face of Flight Surgeon Canipelli. "Welcome to the land of the quick, Lieutenant."

Matt's first attempt to speak was without result. Laryngitis. The only speech comfortable for him was a whisper. "Wh... about ma' leg, Doc?" he managed.

"Nasty gash. Took a hunk of flesh out of you, but it should heal. You've got 20 stitches, so you'll be ambulating with a crutch for a while. It's a miracle the bone escaped major damage." Canipelli sat on the side of the bed and folded his arms. "How you recover from the fumes is the main issue. You can count on one thing, a darn good hangover in the morning."

Matt shook his head dejectedly. "What time is it?"

"Twenty-two hundred. By the way, there're a dozen pilots out in the hall that want proof you're among the living. Feel like a brief visit?"

"Okay," came the labored reply.

# CHAPTER 6

# Getting to Know the Locals

**T**RUE TO PREDICTION, Sunday morning was anything but holy. Matt vowed that if this was a hangover, he most assuredly would never become a drunk. But the world was no longer shaded in green, and the nursing staff had him hobbling around the medical ward. He vaguely recalled a crowd by his bed the night before but none of the conversation, which he had no part in anyway. So Herrington's appearance in the doorway of the ward was a welcome sight: decked out for a mission, the pipe solidly in place, white scarf draped over his shoulder. He was "Hop Harrigan" all over, a fighter pilot who loved his work.

He stood for a moment, hands on hips, beaming down at the patient. "You better get the crap out of here. They're casting lots for your stuff."

"I'd feel sorry for the sucker who wins it," Matt chuckled back at his superior.

There were things that needed saying, for each had played an important role for the other during the Saturday mission. But such is the nature of men that they must warm up to the occasion. Herrington seated himself on the side of the bed and rested his hands on his knees. "You scared us for a while, you know that?"

"I scared me!" Matt grinned. "But I'm here because you flew me in."

Herrington glanced at his watch. "And if you hadn't shot that Hun off my tail? Hey, it's what we do, brother."

They knew well the risks of combat flying. But even in tense moments, there could be outlandish humor when viewed from the safety of hindsight. Matt now learned that during the height of the dogfight, Roger had flown wing for a 109 for several seconds before they recognized each other. The resulting antics, as each jockeyed for advantage, had fueled another of Smaragdis' wild stories at Auger Inn that night. But Roger had nailed the enemy and had his first destroyed.

"Well, Slybird calleth his great warriors to battle," Herrington said as he eased off the bed. "You're in for some R&R, friend. When doc kicks you out, you'll have a pass waiting. Just get your butt well, 'cause I'm short a wingman."

The next few days were an ordeal of another kind for Matt. Boredom set in quickly, leaving him with the restlessness of a caged hawk. His highs came with the visits of fellow pilots who willingly shared their missions and his lows with the roar of fighters rising to the task without him.

By the third day, he had devoured all available reading material and was gaining the reputation of pest as he hobbled curiously around the wards flirting with the nurses and threatening to escape.

Finally the morning came when Dr. Cope sauntered in, minus the ever-present chart, and Matt sensed expectantly the hour of reprieve. "Today's the day, right Doc?"

"Well, Lieutenant, your condition has stabilized, and the leg's coming along nicely. But you're a while from flying," the flight surgeon responded as he pulled the bandage back to check the wound. "There's still some internal healing to come. Can you handle the dressing by yourself?"

"I know the whole routine, sir, and the part about keeping the leg up as much as possible." Matt paused for a moment, hoping he had been as convincing as he was profuse. Cope was smiling, his left hand kneading away the tension in the back of his neck. The flyer assumed he had won. "How long before I can fly, Doc?"

"Depends on the healing. Just don't let it get infected. I'll check it in a week, and we'll go from there," Cope replied as he turned for the door. "And use the crutches. I don't want the stitches pulled, okay?"

Chuck had brought a uniform on his last visit, and Matt was struggling into it within minutes of the surgeon's departure. His condition had been the most serious of the half-dozen patients in residence, and as he swung between the crutches to McDuff's waiting jeep, he was the subject of much attention and well wishing—especially from the nurses, who were a blessing to lonely soldiers far from home. The lipstick smudges on his cheek would serve as mute testimony to an honorable discharge from the infirmary.

Settled in place with his legs stretched out, Matt turned to his driver. "Stop by headquarters on the way, Sarge. I've got a pass coming."

The wounded flyer was none too thrilled with the crutches but found them an asset in the headquarters waiting room where they won him a little faster service. His papers were processed by the hands of a capable young WAC. "What happened, Lieutenant?"

"Flak put me in the hospital. Wasted nearly a week over there."

The WAC noticed the red smudges on the side of Matt's face and a devilish smirk wrinkled her nose. "Pretty nasty scrapes on your cheek, too, sir!"

"Such are the wages of war, ma'am," Matt replied with a smirk of his own.

For a man with a bad leg, he did one heck of a job catching the noon local into Ipswich. Matt prevailed on the driver to wait at the barracks while he stuffed the essentials into a duffel bag. His face brightened when he found a small bundle of mail on his bunk and he fought the temptation to open it, especially the envelope in his mother's distinctive script. Reluctantly, he slipped it all into the bag and hurried out.

This was Matt's first occasion to retrace the route that had taken him from Raydon Wood station to the base. It was a far more relaxed ride than McDuff had provided. They continued through acres of cultivated fields and clustered farm buildings ever so much like his grandfather's. He fought to suppress the tinge of homesickness known all too well to soldiers on foreign soil.

The ride was longer than Matt expected, but then the bus had local stops to make. As they approached Ipswich, the wharfs and quays, with their ancient dockside buildings and warehouses, plainly showed evidence of bomb damage, and at several points he could see the unmistakable protrusion of anti-aircraft weapons.

For some reason, he had not considered England's quaint outer boroughs as war targets, but this was a seaport and North England rail connection. German bombs had left their mark in the gaping spaces between the buildings and in piles of twisted rail. His thoughts went to Vivie, that she would be in service to the defenders during such raids, serving food and water and helping to tend any wounded. *"How close were the bombs to her home?"* he wondered.

Though several passengers offered to let him pass, Matt chose to wait for the bus to clear so he could work the crutches to best advantage. He was about ready to slide his duffle bag down the aisle when the driver offered to help. Matt certainly was willing to let him and followed his bag to the platform. "What's your unit, Lieutenant?"

"Three Fifty-Three Fighter Group at Raydon," he replied before catching himself.

He had broken the vow made after Lord Haw Haw's broadcast. It did seem improbable that this rosy-cheeked, oval-faced "grandfather" intended to betray his England, and his continuing remarks eased the American officer's mind.

"We have quite a few of your lot, you know. Some come down from Martlesham Heath, Debach, even Wattisham."

"Well, this is my first visit," Matt said. "And I really appreciate your help." He adjusted his grip on the duffle-bag strap and began the laborious trudge to the street, then paused and turned back toward the conductor. "By the way, would you know how to get to Falcon's Rest?"

"That I don't, Lieutenant. I'm rather involved with return passengers, so little sightseeing opportunity. A hackney can get you there."

He dropped the bag beside one of the black pint-sized cabs at the curb, which disturbed the extended reverie of its operator. An amusing specimen, this rotund little man in rumpled herringbone jacket with sleeves that covered his knuckles. Folding the newspaper under an arm, he squinted up at his prospective fare. "All right, Lieutenant, you want the girls or the pubs?" It was a sight, the little taxi driver stroking a week's stubble and figuring he had Matt pegged.

"Not today, friend," the American flyer replied. "But you can tell me if there's an inn called Falcon's Rest."

"Aye, I know that one. Henley Road. Most blokes prefer the Butter Market. It's the high street, you know."

"Well, this bloke prefers Henley Road, and I'd like to get there before dark," Matt replied.

The cabbie shrugged, then waddled over and placed the duffle bag in the cab. His passenger preferred the front seat, which seemed to surprise the operator as he scrambled around to the driver's side to clear away a bottle of who knows what. The cab smelled of fried grease, and Matt hurriedly lowered the window. "It's me fish and chips. I couldn't eat it all," the little man offered with another shrug.

The young flyer wondered if he would get the New York treatment from his chauffeur. It was there that he had been driven in circles to raise the fare. "What's your name?" Matt inquired.

"Sims," came the simple reply.

"You lived here all your life?" the flyer said.

"I was born in Rushmere, but me family come into Ipswich when I was a tyke."

As they crossed another yard of railroad tracks, Matt could see how widespread the bomb damage really was. "Looks like the Germans worked you people over pretty good."

"It was plenty bad in '42 and '43. Like two or three times a week. They was mainly after the docks and railway at first. But it spread around after that like they was after the common folks." He paused thoughtfully as they passed by some heavily damaged buildings. "Now, that there was done by them long-range 190 fighters. They slip in, three or four at a time, drop a bomb, and fire their guns."

The damage disturbed Matt as the cab passed along the curious little streets lined with shops and townhouses. Much of old Ipswich remained, with its prominent Tudor architecture. In spite of it all, the people went about: shoppers, messenger boys, those with business errands. The Germans had not made cowards of these people. They were hurt, suppressed for a time, burying those they loved, but they had not broken.

"This here's Cornhill," the driver gestured. "It's kind of the center of things." Matt marveled at the classic old buildings, rather larger than he had expected for the town. The tiny side streets and unique shops beckoned irresistibly, playing on his natural bent to history and antiquity. There were small and great churches, some ornate, commanding lovely campuses. Others, like chapels, sat upon grassy lawns between towering buildings. It was here, he would learn, that

Vivie had grown up, for her family roots spanned three generations in East Suffolk.

St. George Street was so narrow that Matt could well appreciate the tiny English cars, all of which insisted on driving on the wrong side of the road. "All right, Yank, here it tis, Henley. We've but a little way now."

"What's that?" Matt asked as they reached a great open area studied with trees.

"That's Christ Church Park. There's a huge old mansion on the far side of the arboretum. It's an old one if you like such. Dates from the 1500s, they say."

Though some distance ahead, Matt knew instinctively it was Falcon's Rest. He could not yet read the sign, but the charming old building stood out from the rest, more Victorian than Tudor. Three stories it appeared, gray trimmed in white, with deep porches running full width of the first and second floors. It was a stark departure from traditional British architecture. He would learn later the design was deliberate, intended to be noticed and talked about. Its shake-shingled roof, decked with four dormer windows, set an attractive crown. They turned into the parking drive beside a heavily bordered sign, atop which the wooden likeness of a perched hawk surveyed all in regal repose.

Sims was more than accommodating as he hefted the duffle bag to the broad wooden steps. They were met by a lad of slight build, clad in tan knickers, whose fingers combed blond hair that had been captured beneath a brown driving cap. Matt shook his head and smiled to himself at the sight of the knickers. His first experience with them at Monte Sano Grade School in Augusta had spelled adolescent disaster. He had been taken for a Little Lord Fauntleroy by his classmates, much to his mortification, and saw to it that the britches were so damaged they could never be worn again.

What the youngster lacked in weight, he certainly made up for in eagerness. "I'll take your bag, sir," he insisted as he gave Matt a wide-eyed once over. "Do you fly bombers or fighters?"

"Fighters," the American pilot replied with a smile. "What's your name, son?"

"Bobby Brooks, sir," the lad responded, his face masked in awe. He was all questions then, giving Matt little chance to respond. "You got wounded, didn't you? Did the Germans do it, did you shoot down any?"

Matt rested on the crutches and looked down into the expectant young face. A face not unlike his own when, years ago at the county fair, another pilot lifted him into the seat of a biplane. "Well, Bobby Brooks, I did get wounded and I've shot at a few Germans. Now, tell me something. Do you work here?"

"Yes sir. I started a while back. I come by after school and earn a few bobs."

The cabbie had been standing by, his short arms folded over the round belly, enjoying the exchange between man and boy. "I say, Lieutenant, I see you're in good hands so it's off with me."

Matt paid Sims' fare while the youthful bellboy tugged the duffle bag through the lobby door. The pilot's popularity had not waned when he reached the lobby, nor had his young admirer's curiosity. "What kind of fighter do you fly, Lieutenant? How fast will it go?"

"Bobby, you're not to be a pest if you're to work here." Matt was aware that a woman stood behind the lobby desk, but he had been occupied with the young lad. The sound of her voice, more than her presence, drew his attention. It was a specific East Anglian accent, astonishingly familiar to him. When their eyes met, he knew she was the lady on the train the day he arrived at Raydon. Minus the hat and gloves, of course, but her light-brown hair was still rolled just so, with its touch of gray on the sides.

"I'm sorry, Lieutenant," she said. "May I help you?"

Matt started to inquire, but thought better of it, letting discretion prevail. He had been accused once of having the advantage of a lady and he felt it better to feel his way around for the present.

"A room please. On the first floor, if possible," he added. "The fewer steps, the better."

Nimble fingers moved the register around and placed a pen at his disposal. "I should think this level would be more comfortable for you," she replied. "There would be no steps at all."

He had evidently missed something in the exchange. "Well, yes ma'am, the first floor."

The flyer's perplexed expression brought a smile to her face. "You see, Lieutenant, the floor just above is the first floor. I'm sure you mean the ground floor." He shook his head in acknowledgement and returned the smile. The language was still playing tricks on him.

"How long will you be with us, Lieutenant Tower?" she inquired as she checked his entry in the register.

"A couple of days. Probably leave Sunday."

She was studying him from the corner of her eye. It was evident that he was considering her by the moment, but she had not placed him yet. "We serve tea at four in the great room if you would care to join us," she said. "Dinner is from 6 p.m. to 9 p.m., or you may prefer a pub."

By her poise on the train, he had pegged her as the grand lady of a lord, and her position behind the desk required some mental adjustment. She turned to him with the room key, all the while studying him more closely. "Room 3 should be quiet and it has a lovely view of the park."

Matt was about to mention the train. But other guests were arriving, and the stress of travel was beginning to take its toll. He welcomed a nap more than anything. His young admirer stood diligently guarding the duffle bag, a great grin engulfing the bright, attentive face. Matt placed the key in his hand. "Do you know the way, Bobby Brooks?"

He did, and they set off across the spacious lobby, this unlikely parade of tugging youngster and crutch-hung cripple. Matt had time now to appreciate the massive stained molding, a rich walnut that complemented the heavy stairway railings. Large area rugs rested atop shining random plank floors, and the young American had to smile as he contemplated his mother's reaction to the fine old English country pieces placed at intervals around the room.

It took some doing for Matt to disengage from the enthusiastic youngster, but with promises of flying tales to come, he was finally able to shut the door and surrender to the bed.

He had been napping for some time, a shallow sleep that did not blot out a distant mournful wail. Pushing himself to a sitting position, he strained to identify the signal and finally concluded it was an air raid test. Unnerving at the least, awakening in a strange room and bed where long window shadows now streaked the walls. He had slept through tea, and if he lay there much longer, dinner as well.

The cool water revived him as he cupped it to this face, and a few licks of the comb brought order again to his wavy brown crown.

Vivie was much on his mind, and he fought to stifle the tingling anticipation that accompanied him along the hallway. His greatest concern was that she might be at the RAF base, and he would miss her. Activity in the lobby had picked up, with late guests arriving and the evening gourmets taking advantage of the dining hall. The gracious lady was still at her post as Matt crossed the room. She glanced up and a quick smile lit her face. "Lieutenant, pardon me a moment." She covered the few steps that separated them, her hands seeking the lapels of her blue hip-length house coat. On this side of the desk, she was all the more striking. Late 50s, Matt guessed, and she had certainly taken care of herself. "I was certain we had met before," she said. "But I simply could not recall where. It was the train! The train to Hadleigh."

Matt returned her smile boyishly, a quality that endeared him to the senior set in Augusta. "Yes, ma'am. I remember you, too.

Three of us were going to Raydon, and you wished me Godspeed, or something like that."

"Did I now?" she responded, cocking her head thoughtfully. "Well, from the look of things I must say a better prayer for you. Have you been wounded?"

"My fighter was hit with anti-aircraft fire. Took a hunk out of my leg, but the Doc says I'll survive."

"I'm so sorry! I do wish you a speedy recovery. I'm Etta Moore, Lieutenant, and we are delighted to have you at Falcon's Rest. Dinner is being served, and I know you must be hungry at this hour."

The dining room had served most of the guests, and Matt was seated promptly. The proper little waitress, uniformed in black with crisp white collar and cuffs, did her part to complement the setting as she filled his crystal water tumbler. He toyed with the menu for a moment then smiled up at her. "What's good tonight?"

"It's all good, sir. You'll get no stodge at Falcon's Rest!" she boasted.

"Then what's your suggestion for a hungry man?"

"Well, you'd do nicely with the Lancashire pot and greens." His questioning eyes prompted further explanation. She leaned closer. "It's a stew, sir, a meat dish."

"Let's go with that," he replied, folding the menu. "By the way, is the lady at the desk the manager?"

"Oh, a bit more, sir, that's Mrs. Moore. She and Major Moore own the inn, indeed, three of them."

"I thought the Davis family owned Falcon's Rest. Are you certain about that?" he pressed.

"Quite certain, sir. He pays me wages." She retrieved the menu and paused beside the table. "Would you care for a beverage?"

"Just coffee, thanks."

Matt was puzzled. Had he misunderstood? He clearly remembered Mrs. Pearson saying Vivie's parents owned the inn. Etta Moore was speaking with one of the waitresses at the door, her eyes scanning the room to estimate the seatings. This was as good a time as any to clear up the matter, and when her eyes moved in his direction, he smiled and motioned to her. It was a bit awkward for him, but he gained the cooperation of his stiff leg and stood as she approached. "Please be seated, Lieutenant," she said, returning his smile. "I do hope nothing is wrong."

"No ma'am, everything is just fine. I... I wondered if you'd mind my asking a question."

"Certainly not," she replied. "But please be seated. I know it's difficult with your leg."

Matt returned to his chair, and Mrs. Moore rested her hands on the back of the other, a curious smile lingering on her lips. "I hope you won't think me impolite," he began. "But I was under the impression that a family named Davis owned the inn. The waitress said you and Major Moore own it."

"She's quite right. We do. The only Davis is our daughter." Matt held her gaze, his smile slowly receding. "Vivian Davis?" he heard himself ask.

"Why, yes. Do you know her, Lieutenant?" Mrs. Moore eased the chair around and slowly seated herself.

Matt was afraid of what he might hear next. "I met her at the air base, the NAAFI canteen. She was helping a Mrs. Pearson, who later told me about Falcon's Rest. I assumed, stupidly, your name would be Davis."

"So Mary suggested you try to see her again here. Knowing Mary, that's very likely."

"I'm sorry I got things confused. I just didn't realize."

"It's quite natural that you should be confused, Lieutenant." There was no smile now, her blue eyes growing distant. She tucked the rolls of her hair and sighed deeply as one who must relive a painful memory.

"I think you should know this. Vivian was married. A very fine young man, John Davis. When war came, he left his law apprenticeship to join the RAF." Her hands toyed with the table napkin as she labored to retain her composure. "Then came Dunkirk. They were trying to get our soldiers off the beaches, and his plane went down... somewhere over the coast of Belgium. It was his fourth flight that day."

Neither spoke for a time, Mrs. Moore battling her grief and Matt, struggling to put it all together, at a loss for words. When he looked up again, her eyes were shimmering pools. "She was three months pregnant with his child. A few days after we received the news, she miscarried." She pressed the napkin to the corner of her eyes and looked at him again. "Please excuse me, Lieutenant. The last four years have been most difficult."

Matt rested his elbows on the table and buried his face in his hands. "I... am... so... sorry, Mrs. Moore." He could not imagine Vivie in such circumstances. "I wish I had known back at the airfield. I would have understood."

Mrs. Moore continued to dab at her eyes, but she was calmer now. "It was not likely you, Lieutenant, so much as the airport itself. It's been difficult to get her out very often until this last year. Mrs. Pearson has done miracles. You know she was a nurse in the Great War. She felt Vivian could cope more easily if she faced the things associated with her grief."

Matt's dinner arrived, and the waitress began placing the dishes. A true innkeeper, Mrs. Moore surveyed the courses with a critical eye. "Dear! Why did you serve him this?"

He chuckled softly at her concern and offered reassurance. "It was my doing. I was hungry and asked for something filling."

"You men are all alike. You simply eat to live. Next time, you shall dine, and I shall place the order," she replied firmly. Then her face was serious again. "I felt you should know the circumstances early on, Lieutenant."

They talked for a while then, moving the conversation to more pleasant things, about his home in the States and the history of Falcon's Rest. He was nearly finished with dinner when finally she excused herself. Despite her concern, he had enjoyed the meal immensely. The second cup of coffee supplied all the dessert he needed. He placed two half crowns on the table, gathered his crutches, and made his way to the lobby.

It was quieter now, with a few overnighters taking their ease in the lobby's wingback leather chairs. But there was no sign of Vivie. For Matt, the only bright spot then was the rear veranda where the sun, now below the horizon, bathed all in the last glow of dusk. He eased his ailing leg sideways through the French door and rested on the crutches, breathing deeply of the cool evening air. Wooden rockers commanded a splendid view of Christ Church Park with its diverse trees and green meadow, and he claimed one of the chairs for himself, stretching the healing leg in another. He loosened his belt and opened his dress coat, relishing the unbridled comfort. After a time, his hand went to the inside coat pocket and retrieved two letters from his mother and another from his sister. It took him a while to bring his mind to bear on the correspondence, for the new revelations about Vivie were much on his mind.

Elly's letter, containing little Susan's picture, ran on and on about the new baby, while his mother's bogged down in the amusing trivia of Augusta's social and community life. But he loved them both for it, this ever so welcome touch of home. There he sat, drinking in the words, his lips cast in smile. Other guests came and went, having their turns at the view, until Matt ceased to take notice of them.

After a bit the letters lay folded in his lap, and his head rolled back to rest on the chair. His eyes closed slowly as he tried to soothe a frustrated mind. Something roused him, not a noise exactly, but more like a presence. He opened his eyes slightly and scanned the area around him. It was well into dusk, and to his left the silhouette of a woman in uniform stood looking out over the park, her hands braced on the railing. His eyes fixed on the unmistakable coiffure beneath the cap.

The tingle was there again, his chest rising and falling more rapidly, as he debated his approach. If she turned, it would be obvious to her that he had been watching. His must be the first move. "Vivie?" he called above the laughter just inside the door.

She peered over her shoulder and stared in his direction. The last time she had seen him, he was clad in a rumpled flight suit, a considerable difference from the striking American flyer in the dress uniform before her now. "Yes?" she inquired with proper politeness.

He leaned forward to give her a better view. "It's Matt Tower. Do you remember me from the airport?"

She moved closer, her head tilted in question. "Why... yes, I do, Lieutenant."

With some effort he pushed himself to a standing position, balancing nimbly with the aid of a crutch. "How've you been?"

"Just fine, thank you." She was noticeably concerned by his condition, and slim fingers went quickly to cover her lips. "You've been hurt!"

How good it was to hear her voice again, the smooth upper British tones that had echoed through his mind over the past two weeks. "It's not too bad," he responded with a smile.

"Please sit down, Lieutenant. You must be terribly uncomfortable."

He responded willingly for the leg did ache, and his only relief was to elevate it in a chair. "Can I... buy you a coffee or something?" he asked hopefully, since she was still standing.

"A cup would be nice. It is a bit parky, isn't it?" she replied, rubbing her hands on her uniform sleeves for warmth. He could tell that she was as uneasy as he in this new encounter. As he moved to get up again, her hand darted out in caution and the little half smile, which fascinated him so, crept across her lips. "No, no, Lieutenant. Since you're a guest of Falcon's Rest, it shall be my treat."

Before he could argue she was gone, moving briskly through the French doors to the lobby. In reality, he needed a moment to collect his thoughts. Their meeting had not been as he envisioned it, and he was still sorting out the details of his talk with her mother. He was anxious about the effect on his feelings and about Vivie's response to that invasion of her privacy, though it was not of his doing.

The answer to his feelings lay beside his elevated leg, where she had placed the small leather purse and gloves. It pleased him that she had left so personal an item nearby, a comforting assurance that the owner would return. She was becoming special to him, and her reappearance confirmed it all the more.

As he watched her balancing the cups in his direction, he vowed that if the past came up, it would be by her choice. He quickly slid out the small wicker table to receive the cups. "You're an angel to run that little errand," he said, smiling up at her.

"An angel, I fear not, Lieutenant. But happy to oblige, I am," she replied, seating herself across the table.

He took a sip and ran his tongue over his lips. "Black with sugar! Did I tell you that?"

"No," she smiled back. "It's just that most men seem to prefer it that way. If you wish I can fetch another." He took another sip. "No, it's really good! These cups are beautiful."

"I borrowed from Mum's private stock. She likes good coffee and good tea. That's a Spode pattern that belonged to my grandmother. I don't think they make it anymore."

He turned the china cup slowly in his hands, following the crisp blue band capped by a gold rim. "My mom would flip over this. She collects china cups, special ones, from estate sales: famous settings. I'll bet she's got 200 of the things, a whole cabinet full."

Vivie smiled at his appreciation of the fine china. "Mum just told me that you two met on the train."

"More like our paths crossed, I guess." Matt leaned back with the saucer and sipped the coffee again, wondering what else she had been told and how he would handle it. "You know, she didn't know me from Adam, but she gave me her blessing as we left the car. I remember her sitting at the window as the train pulled away, but I never expected to see her again."

Vivie put the cup down and touched the napkin to her lips. "For some reason she singled you out. She remembers that you were like three overgrown scouts arriving at camp, and it concerned her that you might not appreciate the danger." Her eyes drifted confirmingly to his elevated leg, a matter that had not been resolved for her yet. "How... how were you wounded, Lieutenant?" she asked hesitantly.

He placed the cup on the table and shifted his weight for comfort. "We caught some flak over the target area, and I got a little scratch on the back of the leg. It's not all that bad," he replied, keeping the tone as light as possible.

But she was one of an English generation all too familiar with that sport. Keeping it light had not stopped the bombs or the other realities of war, the deeper truths recorded in tragic statistics. Her eyes fixed on the cup and saucer in her lap, her face expressionless, and Matt knew the ball was in his court. "Hey, can a guy have equal time on this question-and-answer show?" She nodded her head as she brought the cup to her lips again. "Well, I was wondering about the uniform. I saw some like it near London."

She ran her fingers down the lapel of the soft green jacket and smoothed it caringly at the waist. "It's the Women's Voluntary Service. That's where I've been this afternoon, working on a mobile canteen for the batteries around the docks. Yesterday we were sorting children's books and clothing at the WVS shop."

"For some reason I thought you might be a nurse."

"Not quite, but I've had most of the training. It's been indispensable a number of times. The men work the batteries right through the raids."

She rambled on about the service, which pleased him because it allowed him to look her full in the face without staring. Her eyes were captivating, the smooth high arch of the brow, the bright level gaze that demanded utter honesty from her converser. He found it difficult to concentrate on anything else and promptly lost his place in the conversation.

She had paused without his being aware, and he quickly blinked himself to consciousness. "Are you all right, Lieutenant?" she inquired with a questioning tilt of her head.

Matt scrambled mentally to cover the flub, to keep her comfortable in their chatting. "I... I'm fine. I was just thinking about Mrs. Pearson. Did she ever hear from her son?"

"Oh, yes, she did!" Vivie seemed pleased by his inquiry. "Would you believe two letters on the same day? Little things bother her, you know, and she was so concerned that they were dated a month apart."

"That flight lieutenant, Cobbs, he really had her pegged right. The base mother," Matt said with a chuckle. "I really liked her."

Vivie folded the napkin and placed it beside the cup on the table. Her eyes avoided him, shifting to the end of the porch. "I'm afraid I wasn't very pleasant that day, Lieutenant. Mary chided me about it, you know. I must have seemed a perfect twit."

"No.... No, no," he breathed, a worry wrinkle appearing on his forehead. "We were the intruders, remember. I'm sure we weren't on our best behavior."

Matt had tried to ignore the muffled rattling at the window behind him, certainly ill-timed and persistent enough now to stir his curiosity. He twisted in the chair as best he could to get a look. "What are they doing in there?"

"Putting Falcon's Rest to bed," she replied with a sigh. "And all Ipswich for that matter. They're air raid curtains."

It seemed to Matt that the war interrupted just about everything, for Vivie was growing restless, as one might with so nightly a reminder of danger. "Are they still bombing here?" he asked, his voice sober and deliberate.

"Rarely are we spared a week, it seems. It's not the bombers so much now, but those FW.... somethings," she replied, as nervous hands retrieved the napkin and rolled it up tightly. "They slip in from the Netherlands, small packs of them, and they seem to care less where they strike. Colonel Burgess—he's an intelligence officer—says the German tactics now are designed to weaken the will of our people."

"Focke-Wulf 190s," Matt injected. "Long-range fighters rigged with bombs."

"They're horrid! They fire into the streets, no longer content to bomb the rail yards and docks." Her delicate hands had become fists, crushing their tension into the twisted napkin. If she was to remain on the porch with him, Matt would have to lighten the mood quickly.

He leaned forward and gathered the correspondence that lay on the table, folding each page neatly to allow Vivie time to wind down. "Letters from home," he volunteered, smiling up at her.

She gave the napkin a reprieve, allowing it to repose limply on her lap. The trace smile returned slowly as she watched him put the letters away. "From your Mum?" she inquired.

"Yes," he chuckled, amused at her expression. "From my Mum and my sister. She's made me an uncle."

"They must be quite proud of you. Will it distress them terribly to know you've been wounded?"

"Mom would pass out. Dad and I developed a neat code before I left, and we can get a message to each other if we need to."

"Doesn't sound very fair to your Mum!" Vivie snapped.

"You don't know my mother! She'd have our congressman on the line in a minute, telling him things were getting out of hand with the war, and her son was to be sent home immediately."

"Noooo," she moaned mockingly in disbelief.

"Yesssss," he moaned back, excited by the first real twinkle he had seen in the questioning eyes.

Matt was feeling much better about his time with Vivie. He had tried hard not to rock the boat, and what he learned that evening made him the better at it. The sun retired for the day, and a chill breeze drifted over the porch, sending all but the two of them inside. Vivie's features were barely visible now as she sat with arms crossed and hands tucked inside her jacket. Their time together that evening was ending, and he must plan quickly for the morrow.

"You know, that cab driver was a walking chamber of commerce when I rode up here from the station. I've never seen so many old churches in one town before. I wish I'd been able to walk around those streets, get into some of those quaint little shops. And this park out here... it's really something else. You're one lucky girl to grow up around all this."

"It is lovely," she replied. "But I daresay you haven't seen the half of Ipswich. This park has been my special place from the time I was a child. There's a marvelous old mansion on the other side."

"Look, I have until Saturday night before I report back. Would you have some time tomorrow to show me the park and some of the sights?"

Vivie grew silent, her eyes turned to the park. It was a terrible wait, for he could not read her face in the dark. After a time, he was ready to concede defeat, to take his licks for pressing again.

"I'm sorry," he sighed. "That's a lot to expect on such short notice."

Her face turned back slowly in his direction. "I don't know, Lieutenant. Why would you ask me?"

It was a struggle to keep his thoughts to himself, fighting the urge to let his heart hang out. With just a little prodding, he could have answered, *"Because you're the most fascinating woman I've ever met. You're beautiful and I want a chance to know you better."* But he knew how far that might get him, so discretion prevailed in a half-truth. "I can't think of anyone who knows the area better. I'd get the best tour available! Besides, it would be you or the taxi driver."

Her reply was a simple, "Oh." She leaned forward in the chair, gathering her purse and the coffee cups. It was the signal he had feared. The evening was over, and she was getting up to leave.

"I'm sorry, Lieutenant, but I'm quite chilled. I must go inside."

Matt did the only thing he could. He agreed reluctantly, admitting that his leg was not all that comfortable in the weather, either. She held the door as he hobbled through to the warmth inside. The great old fireplace lit the lobby, serving as a beacon for the uniformed and civilians gathering around it. He turned to her and looked down into soft blue eyes, willing to beg her to be with him on the morrow.

"Thank you for the coffee," he said, smiling his boyish best. "Thanks to you, I completely forgot the leg for a while."

"It was my pleasure," she replied, a trace smile returning to her face. "Do rest well."

He watched her cross the lobby to the stairs, convinced amid great dejection that he had simply been her last WVS project for the day. It would be a restless night for this American flyer now aching in the heart as well as the leg. He hung forlornly on the crutches, eyes studying the intricate pattern of the oriental carpet beneath his feet. How he hated for the evening to end this way.

It was a struggle not to take one more glance at Vivie. Logic told him he had waited too long anyway, but the compulsion could not be stemmed. He rolled his head toward the stairs, chiding himself all the while for giving in. But she was there, paused on the third step, her expression quite serious, looking back at him. For the longest moment they faced each other, neither moving nor speaking until she broke the silence. "Elevenish," she called to him.

His brow wrinkled and he shrugged. "Elevenish?"

"Elevenish," she repeated. "Here in the lobby, for the park."

He grinned broadly then and waved his acknowledgment, barely able to believe what he had just heard. With his grin permanently in place, he watched her nimbly mount the steps, the tailored uniform doing fair justice to its wearer. He shook his head slowly in the speculation that courting was not unlike piloting a fighter. One minute you were in dire straits and the next, sailing over green pastures.

# CHAPTER 7

# A Day in the Park

**T**HE ROOM WAS dark when Matt awoke, and he tossed for a time trying to doze off again, a fruitless effort that soon had him reaching for the flashlight to check his watch. The hands spread to 7:50 a.m. but the lightless room caused him to doubt the timepiece. He rolled to a sitting position on the bed and tested his footing with his one good leg, then limped to the window to pull back the thick curtains.

Even with them aside, the glow was subdued, a symptom of an overcast sky. But his spirits were high, undaunted even by the sight of an unkempt face in the mirror. He hurried through the personal chores of the morning confidently, sliding the shiny Gillette over his face. All went well until he tried the bathtub, where he chuckled patiently at the awkward configuration required to keep his injured leg dry. Eventually he got it all together, fresh uniform buttoned and belted, then headed for the lobby.

After a tasty breakfast of kippered herring, toast, and marmalade, he was ready for the day. The night's rest had done his leg a world of good, and he moved effortlessly around the lobby wishing the minutes away. By 10:30 he had perused the *East Anglian Daily Times* and a week-old London paper, both boasting the first real Allied momentum of the war. British and American troops were fighting behind German lines in Italy, cutting off supply routes. U.S. Marines followed up victories in the Marshall and Kwajalein islands with landings in New Guinea. Even the Russians were making advances, recapturing the naval base at Sevastopol.

How nice if the headlines had stopped there. But others spoke of a determined enemy, with Nazi forces invading Hungary, and London visited twice in the week by medium bombers of the Luftwaffe. Even so, Matt was able to fold the paper on a light note. It seemed that Mrs. Porter, a 79-years-young widow on Spring Street, had to be forcibly subdued by Air Raid Precautions personnel when she took a broom to them. She insisted they not erect a neighborhood siren in front of her home, according to an ARP spokesman.

It was quarter after "elevenish" by the elegant grandfather clock across the lobby, and Matt was concerned that Vivie might have forgotten. But she hadn't. From the corner of his eye, he saw her coming through the dining room door, prettier than ever in a soft light-blue blouse, with an open vest sweater that matched her beige mid-calf skirt. A small wicker basket swung gently at her side as she crossed the lobby. She had not appeared to look in his direction, and it surprised him that she seemed to know instinctively where he was seated. "Good morning, Lieutenant," she smiled in greeting. "I'm sorry I've kept you waiting."

Her tapered-collar blouse was open to the point of discreet cleavage just below perky twists of light golden-brown locks that rested softly on her shoulders. It was quite an effort for Matt to conceal his appreciation. "Good morning!" he replied, rising to his feet. "Boy, do you look great!"

But she was not attentive to the compliment and tactfully kept the drift to their outing. "I had cook prepare some tasties should we get a bit peckish," she explained.

"Are you always this organized?" he chuckled, glancing at the basket.

"There're certainly no eateries in the park, Lieutenant." Her eyes darted nervously to avoid his. "Shall we go?"

Vivie's defensive wall, so solidly in place, was disheartening to Matt. He had been searching for the gate ever since they met, with evident failure. At least now he knew something of her circumstances and what she had been wrestling with. She was not yet ready to risk another caring relationship, and it would take infinite patience on his part with no guarantees at the end.

So they set out, the lame American swinging on his crutches and the pretty English girl, along a path beneath the great shade trees of the arboretum. Taking her time for Matt's sake, Vivie would pause to show him favorite spots in the park. Gardens along the way could give but a hint of their peacetime grandeur, for the war now directed Ipswich's priorities. The couple rested for a time by one of the ponds and watched two intent young anglers at their sport. The lads handled their tackle quite well but were never rewarded with a fish.

Matt leaned back on the bench, a smile on his lips, as he reflected on the hours spent on his grandfather's ponds. There was no shortage of fish there, and an afternoon could provide a fine mess of bream and crappie with a bass or two thrown in. "It's probably the phase of the moon," he suggested.

"Phase of the moon?" she inquired.

"Yeah. Fish don't bite sometimes if the moon's not right."

Vivie stared out over the water with wistful eyes. "There're no fish in the ponds, Lieutenant. Before the war there were geese and

ducks. We fed them bits of bread after church on Sunday after-
noons. But they disappeared, one by one, to the pots of the hungry."

He looked away. He was learning. "Sorry," he sighed. Symbolic of
the British, she had lost much in the Nazi madness: husband, baby, and
even the pets of her special playground. But she was learning to recover,
to table such thoughts. The trace smile he liked so much returned to
her lips. "Come, Lieutenant. I'll show you my special hideaway."

The topmost branches of the trees were swaying about in a leafy
ballet as though frightened by the great gray clouds sweeping above
them. It was darker now and cooler. "I think we're going to get a
shower," Matt cautioned his tour director.

"And maybe not," she smiled back. "It's that way in England,
you know." She pointed to a stand of trees across the meadow. "It's
there. I think we can make it."

In the distance, Matt could see sheets of rain moving rapidly
across their path. It would be a race to Vivie's hideaway, but there
was no way they could make it back to Falcon's Rest. The wind carried a few drops ahead of the shower, and Vivie squealed like a
schoolgirl with each one that caught her. "Oh dear," she moaned.
"My hair will be ruined!"

Matt was working his crutches as best he could considering the
hilarious spectacle before him. Sheltering her head with a napkin,
Vivie was trying to run and stay back with him all at the same time
while nursing the basket of tasties. It was increasingly evident that
they were not going to make it. "Go on, run!" he called over her
shrieks. "I'll be fine! Go, go!"

She had thought to wear flats, which made her nimbler, but a
mere 10 yards short of the old gazebo, she was captured in a full
torrent of rain. Matt bit his lip to hide his amusement at her antics
as she scurried up the steps. "Hurry, Lieutenant!" she called, frantically waving him in.

The rain felt good to Matt as it splashed across his face. He wasn't as upset by the shower as she was, but his clothing was thicker and he didn't get as wet. Putting on a show of manly prowess, he intended to take the two short steps in a single bound. But a crutch tip broke through a rotted board and he pole-vaulted onto the floor of the gazebo in humiliating prostration. Vivie whimpered at the sight and dropped to her knees beside him. "Are you hurt, Lieutenant?"

"I... I think I'm okay," he replied, rolling over to a more dignified position. "A significant dent in my pride, maybe." The back of his hand had been scrapped in the sprawl, and damp dust from the floor smudged his palms, face, and uniform. "Just look at you!" she exclaimed. "You're quite the mess, you know."

Vivie was no better off—hair matted, makeup running—and she was drenched. Her hands had brushed the floor in the excitement, transferring smears of the pasty dust to her own face and clothing. The absurdity of the situation reflected in the grin spreading across Matt's face. "You don't look so hot yourself, Cinderella!" he shot back playfully.

She retrieved another napkin and gently wiped his face, pushing the mussed locks of his hair back in place. It was the first time he had felt her touch and he dared not disturb it. She knelt there beside the seated flyer, her smile broadening every second as the absurdity caught up with her. Finally she could no longer restrain a chuckle, which easily triggered his own, reducing them both to rounds of laughter.

The exertion soon had them both collapsed against the spindle railing. As their laughter reluctantly died, he pulled himself onto the nearest bench and extended his hands to place her beside him. There they sat, panting and grinning, afraid to look at each other lest the painful laughter return. It had been a very long time since Vivian Davis had abandoned herself to such merriment.

The breeze was light but persistent and Vivie, being wet, felt it all the more. As her arms crossed against the chill, she became aware of how revealing her clinging blouse had become. Matt was quick to sense her uneasiness and when he turned to her, he dared not let his eyes wander. It was a paragon reply to the circumstances, for she felt very vulnerable just then and watched his response intently.

Appropriately, he made her comfort his concern, for she was shivering, and a faint blue showed through her thinly applied lipstick. Unbuckling his belt, Matt slipped off his dress jacket and placed it around her. "Here, we'll make you a lieutenant in the U.S. Air Force," he chuckled as he fastened the top button. He reached back and lifted her hair from under the collar and spread it over her shoulders. "Better?" he inquired.

"Much. Thank you," she nodded.

The basket produced a vacuum of hot coffee, and Matt prepared a cup for her. She accepted a sip, then slipped her hands from beneath the jacket to gain warmth from the porcelain container. "This was my special place," she said, gesturing around the gazebo. "I'd come here as a child with my dolls. Especially Paladin."

"Paladin?"

"Yes," she smiled, staring across the park. "Paladin… about so tall," her hands indicating a foot or so. "And dressed like a royal guardsman, complete with sword. He was really quite grand. The gazebo was our ship, and we sailed to all the continents of the world."

Matt poured himself a cup, careful not to break the mood, for he relished every word. "Did you make it to America?"

"Of course!" she chuckled merrily. "We saw Indians there. And in Africa we went on safari, through the arboretum forest, naturally. Paladin was always there when I needed him. To share joys and secrets… and sometimes to console me when things went amiss." Her eyes were dreamy as she sipped coffee in deep contemplation. "Then as I grew up," she sighed. "Paladin's powers seemed to grow weaker until one day he couldn't help me at all, and HMS Gazebo seemed dry-docked forever."

Matt's elbows rested on his knees as he leaned forward to sip from his cup. He knew very well what she referred to, and he could tell she was on the brink of tears. His mind raced for suitable encouragement, something to lift the mood, but he felt her hurt so much that nothing seemed adequate. It would be Vivie who changed the mood in this instance, determined—with Mrs. Pearson's encouragement—that she could survive and regain her life in spite of. She turned to Matt, eyes clearer and stronger now, granting him a warm smile. "I'm sorry it turned out so terribly today."

It was the cue he had been waiting for. "I don't know. I've always dreamed of being marooned on a deserted island with a beautiful girl. This is pretty close to it."

"Beautiful?" she laughed. "More like the wretched witch of the North! And your island has leaks in the roof and dirt everywhere. We're probably catching our death as it is."

The rain settled down to a steady drizzle, so they opened the tasties and made the best of it. Vivie seemed more at ease than Matt had ever seen her: talkative, inquisitive, reconciled to their misfortune with the weather. "Tell me about America, Lieutenant. What's it like?"

There was one matter that Matt wanted desperately to clear up, and this was as good an opportunity as any to do it. "Well, first of all, in America, it's traditional to call your friends by their first name." He waited and watched to get her reaction. "Would I be classified as a friend, Vivie?"

She chewed the sandwich bite she had just taken and studied his face. He could detect no reservation on her part, but he went on chewing his own food without pressing for an answer.

"And you wish me to call you by your Christian name," she replied, still nibbling.

When had he heard that expression? "Well, the whole thing is Gerald Mattlowe Tower Jr., but I'll answer to Matt."

Her head cocked thoughtfully as she drew the words out for

effect. "Gerald... Mattlowe... Tower... Jr. A rather impressive moniker," she smiled playfully.

Pleased to be over that hump, he stared with placid grin at the lips that formed his name, quite forgetting her question. "All right, Matt, I've done my part. Now, tell me about America."

Matt leaned back and folded his arms. "America," he began with a deep, thoughtful sigh. It was difficult to continue, a sobering discovery for him. He lived there, loved it, but had never really considered how to describe it to someone. "You know, America looks a lot like England in places. Near my base, there's a farm so like my grandfather's that it made me homesick."

"And there are many great cities like London," she broke in. "And majestic mountains, Great Plains, and the Mississippi River." She paused for a second, index finger probing thoughtfully at her chin. "Manufacturing in the North, livestock in the West and agriculture in the South." She smiled in satisfaction as one who might have completed their ABC's correctly.

It left Matt with his mouth open, for she had said it so quickly and authentically. "Pretty good!" he exclaimed. "How'd you put all that together?

She cocked her head knowingly and fired right back at him. "I was educated, Matt Tower, after all!"

He couldn't help but smile at this self-entrapment and held up his hand in a gesture of peace. "I didn't mean it that way. It's just that you did a better job than a lot of Americans. Where did you go to school?"

"Queen Elizabeth. Not far from here. Then it was off to Roedean for girls in Sussex. To be properly finished, of course," she added, mimicking a decorous air with her hands. "Then college in London."

"And how did it go?" he teased, his hand smothering a budding grin.

"How did it go, indeed!" she gasped, her back straightening in dismay. "Here I am! And I know more about your own country than you do!" She paused to nibble the sandwich again. "Mum attended; she was a Roedean girl. Would you believe they've billeted soldiers in our rooms there? Of course, no one can attend just now with the war going on. It's too near the coast."

They talked on into the afternoon, asking, telling, laughing, discovering what they had in common. If he had accomplished nothing more than friendship, Matt was grateful, for it would be a base to build on. The rain had stopped, and in its wake a muggy dampness formed all around with fog in the lower areas. Vivie was becoming restless. She had been drenched, wet through, and by this time was very uncomfortable. "Would you mind terribly, Lieutenant..." she caught herself, still not accustomed to his name. "Matt... if we went back now?"

He agreed and waited as Vivie packed everything neatly back in the basket. She was something to watch. He had known many girls who were pretty, but their countenance lacked a balancing decorum. With Vivie there was the touch of class, a quality that earned a girl the title of *Queen* with Matt's fellow cadets at Richmond Academy in Augusta. One other had come close, Virginia "Ginger" Ellison, on whom he had a senior-year crush though he was at all-male Richmond and she at all-female Tubman High School. But there were joint social events, and the two took advantage of them.

But like a garden bee, that pampered daughter of prominent Augusta attorney Randolph Ellison would hover near the flower so long as it served her needs. Matt, purposeful, intent on college and flying, struggled to keep his priorities in order. Ginger had responded by transferring in her junior year from the University of Georgia to Agnes Scott College. The crush had been long in dying, but by the time he began air force training, her senior high picture had found its way from his wallet to the back of a dresser drawer.

The stroll back to Falcon's Rest was more taxing for Matt than when their excursion began. Vivie, uncomfortable as she was, shortened her stride to accommodate him. "This is horrible!" she injected. "Some tour you've had."

"If I can get back here again, would you finish showing me around?"

She walked away without replying, another of those long silences he had learned to endure when she was uncertain about something. Instinctively he felt she wanted, indeed needed, to bring up her past before much more time was invested. But he didn't know just when or how. "Perhaps," she offered at last, her tone less than encouraging. "It would depend."

"On what?"

"Well, on when you might return and if my schedule is free."

"I could phone you ahead at the inn," he offered, hoping for agreement.

A new dimension was evolving for Vivie. Emotions—over four years dormant—had been stirred, which surprised and frightened her a little. It had happened despite the promise she made, that she would not risk such hurt again. But this attractive, disarming American made that difficult now. Yet he was a pilot, and one who had been wounded at that.

Vivie left his question dangling, and they proceeded to Falcon's Rest in silence. She led him to the rear door of the kitchen, having no intention of parading her discomposure through the lobby. He followed laboriously up the steps and through the broad door to the service hall, where they slipped in as inconspicuously as possible. Alas, to no avail, for they entered upon Mrs. Moore conferring with members of the culinary staff. A half-dozen sets of eyes turned to the couple, none more perplexed than Vivie's mother.

"Good heavens, Vivian! What happened to you two?" she asked, her hands resting on her hips in concern.

"We've been playing in the mud, ma'am," Matt offered with a grin.

"Codswallop!" Vivie corrected. "We simply couldn't escape the rain and ended up in that old gazebo in the park."

Mrs. Moore glanced skeptically at the two young people, a half-smile taking her lips. "I daresay Lieutenant Tower's explanation is more befitting. You both need a long bath and a change of clothing or you'll be ill."

Shaking her head in parental dismay, Etta Moore herded the snickering staff into the kitchen, allowing the young couple to repair their dignity. Matt turned to Vivie and they exchanged smiles as might two prankish youngsters. "I did have a good time in spite of the weather," he reassured. "I wish I didn't have to leave in the morning."

She was still encased in the warmth of his jacket, her hair matted, makeup ruined, and he was glad she could not see herself, for their time together would end abruptly. She was hesitating, as unable as he to break off properly. "There's a USO bus leaving from Town Hall at 9 a.m."

"There is?" he inquired, hoping to prolong the conversation.

"Quite. We have friends at Great Wenham: the Walldons. They have a lodge there. The road's a bit rough in places, but I've traveled it often."

Matt mustered his nerve for the next question and hoped for the best. "Could we have dinner this evening? I'd like to thank you for the day."

"Oh... I'm sorry, Matt," she replied softly. "My unit is on duty. We've quite an evening ahead. But I shan't forget today. It was great fun." Her soft blue eyes searched his face questioningly, and he could sense the mixed emotions in her deliberation. "Please... could we leave it there just now?"

He glanced around the room struggling for words, wanting very much to let her know how he felt. He would have given anything for just a spark of assurance. "Vivie, I just want you to know how I...."

She interrupted quickly, laying her hand on his arm. "For just now... please... for just now?" her eyes pleaded.

He nodded his head in understanding, forcing a half-hearted smile. "Okay... maybe we'll see each other in the morning."

She slipped the jacket off and draped it over his shoulders, smoothing the lapels with her hands. "There, you're a lieutenant again!" Stepping back, she offered a flicker of the little trace smile that bewitched him so. "I must go."

Vivie scurried up the stairs leading to the family wing of the inn, and Matt found himself alone, still damp, and a bit dejected. So it was back to his room and another bath to get comfortable. Comfortable except for the leg, which seemed to pain him more in the evenings. He had been diligent with the bandage and dressing because healing meant he could fly again. The results were there as he examined the wound. It was healing nicely.

After dinner Matt took a chair in the lobby, which he hoped would provide him a glimpse of Vivie should she pass that way. It was also an excellent location for his passive hobby of character study as the evening regulars began drifting in. A chilly English night made the glow of the great fireplace all the more inviting, and in time the regulars arrived, meeting their established friends and settling in their established places. They were all up in age, from the portly middle aged to crotchety old codgers. The young were few and easily identified by uniform.

Matt's favorites among the lot were two in civil-defense gear who seemed to have an ongoing grudge match at the game of draughts. Because their defense posts were within the block, neither felt required to stand guard in the dark cold unless some action was taking place. Usually, after a game or two, they began jumping the checkerboard with a mounting vengeance that served to establish and divide their cheering sections among the gathered audience.

Nearby, without disturbing the players or viewers, the Falcon's Rest custodian drew the long heavy curtains, thoroughly tending each window around the lobby to hide from enemy eyes the great fire and the flicker of paraffin lanterns. Crackling hardwood under flame and the drone of conversation soon did their work on the tired American flyer, and he fell asleep in the lap of a great stuffed chair.

His reverie would not go unchallenged, however, and a while later he awakened to a bewildering concert of clambering feet and wailing sirens. Much the victim of twilight blahs so characteristic of one in unfamiliar settings, he sought to gain his bearings. The grandfather clock showed 1:30 a.m. and the game table was empty, its players long since out the lobby door. Across the room, an elderly gentleman with a pearl-white mustache slid the newspaper from his well-padded lap and looked up at Matt. "Bloody air raid, Yank. They're after the docks again, I'd say."

Matt stared in disbelief as the old gentleman adjusted his position in the chair with a wheezy cough and flipped the paper into reading position again. He had expected people to swarm out of their rooms like ants, but only a few wandered into the lobby area. The young flyer followed a couple of the more curious men, one an RAF pilot officer, to the doorway beside the desk and stepped onto the rear porch. He could feel the vibration through his feet though the explosions were some distance to the south. The scene was nothing like his experience outside London, but the flashes were there along with the *whoomph, whoomph* of anti-aircraft.

The British flyer stood with arms folded beside his American counterpart. Neither spoke as they gazed beyond the park at the distant spectacle until the sound of aircraft engines grew louder. "It's a blooming Junkers!" the Britisher injected.

"I don't know," Matt shook his head. "I've never heard one."

"Oh, it's a Junkers, all right. That's Jerry's favorite trick around these parts: a light bomber with a flight of long-range fighters for good measure."

Matt's ear caught the change of tone as the planes turned away from the target. "Okay, I can hear the fighters now."

"That's likely it," the pilot officer concluded. "They'll save a few for Felixstowe on the way out."

"How the devil do they get this far in without being detected?" Matt inquired.

"Right up the bloody River Orwell. That kite will do over 400 miles an hour. They'll come across just like we go over there, 300 feet above the sea."

As the drone of the planes subsided, Matt's mind turned to Vivie. Where was she during the bombing? He tried to reassure himself that she had experience with these things. After all, had she not survived the last four years before he even met her? There was nothing he could do but turn in for the night, though sleep would come only in short, shallow attempts.

Then at 5 a.m. the rising roar of approaching planes sat him up in bed until he recognized the distinctive rhythm of B-17 radials. They were heading for the coast and Europe. He pulled back the curtains, but there was little to see. What was happening back at group? Were the guys even now suiting up in the ready room? Was this gaggle of bombers to be their responsibility? Matt knew one thing: this was not the side of the fence he wanted to be on. He could not remember when he had spent a more miserable night, and he longed to get back into action.

At last, daybreak, and was he ever glad to see it. The only thing troubling him now was whether he would see Vivie. He was dressed and in the lobby by 7:30 a.m., but neither Mrs. Moore nor her daughter were in sight. Except for a housekeeper and the desk clerk, no one else was available. The little woman tried to be helpful, but she did not have the answers he wanted. "I'm sorry, sir, but Mrs. Moore was up most of the night, and Mrs. Davis did not get back until 6 this morning. There was a bombing, you know."

He knew that, all right, and the only consolation lay in the fact that Vivie was safe in her bed. "Well, I'd like to leave a message for Mrs. Davis if you'll see that she gets it."

"Gladly, sir."

His hands went to the pencil and pad on the desk. "Tell her that Matt Tower would like to...."

The desk clerk waved her hand to interrupt. "Oh, if you're Lieutenant Tower I do believe she left something for you, sir."

She reached back to his room key slot and produced a small enve-lope. The feminine script simply spelled "Lieutenant Matt Tower." He popped the seal quickly and opened the small sheet of paper, which showed a short series of numbers. "Would you know what that is?" he asked, turning the paper to the desk clerk.

"Yes, sir. That's Falcon's Rest's telephone number." A broad smile eased across Matt's face, and he thanked the little woman behind the desk. "You're welcome, sir. Is there a message for Mrs. Davis?"

"No, not now," he sighed contentedly, his fingers carefully folding the paper away. "It appears she got my message earlier." With a renewed vigor he retrieved his duffle bag and prepared to leave. "I'll see you next trip, ma'am."

# CHAPTER 8

# The First Swastika

IT WOULD BE two weeks before the flight surgeon released Matt for flying duty. It seemed a boring eternity for the restless pilot, who took on a variety of projects from sorting books for the American Red Cross library to being secretary for Herrington. Anything to keep himself occupied. The latter would prove quite valuable in the months to come when Matt's responsibilities increased.

It rained frequently and when it did, the base became a gummy mire, adding to his general discomfort. He thought about Vivie and when he might see her again. Their time together confirmed all the more the rightness of his service against the Axis, and when the news of his flight status came, he was ecstatic.

"Sit down, soldier," Herrington told his anxious charge. "It's been better than three weeks since you were behind the stick. You've got some catching up to do."

"I'm ready, sir!" he replied, sitting on the edge of the chair.

"Then check out a fighter and don't come down until your butt is beat," the captain grinned back at him.

It was a jolt to find that another pilot was using *Sweet Pea*. Like most flyers, Matt had become attached to the plane that first took him into combat and brought him back. His only comfort lay in the fact that the big jug was still operational. He would see Herrington about it since he certainly had enough seniority to claim priority with that P-47.

The first sunshine in a week beamed down warmly as Matt took the signal to start the engine. All the instruments of a perfect aero symphony harmonized when the fighter's powerhouse whined shrilly and roared to life. Reluctantly, he slid the canopy shut, for the wind and sound of the surging warbird really set him free. The smell of the cockpit, the feel of the stick, the sway of liftoff—all reminded him how much he had missed the experience. He kept his appointment at the target areas, firing on pass after pass, putting the fighter through every turn and roll possible until an hour later, he was wrung out.

One last maneuver seemed to be in order. Indeed, irresistible. On the return to Raydon, the River Orwell lay broad and beckoning, pointing like a crooked finger to the Borough of Ipswich. Matt circled the town and lined up as low as he dared on Christ Church Park. He could see Henley Road but was traveling too fast to easily sight Falcon's Rest. No matter, for his slow roll was timed for the length of the park and culminated with a rocket-like climb straight up. "Spectacular!" he complimented himself. If she hadn't seen it, certainly she would hear about it.

The first mission he flew—withdrawal support for B-24 Liberators over Belgium—was without incident. But the next day would be a major milestone in Matt's Air Force career.

Thirty-six Slybirds roared into the sky that morning to join two other fighter groups in support of a large bomber formation destined for targets around Frankfurt, Germany. This was the Augustan's second time out with *Sweet Pea* since his return to flying status, and Colonel Duncan was leading. It would prove to be a rewarding combination in the future, for Duncan was an aggressive stalker of the enemy and long on experience.

The first group of bombers worked over industrial targets around Brussels then returned to England. The larger formation continued to Frankfurt, where such depth of penetration insured a greeting from flak and fighters of the Luftwaffe.

In the weeks Matt had sat on the sidelines, a strategy change had occurred in escort tactics. No longer would the fighters hover around the bombers exclusively. The new directive meant most of the escorts would pursue the enemy fighters to the limit of fuel and ammunition.

Before the flak faded, Matt picked up the tiny dots circling into the sun for attack. It was he who called out the warning this time. "Bogies at 1 o'clock!" His fingers tingled as he turned with Red Section to their defensive position near the front of the bomber formation. Amid the subsequent chatter he heard a Slybird pilot on the enemy flank blurt out, "Son of a gun! There must be 50 of 'em!"

Not to be outdone, eagle-eye Smaragdis picked up more of the Germans forming for a frontal attack. Nose and turret gunners on the lead bombers were already at work as the first Messerschmitts zipped through. Herrington's husky voice crackled sharply, "All right Tower, let's go!"

The flight divided, and Matt clung to his leader's wing obediently as they picked up three 109s coming out of the bombers. Herrington's contentious aggression beat anything the junior officer had witnessed since joining the group. A fresh kill the week before had ignited the captain's thirst for blood. Though Matt's mouth was dry as a desert, he shared his superior's sense of urgency and set his jaw to do battle. The three 109s saw the Americans coming and banked sharply beneath a cloud formation. It didn't slow Herrington even a little as he anticipated the point of their emergence and put his element right there.

They were less than 300 feet above the enemy when the 109s broke out, and Herrington headed for the nearest with guns blazing. Matt followed him down as the trio broke up. "When my tail's clear, get yourself a Hun, Tower! I want trophies!" he bellowed. Matt rubbernecked the area and saw plenty of action but no threats to his leader. The two Messerschmitts were still flying straight, as though unaware the third was in trouble, and Matt pulled in right behind them. As tail-end Charlie drifted into his sights, Matt squeezed off a long burst, spewing strikes across the left wing and cowling of the Messerschmitt.

The German dropped off so suddenly that *Sweet Pea* overshot him. Matt had been warned about diving with a 109 and quickly chose the third enemy fighter. Within seconds he knew this flyer was no neophyte but a slippery pig applying every trick to stay out of his attacker's sights. But Matt wasn't up for the first time either, nor was he content to dust his targets and lose them to evasive stunts. A single-mindedness of anger flowed over him as the flustered puppy turned into attack dog.

The German was barrel rolling, a favorite tactic to throw the pursuer off. Relying on Will Cobbs' instruction, Matt rolled once with his prey. But on the second attempt, he followed the 109 only a third of the way into the roll, then straightened up and rammed the throttle into emergency power. By the time the German was at the top of his roll, Matt was at close range just beneath him. In split-second timing he nosed up the P-47, squeezing the trigger until his hand ached. The results were devastating as the enemy's cockpit disintegrated into flying glass and twisted metal.

Matt was still firing as *Sweet Pea* roared above the stricken 109. When he leveled off, the Messerschmitt continued on its back, slipping sideways, the powerless prop rotating lazily and thick black smoke belching from the cockpit. Oblivious to the frantic chatter in his headphones, he watched his first destroyed enemy aircraft sink to the earth. He knew there could be no parachute, for when it was timed right, Cobbs' tactic was terminal.

His heart pounded as *Sweet Pea* made a wide, steady turn back toward the bombers. He had killed, intentionally and with acquired skill, but not comfortably. Sweat poured from his brow as he struggled for emotional control. He had known this time would come, but the sane are not easily reconciled to the termination of life even when justified. *"God, forgive me!"* he whispered into the ears of the Omniscient.

The merciful antidote came with the image of the first plane he had seen fall from the sky. There was that flash again in his mind as the B-17's tail separated from the doomed bomber and it spun away helplessly beneath its sister ships. The seconds slipped by while Matt's mind clamored for reassurance, gradually accepting the fact that the Hun had to be stopped. All of them! That was easily confirmed, for as he neared the formation of tall-tailed Big Friends, one was struggling to stay with its unit, smoke pouring from a starboard engine. There were 10 men in there, fully aware of the danger but faithfully manning their stations. Matt had yet to see a bomber able to fly that did not try to complete the mission.

The 17s delivered their packages and began the long run for home, lighter and a bit faster but still tasty to the Luftwaffe. Matt could not recognize a Slybird among the crisscrossing P-47s and would make the return trip on his own. He flew for a moment with two other Thunderbolts that appeared as orphaned as he was until oncoming flashes from the wings of four 109s dissolved the partnership. Diving would expose *Sweet Pea's* cockpit, and climbing would offer its tender belly as a broader target. Matt committed himself to a standoff and returned fire head-on.

One of the P-47s made the mistake of breaking away, which

enticed two of the approaching enemy to take him on. The other 109s flashed by Matt so closely he could see the pilots' faces. What happened to the wingman of the diving P-47 he never knew, but the diver was in serious trouble, heading for the deck with two killers on his tail. Matt checked the rear mirror and found that his attackers had not turned back, so he nosed over and went down to help the distressed American pilot.

The Messerschmitts were on him, and the only hope was to even the odds. Matt finally got the trailing 109 in his sights and poured a burst into him. The German broke to the left and headed for cloud cover. *Sweet Pea's* 50s dusted him good, ripping off chunks of the left wing as the 109 slipped into the white fluff. A second more and there might have been a double for the day.

It was unsettling to find himself alone in the skies over enemy territory, and Matt instinctively nosed up for that all-important altitude. Bomber missions left great highways of vapor trails coming in and smoke streams from the damaged going out. He could trust the drifting trails or set his own course. He reckoned the bombers would take the shortest route, and since it seemed logical on the compass, he followed. It was eerie that all the winged warriors seemed absorbed into the sky so quickly. But his time spent in the dogfight had dragged on longer than he imagined, and any friendly ship would be welcome company now.

One aircraft lay just ahead, a tiny dot on the horizon trailing a ribbon of thin brown smoke. Matt gave chase until he saw the unique tail of a B-17 at about 5,000 feet where the bomber struggled along on three engines. A pair of 109s were stalking, making alternate passes at the disabled Flying Fortress. The rudder was shot up badly, and it appeared the enemy fighters had taken out the tail gunner. There was no time for up-sun position or other fancy approaches, and he dived straight into the first Messerschmitt with a recklessness born of anger. The combination of gunners in the cripple and an able American fighter raised the risk for the enemy, and they broke off after several attempts to get back at the bomber.

When Matt pulled up beside the Fortress, he was pushed away with a shower of tracers, evidently lacking a proper introduction to an edgy crew still shy of single engines. He wrestled with the radio channels until he heard the pilot calling down the gunners and broke in. "Hey! Over here, I'm on your side! Check the star on the side of this jug, will you?"

"Sorry, Little Friend! We've had the crap shot out of us. Boy, are we glad to see you!"

"Where you guys from?"

"Rattlesden."

"Can you get any more altitude?" Matt inquired.

"I doubt it. One engine out and a second not pulling its weight."

"Well, try to stay away from the cities and ease it up as much as you can. I can't do as much for you down here if we get bounced again."

"We'll try, Little Friend, but having you around is mighty comforting. You've got 353rd markings. You at Raydon?"

"I am."

The tail of the Fortress was thoroughly punctured, the rudder in shreds, marring the sporty yellow striping. Only the *K* of its group designation seemed intact. But the Georgia boy had problems of his own. The escort had taken the fighters to their maximum range, even with belly tanks, and the needle of the 47's fuel gauge nestled near empty. He applied every fuel-saving procedure, and lagging with the distressed bomber was not one of them. He determined to stay with it until the coast was sighted, which offered a better margin of safety from enemy fighters.

A few minutes later Matt called the B-17's pilot. "There's the channel, Big Friend. I'm low on fuel. Afraid I've done all I can for you."

"Many, many thanks, Little Friend. Try *two seven zero*. That should show you the White Cliffs, the closest beach."

*Sweet Pea* cleared the French coast, then headed out over the channel. Matt could barely distinguish a hair of space between the needle and Empty. Flashes of Andy Johnson's adventure in the deep kept him ever attentive to the fighter's performance. He wanted to gain altitude for as much glide as possible if the engine stopped, but that would have taxed his fuel the more. The sight of broad, white cliffs was the next best thing to the end of a runway, and his hope welled. "Come on, *Sweet Pea*.... Do right by me, baby," he coaxed, remembering his crew chief's promise.

He was not the only late arrival, for at the foot of the cliffs lay the wreckage of a fighter where steady winds carried a stream of smoke down the coastline. Military vehicles parked at the top of the cliff, and men were engaged in recovery efforts. But Matt speculated if the pilot was in the plane when it crashed, there would be little to recover. His engine sputtered then caught again, sending a chill through the young flyer's body. Out of the corner of his left eye he saw it, the tell-tale triangle of an airfield. Would it be too far? *"Gear down, Tower, while you have power."*

Four miles... three miles.... *Sweet Pea's* engine was alternately sputtering and catching as the hands on the altimeter wound down ever more rapidly. Then only the sound of the wind as the engine quit. *"Airspeed, Tower, airspeed,"* he instructed himself as he eased the fighter's nose down. Three flairs in rapid succession rocketed into the air from the descending fighter, for he had no time to circle the traffic pattern. His glide had extended as far as possible; *Sweet Pea* was coming down. The P-47 dropped roughly onto the grass 100 feet from the runway, bouncing into the air in three pounding leaps, the last touching its wheels to pavement. He held it steady, using as little correction as possible as the fighter finished its rollout.

Matt slid the canopy back and, pulling off his helmet, sucked in a

deep breath of air. Wherever he was, he had created quite a disturbance, for a parade of British vehicles was racing across the field in
his direction. An RAF airman bounded onto the wing and peered
into the cockpit. "I say, Lieutenant, are you all right?"

Matt nodded affirmatively and cleared the fighter's switches.
"Where the heck am I?"

"An RAF base near Hawkinge, sir. Do you need help?"

The American pulled himself to a standing position and stretched
away the hours of cramped quarters. "How much do you charge for
petrol these days?" he asked, smiling at the sober-faced sergeant.

# CHAPTER 9

# Getting to Know Vivie

**M**ATT'S WELCOMING PARTY at Raydon was a bit more enthusiastic. As he taxied *Sweet Pea* into place on the dispersal pad, Milt-the-Stilt lowered his lanky body from his perch atop an oil drum. He and his crew had waited for an agonizing three hours after the other fighters returned. Matt responded to the shuffling Tennessean's grin with one of his own as he dropped to the ground from the fighter's wing.

"Where you been with ma' airplane, Lieutenant?" the crew chief drawled.

Herrington's arrival by jeep cut Matt's reply short. "What are you trying to do, Tower, grandstand?" He tried to keep a straight face with all his might. "Don't you know U.S. Government property is to be returned promptly after use?"

"Well, sir," Matt replied. "A funny thing happened on the way back...."

"Some dang fine flying, that's what!" the captain interrupted. "Milt," he said, turning to the crew chief, "this man bagged his first destroyed today!"

Matt briefed his crew chief, sharing the excitement of *Sweet Pea's* performance, then headed for debriefing with Herrington. The 350th Squadron had several dusted and five destroyed, one being Matt's. While Herrington was thrilled with the trophy, Colonel Duncan had a call from the 447th Bomber Group commander with a special commendation for an *LH* fighter that had pulled one of his Flying Fortresses out of the tights over France. The 353rd Fighter Group had scored a total of five enemy destroyed, and the resulting party that night pulled out all the stops.

As the evening wore on, Matt, already taxed to the limit, soon tired of the backslapping and mutual praise about the day's performance. There was but one person he wanted to share his feelings with. He slipped out of the officers' club unnoticed and took a grateful breath of the crisp night air. Making his way to the Operations office, he found only the Officer of the Day and a couple of clerks in residence. Under the pretense of completing mission forms, Matt made his way to a private office in the rear and shut the door. Out came the neatly folded memo, and he placed a call to Falcon's Rest.

"Mrs. Davis, please."

"One moment, sir," the receptionist replied.

Matt tapped his fingers impatiently and glanced through the glass partition to see if anyone was getting nosey. They weren't, so he relaxed a little.

"May I help you?" the distinctive voice of Mrs. Moore inquired.

"Mrs. Moore, this is Lieutenant Tower. I was calling for Vivie. Is she available?"

"I'm sorry, Lieutenant, but she's not in presently. Would you like me to tell her you called?"

"Well, I may be coming into town later this week, and she gave me the number there to call ahead. Do you know if she has plans Wednesday or Thursday?"

"I'm not certain about Wednesday, but she's not mentioned anything for Thursday. If you come Wednesday, would you care to take dinner with us?"

The unexpected invitation pleased him greatly, and he paused to collect his thoughts. "Thank you! I'd like that very much. Please tell Vivie if nothing comes up, like I can't get a pass, I'll be there by early afternoon."

He still had the receiver to his ear when the OD knocked and entered the office. "Excuse me, sir, but do you have clearance for off-base calls?"

Matt's expression changed to one of sober concern as he slowly and deliberately swiveled the chair to meet the enlisted man's inquiring eyes. "Do you have any idea of the nature of this call, Sergeant?"

"No, sir."

"Did you hear even a word of the conversation?"

"No sir, not really."

"Good! Because if you had it would be necessary to confine you to quarters for at least the next three days."

"Well sir, it… it just seemed like a personal call, and I'm supposed to watch out for that kind of thing."

"Of course it's to sound like that, Sergeant! Do you think we can rest securely even on a base phone regarding matters as important as this?"

"Probably not, sir."

Matt rose from his chair, maintaining an air of urgent security as the OD came to attention. "You're doing an excellent job here, Sergeant. It's comforting to know that we in the line of fire have such dedication to duty in our support team. Rest assured that Colonel Bailey will get word of this."

"Thank you, sir," the skeptical OD replied with a smile.

Matt allowed the sergeant to escort him to the exit, where he returned the snappy salute. As he heard the door closing behind him, he wiped the sweat from his brow with a sigh of relief. "We better win this war in a heck of a hurry," he mumbled, reflecting on his little drama with the gullible OD.

The emotional impact of the day had Matt under his blanket 30 minutes later. He was asleep almost instantly, but at 2 a.m. he awoke with a start, frantically attacking the bed covers. In his dream, the shadowy form of a German officer, in full uniform and cap, walked out of the fog with arm raised in a Nazi salute. As he approached Matt, the extended hand grew into a great black-gloved fist. So real was the dream, Matt could smell the leather as the gloved hand attempted to overtake him. After running for a time, he turned to find no trace of the phantom. But when he stopped to rest, panting for breath, the arm emerged again from another direction.

After repeated confrontations, Matt was unable to run further and collapsed as the silhouette of the phantom dropped rapidly over him. Painfully awake now, he had wadded up the German in his blanket and sat on the cot in a lather of sweat. *"Oh, God!"* he prayed in the semi darkness, *"must I fight 'em in my sleep?"*

As composure returned, he eased out of bed and moved quietly to the bath house where he let the cool water cascade over his head. A quick wipe-down refreshed him and brought his heart to a normal beat. But it was another hour before his tossing body would submit to sleep again.

Mercifully, his element was not on the day's mission roster, and he ended up working on reports with Herrington.

By noon, the captain suggested a break and the two men strolled outside. The base was quiet, with most of the 353rd Fighter Group on a bomb-and-strafe mission somewhere over the French coast. Not by accident the two pilots ended up on the dispersal pad beside

Herrington's P-47, *Wicked Wanda*. Matt felt something was in the air and sought to loosen up Herrington and see what gave. "How'd you come up with that name, Captain?"

Herrington pulled the pipe from his mouth and glanced up at the reclining model on the fighter's cowling. "*Wanda*?" he grinned. "Meanest woman I ever met. She kept the guys all hot and bothered, cheerleader, you know... and an exhibitionist."

The captain fired up his pipe and leaned against the fighter's wing. "Tower, stuff's getting ready to break loose. There's every indication Eisenhower's going to let the invasion roll this summer. Duncan wants the group ready, the squadrons, flights, elements in capable hands. They're bumping me up a notch to Ops, and I need someone to handle Red." He paused to pack the pipe with his finger, then glanced back at Matt. "That's you."

Matt was caught by surprise. He hadn't expected the opportunity this early and struggled to harness the smile creeping across his face. It would mean a command, something he had yearned for from his first day in training. "You're not pulling my leg, are you, Captain?"

"Nope. Unless you think you're not ready."

"I'd never let you know it, sir."

Herrington chuckled and drew on the pipe. "Didn't think you would. You have any questions?"

"I'm wondering about Chuck and Roger."

The captain folded his arms and nursed the pipe in smooth, easy draws. "You're wondering if it will bother them."

"Yes, sir. We've been together since basic and shared a lot, always on equal terms. They're good men. They'll want to know why me instead of them."

"Well, I'll tell you up front it's just a matter of time for Shilling. He'll be ripe for an element when it's available. Baker's a horse of another color. Good pilot, but he's too dang reckless."

"I don't mind Roger, but I'd prefer Chuck on my wing for as long as possible," Matt replied.

"Done. I'll handle it and we'll go from there," the captain offered.

"Thank you, sir. If you state how it's going to be, they can make up their minds without any hard feelings toward me."

Herrington stuck the pipe between his teeth and fumbled in his jacket pockets until he retrieved a small box. "Here, you'll need these."

Matt slipped the top off to reveal two silver bars sparkling in the midday sun. To this eager young pilot, diamonds would have been no grander. "Captain.... I... well, this is all so fast I don't know what to say!"

"Don't give me a lot of your lip, Tower. All I want is trophies. It'll be official in the morning. But what the hey, put 'em on now."

"When do I take over, sir?"

"Saturday, as soon as you arrive back at the base."

"Back? Where am I going?"

"Into Ipswich to take care of that piece of business you phoned about last night," Herrington replied dryly.

Matt concluded quickly that the best defense was innocent admission. "It was just a short call, sir. How'd you know about it?"

"Tower, I take responsibility for my men seriously. In the future abide by regulations. Understood?"

"Yes, sir," the new first lieutenant acknowledged soberly.

"Then get some chow and come by my office so we can start things rolling on the changeover."

The officers worked diligently over the next two days, sandwiching their time between missions. Roger and Chuck had no problem with Matt's promotion to element leader, and he was able to leave for Ipswich on Wednesday with his mind at ease.

This time, more familiar with the town, he noticed that despite the terror from above, many of the homes had flowers, and cultivation of the abundant allotment gardens showed promise of a decent harvest. The remarkable spirit of the English people impressed the American flyer at every turn. Churchill's reply to Hitler's taunt that he'd "wring the English chicken's neck," was right on target.

*"Some chicken, some neck!"* the prime minister shot back.

It was late afternoon when he arrived at Falcon's Rest. His young fan, Bobby Brooks, was hard at work sweeping the great front porch. As Matt headed for the steps the lad recognized him immediately. He was all smiles as he ran to the rail to greet the flyer. "Hey, Lieutenant, do you remember me? I'm Bobby Brooks!"

Matt placed a hand on the boy's shoulder and smiled down at him. "I sure do. You're the guy who wants to be a fighter pilot, right?"

"Your crutches are gone. Are you well now?"

"Much better, Bobby. And how have you been?"

"I've been fine. Did you know we had a real dogfight right over the town?"

"No, I hadn't heard about that. What happened?"

The youngster was beside himself now. He was giving firsthand information of great significance to a bigger-than-life fighter pilot for whom he had the highest regard. "Well, sir, we were all up early at my house Sabbath morn, the very crack of dawn, when all this screaming roar come right down our street!"

Matt bit his lip to keep from laughing at the youthful excitement as Bobby gasped for breath and swallowed between sentences. "It was a German, all right, rolling and turning, and right behind him was two Spitfires! They was firing at him. You could hear the guns way up there!"

The boy reached into his jacket pocket and pulled out a shiny metal cylinder. "See!" he said, handing it to Matt. "It's one of the shells. Some of them bounced into the street."

"Well, you've had quite an adventure, little buddy. How did the fight come out?"

"Oh! They shot him down, Lieutenant! He crashed in a field near Dale Hall. Everybody's been there to see it. Do you want to see it, too?"

"Maybe, if I have time. By the way, have you seen Mrs. Davis around?"

"Yes, sir. She was in and about this morning." A crease settled on the youthful brow as he cocked his head questioningly. "She seemed different today, singing to herself and all, a bit dotty like. You know?"

"Is that so?"

The youngster drew his jacket sleeve across his mouth and looked up questioningly at Matt. "Do you like her, Lieutenant?"

"Now what makes you ask something like that?" Matt replied as he hid a grin with his hand.

"Because I can't think of no reason why you'd come back here if you didn't. Most of the soldiers likes it down around Corn Hill and Butter Market."

Matt, stroking his chin thoughtfully, had not expected to be so questioned by his nosey admirer. It was important that this young-ster not pop off his mouth in some naive blunder. The American decided to take the little guy into his confidence. He seated himself on the top step and motioned for Bobby to join him. "How good are you at military secrets, young man?"

"I'm quite good at secrets, Lieutenant!"

"What would you do if you had a girl that you liked a whole lot, maybe at school or something?"

"Like you likes Mrs. Davis?"

"I'm asking the questions here," Matt reminded.

"Well, I'd tell her right out!" That wasn't what Matt wanted to hear and he questioned the youngster's thinking. "Why would you do that?"

"Cause I wouldn't want another bloke to get her first."

Matt couldn't argue with that, but it had not addressed his

concern. He folded his hands and rested his arms on his knees to impute a proper seriousness. "Suppose you're not sure the girl likes you as much as you like her?"

The young head lowered a bit and the sleeve went across his mouth again. "I don't know, Lieutenant. I guess it would be best to wait a bit."

Matt straightened up and put an arm on the boy's shoulder. "Thank you, Bobby. That's the best advice I could have. A fellow needs another man to discuss these things with. So that's our secret now. I'm going to wait awhile before I tell her right out. Agreed?"

Young Brooks nodded his head and Matt breathed a sigh of relief, more confident now that youthful impetuousness would not do him in. He returned the spent cartridge to the boy, telling him he had a very special keepsake: a reminder of the days when men risked their lives to protect England.

The youngster's attention span had endured all the deep talk it could. There were far more important items in his youthful perspective, and he moved right to them. "Did you shoot down any Germans yet?"

"As a matter of fact, I did."

"Wow!" the youngster gasped. "What was it?"

"A Messerschmitt 109."

Bobby was fine-tuned to the American flyer, taking in every word. "How did you do it, Lieutenant? Did they shoot back?"

"They were shooting at our bombers," Matt replied, smiling down at the jubilant boy sitting beside him. "Three of them came right out of the formation and dived under us."

"Wow! And you got one! Wow!"

"Sure did. I dusted another pretty good, but he slipped into cloud cover and I was low on fuel."

Bobby pressed for details, which Matt provided willingly until he became concerned that the little guy was growing hyper with excitement and neglecting his chores. "Tell you what, Bobby. Let's save some for later. I don't want to get you fired from a good job."

Reluctantly, the youngster resumed his position with the broom, and Matt escaped into the lobby. None of the ladies was present at the desk. In their place, a rather ruddy gentleman of noble bearing manned the station. Crowned with thick, wavy white hair and sporting a slightly rumpled tweed jacket, he worked intently over a set of leather-bound ledgers.

"Excuse me," Matt interrupted. "Is Mrs. Davis in?"

The elder man turned slowly and glanced down his nose through black-rimmed glasses at his inquirer. "Mrs. Davis is away," he replied, his voice a rather deep resonant British that offered no additional comment. The steady gaze left Matt ill at ease.

"Would Mrs. Moore be in?" Matt tried again, a trace of hopeful urgency filtering through his voice. "They're expecting me."

"Are they, now?" the silver-haired Englishman retorted, his dark-blue eyes skimming the uniformed flyer. "Well, I'm Mrs. Moore's husband and Mrs. Davis' father, and I'd jolly well like to know who you are."

This unsettling disclosure brought up the young officer abruptly. There had been no mention of Major Moore by any but the waitress taking his order on the first visit. Of course, with his casual arrival on that date there would have been no particular reason for Matt to gain the family history. Now he hoped to conduct himself in a manner befitting this first introduction to the paternal entity. "The name is Tower, sir, Matt Tower. I was here a couple of weeks ago and met Mrs. Moore."

"Tower.... Oh, yes, she did mention you. You met Vivian at an RAF base sometime back if I remember correctly."

"In the NAAFI canteen there," Matt volunteered. "I'm sorry I didn't have the pleasure of meeting you on my last visit, sir."

Major Moore continued to size up Matt, standing at last to get a full view. In a rather strained gesture, he extended his hand. "Robert Moore, Lieutenant." The grip was strong, testing the American's steel. "I was likely on hunt when you were here."

"Do you ride to the hounds, sir?"

"Not for some time," the major replied, impressed with Matt's awareness of the sport. "These ancient bones much prefer fowling. Are you much of a shooter, young man?"

"Yes, sir." Matt was quick to see that Vivie's father placed importance on the game sports, and he was grateful to find common ground. "I've been hunting since I was a youngster. My grandfather has a farm near the Savannah River, and we shot dove, quail, and duck in season."

"Good!" Mr. Moore exclaimed. "Quite healthy for mind and body, you know."

Matt knew he was being evaluated and he half-smiled, remembering his father's technique when the suitors came calling on his sister. *"Vivie must be quite a daughter,"* he thought to himself.

In England, conversation always came around to the war, and Matt was treated to a colorful discourse on the senior Moore's tenure in His Majesty's artillery during the Great War. The major was quite into it when he paused suddenly and gestured toward the lobby door. "Your patience is rewarded, Lieutenant."

Vivie entered the lobby with a friend, a perky, attractive young woman of creamy complexion and wavy black hair. Lost in girl talk, the uniformed pair reached the lobby desk before Vivie noticed the American flyer. She stood there at first, hands by her sides, a bit awkward with the encounter. "Matt?" she questioned, a trace smile and arched eyebrows exposing a definite, if somewhat restrained, excitement.

"Hi," he smiled in return. "I made it."

"Mum told me you were coming."

The brunette, whose babbling had ceased abruptly, did little to conceal her appreciation of the handsome Air Force officer. "Vivie!" she interrupted, her elbow jabbing playfully. "Aren't you going to introduce us?"

Vivie pretended to be unaffected by the brunette's assertiveness. "Lieutenant Tower, this is Ruth Hardy, a friend of mine."

"Delighted, Lieutenant!" Ruth injected, extending her hand in such a way that the smiling officer must hold it instead of shaking it.

If anything surprised Vivie more than Ruth's coquettish behavior, it was her own feelings in the matter. She grew quite uncomfortable at the sight of Matt in the clutches of her friend. "Have you met my father, Lieutenant?" she interrupted quickly.

"Yes, I have. We were talking just before you two came in," he replied, looking toward Major Moore, who sat by the ledgers peering over his glasses. It was evident he preferred his position of neutrality to becoming further involved.

"I see there are no crutches now," Vivie said. "You must be all well again."

"I was fortunate, I guess. The wound was clean. They put me back on active a week ago."

"Oh, how heroic!" Ruth squealed, pressing her hands to her chest. "A real flyer! I do so love bravery in a man. Isn't he marvelous, Vivie?"

Matt was vulnerable as any to such feminine prattle. But seeing Vivie's eyes, his response was careful. "Well, you don't have to be heroic to get hurt," he offered, attempting to smooth the matter over. "Sometimes stupidity does the job."

But the giddy brunette wouldn't let it die. "And so modest and strong!" she swooned.

Knowing her old school chum's nature, Vivie might have been more tolerant in another setting, but the brunette was interfering with a delicate moment. "Ruth, fetch the clothing while I see that the lieutenant has a comfortable room." Ruth's hesitation served only to fan Vivie's impatience. "Beetle off, dear!" she prompted.

As the impulsive one moved away, Vivie placed her purse on the desk and pulled the registration book to her. "I'm sorry about that. She's a dear friend but such a dolly-bird at times."

"No harm done. She's so brash, she's cute."

"Cute?" Vivie questioned dryly, cutting her eyes at Matt. "Would you like Room 3 again?"

"That'll be fine. I've really been looking forward to this."

"Mum said you're to have dinner with us. I hope it's something you like."

"I trust your mother implicitly. Every meal I've had here has been great."

Vivie looked so good to him, and Matt felt an inexplicable contentment in her presence as though he had known her for a much longer time. Pleasant memories of the park made him yearn for another time of privacy with her.

Ruth Hardy, struggling with a box of dangling clothes, crossed the lobby inches from Matt, leaving the instinctive gentleman no alternative. "Here, let me help you with that."

"Oh, thank you, Lieutenant. It is a bit much for little ol' me."

Vivie watched the two transfer the clothes into boy and girl piles destined for the WVS shelter. Retrieving her purse, she marched toward the lobby door and propped it open. "It's a bit much for me as well!" she retaliated. "Let's get on to the service van, Lieutenant."

Ruth swayed along in front, quite evidently for Matt's benefit, as she rummaged her purse for the vehicle's keys. It didn't take a psychologist to detect Vivie's mounting impatience. Matt felt the coolness as he brushed past her to the front porch, but there was no tactful way to abandon the chore he had undertaken. It was not what he had intended at all, and once the boxes were in place, he positioned himself safely behind Vivie.

In spite of being outflanked, Ruth sported a generous smile as she leaned out the car window. "Thank you, Lieutenant," she breathed, drawing the words out. "You're such a dear. So gallant!"

Vivie's eyes rolled heavenward, her arms folding critically across the WVS jacket. "Buzz off, Ruth. You're late for the shelter as it tis."

The brunette shrugged and slid to the driver's seat. "Ta-ta, one and all," she cooed, offering a prissy wave as the Austin van pulled away.

Vivie, with her arms still folded, turned back to Falcon's Rest. "I'm sorry, Matt. She can be such a twit at times!"

"How long have you been friends?"

"Until a few minutes ago!" Vivie snapped. "She went to school in London when I was at Roedean. She was my maid of…." Vivie's words ended abruptly. She paused at the foot of the steps and turned to him. Her lovely blue eyes searched his face as she bit her lower lip. He knew what was on her mind and let his gaze drop to the ground so she might recover.

"Hey, Lieutenant! I see you found her right enough!" It was young Brooks, staging yet another untimely interruption. "Did you tell her yet?"

Vivie's head turned toward the noisy intruder. "Bobby, have you finished with the porches so soon?"

"And the storage room too, ma'am!" the youngster replied as Matt waved him to secrecy from behind Vivie's back.

She almost caught him in the act, but he quickly moved his hands to less evident gestures. "And just what is it that I should be told?" she questioned the guilty faces.

"The Messerschmitt! He got a Messerschmitt, Mrs. Davis!"

Matt sighed, grateful that the lad had not breached their earlier agreement. "I have two surprises. That was one."

Vivie's face was quite sober. She knew only too well that such engagements bore great risks for both sides. But she would not deny him his moment. "Good!" she congratulated, her voice conveying unchecked contempt for the German enemy. "I know you must be quite proud."

"Well, the second surprise might be more to your liking. Come on, let's sit on the porch."

Bobby Brooks tagged along characteristically, assuming the invitation was inclusive. Matt seated himself in one of the rockers beside Vivie, whose charming smile was already reflecting the youngster's anticipation. "Is this better than the Messerschmitt?" Bobby pressed.

"What do you say we let Mrs. Davis decide that?" Matt replied, pressing a small package into her hand. She fingered the box, speculating on its contents.

"It must be quite small, whatever it is." Impatiently, she pulled off the top, and two silver bars sparkled in the sunlight.

"He's been promoted, Mrs. Davis!" young Brooks bellowed as his arms shot upward. Excitement crept across Vivie's face and culminated in a puckered "O" of her lips. "They're beautiful, Matt," she breathed.

He anticipated the question when her gaze turned to his shoulders, then back to the box. "First Lieutenant," he explained with a smile. "And I'll have an element of fighters when I get back to base."

"I'm so thrilled for you! I simply don't know what to do."

He could have given her one good suggestion for the tempting lips inches away. "Well, you could pin them on for a start."

Sitting at their feet, young Brooks fell silent, an enormous smile plastered across his face, arms encircling his drawn-up knees. Vivie leaned over to detach the gold bars, drawing quite close to Matt as she worked the pin clips. She was smiling, her blue eyes darting coyly to and from his, as though she might be aware of his wish. Had the British youngster not been on hand, Matt probably would have kissed her despite the risk. She attached the new silver bars and patted them in place. "There now, everything is in order, First Lieutenant Tower."

"Almost everything," Matt replied. He winked at Vivie and rolled the gold bars around in his hand. "I've got to do something with these."

Bobby followed the American's gesture intently, his smile having dwindled to a serious, thin line. Matt grinned down at the questioning young face and opened his hand. "You know what I think, Vivie? I think these would look just right on Bobby Brooks' jacket."

The response surfaced immediately in the boy's eyes, which seemed to double in size. "Wow! Do you really mean it, Lieutenant?"

"I certainly do. I'm going to make you an honorary lieutenant in the United States Army Air Force."

By the time the bars found their place on the youngster's jacket, he was beside himself with excitement. "Thank you! Thank you! Thank you!" he stressed over and over. There were friends he needed to tell, to whom he must show this great prize, and he fumbled for an excuse to leave. "Wow! I've got to tell my dad and mum! I can't stay any longer, Lieutenant."

The lad sprang to his feet and bolted down the steps. "Hey, soldier," Matt called out. Bobby stopped short and looked back at the couple seated on the porch. "You're supposed to salute a superior officer when you leave!"

That was the icing on the cake for the boy. He snapped to rigid attention and popped his hand to his forehead. "Yes, sir!" he called back, then broke into a run.

Vivie sat smiling, hands clasped in her lap. "That was a grand thing you did, Matt Tower. His father is in naval service, you know, and the lad misses him terribly."

"I didn't know. He certainly latched onto me. When I was here before, I had to dodge him to get a minute's peace."

"We'll have tea shortly," Vivie said as she stood up. "Would you care to walk in the garden first?"

"If you promise no rain or dirty gazebos," Matt chuckled.

She accepted his arm as they descended the steps and then clasped her hands behind her back. Matt very much wanted to hold one of them as they walked along, but she was not ready for that. So he slipped his hands in his pockets and followed her lead along the garden path. Neither spoke for a time until they came to an iron bench secluded in the hedges at the far end of the grounds. "Could we sit here for a moment?" Vivie asked.

Matt could sense that her mood had changed as they walked along, and he grew uneasy, much as he had as a boy when his Dad would say, *"I need to talk with you, son."* Vivie leaned back on the bench and folded her arms and looked up into the spreading branches of the trees. "Matt, I must ask you something."

"Okay."

"Why do you keep coming here?"

He thought for a moment, then grinned. "For the cooking. Hands down!"

There was no responding smile at his humor, and he realized Vivie's question was in all candor. She simply waited until the gravity of the moment showed on his face. "Why?" she repeated calmly.

Her honest, level gaze could strip one's soul naked, and he knew she was ready for the talk they had delayed so long. "Because of a woman I met in a NAAFI canteen awhile back."

"You know very little about that woman," she replied, gazing again into the spreading limbs.

"Maybe so. But when I first saw her, I knew she was different from anyone I ever met, and I wanted to see her again."

"How did you know to come here?"

"Mrs. Pearson gave me a note."

"Mary," Vivie whispered, cocking her head knowingly. She slumped back on the bench and sighed. "I feel smothered," she said softly. "Everyone's directing my life. Mrs. Pearson, Ruth, Mum, the Vicar, but none of them understand how bloody awful it is for me!"

As she dabbed at her eyes, Matt looked away to give her time. He could not think of one intelligent thing to say. "And now here I am causing all these things to come up again. I didn't mean to do that."

"No. You must know," she said, turning in his direction. "It's only fair." He could see that she was determined to deal with the matter and settled back to let her continue. "John and I were married a few months after war was declared. He took leave from his law apprenticeship to join the RAF. He'd always loved flying, and England needed pilots desperately."

It was a difficult moment for Matt. Compassion urged him to caress her hand, to signal his sympathy with a physical gesture. He withheld his touch reluctantly, lest it be ill-timed, and let her continue. "Then came Dunkirk. The Germans had pushed our troops back against the sea. They lined the beaches, huddled in the open. Everyone was trying to save them. It was up to the RAF to keep the Germans back while the ships worked to ferry the soldiers across the channel. For days they flew. Commander Chumley told us John was on his fourth mission the day his plane was seen to go down."

Face buried in her hands, she turned aside as silent sobs jerked her body. His arm was already on the back of the bench and he reached over to steady her, his face soberly mirroring her hurt. "Vivie, Vivie," he called softly. "You don't have to do this. You don't owe... I don't need any explanations."

"Yes, you do," she replied as she held his handkerchief over her eyes. "I was carrying his baby." The sobs returned.

She rested against his arm until her breathing returned to normal, then slowly straightened up. "Four weeks later, I miscarried. I lost the baby."

Matt looked out across the grounds as though he had awakened from a dream. It was then his eye caught a form in a second-story window of the inn. It was not a clear image, but he could tell it was large. It remained for a few seconds, then disappeared. Matt was certain it had been there for some time before he saw it. He did not call Vivie's attention to it, feeling it would upset her further, but he was concerned by the spy's callous liberty.

"It's been difficult for me since then," Vivie said. "I had to push myself to do something, and the women's service seemed to fill a need. I saw so many others with great problems of their own. That's how I met Mrs. Pearson, and she has been just a dear to me."

Vivie paused to dab at her eyes again, her chest rising and falling in a deep sigh. "Friends have tried arranging dates for me, but they were all alike. They just see a young widow with all the implications one might expect. I think that's what surprised me when we were in the park. I've not had a time like that since I can remember," she said as the makings of a smile toyed with her lips.

When she paused, Matt gently brushed her cheek with his fingers. "The first time I saw you, Vivie, I felt something very special. You were different in so many ways from most of the women I've met. I guess I'm not doing a very good job of saying how I feel about you, but more than anything I can think of, I wanted a chance to know you better."

"That's just it," she replied with a sigh. "I'm not certain what I feel, Matt." Vivie gathered her purse and attempted to repair her makeup. "I do feel comfortable with you. Not pressured so much as with the others. But I wanted you to be aware that things in my life have been quite out of sorts."

"I know it must be difficult for you, and I care about that a great deal," he replied. "I can wait awhile if I just know you're willing to give it a chance.... *At least I think I can,*" he added under his breath.

"Then it's very good friends, just now?" she asked assuredly.

"The very best!" he replied, returning her smile.

Vivie stood and looked at her watch. "Dear! We'll miss tea. Come on, I'll race you to the door!"

To Matt's utter surprise she lifted her skirt just above the knees and sprang away like a startled doe. He responded quickly and chased her but soon decided not to pass the lovely legs, for the view was unbeatable from his position. He had every intention of waiting as long as it took.

They were both laughing as they reached the porch. She knew he had let her win, but she claimed victory anyway. "Foul!" he cried, panting up the steps. "I demand a referee's opinion!"

"Whatever for?" she giggled breathlessly.

"There must be a rule somewhere that it's unfair to run in front of your opponent with your skirt up!" he replied.

"Works every time!" came the teasing tones of Ruth Hardy's voice from the doorway. "Have the boys and girls been out to play?"

Vivie's embarrassment was momentary. "What are you doing here?"

"It's jolly well your fault, Vivie dear. You didn't tell me what to say to David about the dance tonight." Vivie was winded and off-guard, so Matt figured he would take the pressure off. "Mrs. Davis already has a date, and if she wishes to attend the dance, he'll see that she gets there."

Ruth flashed a cunning little smile as she stopped in front of Matt. "Well, I can see that you're in very good hands, Vivian. Very good hands, indeed!" she added as her seductive eyes outlined the American flyer. "I'll supply a suitable alibi."

"Just say I'm engaged for the evening," Vivie directed.

"Very well," the brunette replied, her tone more sympathetic now. "I'm sorry I interrupted. I do hope you can make it, though." She hurried to the Austin van and drove away, waving merrily through the window.

"David?" Matt inquired. "Have I caused another problem?"

"Heavens, no," Vivie sighed. "David Walldon is the son of family friends at Great Wenham. I met him years ago and he hasn't changed a bit. Still the clever dick!" She smoothed her uniform with her hands and patted her hair in place. "Come along now. We'll be late for tea."

# CHAPTER 10

# Courting

**D**INNER WITH THE Moores gave Matt entrée to the family's private quarters for the first time and one delicious Etta Moore meal, which she had promised him. The evening was quiet, congenial as concerned the ladies. Mrs. Moore showed particular interest in the States and his home and family, but Major Moore's participation seemed civil at best, which strained his wife's tactfulness considerably. Though Matt was hard pressed to understand the change in disposition, he did a masterful job of patronizing the older man, pulling him out on the Great War and fowling.

It was near seven o'clock when they completed dessert. Her father's attitude concerned Vivie as much as it had her mother, and in an effort to escape the tension she mentioned the dance again. Matt gratefully picked up on it and they excused themselves. *"Le repas etait delicieux,"* he smiled as he eased his chair back from the table. *"Mes compliments au chef."*

Mrs. Moore straightened and returned the smile, pleasantly surprised by his French. *"Merci tant, Lieutenant. Tu parles bien le francais."*

With that fluent response Matt knew who had better command of the language, but he made a good show for himself as the two continued their exchange. It seemed to amuse all except Major Moore, who toyed with his fork and stared skeptically over his glasses at the three before him.

Only after Etta echoed Matt's *"Bonsoir"* and the young people had left did Vivie's father drop the silverware and sink back in his chair. Etta could hardly contain herself until they were alone.

"Robert, you were quite inhospitable this evening. Whatever is the matter?"

He leaned forward, resting his elbows on the dining table. "That bloody Yank you're so taken with! That's what!"

"Lieutenant Tower?" she implored.

"Indeed!"

Etta's lips pursed inquisitively. "And just what is it about him?"

"He had your daughter in tears just before tea. I saw them from the library window. Then she ran to the inn in tears."

"Whatever for?"

"I haven't the foggiest," he replied. "But I've seen her cry and I'll not tolerate anyone interfering with her. These Yanks have a way of chatting up and Vivian is not a war trophy!"

Etta Moore's hands pressed the linen napkin folded before her as she weighed her husband's implications. "I'm quite certain the lieutenant did nothing wrong."

"Then you can jolly well explain the matter for me."

"I'm not certain I can just now," she replied. "But they've been together a number of times of late, and my intuition tells me a bit of getting to know is taking place between them."

"Aye! And then?"

"Robert!" Etta gasped. "I think you're overreacting. Your daughter is a responsible young lady if ever there was one. You didn't raise a dimwit, Robert Moore!"

She rose and pushed her chair to the table with a solid bump of displeasure. The major never changed expression, holding his ground quite firmly as Etta turned to leave the room. Her angry stride slowed at the door, where she stood with her back to him. "Very well, I'll speak with Vivian when the time's right. But I think you're a bit nervy over nothing."

"Nervy, is it?" he responded, settling back in the chair. "I tend to agree with Colonel Burgess: they're over-paid, over-sexed, and over here!"

Matt and Vivie, in youthful enthusiasm, had long since departed and were not privy to the exchange between her parents. But Vivie still retained some reservations about the mood at dinner. "I must apologize for my father," she said as they drove along. "He wasn't very sociable this evening."

"I think he was just preoccupied. Maybe it was business. I saw him going over the books in the lobby, and I remember how my Dad was at audit time."

"Perhaps. But I know my Father, and he's usually a splendid host at dinner," she replied in thoughtful tones. "You handle French rather well. How did you learn?"

"Oh, that was high school at best. Your Mum really has it down. Roedean, right?"

Their progress was slow as Matt eased along, squinting into the meager light from the car's blackout-masked headlamps. Except for wardens milling about, Ipswich seemed deserted. It wasn't long, however, before pedestrian traffic exposed the entertainment haunts, and Vivie motioned toward the next corner. "Turn left there. The palais is just a few doors."

Matt found a suitable place to park and braked against the curb.

Several couples, variously entwined, moved to and from the obscure doorway of a quaint but darkened building. "What is this place?" he inquired as he helped Vivie from the car.

"It's called *The Bolt Hold*," she smiled back. Even in the dark she could sense the questioning expression on his face. "It means a safe place where one might hide a valuable. Quite appropriate, I'd say, for everyone goes there to dance, sip a bitter, and get away from the war for a time."

The building's double-door foyer prevented interior light from spilling into the street and was, together with the heavy curtains, an ever-present reminder of the German threat. The spacious room offered a wooden dance floor, bandstand, and a well-attended bar at the opposite end. It appeared that every British and American military service was represented, a large number of which were finishing a riotous musical version of follow-the-leader. At the last chord the participants applauded and cheered loudly, suggesting they could have endured another skip around the hall.

It was break time for the band, and the newcomers stood aside to get acclimated and allow the swirling humanity to find their places. "Would you care for something to drink?" Matt inquired.

"Perhaps a snifter of ale. It is a bit stuffy."

He seated her at one of the smaller tables and made his way to the bar. An unlit cigarette dangled from the lips of the thin-faced barkeeper whose jet-black hair had been slicked into submission. This classic Norman Rockwell character flipped a towel over his shoulder and leaned on the counter. "All right, Yank, what'll it be?"

"Two snifters of ale, whatever that is."

Without explanation the tender filled the glasses and sat them before the American. "Ten shillings," he mumbled with as little enthusiasm as his earlier greeting. Matt retrieved the drinks and squirmed through the waiting belly-uppers.

Vivie had company, and the American flyer winced as he

recognized Ruth Hardy's unmistakable profile bending over the table. The Women's Voluntary Service had given way to a silky blouse, which clung for dear life, and a pleated skirt cascading from her curvy hips. Comparatively, Vivie was no slouch, but she had not battle-dressed for major competition. Matt made certain he arrived with the table between the vamp and himself. "Well, hello again," he opened as nonchalantly as possible.

"This is wonderful!" Ruth replied. "I was so in hopes you two would make it!"

"Where's your date?" Matt said, hoping she had one and that he was nearby.

"He's taking care of David. The dotty bloke's one-over-the-eight again and a bit gammy for it. Do you mind if I sit this one out?" she added as the band came alive again.

Gentlemanly, Matt assisted with her chair and the three, muted by the din of music and voices, sat back to watch. "And now, ladies and gentlemen," the band leader began. "For your listening and dancing pleasure, a medley of favorites from the States. *Anything Goes, Little Brown Jug, Stardust,* and to quiet the beast, *Blue Moon.*"

The band was good. Within minutes, even the non-participants were rocking and tapping to the sound. Matt leaned over and asked Vivie if she would care to dance, for he had cut his teeth on these pieces and longed to get her on the floor. "Not just now," she replied, occupying herself with her drink. "Later, perhaps."

He was disappointed, beginning to feel the music, but stopped short of asking Ruth, who gave every indication of being available. When the first number had ended, the black-haired vamp was still without her date. She appeared unconcerned, for as Matt would soon learn, it was extremely convenient to her plan. She wanted contact with the American lieutenant, and if he wouldn't see to it, she would. She knew he would come to his feet when she stood, so she did just that. "Oh, Vivie dear, would you mind terribly if I borrowed the lieutenant for this one?"

Matt looked down at Vivie and shrugged. "I'd rather dance with you," he whispered.

"I don't mind, really," she replied, nodding at Ruth who was already swaying to the opening bars. "You're a big boy. I'm certain you can take care of yourself."

Vivie's eyes drifted to the dance floor, avoiding Matt. Uncertain of how she really felt, he was ready to rethink the matter when his hand was suddenly locked in Ruth's firm, warm grip. "Come on, Lieutenant. We'll miss it!"

Ruth had the experience. He could tell that right off. She took to the jitterbug as naturally as a duck to water: feet, body and arms in fluid rhythm. The band was not Glenn Miller's, but it did a commendable job with *Little Brown Jug*. They danced well together, the vamp and the American flyer, her skirt billowing out like an umbrella with each spin. Their exhibition was so good only three couples tried to keep up. The rest of the hall moved back in appreciation to clap their approval.

By the time the starring couple gained the confidence to side roll and lap straddle, they had the exclusive use of the floor. Beyond the fact that her date was making a spectacle of himself with another woman, Vivie could not help but appreciate Matt's ability. Even dancing, he mirrored the same calm, can-do confidence that had begun to attract her. The men her little helpers provided were, for the most part, shallow opportunists with whom she could share little. Matt was sensitive, caring, and quite surprising in a modest way.

Vivie had been denying her evolving feelings toward him in spite of her compulsive pause on the stairs in Falcon's Rest's lobby, a pause that was singularly responsible for their day in the park. He had invaded her thoughts frequently in the intervening days, and now she was trying hard not to acknowledge the subtle stirring of the "green-eyed monster." She lost that battle at the conclusion of the dance, when the couple's colorful finale left Ruth astraddle her partner's lap.

As the applause died, it took some tactful doing to disengage Ruth, for she milked every moment of the embrace. Adjusting his uniform and tie, Matt hurried Ruth back to the table where Vivie sat in mock approval. Her forlorn vibes were loud and clear when she addressed him by rank, an all-to-familiar sign of displeasure. "Well, Lieutenant, you two seem to have made quite a bomb of it."

Ruth was rubbing her hands together and wiggling with excitement. "He is marvelous, Vivie! You simply must try him!"

Matt pressed a handkerchief to his brow and moved to Vivie's side. "You cut a mean rug yourself," he sighed. "Very good!"

"Ohhh! I'll wager you're good at every little thing you do, Lieutenant!" she cooed suggestively.

Suddenly, out of the milling throng, two arms slipped around Ruth's waist and lifted her slightly off the floor. She squealed approval as the grinning face of a junior-grade naval officer nestled her cheek from behind. "Hello! Who've we here?"

"Mind your manners!" Ruth joked. "These are my friends. Phillip Browne, this is Lieutenant Matt Tower and Vivie Davis."

"Delighted," the navy type replied, extending his hand to Matt. "Sorry I was delayed, but we had to find a place for David."

"A place?" Vivie inquired.

"He was blooming drunk! Fagged-out. We put him in a storage room on top of a pile of mops. He'll be fine."

The tall sailor and the vamp claimed two chairs and joined the table. He was a pleasant-looking chap, easily met and very taken with Ruth, a fact that pleased Matt no end and earned him some time to mend fences on his side of the table. The Royal Navy offered drinks all around, but the band was warming up again, and Matt preferred to claim his turn with Vivie. "May I have this dance, Mrs. Davis?"

"Are you certain it won't be too much of a letdown?" she replied, her steady, unsmiling gaze testing him.

"Uh, uh! In my country, we save the best till last."

"Twit that I am to believe it, Matt Tower," she chuckled, rising from the chair. "Mr. Roosevelt would do well to reassign you to the diplomatic office."

The opening notes of *Stardust* greeted the couple as they reached the dance floor and eased smoothly into the waltz. For just a moment, Matt's thoughts flashed back to high school proms when guys relished the waltz numbers. A chance to hold a live girl close, low-cut gown and all. There were layers of crinoline and petticoats to deal with, though they did fashion each dreamy daughter into a Cinderella for the evening.

Vivie followed her partner's lead smoothly, but Matt sensed tension in her shoulders and hands, even a slight tremble. She was dancing at a very formal distance, unlike the couples around them. "I'm a bit out of practice," she apologized through a timid smile.

"So am I."

"I should doubt that after your smashing demonstration just now."

"Oh, that's easy. You can make a bundle of mistakes doing that and no one can tell." He led her into a series of graceful turns through which she stepped smartly. "Hey, you are good, Mrs. Davis!"

She was warming up, and as time went by, the distance between them narrowed. He had coaxed her in gently at the end of each turn until her cheek touched his shoulder. Though the band rolled into the next number without pausing, Vivie seemed willing to stay on the floor, which pleased him immensely. But this particular piece possessed a special meaning, a universal spirit most assuredly shared by the clientele of The Bolt Hold. Matt would learn that the war-weary English were often moved to join in prayerfully, almost as a hymn.

One by one, a few at the time, they began to sing softly until the hall filled with a mellow chorus of yearning Limeys and Yanks, and only the dancers moved. *"When the lights go on again... all over the world... and the boys are home again... all over the world... And rain or snow is all... that may fall... from the sky above... and a kiss won't mean goodbye... but hello to love."*

Vivie's lips were thoughtfully silent, so Matt whispered the words to her. And then, for the first time, he felt the growing pressure of her body. *"When the lights go on again... all over the world... and the ships will sail again... all over the world... Then we'll have time for things like... "* His voice trailed off when he saw the tear glistening on her cheek and he just held her, and they danced... and listened.

When the final notes died away a great hush fell over the hall. Not a clap was heard, for every hand had joined a neighbor's in silent partition that by their common will, fate might be directed to alter the course of events so devastating to the world.

Phillip the British sailor had freshened the drinks as conversations rekindled and the band tried to lighten the mood. Vivie sat beside Matt, hands folded in her lap, her melancholy eyes still damp. "I'd rather not dance again just now, if you don't mind." She fanned her face with a napkin. "Is it warm in here or is it just me?"

Ruth, old friend that she was, knew Vivie's danger signs and was quick to seize the moment. "I think we girls will repair our makeup, gentlemen." She moved quickly to Vivie's side and led her away. "We'll be back shortly. You gents chat a bit."

This once, Matt was glad to have Ruth around, for she could best fill the role of confidant just now. The sailor had no comprehension. He had his bitter, and perhaps the sexiest woman in the place, and a two-day pass. Matt wasn't that interested but talking was better than grinning over the mugs. "Where are you stationed, Phil?"

"Felixstowe," the midshipman replied. "Communications officer. Are you flying bombers or fighters?"

"353$^{rd}$ Fighter Group at Raydon."

"353$^{rd}$ is it. You know, I think we pulled one of your chaps out of the drink awhile back. We're a unit of Naval Rescue."

"Well, brother, my hat's off to you fellows," Matt toasted with his mug. "I've never crossed the North Sea that the idea of ditching didn't raise the hair on my neck. Hope I never need your services."

Meanwhile, Ruth steered her friend past the ladies' room and out a rear door. "Come on, love. We need some fresh air." The tile porch, overlooking a small courtyard, ran the length of the building. Several couples, in various degrees of intimacy, took advantage of the blackout, and the two women ended up in the garden for a little privacy.

Vivie sat on the short wall by the pool, dabbing at her eyes with a handkerchief as Ruth lit a cigarette from the silver box in her purse. "Are you all right, Viv?"

"I'm better now."

They sat for a while listening to the sounds of the night until Ruth felt her friend was more composed. "Just what happened in there to upset you so? Did Matt say or do something wrong?"

"Whatever made you ask that?"

"Well, you were rather distraught when you came off the dance floor."

"No," Vivie replied with a deep sigh. "He's always been a gentleman." She lowered her head. "I guess it was the song, Ruth."

Ruth reached over and hugged her friend, rocking her gently. "You know what I think?" she questioned. "I think you're feeling guilty. You're having a delightful evening with a wonderful man and you're upset because of it."

Ruth could feel the pressure of Vivie's hands increasing and she hoped it meant the problem was about to come out in the open. "I do feel guilty, Ruth. For the first time in I can't remember when, I haven't been able to control my feelings."

"About what?"

"About a man! That's what!" Vivie set her lips and jaw, determined to hold herself together in what was a painful and trying disclosure. "My boy's not coming home again, Ruth. I know John's not coming back." The tears welled and she struggled to hold them back. "I've waited and worried for so long. I feared for a time I wouldn't survive the hurt and I'm frightened now."

"And you're attracted to Matt Tower. But you're concerned about John's memory, concerned that it's a flyer again. And yet something deep inside tells you not to turn your back on this man. Did I leave anything out?" Ruth concluded breathlessly.

"Bloody little," Vivie responded, half crying and half laughing in a paradox of frustration and release. "Dear Ruth, what am I to do?"

Ruth crushed the cigarette in the ashtray. She was no longer the flitty flirt when she took her friend's hands in her own. "All right. You've asked this nosey parker and I'll tell you quite bluntly. Naturally there will be thoughts of John. Why not? He was part of your life. But there's nothing wrong with your feelings toward Matt. It's been a long time, Vivie!" She used her own handkerchief to dab at the teary eyes, then pressed Vivie's hand against her cheek in a gesture of sympathy. "He's a handsome bloke, and he really seems to care for you. I'd be after him in a minute!"

"I'd say you jolly well have been!"

"Dear, dear Vivie," Ruth replied, shaking her head assuringly. "That's before I knew you cared. He doesn't give a flip for me. But he looks at you like the last doughnut in the box."

"Oh, Ruth, and what if...."

"What if! What if!" the dark-haired vamp exclaimed. "What if my Tommy hadn't chosen submarine service? What if this ruddy war had never started? Give it a chance. In time, you'll know. But stop torturing yourself like this. You've done nothing wrong!"

The sisterly talk had done much to ease Vivie's anxiety. She was beginning to feel that she could just be herself, not presuming quite so much, giving her feelings permission to develop as they would. She knew it would not be easy. There would be nostalgic moments to overcome, but Ruth was right. She didn't want to turn her back on the American lieutenant. Vivie reached over and rested her hand on her friend's arm. "Ruth... thank you!" she whispered, a tiny smile stretching her lips.

"Well now, we had better be getting back to the men," Ruth replied as she returned the smile. "We'll talk again."

The return of the ladies interrupted a deep war-strategy session between the Royal Navy and the United States Army Air Force. But it seemed to be a welcome intrusion as the officers rose to greet them. "We were that close to sending a search party," Matt chuckled as he measured a half-inch between his fingers.

"Aye. We figured you were on the arms of two French sailors by now," Phillip added.

"Well, they were all taken, so we had no choice but to return to you two!" Ruth responded in like candor. "I have a suggestion, though. Let's stop by the chippy."

Vivie took her place beside Matt and asked his preference. "You're on leave, Matt. I want you to have a grand evening."

He took her hands and gazed into the lovely blue eyes. "You're my evening," he whispered softly. "Whatever you'd like to do is fine with me."

She kissed him with her eyes. One thing was certain now, she determined to give it a chance. "Then we best get cracking before curfew," she suggested cheerfully.

A damp chill had invaded the night, and Vivie shivered as the four reached the sidewalk. Matt adjusted her sweater and wrapped an arm around her against the weather as they made their way to the Fish & Chips at the end of the block. That very area seemed straight out of a chapter of Charles Dickens with its crude building lines and quaint, old lamp posts.

The shop windows were dark now, and only young couples comprised the late-hour pedestrian traffic. By the time they reached the chippy, the women were rubbing their hands in anticipation of the warmth behind the door. Beads of condensation blurred the windows of the little shop, and as they entered, Matt got a whiff of the classic English dish in preparation. Waiting their turn, the four laughed and joked among themselves.

The short, portly proprietor, with an accent thicker than molasses, was quick about his work and greeted them with a toothless grin.

"I can't understand a word he's saying," the American flyer confessed. "Look, I'll buy if somebody will order."

"I'll take you up on that, mate," the sailor responded. "He's an old Scot. If you were a native, you'd get it, all right."

"Scot, huh. Those guys who wear the funny skirts?"

"Store it, mate!" the sailor whispered in good-natured caution, placing a finger to his lips. "They get rather barmy about that, especially coming from a Yank. It's called a *kilt*."

The fish came hot, clothed in crisp batter and wrapped with chips of fried potato in a fold of newspaper. Vivie and Ruth had appropriated a table while the men collected the tasty meal. "Now, sprinkle a bit of this over the fish," Vivie directed, pushing a thin bottle toward Matt.

"Well?" Ruth inquired as he took his first bite.

The expression on his face reflected sheer delight. He was learning the language and the ways a bit at the time and loving it. As the four talked on into the evening, Matt leaned against the back of the narrow bench, content to let the others carry the conversation. Just as well, since his fascination with the women at his side blotted out much of what was said. *"How lovely you are, dear lady,"* he thought to himself.

She had grown much less inhibited, less conscious of being near him in the merriment of the hour. It pained him that his time with her was quickly slipping away. But then somebody had to fight the war. A rap on the window by their table startled him. He turned to see a stern-faced warden pressing his pocket watch against the glass. The proprietor knew the signal well and waved a hand at the persistent official. Matt could distinguish the word *curfew* in the rush of Gaelic jabber directed at his table, and the two couples knew the party was over for the evening.

"Great fun, Yank," the midshipman grinned as they prepared separate ways. "Perhaps we'll see each other again."

"Socially, I hope," Matt replied, referring to the Britisher's rescue squadron.

Vivie was silent as Matt held the door for her and then slid behind the wheel of the blue Morris 14. They were well on their way back to Falcon's Rest before either spoke. "Must you return in the morning?" she asked.

"No choice, I'm afraid. I have to be on base by 1200 hours."

"This new command, it is more dangerous, isn't it?"

"No, not really," he lied, pleased by her concern. "More responsibility... and accountability, I would say." How could he tell her there was no safe position up there?

For a while there was only the sound of the car as they drove through the darkened streets. Vivie had been an RAF wife, and she knew full well who led the attacks. But she suffered the all-too-familiar churn in her stomach in silence, since men of that caliber would not negate such challenges to duty. She was determined, then, that the day must end on a high note. "I hope you enjoyed your evening, Matt," she said, slipping her arm through his.

It was the first intimate initiative on her part and he would build cautiously on that. "It was super, thanks to my faithful tour guide," he replied, squeezing her arm briefly with his own. "Do you have any appointments open in a week or so if I can get back over?"

"I don't know, just off," she replied playfully. "I must consult my tour calendar. I'm certain something could be arranged."

The more she was with Matt, the more she wanted to know about him, and she began to probe gently. "Would you mind if I asked a personal question?"

"If you can stand the answer, I guess I can stand the question," he chuckled.

"It's really none of my affair, but I am curious. Is there someone back home?"

Such an inquiry was the furthest thing from his mind. The fleeting but unwelcome image of Ginger appeared, which irritated him. "A fair question. That would make a difference?"

"Yes," she replied softly, aware that the matter was delicate. "It's quite stressful when someone you care about is away."

It was a salient question from the feminine perspective and he had to answer. "Well now, you said girl, not girls!" he chuckled.

"You men can be just as vain as you claim we women are," she responded dryly. He wasn't off the hook. "Is she pretty?"

"Yes," he replied, hoping honest brevity might change the subject. But it didn't.

"Did you tell her to wait for you?" Vivie pressed.

"We broke up a good while before I shipped over. It wasn't pleasant. More like a school thing, I guess." He waited for the verdict. The silence moved him to a last reassuring plea. "Look, I'm not burning any candles over it. That was a long time ago!"

Vivie stared silently ahead, the delicate silhouette of her face barely visible against the side window. Then slowly, deliberately, her hand slid down his sleeve seeking his palm and their fingers interlocked. The verdict was in.

Chilly air greeted them as they left the car. "Ohhh, I'd love a cup about now!" she giggled. "Would you care for one? We'd have the kitchen to ourselves at this hour."

"You bet I would!"

Inside, the great fireplace held only glowing embers now. It was quiet, deserted, except for one old geezer, softly snoring in a wing-back chair.

They smiled at the sight as Vivie led him across the room. "Oh, we jolly well have our characters, all right. You should have seen the lobby early in the war. My dad took in dozens of the homeless. They slept on the floor for the most part. It was winter and they had nowhere to go."

The ancient grandfather clock announced midnight as the couple entered the darkened kitchen. She stopped his hand as he reached to turn the light on. "We leave them off at night when we can. There's a lantern on the hunt board there. Would you light it for me?"

Matt fumbled for the matches as she set the kettle and eased her way cautiously toward the cupboard. The little wick finally flickered to life, its dim glow just enough for the chore at hand. He leaned against the counter as she returned with the crockery. She was quite near him now, the soft light catching the highlights of her hair and face. His silver shoulder bars and pilot wings winked in the glow from the lamp as he looked down at her. His lips were unsmiling but gentle, the strong chin set intently as his eyes found hers. She could not turn away when he leaned slowly toward her until their lips touched.

It was a tender kiss, lingering, though neither used their arms. Vivie moaned ever so slightly, for her body remembered what her mind had hidden away. His lips were tender, kissing quite adequately, but not demanding. Had her hand not nudged one of the cups, tipping it out of its saucer, it would have lasted longer. She retreated slowly, as though she was surprised to have actually gone through with it.

They stood there facing each other, her eyes never leaving his. Vivie could not think as her senses were too occupied relishing the moment. She watched his lips whisper her name as they drew near again, and suddenly there was the pressure of his hands on her waist. This time she kissed him back, her hands sliding up the arms that now encircled her until they caressed his broad shoulders. The bulk of him in her arms was overwhelming, for she had not been handled thusly for longer than she cared to remember. Hesitantly, her lips withdrew and she placed her cheek on his chest. "Oh, dear," she whispered.

"What's wrong?" he questioned.

"It's... it's just that I didn't expect this to happen, Matt."

"What?"

"You and me... this way."

"Oh, dear lady, I prayed that it would!"

"And I tried just as hard not to let it," she replied, brushing the hair back from her cheek as their eyes met again. Eyes so moist, so vulnerable just now that he felt a twinge of guilt for having pursued so relentlessly.

His embrace was becoming too comfortable. Slowly, she slipped out of his arms and turned again to the kitchen counter. "I think it best that I put you to work for the moment. Will you place the cups for me?"

Matt balanced the saucers to the table, unbuttoned his jacket and pulled up a chair. He watched as she busied herself about the whistling kettle, so intently that she became aware of it. "One might think you've never seen coffee made before, Matt Tower."

"I've never seen you make it before."

"Oh, then I hope I did it well," she replied, filling his cup with the steaming brew.

He added some sugar, stirred, then sipped the hot liquid cautiously. "You make a fine coffee, Mrs. Davis!"

She beamed as she settled by him with her own cup, for she did want to please him. He leaned back in the chair, letting the crockery warm his hands. "What's your week like when I'm not around? You always seem so busy."

"Not as exciting as yours, no doubt," she replied, tapping her lower lip thoughtfully. "Let me see now, I'm with Women's Voluntary three days, the hospital one day, and I try to spare Mum and Dad a day at the lobby desk. Then there's church on Sunday. You cannot imagine what Vicar Hurden has meant to our family, Matt." She paused in reflection for a moment. "And then a day for Vivie. Of course, I'm never certain when that day will be."

"I think about you. Even at 20,000 feet over Europe," he chuckled. "And I'm thinking, is she trying not to think about me?"

She couldn't hide the quiver in her voice. "You can't know what the last few years have been like, Matt, and it seems that I'm doing it all over again."

He reached over and took her hand. There was no resistance, but her eyes searched his entreatingly, trusting for an answer that would still her fears. "Look, John Davis must have been some kind of a man if you married him. Everyone's made that very clear: your mother, Mrs. Pearson, even Ruth Hardy. It was a wonderful, cherished time in your life and you'll always have those memories. But I don't think he would expect you... would want you to go through life with never a second chance."

Her grip tightened on his hand as she looked away, a thin, teary smile on her lips. "And what if I lose you?"

"And what if I lose you, Vivie? This war has everybody paranoid. Sure, there's risk. The special services van could turn over on the way back to the base. You could be serving those gunners in the anti-aircraft batteries at the wrong time. I worry about you, too!"

He paused to sip from the cup and collect himself as Vivie touched a napkin to the corner of her eye. "Do you remember the air raid last time I was here?" he said. "In the middle of the night, this RAF officer and I are leaning on the porch railing watching the flashes against the sky. I knew you were out there somewhere, but there was no way to check. It was the next morning before I got your note and knew you were okay."

Vivie turned back to meet his gaze, her head shaking slowly. "Matt, that's been going on for five years. If we had let the Luftwaffe have its way, all England would have been immobile!" She took another sip from her cup and placed her hand on his. "They bombed the lower wharfs that night. Eagle Wharf had the worst of it. The first plane laid a path of incendiaries for the others to follow. Some of them fell along Acton Road, setting homes ablaze. We worked well into the morning hours arranging shelter for the families."

"Okay," Matt said, rolling his hands over to more readily encircle hers. "So we're victims of the times. If all England can handle it, surely you and I can! There'll be some pretty anxious moments for both of us, Vivie. But I'll be a dang sight better off knowing that... that... you and I...."

The resonant chime of the old grandfather clock drifted into the kitchen announcing 2 a.m. "Oh dear," Vivie sighed dejectedly. "It's later than I thought. I've an early call this morning. Would you mind dreadfully?"

Yes, he minded. Dreadfully! It had taken forever to get this far with Vivie. But he had responsibilities also, and it would be a full day for him as well. He helped her rinse the cups. "I don't know when I can get back over. Things have tightened up on base in the last couple of weeks."

"Do you think it's the invasion?" she inquired, her hands working nervously with the towel.

The question surprised him. "Where did you get that idea?"

"It's hardly a secret. Even Lord Haw Haw jests about it. Colonel Burgess thinks it's quite imminent."

"That's amazing. The civilian quarter seems to know more about this plagued war than the people fighting it!"

"Oh, I doubt that!" she retorted. "But we do so want the war to end, and it won't until the Germans are defeated." She sought to change the mood with a bright smile and took his hand. "Come on, my little poppet. See me to the stair."

There was still the uncertainty of his next visit. "I'll call you when I know my assignments, okay?"

She turned to him as they reached the back steps to the living quarters. "You will be careful?"

"Yes," he whispered, taking her hands in his. "I have something to be careful for."

"Perhaps I can come to Great Wenham," she offered. "It's nearer the base and we haven't imposed on the Walldons in some time. I can get a message to you."

"That's music to my ears, lady, because I'm going to miss you something terrible!" His arms went around her waist as she brought her hands to his face, caressing it tenderly.

He started to speak again, but her finger rested on his lips. "As soon as I can, I'll come. Just fly carefully for me, please." He nodded in agreement and their lips met again for the last time. "Soon," she whispered, blowing him another kiss.

She mounted the steps, humming softly the music they had danced to earlier. The light was on in the library, and though she was ready for her bed, curiosity required she look in. Etta Moore sat in her long robe nodding over a book, "Mum?" Vivie inquired, surprised that she was still up.

Etta looked up slowly and smiled at her daughter. "My, aren't we the chipper one at this late hour. How was your evening, dear?"

"Quite nice. We danced and had chips after. Of all people, Ruth was there. She's dating one of His Majesty's naval officers."

"And your American lieutenant?"

Vivie sat down across from her mother, her eyes staring off in space, "He's quite unlike the others, Mum."

"I surmised as much," Etta replied, lowering her book so that she might read her daughter the better. "Your father was a bit concerned last afternoon."

"Concerned?" Vivie asked, her attention no longer divided with daydreams. "Whatever about?"

"Oh, it seems he caught a glimpse of you two in the garden. It appeared you were upset about something, and then you ran to the inn."

Vivie sighed deeply, shaking her head in annoyance. "So that's what dinner was all about!" She wasn't angry with him, for he had been all a father could be. She was his only daughter, the only baby he had ever known. It was his strong arms that held her for an eternity on the hospital bed as they cried away the double tragedy that had so devastated her life.

Vivie leaned back in the chair, a pleasant, tongue-in-cheek smile creeping across her face. "You may tell Major Moore that his daughter's honor is very much intact and that her escort was quite the gentleman!"

Etta's head rolled back against the chair, her elegant blue eyes sparkling in concurrence as she struggled to keep her laughter as subdued as possible. "Smashing, my darling daughter. Absolutely smashing!"

They snickered together for a time and then it grew quiet again. Vivie leaned forward and reached for her mother's hands. "He's so strong, Mum, inside. And not at all pushy. I do like him very much."

Etta smiled at Vivie and reached up to tuck in an unruly lock of her daughter's hair. "I've been quite impressed with him," she confessed, "though he's not British. Just promise me that you'll take it slowly. There's much you need to know about him and his family."

"I know," Vivie concurred as she left the chair and stretched her weary limbs. "By the by, do we have the Walldons' number?"

"The Walldons?" Etta repeated, her brow wrinkling in question. "It should be in the directory in your father's office. Are you planning to ring them up?"

"I thought I might. It's been a while since I've been in the country."

"Especially the country around the American air base," Etta replied as she hid her smile behind the book.

Vivie extended her hands and palms up. "Soooo?"

"Soooo!" Etta teased back, peering over the book.

The grin was irrepressible, even though the spoof had gotten under her skin, and Vivie slipped out the door to conceal it. "Good night, Mum!" she sighed, feigning irritation.

"Good night, daughter," came the merry reply. "Pleasant dreams."

# CHAPTER 11

# Preparing for the Big One

**R**ETURNING TO BASE after a 48-hour pass was always a cultural shock. Only a late lunch had separated Matt's return from a major briefing of the 350<sup>th</sup> Squadron's flight and section leaders. Newhart, Captain Herrington, first lieutenants Smaragdis, Maxwell, Lee, and Tower encircled the conference table. Newhart, the systematic planner and by now a major, allowed a proper interval for coffee cups and ash trays to be settled then swore the men to secrecy.

"We're close to an invasion, gentlemen. Pine Tree won't be specific, but you'll find our strafing and patrol runs taking on a new pattern in the coming days. They want us to do a real job on these target areas, attract all the attention we can get."

The senior officer pulled down a new wall map, which showed several shaded areas along the French coast. "Except for bomber escort, the 353<sup>rd</sup> Group will be concentrating here in the Pas-de-Calais area. Other groups will take on areas inland. You'll be after any-thing that moves, with special attention to rail targets and bridges. The object is to keep Jerry guessing about the probable landing site and to damage his transportation on as broad a range as possible."

Newhart distributed folders to all in attendance and resumed his place at the table. "I want you to study the map and aerial photos in these packets. Learn it so you can recognize any point from any direction. Get the natural landmarks down pat." He took a sip from the steaming mug and settled back in his chair. "Now, some of you will have new men in your units who've never seen combat. You'll have to bring them along fast, especially in low-level work. I don't want anybody getting lost or homing in on a flak tower."

When the floor was opened, questions came in torrents, drag-ging the briefing through another half hour. Matt took full advan-tage of the experience around him, for not only did he have a new command, one of the replacements would be in his section.

Herrington made a point of walking out with Matt as the briefing concluded. The captain's hands were pushed deeply into his flight-suit pockets, a familiar gesture when there were weighty matters on his mind. The new first lieutenant was reading all kinds of omens into the situation and quickly broke the silence. "Something on your mind, sir?"

"There's some bad news," the captain admitted. "And a bit of good news, but I wanted you to get it from me." He freed a hand to hold his pipe before continuing. "Old *Sweet Pea's* had it, Matt. Andy Johnson pranged it good the day you went on leave."

Matt's face sobered quickly, his mind not ready to accept Herrington's disclosure. "You've got to be kidding, Captain." But the flight leader's silence was a chilling confirmation.

"Well, how bad is it? Can it fly again?"

"Not in this life, it won't. We were on withdrawal support near the Dutch border when two squadrons of 190s found us. Andy was flying tail-end and they shot him up pretty bad. He barely made it to base, but the gear wouldn't drop and he smeared it all over the runway."

"Was he okay?"

"Cracked his head pretty good. Looked like an Indian with red war paint when they got to him." Herrington chuckled as he relit his pipe. "He told the medics he was dang glad it was his head or he might have been seriously hurt." The captain motioned for Matt to climb into his jeep. "Come on, we'll go have a look."

The images Matt conceived as they rode to the hangar did not prepare him for what he found. *Sweet Pea* lay on its belly, listing to port, the smooth skin buckling at points. Bullet-hole patterns curved randomly across wings and fuselage. The guns had been removed, and cannibalizing of parts was well underway. He circled the broken hulk silently, then stepped on the wing for a look at the cockpit. He reached instinctively for the disengaged stick, which gyrated effortlessly in his hand.

After a time he stepped back, slapping his thighs in despair over the humiliation of his gallant old war bird. "You said something about good news, Captain. I could sure stand a little."

"Well, take a look at this and see if it lifts your spirits," Herrington replied, leading Matt inside the hangar. A half-dozen silver-skin, bubble-canopy Thunderbolts angled along the wall where the two officers paused. "D-25s, Tower. A little hotter and 360-degree vision."

Matt walked over to the fighter nearest the hangar door, hands at his hips, as his hazel eyes feasted on the sleek aircraft. A ground crewman put the finishing touches to the black and yellow cowling insignia and grinned down at the approaching flyer. "Is this one yours, sir?"

"What about it, Captain?" Matt inquired without looking back.

"Pilot's no dang good without a plane. Put his name on it!"

The smooth, bright skin of the fighter was cool to Matt's touch. She would be something to fly, and like any combat pilot, he wanted her. But as his appreciation of the new Thunderbolt reached its zenith, the vision of *Sweet Pea* crumpled among the relics, its drab coat blistered with wounds, wrenched a mournful sigh. He shook his head to clear his thoughts and mounted the wing for a look in the cockpit of his new surprise.

"Take her down to the firing butts and get your guns set like you want them," Herrington called up from the floor. "Give her a checkout spin, then meet me in the ready room at 1500."

Matt saluted from the pilot's seat and settled back to go over the gauges and controls. His eager eyes roamed the interior, still fragrant with new leather, rubber, and electronics, until they rested on the rear-view mirror. *"What's this?"* he mumbled, squinting into the tiny oval glass. *"That's a joke! Whoever stuck that up there never had a Messerschmitt on his tail!"* He stood up and called to the crewman. "Roll this baby out for me, will you? And let me have a screwdriver."

It took some doing to loosen the bolts, but Matt persevered and slipped the mirror out of its mount. He double-timed through the hangar's side door to *Sweet Pea's* resting place and repeated the work. The old mirror was nearly twice the size, wide enough to do some good and goose-necked for easier viewing. "Okay, old pal," he chuckled, giving the retired fighter a love pat. "A piece of you is still gonna fight this war."

An hour and a half later and 10,000 feet over the English coast, Matt didn't want to come down.

But down he came to the less-glamorous routine of paperwork and administration that accompanies promotion. Herrington was waiting in the company of Red Section's replacement, a typical neighborhood kid with hat in hand and black curly hair. Slightly protruding ears made him appear an unlikely candidate for combat flying. But he knew better than to judge too soon, for the base was loaded with pilots who looked like Boy Scouts.

"Barry Stockton, this is your element leader, Lieutenant Tower." The men shook hands, and after Herrington covered some matters with Matt, he excused himself.

"Have you met any of the pilots?" Matt inquired of the recruit.

"Yes, sir. Lieutenant Baker. I flew with him yesterday. We strafed some barges. They seemed to be holding me back a little. Guess I'm not a member of the clan yet."

"No, they're trying to save your backside. You've a lot to learn that they can't teach in flight school. I know the feeling. But you can bet it'll wear off. Where are you from, Barry?"

"West Virginia, sir."

"You fly before the war?"

"No sir."

"How'd you build up all these hours?" Matt asked as he looked over the young pilot's folder.

"Well, sir, whatever needed to be done, I'd volunteer. We got delayed in the States and they let us fly every day. The 357th Group at Leiston was our original destination, but by the time we shipped out, the openings were here."

"Glad to have you on board, West Virginia." Matt gave the new flyer's shoulder a welcoming squeeze. "I'm going to give you a couple of hours more this afternoon. We all need settling in after all these changes. Get suited up and we'll meet Shilling and Baker on dispersal at 1700." Matt chuckled to himself as he left the building, for he was sounding more like Herrington every minute and feeling the first pressure of his new responsibilities.

What combat experience the new flyer lacked, he made up in general skill. After some formation flying and gunnery practice over the range, Matt's confidence in Stockton increased. There was plenty to work with in Baker's wingman, and he felt that Red Section would be ready for what was required when the time came.

And in the following days, six of those times came. Again and again, sleepy pilots were roused from their bunks to face the chilly English mornings, most often in the dark. Roger Baker bagged a Messerschmitt, his second confirmed kill, though he had already sent several home smoking. He was a charging warrior in the heat of battle, making Barry Stockton's steady hand a godsend in keeping the Luftwaffe off his leader's stern. Red Section had grown into a capable fighting unit.

But there were other things on his mind, for as they returned from the missions, Vivie's smiling face was a frequent reflection in the canopy glass. It was a great comfort to know that he was now in her thoughts as she had been in his. As the weekend approached, he would check faithfully each day for the message she had promised. He looked forward to showing her off at the officers club and to surprising her with the artwork on his new Thunderbolt.

He had commissioned the squadron artist to paint *Paladin* in bold arched letters with a horizontal gold Roman broadsword in a knight's gloved hand beneath the arched name. All neatly outlined in black. The fighter was a handsome sight standing at dispersal with the likes of Dewey Newhart's *Mud N Mules*, Ken Gallup's *Fern Marie*, Bill Tanner's *Prudence V*, Colonel Duncan's *Dove of Peace,* and a battery of others that faithfully carried their pilots into the wild blue yonder.

True to her promise, Vivie had arranged with Katherine Walldon to spend a few days at their lodge. The couple once operated two enchanting Tudor inns. But as retirement neared, the one to the south, on Colchester Road, was sold. Vivie knew little of it, for the pleasant memories of a young girl on holiday had always centered around visits to her adopted aunt and uncle at Manor Lodge in rural Wenham.

Emergencies from repeated bombing of the Ipswich docks had delayed her arrival until Sunday afternoon. She had hardly unpacked her valise when the distant rumble of aircraft engines sent her scurrying to the window. Haze above the cultivated fields restricted her view from the second-story room, and she was unable to see the source of the noise. "They'll circle over, dear," Kathrine assured her as she helped put away the younger woman's clothing.

The rumble grew louder as Vivie craned her neck to get a glimpse of the fighters forming up. Speculating if Matt might be in one of them, she watched intently, fist pressed against her chin, while the windows rattled their customary greeting to the passing squadron. When the fighters had droned out of sight, she stepped back reluctantly from the opening to face the sympathetic smile of her mother's close friend.

Katherine Walldon was a slender woman, her graying hair always in a royal roll around her head. Many was the time Vivie had looked up into that oval face, with its twinkling eyes and warm smile, as she was tucked in for the night. Uncle Cecil would stand by in open vest and rolled sleeves, an old pipe smoking away, and nod approval. As long as Vivie could remember, his head had been bald except for the fluffy white around the sides.

"Well, now, you must tell me about your American flyer," Katherine implored. "What's he like?"

Vivie plopped on the bed and leaned back on her hands to kick her shoes off, face brightening at the thought of the new man in her life. "Oh, he's quite nice, Aunt Kate! Very much the gentleman."

"And?"

"And..." Vivie repeated, gathering her thoughts. "Well, he has hazel eyes, light brown hair, and he's about as tall as Dad."

"I take it, then, that you like him."

"Yes, very much. I'm to leave a message at the base for him. I do so want you and Uncle Cecil to meet him."

"Nothing would give us more pleasure, dear. What does Etta think about him?"

"I think Mum likes him. She met him briefly on the train with no idea she'd ever see him again. Dad is another matter. He's a bit skeptical as yet. Rather concerned for my honor, the poor dear. I do so want him to like Matt."

"All in good time, dear, I'm sure. I'll cycle over to the base with you if you like. There's an old cart road that leads to one of the entrance gates. But first we'll freshen you up and have a bite to eat."

Vivie pecked at her food out of respect for her host, but her heart wasn't in it. It was at the base. "Where is Uncle Cecil, anyway?"

"He's at St John's. Some of the vestrymen promised the Vicar they would search out a pesky leak in the roof. And you know Cecil, ever eager to put his hands to work for the Lord."

How such a loveable couple could have birthed a prankster like David Walldon puzzled Vivie. While he had matured a bit in the war years, there was still room for improvement. Vivie let him know that in no uncertain terms a few days earlier when he accused her of avoiding him for a *"bloody Yank."*

The haze had grown no worse as the women took to the road with their bicycles. It was a pleasant companionship peddling along the lanes, squealing with laughter when the bikes coasted through an occasional shallow ford. They waved to Katherine's friends at Lodge Farm and took the turn that would bring them to the base.

"Good heavens!" Vivie exclaimed. "What have they done to Raydon Wood forest.... And Notley Farm? It's not there anymore!"

"The price of freedom, I'm afraid," Katherine answered with a sigh as they dismounted.

The older woman noticed the difference at once. The airfield was ringed with sentinels posted at regular intervals. Two MPs, though smiling pleasantly, showed no indication of allowing the bikers to proceed another foot. "Can I help you ladies?" one of them asked.

Vivie had not yet grasped the situation and stood by her bike returning the smiles. "I was to meet one of your pilots. Lieutenant Tower. I'd like to get a message to him. Can you assist me, Sergeant?"

"I'm sorry, ma'am, but the base is restricted. No one can come in or out without proper authority."

"But I only wanted to get a message to him," Vivie insisted, concern growing in her voice. "Can't I leave a message?"

"No, ma'am. No communication goes in or out without authorization." Having no other ploy of her own, the younger woman looked to the older for some magical recourse. But Katherine was preoccupied. She could not remember so many aircraft gathered around the field in the past, nor such hurried movement of personnel. "I think it best, dear, that we wait."

The ride back to Manor Lodge held none of the joviality the women experienced earlier. It was not enough that Vivie had been late arriving for the weekend, but the inability to let Matt know she had made it left her extremely dejected.

"Now don't be so concerned," Katherine reassured as they put the bikes away. "Your lieutenant must be quite aware of the circumstances."

Vivie would not be consoled easily. A more intimate relationship with Matt had heightened her anticipation. "Isn't there someone we might call, Aunt Kate?"

Katherine placed a call or two but only learned the base was placed on restriction that Friday, the day before their bike trip. "There's nothing more we can do just now," Katherine sighed. "Perhaps Cecil will have some news when he returns. Why don't we make tea while we wait?"

Vivie's hands performed from habit, but the British ritual could not suppress the bits and pieces heard in recent weeks. Either the invasion was in progress or shortly to come. Matt would be in the thick of it, and it distressed her greatly that he would not know she was there for him.

The mood on base was no less tense, for the squadron had been alerted at 0300 that morning and hurried to special briefings. Then came the long wait until dawn, only to have the mission aborted due to weather. Invasion postponed. In spite of the delay, Slybird would carry out its diversion role, and by 0826 hours, 36 fighters lifted off under the command of Major Kenneth Gallup. War is no keeper of the Sabbath, and the rattle of machine-gun fire and rocket explosions would compete with the church bells of Calais once more.

During the delay, Matt caught up on his letter writing. Many of the guys passed the buck to the chaplain, but this young flyer found great pleasure in communicating with his family, especially in sharing war experiences with his veteran father.

*"Dear Mom & Dad, By the time you get this something really big will have happened in the war. We have been on alert for three days now and the anticipation is awesome! Your son has had a big month. I bagged my first enemy fighter, a Messerschmitt 109. I've made first lieutenant and am in charge of a fighter element. We've become a pretty good team in our six missions together. The two guys I came over with, Chuck Shilling and Roger Baker, are still in my unit. Chuck flies wing for me. We got some of the new P-47s and they assigned me one. I bought a camera—German of all things— from a guy finishing his tour. Maybe I can get some photos back home so Mom can see that I'm holding my weight okay. England is just as charming and quaint as you said it was, Dad, but I'm nowhere near your old quarters."*

Matt was not ready yet to spring Vivie on his parents, which would have put his mother in a tizzy. And certainly not his wound. So the letter rambled on about what he had seen in his travels. *"Tell Pearl hello for me and that I want a six-inch stack of her pancakes the day I get back. I'm writing Sis and Grammar, so won't include anything for them just now. Can't get over becoming an uncle! I miss you all and thanks for the letters. Love, Matt. PS: Mom, we have excellent officers and they take very good care of us. Not to worry!"*

He liked to write before going to sleep. It relaxed and cheered him to think about those in whose hearts and prayers he was kept. Stretched out on the lumpy English mattress, he stared at the ceiling curving above him where faint flickers of light from the stove danced about. As his mind wandered, the flickers became tiny flashes of countless bombs and cannons, and the orange puffs became enemy wing guns. His soul told him the invasion most certainly would come in the morning. A paranoid paper hanger in Berlin would cause the death of thousands of men in that one day as the Allies struggled for a beachhead.

Matt began praying there in the dark. For the group. For the men under his command. For those he would never know who would splash from the landing craft onto the beaches below his wings. Air cover was an awesome responsibility, and as he prayed, he thought on the words of Jesus when He had faced His ultimate test. *"Oh my Father, if it be possible, let this cup pass from me."* [Matthew 26:39 KJV] As a youngster, it had puzzled Matt why the Father had not spared the Son until the day Grammar Mattlowe lifted him onto her knees and from the books of Isaiah and John explained it. In the comfort of her words, he finally slipped from his season of prayer into the peace of dreamless sleep.

The scenery had not changed when the barracks was awakened at 0300. Matt heard the familiar grumbling of fellow pilots before the sergeant shook his bunk. "Briefing at 0400, gentlemen! Colonel Duncan himself. Shake it now, shake it!"

On this morning the men, prodded by nervous energy, had dressed in record time. The briefing room was crammed, with every squadron responding in full strength. The brass was there in strength: Duncan, Bailey, Rimerman, Blickenstaff, Gallup, Christian, and a half-dozen others who would be logged in history as outstanding mission leaders of the 353rd Fighter Group. A hush fell over the room as Duncan stepped to the platform. "This mission won't be aborted, gentlemen. The weather's fine where we're going."

Whispers among the flyers brought the tall Texas colonel's hand up. "I'm sure you know this is the big one. We'll fly as long as there's light. Most of you will get two or three sorties out of this. When you've exhausted your ammunition, high-tail it back to base so your crew can ready the aircraft for another flight."

Standing before the map, Duncan positioned his pointer. "Our sector is this area between Bernay and Compiegne just west of Paris. Dive bombing and strafing of transportation and communication targets is our job. Bomber groups will concentrate on coastal fortifications to complement the naval bombardment. Your squadron and flight leaders will provide details for each run we make." The senior officer rested his hands on his hips and surveyed the audience of eager faces, reverently hushed in awe of the task before them. "I don't need to remind you that it's not just our hides this time around, gentlemen. The men on the beaches, the paratroopers, and those in the gliders will be looking to the Air Force to tie Jerry down."

Subsequent briefings filtered down to the element level where Matt, following Herrington's example, closed the time with Chuck in a moment of silence. Twenty minutes later the squeaking personnel carriers delivered the pilots to their planes, the wings and sides of which sported bold stripes of black and white for Allied identification in the coming confusion. Milt-the-Stilt, making the ground check with his pilot, was as caught up in the adventure as those who would be taking off soon. "Hot dang, sir, we gonna git on with it now, ain't we!"

Matt patted his crew chief on the back as they squatted beneath the Thunderbolt. "Will all this stuff work?" he asked, pointing to the bombs, rocket launchers, and belly tank burdening the aircraft.

"If you can git it off'n the ground, it will," Milt replied through a face-consuming grin.

Red Section was in place along the runway where Matt sat, as he had countless times before, shivering in *Paladin's* cockpit as much from anticipation as chill of the night; he could not be sure. A persistent haze over the field would allow just enough visibility for takeoff when the signal flair soared from the tower. Matt pressed his engine to join the whining and coughing of P-47 powerhouses coming to life across the field.

He didn't like the waiting. Once in the cockpit, with checkout completed, Matt was ready to roll. "Milt," he called down to his crew chief. "Come up for a minute." As Milt stood dutifully by the cockpit, Matt slid to the hard stand and trotted behind the service barrels. "Hurry up, Lieutenant, they's piling up on the tower roof."

Launching three heavily-armed squadrons before dawn, in 1,000-foot overcast sky, demanded infinite patience. Vivie helped tremendously in that area. He had but to think of her, the smile, the touch, the smell, and he was calmed. If only he could have spent even a little time with her before the base was restricted, to hold her, to reassure her, for by now she must surely have guessed what was happening. But alas, reality returned abruptly when the second signal flare rocketed into the sky and engines revved down the line.

It was a fearful machine under his hands, loaded with destructive power, and he was never more ready to use it. For Vivie, for England, and for his country. *Paladin's* turn came and the four great blades dug into the air. Matt labored against the engine's awful torque and trusted the instruments to lead him through thick dark mist to clearer skies. If they were lucky, the clouds over Europe would be broken so they could search for the enemy.

Timed to the break-of-day in France, this proud group of Slybirds found the ceiling higher than in England, and Colonel Duncan turned the squadrons loose to sweep their target sectors. Herrington led his flight to the south and the Bernay sector. "All right, Red One," he called to Matt. "Run that rail line and see what you can find. We'll check the field at Rouen in case the Germans are using it again."

Matt banked Red Section away and lined up on the tracks that led to Le Havre and the coast. The first light of day had been hampered by persistent overcast that bathed the earth and its vegetation below in a monotonous pall of gray. A friend to the camouflaged enemy, such conditions frustrated these weary-eyed pursuers who squinted and blinked at the countryside for a possible target. They had flown but a few miles when Roger Baker broke the silence. "Red One, see those haystacks around that field at 10 o'clock?"

"What about 'em?" Matt asked, his eyes searching the dozen or so piles lining the edge of the woods.

"Too early in the season and stacks way too big," the country boy explained. "Any clod kicker worth his manure would know that!"

The whole section got the point in an instant. "Red Three, take your element down there and bust up one of those stacks," Matt invited. "Let's see what happens."

Roger peeled away with Barry Stockton and dropped to strafing level. As the two fighters turned to make a run at the nearest stack, Matt saw figures dash from the trees and scramble onto the haystacks at the end of the field. "Watch it, Red Three! I think you're onto something!"

Rockets streamed from Roger's fighter, catching the nearest stack broadside. He didn't have to wait for the dust to settle. His guess was right. The tanks on the far side broke cover as Stockton got a round into the second panzer. By the time Matt and Chuck were in position, the targets were backing into the forest as German turret gunners returned the fire. Too little and too late, though, for a third piece of armor drifted into the sights of the attacking duo with predictable results.

Red Section circled the wooded area hoping for an opening, but the trees were too thick. "Let's save what's left for a better target," Matt ordered as he turned his pilots back to the rail lines.

They were near the sea now and in the distance, off their port wings, billows of brownish smoke leaned with the wind from a hundred points just inland. As his element drew nearer, the wide gray beaches melted into channel waters seemingly peppered with ships of every description. Above this great amphitheater of war, miniature bombers circled lazily, discharging their sticks of tumbling bombs on German coastal defenses. It was the most compelling thing Matt had ever seen, this classic battle, employing every method of warfare then known. Only his first thousand bomber missions could hold a candle to it.

They had a distant but adequate seat to monitor the first efforts of British and Canadian soldiers establishing a beachhead on the shores of France. Thirty miles down the coast, their own countrymen waged the same battle on Utah and Omaha beaches. For certain, the spectacle fathered an urgency previously unknown by the men of Matt's unit, and they returned to their task with sober but silent vengeance.

The Germans had camouflaged repairs to the bridge west of Rouen, but Red Section didn't take the bait and six of its eight bombs left the overcrossing in shambles again. Until fuel became critical, the four attacked every communication target they could identify. And when the rockets were exhausted, parting shots from their wing guns littered the Normandy countryside with wrecks of a dozen assorted enemy vehicles.

Heavy flak forced the flyers to oxygen altitude, for the Germans had come to life and were throwing all they had at anything that flew. At mid-channel, high above the ongoing drama, it appeared the world's harbors had deposited every ship afloat into the murky waters below. Some of them oozed the smoke of damage where German coastal guns had found their mark. But still they came like ants, pouring from the countless ports of Kent, Sussex, Hampshire, and Dorset on the southern coast of a war-weary England.

Matt was well pleased with the performance of his element.

Fighter sweeps provided the best opportunity for the men to work as a unit, backing each other and bringing concentrated firepower on the targets. Much later, they would learn that Red Section was one of more than 14,000 aircraft launched by the Allies on that first day of invasion. And as they returned to England, the outbound air traffic confirmed it.

Operation Overlord, as it would go down in history, had been a surprise to the enemy. Intelligence trickery by the Allies confused the German high command as to the probable landing point. Hitler slept through the early hours when General Keitel, unfazed by the reports, refused to awaken him. Misjudgments prevented the Luftwaffe's effective participation as well, for Luftflotte III had barely 500 operational aircraft in the area concerned, most of which were pinned down by continuous Allied fighter cover.

Slybird flew seven sorties that day as the dedicated pilots of the 353rd Fighter Group rotated to the cause. Matt would sleep a few hours, eat what his nerves allowed, then take *Paladin* back to France on the final mission of the day.

# CHAPTER 12

# Doing His Duty

T HE RESIDENTS OF Great Wenham were accustomed to aircraft, but never on the scale of June 6, 1944. Hardly an hour
passed when the sound of planes, coming or going, did not
fill the air. By late morning, BBC was backlogged with reports on
the invasion. All England, from its great cities to its tiny hamlets,
was in a state of jubilation.

People were out in droves, the women clutching sweaters across
their backs against a chilly morning. Visitation was the order of the
day as neighbors stopped in to give their opinion on the unfolding
events. Others, clustered at road crossings, stared over the horizon
as though they might obtain a glimpse of the landings.

It had taken Etta Moore nearly two hours to get a line through
to Manor Lodge. She wanted news of Matt's unit, which Vivie was
unable to provide, and to give her daughter moral support in the
tense hours to come.

By late afternoon, the excitement had taken its toll. Katherine Walldon left the remaining visitors with her husband and retired to the relative quiet of her second-story bedroom to rest before tea. There she found Vivie, perched on a chair with duster in hand, cleaning the huge picture frames on the hallway walls. "Vivian, what are you doing?"

"Oh, just tidying up a bit."

"That's very thoughtful of you, dear. But you don't need to play Mrs. Mop just because you're staying with us. Tea will be served shortly. Why don't you step down and freshen up?"

"I think I would rather finish these, if you don't mind. The busier my hands, the better just now."

Katherine scolded herself silently for neglecting her special guest at so trying a time. Leaning on one of the door casings, her arms folded, she watched the tedious efforts of the self-appointed maid. "I daresay they haven't been that well cared for in some time. If you were any more thorough, I should think they would need gilding again!"

She paused as the chair was moved to the next frame, her heart going out to the industrious young woman. "He's going to be just fine," she heard herself say with such authority that Vivie stopped to meet her gaze. "I'm quite certain of it. Really!"

"I'll be fine, Aunt Kate," Vivie replied as she stepped from the chair. "But he is on my mind."

"I'd say more like your heart, dear child. I remember all too well when Mr. Walldon went off to war. We were married one weekend and he was gone the next. I rode the train to London with him and watched him march away from the station with his unit."

Like her peers, Vivie had seldom considered the older generation in a romantic sense. But her present circumstances, coupled with Katherine's disclosures, put their relationship in a new light. Here was a woman who still carried the memories of a painful separation engineered by yet another war. "I didn't know that, Aunt Kate. How long was he away?"

"Nearly two years. Weeks would go by without a letter. The waiting was dreadful!"

"Well, at least he returned safely," Vivie said as she rolled the sleeves of her blouse back in place.

"Returned, yes. But he was wounded twice. The second time he spent a month in the hospital." Katherine began to chuckle softly, shaking her head. "The first time was his own fault, you know."

"His fault?" Vivie inquired as she took a chair beside her host.

"You might say so. He was crawling along in one of the trenches near dusk and thought he had reached the end of it. In fact, it was simply a sharp turn. Anyway, he placed his rifle on a support timber and set about relieving himself." Katherine's hands rushed to her reddened cheeks, fingers spread to stifle a smile. In all her time at Manor Lodge, Vivie had never seen this side of her aunt and her eyes widened as the older woman continued.

"Well, just as Cecil was in… position, this German appears round the turn, evidently thinking he's within his own lines. The confrontation was a shock to both, as you might expect. Fortunately, the German's holster was stuck somehow, giving your uncle time to adjust his circumstances." Katherine was chuckling aloud by now and Vivie was not far behind. "But the German took one of those grenade things from his belt and in the ensuing struggle, the thing was triggered. Well, they both knew the consequences of that and were forced to cooperate in a tussle to rid the trench of the horrid thing."

"Anyway," Katherine said, "the two of them pressed into the bank awaiting the explosion, which sprayed them with dirt. There were uncertain moments when they faced each other again, both without guns at hand now. So Cecil pointed at the German, then the exit behind him. Then he pointed to himself and the pathway to his rear. The German got the message and they cautiously backed away from each other. Your uncle was so concerned the enemy would return, he backed into his own bayonet!"

"Oh, dear!" Vivie cried. "How badly was he hurt?"

"Fortunately, it just stuck his bum about here," Katherine replied, her hand covering a spot just below her hip. "The bomb is he was seriously wounded sometime later, but the medal was erroneously awarded for the bayonet incident."

Vivie's reward from this session of merriment was a pain and both were blotting tears between their sighs. Their antics did not escape those below. The booming voice of Cecil Walldon filled the stairwell. "I say, up there, have you taken leave of your senses?"

His wife assured him they most assuredly had not and they would be down presently. Vivie took the older woman's hand and pressed it gently between hers. "Thank you, Aunt Kate, for sharing such a thing. The laughter was a marvelous balm!"

The mood did carry Vivie through the evening until bedtime, when she would fall victim again to her worries. The lonely darkness told her one thing: that her feelings for Matt had advanced well beyond simple affection.

The roar of departing aircraft greeted Great Wenham at the crack of dawn the next morning. But it would be the second wave, two hours later, that took Matt back to Europe. Hazy skies prevailed over the channel, keeping the choppy waters below in a pale dishwater gray. The Germans had mobilized swiftly in the past 24 hours, and the high priority of support for their front was evident along roads and rail lines. Good hunting for Slybird, but all the more dangerous with anti-aircraft batteries beefed up and attached to nearly every moving target.

Day 2, however, would not be exclusive air-to-ground warfare. Field Marshal Hermann Goering, asleep at the switch with pre-invasion air cover, was still reeling from the Fuhrer's tongue lashing as he corrected the blunder. The Luftwaffe was well represented at points across Normandy, their bombers attempting to suppress the advancing British and American forces.

As the 353$^{rd}$ Fighter Group neared Paris, it intercepted a flight of Junkers 188 Schnellbombers with some fighter cover. The Americans could not know of the near-suicidal orders their enemy flew under. They found themselves immediately challenged by sleek Focke-Wulf 190 fighters. They had no choice but to drop bombs, rockets, and tanks in a hasty effort to survive the attack. Most of the fighters Matt had been up against were Messerschmitt 109s, and he could tell the difference immediately as the two sides positioned for advantage. Captain Wayne Blickenstaff, already logging an impressive score of air kills, was leading the Group on this second sortie.

"Blick" loved the fray more than leading and quickly directed the 352$^{nd}$ Jockey Squadron to hold off the fighters while he led the rest after the bombers. Assigned to the 350$^{th}$ Squadron, he would put Matt's element on the cutting edge of the engagement. "All right, you new guys, don't get in front of these 190s. They've got more firepower up there than you have."

The German bombers were in Vic formation and boxed close for mutual protection. "Okay, Red and White, let's bust that formation so we can pick 'em off!" Herrington barked.

Holding a brace of Focke-Wulf fighters in check is not unlike cornering wet soap in the bathtub. After a few minutes of sparing with Jockey Squadron, the crafty Focke-Wulfs broke away to the aid of their bombers. The lead pilots rolled in over the Junkers to meet the Americans head on, seemingly without an ounce of fear. Blickenstaff faced them down holding to his target, but his wingman, calling for his leader to break, made a fatal turn to the right.

Tragedy struck instantly as the first 190 sailed over Blick and caught the turning Thunderbolt with a full charge of 20mm cannon. Debris spun off the doomed fighter seconds before an orange flash dislodged its engine. Matt, helpless from his position, fought rising anger lest it cloud his judgment.

"Somebody get the devil down here and help me with these bombers!" Blick yelled into his mike. He had lost his wingman and he would extract retribution before the chance was lost. Tears must come later over scotch and water at Auger Inn.

The German charge, line abreast, scattered the Thunderbolts, and the sky became a maze of darting fighters. Blickenstaff, below the enemy attack, was able to reach the trailing bomber and smoke its starboard engine. The radio was a jabber of confusion, unavailable for intelligible orders, and Matt hoped Chuck would read his hand signals as their fighters closed ranks again. In all the distraction, he had not forgotten Blick's call for assistance and nosed down in the hope Baker and Stockton could follow.

But the Huns were good. On his left Matt saw two Focke-Wulfs closing rapidly, determined that he not reach his target. "Chuck!" he yelled onto his mike. "Ten o'clock! Can you keep 'em off me?"

They were close enough that the transmission got through, and Chuck turned into the approaching enemy. Breathing a sigh of relief, Matt continued his shallow dive, closing fast on the bombers. In a split-second decision he passed up Blick's target, which now had fire streaming from its damaged engine, and headed for the next in line. Close enough to see the swiveling barrel of the rear cockpit gun, he concentrated his first burst of fire at that point. Still, tracers circled around *Paladin*, and Matt was forced to drop lower out of the gunner's angle of fire.

The German bomber pilot tried to maintain a tight formation, hoping to get assistance from the other Junkers. But Matt was closing at nearly a right angle now, and the broad blueish-green wings of the bomber filled his sights. *Paladin*'s reassuring shudder told him all guns were working, and strikes flashed across the bomber's back and out to its port engine. Nothing! He throttled back so as not to overshoot his prey then repeated the attack. At just under 150 yards, the Thunderbolt's tracers merged on the port wing, which crumbled in flames and spun away from the bomber.

In a second Matt had passed it, diving beneath the remaining formation with the fear he had pressed his luck with the Focke- -Wulfs. Turning back to the action, he saw his target dropping straight down in a ball of flame. Nearby, two figures rolled from Blick's kill, their parachutes blossoming into white canopies. Chuck Shilling had done his job and was well below it all, jockeying with the German fighters he had engaged. The farther down they dived, the worse it was for Chuck, who found himself losing the defense game. *Paladin*'s great silver wings rolled over into a steep dive as Matt went to the aid of his wingman.

Shilling's only hope was to keep crossing between the two 190s, but that wouldn't work forever. There was no longer room to fight and his mind turned to survival. He would bail out before the enemy's cannon blew him out of the sky. As his hand grasped the canopy latch, the saving sound of Matt's voice reached his head- phones. "Hang in there, Red Two! I'm right behind 'em!"

It was a long shot, at least 250 yards, when Matt fired on the left Focke-Wulf. It took a sustained burst to get a hit, but it was enough to make the German break off. "The match is even, Red Two! Have at it!"

Matt followed the 190, getting in two more short bursts before it ran for the deck. Just as signs of a vapor trail tempted him to hound the enemy to the ground, a flaming Thunderbolt streaked past *Paladin*'s left wing. It was raining death, and the deck was no place to be alone in enemy territory. There were six parachutes hanging against the gray sky as Matt turned to catch up with his wingman. Before the day was over, three Slybirds and 11 Germans would miss taps that night.

Chuck had locked on the other Focke-Wulf, chasing it down to less than 1,000 feet. The enemy pilot was capable, running his pur- suer a dangerous race deeper into German territory. But the pilot of Red Two, so far without a kill, intended to get this trophy and he matched his prey turn for turn. Matt was too far out to help Shilling, but in good position to fly security for him. And it was from that vantage point that he watched his friend set the 190 on fire. Down it went, skidding across the field below, then pin-wheeling into a bright-orange explosion.

"Confirmed, Chuck baby! Confirmed!" Matt yelled into the radio. Shilling wagged his wings and nosed the fighter up in a spiraling climb of exhilaration before the two joined up again. "Beautiful job!" Matt added as he shot his wingman a stiff thumbs up. They had liked each other from the very beginning, nearly a year ago, when they trained in Florida skies with Curtiss P-40s. Roger had come into the trio later, something of an enigma, for the other two were closer intellectually.

The dogfight spread all over the sky and they could hear transmissions from pilots still engaged where battle lines had dissolved. It would be fruitless for the two to spend precious fuel trying to regain their position above. Coming up from the deck slow and vulnerable was a suicide expedition. Better to turn for home and pick off what targets of chance they might encounter. And encounter they did when a small convoy outside Calais cost them the rest of their ammunition, a condition that never failed to hurry a pilot on home.

They were the first of their sortie to return, full of themselves, streaking in low over the runway in flashy victory rolls. This was good medicine for crew chiefs, who gained a certain status among their peers when they serviced a hot pilot. As *Paladin* rolled to a stop, Milt-the-Stilt performed his Tennessee soft shoe reserved for such moments. An ecstatic Dewey Newhart learned of the two kills on the tower radio as Matt's element crossed the channel. They would be the first of eight that day for the major's 350th Squadron.

Lunch followed debriefing, then came the lumpy English mattress where Matt lost consciousness for the next four hours. Every squadron scored victories that day, and the pilots of Slybird would record 12 German fighters destroyed and six damaged for the record. But the evening celebration at Auger Inn was tempered profoundly by the absence of three flyers. These tragedies plus 16 severely damaged fighters were but a prelude to coming events, for the 353rd Fighter Group would face additional losses in the weeks to come.

Even in war there were little pleasures, like not being shaken out of bed before the sun peeked over the horizon. Matt realized he had missed the early missions and held his breath as he checked the day's assignment roster. He wasn't there! Restrictions had been lifted and pilgrimages to area pubs were in a high state of preparation. Roger Baker quivered with the anticipation of a Lowcountry bird dog on the first day of quail season. It's doubtful that he even missed his section leader as he led the bicycle brigade to Wenham Queen.

But Matt Tower had higher priorities than cheap English beer and the Piccadilly Commandos on city streets selling their favors. Within the hour he was open collared, in flight jacket and officer's hat, cycling through neighboring farms in search of the Walldon place. At this late date he could understand if Vivie was not there, but it would be good to meet her hosts and perhaps use their telephone to arrange a reunion.

Manor Lodge was unique, standing out from the small country cottages and inns of the area. Even at a distance Matt could see why anyone passing through would be drawn to an evening's rest there. Great old trees posted themselves at intervals around the white Tudor with its rustic wooden trim. A handsome carriage barn and small pasture completed the picture. He smiled as he envisioned the heydays when traveling coaches would have deposited horses and passengers there for the night.

Two skirted figures walked in the courtyard, and Matt's heart raced with anticipation. One was Vivie! A simple blue dress, her light golden-brown hair pulled back and secured with a ribbon, gave clear evidence no visitors had been expected. Though she noticed his approach, he was still shaded by the arching trees along the lane. But as he drew nearer, her hands rushed to her cheeks and she moved hesitantly down the short patio steps.

Katherine would have paid little attention had Vivie not reacted so, for it was not uncommon that servicemen regularly passed along the roads. The older woman, slowly drying her hands on her apron, watched the younger trot to the corner of the yard in that gait so typical of the delicate sex. The serviceman dropped his bike and cleared the small bordering wall in one flowing movement.

They did not embrace at first, preferring to let thirsty eyes drink their fill. "Matt! Oh, Matt," Vivie breathed. "I tried to reach you, but the base was restricted."

"I knew. I knew you were there, sweetheart," he smiled back, folding her gently into his arms.

Katherine, unexpected but willing witness to the intimate moment, returned to her window washing but could not erase the knowing smile consuming her face. *"So,"* she chuckled under her breath. *"Mr. Wonderful finally arrives."*

With the enthusiasm of an adolescent, Vivie presented Matt to Katherine. "Aunt Kate, this is Matt Tower. I've wanted so much for you to meet him."

"I am delighted," Katherine replied, extending her hand. "I'm Katherine Walldon, and you are every bit as Vivian described you. Welcome to Manor Lodge!"

"Thank you, ma'am. I've really enjoyed meeting Vivie's family."

"Well, as much as I would relish such glory, young man, I am a mere godmother to this precious child."

Vivie clung to the flyer's arm as though fearing his eminent escape, which amused Katherine greatly. "Dear, the extremities must enjoy circulation to prevent tingling numbness or, heaven forbid, gangrene. Give the lieutenant some freedom."

Katherine led them to the great country kitchen and its long dining table where the young couple sat with hands joined, their eyes not yet satisfied. Vivie's concern was quite evident in the tone of her voice. "You look tired, sweetheart. And thinner. Haven't they been feeding you?"

His smile was as reassuring as he could make it. "The food's not as good as your mother's, but there's plenty of it. We've had a few hectic days, that's all," he confessed, relishing the stroke of her smooth palm on his cheek.

Unaware he had a new guest, Cecil Walldon backed into the kitchen, his arms loaded with firewood. Matt was the first to see him and rose quickly to assist. "Let me help you with those, sir."

"By Jove!" the older man exclaimed, somewhat surprised. "Indeed, you may." He surveyed the trio before him, his brows arching in question. "Humm. You must belong to Vivian."

Vivie's smile was generous as she took the American's arm. "Uncle Cecil, this is Matt Tower. You know, the flyer I was telling you about."

"Quite evidently!" Cecil grunted as he lowered the logs. "It's a pleasure to meet you, Lieutenant."

The handshake was that of a hardy Englishman, genuine, firm, cordial. Perhaps it was Matt's uniform, new soldier to old soldier, but there was a mutual appreciation.

"Come lad, sit here," the old major motioned. He obviously was pleased to have male companionship, especially one so involved in the great conflict. Seating himself amid the wheezes and grunts of his years, he circled the cup with his weathered hands and took a lengthy sip. "She makes the tea of kings," he smacked, nodding at his wife. "What kind of plane are you flying, Lieutenant?"

"P-47, sir. Thunderbolts."

"Humm," came the reply as Cecil drew again from the cup. "Pity. You should have a Spitfire 9. Now, there's a fighter!"

Matt smiled politely, for he was well pleased with his own new warbird. "That's a fine aircraft, sir. I've seen them in action."

"Tell me now, did you see any of the invasion?"

"We flew over some of it just west of Le Havre. I think it was a British position," Matt added with a grin.

"Quite! Quite!" Cecil responded. "Miles Dempsey, no doubt."

"Miles Dempsey?"

"Oh. General Sir Miles Dempsey, now. British Second Army. We go back a bit, the general and I."

The women had been content to play spectator to that point, but Katherine knew her husband. If allowed to gain momentum, he would have the war maps out presently. "Now, now, Cecil. I'm quite certain Lieutenant Tower prefers to spend his leave free of the war."

The old soldier's stare inferred that his spouse spoke for herself, but Aunt Kate held her ground. "Will you be staying the night with us, Lieutenant?"

"No, ma'am. I have to report back tonight."

"Oh, Matt," Vivie moaned. "I was so in hopes." She had taken his arm again and he covered her hand with his own.

Katherine mirrored the disappointment. She would like to know the American flyer better, but time was precious to the young couple. "Well, if that's the case, you shan't spend your time with old Darby and Joan. Vivian, why don't you show Lieutenant Tower the grounds? Perhaps see to Bertha in the far pasture." She paused to glance at Cecil, who sat rather discontentedly while nursing his tea. "If a certain party would tend the fence, we would have more milk. You see, when the neighbors return the old cow, she's always dry."

Katherine placed fresh buns in a napkin with a vacuum of tea and sent the young people out into the reappearing sunshine. The pasture, responding to midsummer, was clothed in tender tints of green. Chains of wildflowers wound their way along the fences and dotted the natural boundaries with a dash of lavender and red-and-white petals. For Vivie, smiling up at the man walking beside her, it made all complete. There was time now to be alone, to talk, perchance to wish together.

Matt, breathing deeply of the country air, was at home in the spacious fields. He showed no hesitation in greeting old Bertha, who had succeeded in dislodging another fence rail. Smart cow. Bertha turned away from it as the couple approached, pretending contentment with her cud. Matt gave the soft brown hide a good slap for discouragement, but she refused to be intimidated. "She's a healthy specimen," he laughed. "Bet she'd calve a fine calf. You know, it takes about nine months."

Vivie seemed impressed that he understood such things. "How do you know all this?"

"They run cattle on Grandfather's farm. I spent a lot of time there. Is this their only one?"

"They've thought about it, but I daresay they would be hard put to care for another animal. Besides, knowing Uncle Cecil, he would require the bull that serviced her to be straight out of *Debrett's Peerage*."

"Well, let's see if we can discourage old Bertha." They walked through the gate, and Matt set about the project. "I'll wedge the rail from this side so she can't lift it again."

Vivie took pleasure in watching him. He made things seem so simple, studying the chore for a moment and then moving the parts smoothly into place. "Lieutenant Tower, is there anything you don't know your way about?"

"Very little," he joked. From the corner of his eye he watched her as he worked with the rail. Even in a pastoral setting, with hair pulled back, she retained the regal countenance that had won his heart at their first meeting. "That should do it," he said, stepping back to view the result. "Now there's just one engineering project remaining."

"And what could that be? It looks fine to me."

"Getting you over the fence."

"Whatever for?" she teased, knowing full well that he wished for more privacy.

He smiled slyly and glanced at the ground. "Well, it's plain to see there's no safe place to sit on Bertha's side of the fence. Besides, I'm taking you to my gazebo this time. Right over there under that big tree."

"And just what is your plan, Mr. Engineer?" she questioned coquettishly, enjoying the anticipation of his next move.

"Allow me to introduce a little Yankee ingenuity, madam." In a second, he had lifted her in his arms—basket, vacuum, and all.

Vivie squealed and kicked her legs in delight as Matt stepped to the fence and deposited his package on the other side. It had been so long since a man had taken charge, had planned things for her. He didn't let go when her feet touched the ground but leaned across the fence to caress her. "Tip, please," he paused, his lips puckered expectantly,

"Tip? For what?" she inquired, faking a yawn with the touch of her fingers to her soft pink lips.

"Well, even a bellboy gets a tip for carrying a bag."

"A bag is it, now!" she cried in mock anger. "If that's what you think, there'll be no tip from this bag, my dear sir."

Slipping from his embrace, she moved quickly out of reach, leaving him at the fence with arms dangling over the rail. He saw through her little wile and was sport enough to play it out. "Ah-ha!" he roared in retaliation. "That will cost you double, madam! Observe the vigor of the defrauded bellboy as he seeks revenge!"

Matt planted his hands firmly on the wedged rail and vaulted the fence. Vivie was dancing backward, eyes wide with excitement, knowing full well she was but seconds from being man-handled. He would do his awful tickling and she would have to beg for mercy.

But he would not have his prize easily, for she turned and ran with unexpected speed. The merry chase was on with Vivie taking the lead, skirt pulled above her knees and trim legs churning as they had in her track days. It was a nimble and quick performance but doomed in the shadow of her pursuer's manly stride.

"Noooo!" she was shrieking giddily. "No, you don't, Matt Tower!" But he would and he did.

She took some catching, and they were in the shade of the great tree before his arms finally captured her. Both were winded as they paced down to a stop and faced each other, his arms holding her to him. As deeply as they were breathing, Vivie managed a taunting smile. "You're awfully out of breath for a soldier. You know that?"

"I want my tip," he smiled back, his encircling arms drawing her the more to him.

"Poo! I don't think you could take it in your condition."

They grew quiet then, though their eyes continued the conversation until he whispered, "Try me."

She did. Her arms circled his neck as her sweet, soft, very pink lips responded to the pleading in his eyes. Just a touch at first, much as the connoisseur might sample a vintage wine. His lips took over then, requiring and receiving the surrender, the dream that sustained him in days past 20,000 feet over France.

Vivie found herself without thought, aware only of his presence and the pressure of his arms. The tender weakness that followed gently lowered them to their knees. When they could kiss no longer, they clung there until the quiver of Vivie's soft sobs separated them. She sat back on her heels, fingers covering her eyes.

Matt's hands quickly steadied her shoulders, his voice gentle with concern. "Vivie?"

"I'm fine," she sighed, dabbing at the tiny tears with the back of her hands.

But he would not be so quickly assured and took the small

handkerchief she retrieved from her pocket and dabbed at the tears. "Well, I'd hate to see you when you weren't so fine!"

"I'm sorry, poppet," she replied, smoothing her hair. "It's just that I'm so very happy."

"This is happy?"

"Yes," she breathed through a widening smile. "It's been so long since I dared to feel this way." But the smile did not linger as she sat rigidly before him, her lovely blue eyes imploring earnestly. "Matt, this is all true, isn't it? You do care for me?"

She preferred the reply from his eyes and his heart, but he hung his head. "No, actually I really do not," he replied in the most serious of tones.

Vivie froze in place, her brow wrinkled in disbelief. Then he slowly raised his head to reveal a smile. "No, *care* is not sufficient, my lady. I absolutely adore you! I think I loved you from the first, but there was so much going against us, I was afraid you could never return it."

"It's returned, Matt Tower," she whispered in blessed relief and leaned to place a brief kiss on his lips. "I could never forget your eyes. Quite unnerving, you know. We had never seen each other before, but you didn't seem a stranger to me, as though I had known you at another time. It was so very strange. I've never been looked at like that before." Her eyes drifted to the pasture as she paused. "Not even with John."

"Danged if you can't keep a secret! I'd never have known."

"I hoped you wouldn't. I tried as hard as I could not to get involved. Now look at me. I've done everything I vowed I wouldn't!"

"Sorry?"

"Oh no, my dear poppet. I'm just a bit frightened by it all. If you hadn't seemed so sure, so certain about things, I could never have come this far."

"And if you hadn't come this far, dear lady...."

When Matt removed his jacket and spread it for Vivie to sit on, an envelope slipped to the ground. She retrieved it, glanced briefly at the return address, then handed it to him. "Letter from home?" she asked smiling.

"My mother. It arrived this morning. I didn't finish reading it."

Vivie had spread the napkin and divided the tasty buns between them. "She has a lovely hand. I thought only we English took such pains with our penmanship."

"She's quite an artist, too. Really great sketches and watercolors."

They finished the buns amid the intimate small talk of lovers. The countryside had been peaceful to that point with only a gentle breeze and the chirp of distant birds for company. So engrossed were the young people that they failed to detect the approaching aircraft until the drone of their engines was above them. Matt's eyes sought out the intruders. He recognized his group as it circled to form up for a mission, each plane catching up with its section leader for typical formation.

Vivie watched him intently, the tension in his shoulders and deepening breaths quickly wiping the smile from her face. Goose bumps speckled her arms as she crossed them anxiously. For all practical purposes, she had lost him to the sky.

When the engines faded in the distance, he drew his legs up, circling them with his arms again so a weary brow could rest on his knees. Gently, Vivie's hands slid across his shoulders until her fingers found the taut muscles of his neck. Though he said nothing, his body responded with appreciation as she massaged. "Dear love, you are tired, aren't you?"

"They'll be over the continent soon," he said matter-of-factly. "Right up the Seine and out across Normandy, the new guys hugging their element leaders like chicks to a hen."

"I know," she replied softly. "But you told me yourself, they're in good hands. I think you deserve a bit of R&R, Lieutenant. Come, put your head here on my lap."

He needed little coaxing, since he felt the tension far more now than he had on the base amid the whirl of the last 10 days. Vivie rested against the trunk of the great tree and guided him back until his head found the soft hollow of her lap. "Now, close your eyes and I'll read to you."

"Read what?" he yawned, snuggling his head for comfort.

"Your letter, of course. That is if you don't mind. Your mum seems such a dear, and I do want to know more about you."

He smiled his approval and she opened the voluminous letter with eager hands. "What's this at the top of the page? Psalm 139:9-10."

"She always does that," he said through a widening smile. "Everything she's ever written me, even in school, there's been a Bible verse. She can really pick 'em for the occasion, too."

"And what is this one?"

"I... don't... know," he replied, his words slower now, almost dreamy. "I haven't... haven't checked it yet."

Vivie continued reading, her lovely English voice eager and interested. She would punctuate the lines that especially touched her with thoughts of her own heart. But soon she kept them to herself, for the pressure of his head on her lap told her he was napping. She lowered the letter to look at his face, an evidently weary one, so sober in repose. He belonged to her exclusively now, at least for this special time. Flights and elements, pilots and missions, yes, even the war, must wait.

Gently, she moved a lock of his hair back in place, taking every precaution not to wake him. His head rolled slightly and she sighed contentedly, savoring the innocent intimacy.

It was late afternoon when the wandering pair walked hand in hand along the path to Manor Lodge. Katherine, with no shortage of feminine instinct, sensed the change in their countenance from her kitchen window. She could only imagine how the day had gone for the young couple. But one thing was certain: for each, the world now centered around the other.

They were inseparable at dinner, and Katherine's heart warmed by the glow on Vivie's face. How long it had been since she had seen Etta's daughter so alive. She wished her friend were there, for the Moores had worried so over Vivie's fate after the double tragedy. Robert was, no doubt, less than enthusiastic about Matt's lack of British credentials. But the American lieutenant had accomplished what no other seemed able to.

After the evening meal and a generous dose of Cecil's war theories, the older man left for his turn with the Home Guard. Katherine had hurried him along tactfully to leave the young people as much time as possible before Matt returned to base. "There he goes," she chuckled. "I daresay England is safer from the Germans than that band of old geezers. But they were willing," she added reflectively. "In the early days, with the blitz and the threat of invasion, they would have fought for the king with their bare hands."

Matt took Katherine's hand in his and thanked her warmly for her hospitality. "Your husband's an honorable man, Mrs. Walldon. And a brave one. I'm proud to be included at his table."

Her eyes welled and she sighed deeply, forcing a smile, for Matt's evaluation had complimented a 50-year love affair between the Walldons. "Thank you, Lieutenant. You're always welcome at Manor Lodge." Gaining her composure, she gave her attention to Vivie who was busy with the dishes. "No, dear. No, no, no! I'll see to those and you see to the lieutenant."

Vivie led Matt to the courtyard and its clear, chilly air where a half moon's eerie glow paled the countryside. Katherine had dialed the radio searching for late news, and the soft refrain of Tommy Dorsey's orchestra drifted from the Armed Forces station. *"I'll...never smile again...until I smile at you..."* came the harmony of Frank Sinatra and the Pied Pipers. Vivie accepted the warmth of her flyer's arm as they stood together at the patio wall. "It's rather quiet in the country," she said. "I'm sorry there's not more to do."

She had changed before dinner, taking her hair down and replacing the plain blue dress with the lower-cut green one she had hoped to meet him in. The moon's glow on her light golden-brown locks gave just a hint of the halo he had seen when they first met. He could not remember when he had been this happy. That prim little top lip of hers and the face, with its taunting trace smile, utterly captivated him. "There is nothing I would rather do than spend this evening right here with you, dear lady. And there is something to do. Would you care to dance, Mrs. Davis?"

"Out here?" she laughed softly.

"And why not? Look! It's the grandest ballroom in the world," he proclaimed, waving an arm across the sky.

"Dear!" she exclaimed. "Then we must take advantage of it."

She melted eagerly into his arms, nestling her cheek against his. The music was perfect for their mood and he led her gracefully around the patio. "Matt?" she asked softly.

"Yes?" he whispered.

"I feel just like that."

"Like what, pet?"

"That song. When you're away I don't want to smile. I feel lonely and... afraid sometimes."

Matt smiled reassuringly. "I love you, Vivie. There's nothing to be afraid of."

They danced the song out and sat on the patio wall to spend the time before Matt would leave.

"Oh, I quite forgot!" Vivie exclaimed. "I've an invitation for you. Dad requests the pleasure of your company for a pheasant hunt."

Matt cocked his head skeptically and crossed his arms. "Now, let me get this straight. Your father is extending me an invitation?"

"Quite!" she bubbled excitedly. "I'm so thrilled! I do want the two of you to get along well."

"What brought about this sudden change of heart?"

"Not so sudden," she answered, her tones more serious now. "I think he simply misunderstood some things. Anyway, I know he and Mum talked at length on the matter, and then he asked me to deliver his invitation. They have a delightful time. Usually it includes Colonel Burgess, Sir Charles Tinley, and Lord Havely. It's his estate they shoot on. You will come, won't you?"

The hope in her voice was irresistible. Frankly, he rather liked her father though he never understood what had gotten them off on the wrong foot. "Tell him I would be delighted. I just hope it's not a scheme to set up a hunting accident," he added with a chuckle.

"Matt!" she admonished. "Dad would never do such a thing!"

"I'm only kidding! I'm only kidding!" he pleaded, taking her face in his hands. Quickly he kissed away the tiny trace of hurt on her lips. "When is the shoot?"

"He wants you to let him know when you have leave coming. He'll arrange it then. Lord Havely makes a big thing out of these hunts with British and American officers and some assorted VIPs. It's his contribution to the war effort." Her hands sought his and she pressed them against her cheek. "Oh, Matt, whatever shall I do until then? I don't want you to leave."

They planned, as much as they could, for another time together. A decorations ceremony was scheduled at the base in a few days with a party to follow. Guests were welcome and he would see to it Vivie was there. So they talked, the incidental small talk of lovers and in the quiet moments, comforted each other with a touch, a caress, until at last a parting kiss sealed the evening.

Katherine sat by the fire working with thread and needle as Vivie came in from the patio. "Has the lieutenant returned to base?"

"Yes," the younger woman sighed.

"He seems a very nice young man."

"Do you really like him, Aunt Kate?" Vivie questioned as she perched on the bench opposite Katherine.

"I do, indeed. But more importantly, what are your feelings toward him? Do I detect something a bit beyond liking?"

Vivie gazed into the dancing flames, her brow creased in deep thought. Dainty fingers toyed with the perky locks resting on her shoulder as she drew the courage to ask a troubling question. "Aunt Kate, is it possible to love, so strongly, more than once?"

Katherine had raised a daughter now off and married and a son with all the complexities of young adulthood. Though this child was not hers, she cared for her nearly as much and she felt the full weight of the question. "Yes, I think it's possible," she replied, more from her head than her heart. She had never been attracted to another man as strongly as she had to Cecil.

"I worry about him—where he is, what he's doing," Vivie sighed. "I knew I was falling in love with him awhile back, but I wasn't certain I wanted that."

"And now?"

"Oh, more than anything, Aunt Kate. It's so wonderful when he's near. I feel… well, whole again. It's like… well… oh dear, I'm not making much sense, am I? Wafting away like this."

Katherine leaned forward and patted Vivie's knee, a sympathetic smile creasing her seasoned lips. "You've had quite a day, dear. I think some warm milk and a good night's rest will do nicely." Squeezing the comforting hand, Vivie planted an affectionate buss on Katherine's forehead. "You're a dear, Aunt Kate, listening so patiently and playing the splendid hostess. Thank you!"

Katherine concealed her brimming eyes from Vivie as the younger woman left the room. Brimming not so much from the affection just displayed as the cherished memories kindled by the tender reunion of the couple earlier in the day so like her own special moments years earlier when Cecil would return home on furlough.

At the stairs the younger woman paused thoughtfully and turned back to Katherine. "Aunt Kate, do you have a Bible I might borrow? There's a verse on my mind."

"A Bible? Well, yes. Take mine there on the table," she said, smiling up from her chair. With discerning eyes, she watched Vivie retrieve the *Holy Writ* and fold it in her arms as she returned to the stairs. "Vivian," Katherine called softly. "He'll be in my prayers, too. Good night, dear."

# CHAPTER 13

# Sticking to It

**T**HE ALLIED EFFORT in France saw the liberation of Bayeux, Sainte-Mere-Eglise, Trevieres, Carentan, and a substantial German counterattack beaten off west of Caen. American and British forces had at last linked up, and their close support aircraft were able to operate from fields on French soil for the first time. It was a welcome date for the pilots of the 353$^{rd}$ Fighter Group whose accelerated daylong sorties in support of the invasion had come to an end.

Matt Tower was back in the cockpit, giving Red Section the most inspired leadership of his time in England. Three tiny swastikas shined under his canopy now. He had dispatched another Messerschmitt 109, in the process picking up a few bouquets by shooting it off Lieutenant Colonel Rimerman's tail.

It was a confident element leader lifting off the runway two days later at 0600 hours. The target: communication centers near the

Evreux-Dreux area. Major Dewey Newhart was leading his cherished 350th Squadron. Together with its two sister squadrons, 36 P-47s were riding cover for eight dive bombers. "Pregnant with bomb and rocket and itching to give birth," Newhart had laughed.

At Evreux, Colonel Duncan split up the squadrons for their designated targets. Matt pulled Red Section away from the Group to follow Newhart, who was flying Blickenstaff's fighter while *Mud N' Mules* obtained much-needed maintenance.

Near Dreux, their patient stalking was generously rewarded with a granddaddy of German truck convoys headed for the front. Newhart's voice crackled with fervor as he gave the order to dive. He led the first two elements, which proceeded to administer more than adequate damage to the lead vehicles.

Perhaps it was the excitement of so choice a target that the 350th dropped its guard. However, the report would read, "The squadron was unaware of impending tragedy only seconds away." Responding to Newhart's call for assistance with the convoy, the 350th's remaining elements dived for the target through patchy clouds. All aircraft were committed by the time Blue Section's tail-end Charlie yelled, "Bogeys, nine o'clock!"

Matt's darting eyes rested on a sight that knotted his belly. Just 1,000 feet above his section the sky was dotted with Messerschmitt 109s. Taking advantage of surprise and position, they were quickly raining down on the shallow-diving P-47s. Instinctively, belly tanks and wing bombs were dropped as the Americans scattered in hasty defense.

Though Stanley Herrington had not drawn this mission, he was there in spirit with his pilots. Through Matt's jammed emotional circuits, he recalled the captain's crisp, steady voice, *"When in doubt, turn into the enemy. You'll make less of a target and you'll give the jerks something to think about."*

Trust bonded Matt, Roger, and Chuck, and those two held the

line, awaiting Matt's order. But Barry Stockton, bringing up the rear, had a graphic view of the hell breaking loose around the squadron, and he followed the urge to pull away from the onslaught. "Get your butt back in here, West Virginia!" Baker yelled at his wingman.

"Turn into 'em, Red Section!" Matt ordered. "Line abreast! Return the fire!" They may have been the only flight to try that stunt, but it was clear, from the waver in formation, that the Germans did not expect it. That momentary hesitation in the second Messerschmitt squadron would be credited later with saving a lot of P-47s.

But not all. Glenn Duncan, some distance away, heard the frantic transmissions and headed back to help. Before the reinforcements could arrive, however, three Thunderbolts lay in smoking wreckage on the fields below. Another spiraled down beneath a billowing white parachute. Sandwiched in the panicked combat transmissions came the unmistakable voice of Major Dewey Newhart. "Need help! On my tail…. Dang it, I'm hit! I'm hit!" His race for escape to the channel would fail, and the 353$^{rd}$ Group would never see the spunky pilot again.

Duncan's arrival offered some hope as the capable triple ace led a counterattack. Within minutes, *Dove of Peace* had dropped three Messerschmitts, bringing the colonel's score to 18 killed in the air. But the sleek 109s were nimble and quick. Their pilots stayed around to slug it out, eventually destroying eight American aircraft and critically damaging five others.

It was a standoff to the death, and the Germans had the fuel advantage. What would ultimately end it was the depletion of ammunition on both sides as one after another, the fighters spewed straight tracers indicating their final rounds. Matt succeeded only in clearing the tails of pilots around him, sending two 109s home pouring smoke. He was pulling up from one of those runs when Stockton's voice reached his ears. "Red Leader, break! Break!"

Matt glanced in *Paladin*'s mirror where the distinctive square cockpits of two Messerschmitts closed on him from approximately 300 yards. Before he saw the orange wing flashes, he felt the hits on *Paladin's* left wing. It would be but seconds before they had his range. Then a second spray of hits. *"One Messerschmitt, maybe,"* his mind argued. *"But two at that range?"* He had flown in combat long enough to know the odds and his mouth was cotton dry.

"Break, dang it! Break!" the voice jolted him again. He jammed the throttle and stood the Thunderbolt on wing tip, reducing exposure in the German sights. Frantically, he calculated escape. A thousand yards ahead there were clouds, lifesaving clouds if he could reach them. The enemy rolled with him, but the shooting paused and he gained precious seconds of lead.

Then another spray of hits pelted *Paladin's* wounded hide. Cold sweat oozed through Matt's pores as he checked the mirror again. The 109s were still closing, hotter models than he had experienced. He swore that the cloud was moving away from him, an illusion of urgency but every bit as panicking. There was no choice but to ride it out and pray.

Eight hundred yards, then 700, and another spray of hits and metal strips flew off the wing. If he bailed out, there was a chance. With his heart pounding the breaths in and out of his chest, Matt checked his parachute harness and the canopy release. He thought of his parents, how devastated they would be if he didn't make it. And Vivie, precious Vivie, how would she handle it? A last glance in the mirror.

Blinking in disbelief, he watched one of the Messerschmitts roll out of view, evidently taking hits from somebody. His spirits soared instantly. "Oh, yeah!" he hissed through clenched teeth. "They ain't getting little Mattlowe that easy!" His hand jerked away from the release, for he would willingly take his chances with the remaining 109.

The German was good, staying on his target, and Matt prayed *Paladin's* engine could stand the long burst of emergency power.

Five hundred yards to the cloud. With composure returned, the pilot in him instinctively cleared the sky above and below. Intent on the cumulus ahead, he had missed its lower strata altogether. There, 150 feet below him, its sunlit puffs of white beckoned long and thick. With a grin of relief, he pushed the P-47 into a steep dive. In seconds, the dusty white mist enveloped fighter and pilot, and the ruinous strikes ceased at last.

The radio traffic told Matt that the fight was about over, but he weaved in and out of the cloud just to be safe. Not until he was on the deck racing for England did he fully appreciate the impact of his drama above. Breath came in long, heavy draws and his hands, clothed in sweaty gloves, still shook on the stick. But war has no mercy, and in the distance he saw the railroad yard closing fast, its powerhouse dead in his line of flight. His exhausted body pleaded with its occupant to let the target go, just this once.

Matt's head, resting on the back-armor plate, rolled slowly from side to side with the shifting of the fighter. He didn't want to lift a finger, didn't want to detour an inch, just fly the bulky old warbird straight to Raydon. "Nope," he sighed at last. "You're a fighter pilot, Tower. We don't go home with loaded guns."

Mechanically, he started to set up the run. It was a big target, adequate for a single pass. He could see men running across the rail yard. One leaped from a truck, stumbled, and plowed into the ground. Matt pressed the trigger, and the earth spewed a trail of dirt geysers right into the building. *Paladin* had lost three guns in wing damage, but the functioning five fired the last of the 50-calibers right through the building. He had time only to see some fuel drums go up from the tracers. What happened inside he would never know.

England beckoned on the horizon, its shoreline broad upon the channel and the North Sea, where German PT boats raced in packs at night hoping to pick off ships supplying the invasion. The cliffs of Dover never looked better to Matt as *Paladin* made landfall and banked to the right. He knew the route like the back of his hand, all the points leading to Raydon. Fuel depleted, guns empty, skin punctured, the tough old Thunderbolt dropped its gear slowly and reached for the comfort and safety of runway sixty.

Sluggishly, the wounded jug found its place on the dispersal pad, where Matt cut the switch and left the big prop to spin itself to rest. Milt-the-Stilt had served long enough to know when a mission was particularly rough, and he quickly mounted the wing to assist his pilot. Sliding the canopy back, his eyes rested on a weary stoic face smudged and sweaty with the residue of war. "Sir?" he called in concern to the slumped aviator. "You all right, ain't ya?" Matt stared at his crew chief for a time, then slowly pulled himself up and stepped out of the cockpit. His trousers were soiled and the stench of urine followed him down the wing.

Pulling his helmet off, he rubbed his face and roughed the matted hair. "They shot us up pretty bad, Milt," he replied hoarsely.

The fighters that survived the ordeal settled randomly onto the runway. Many would be late returning and one would crash and burn, its pilot narrowly escaping with his life. Like players retiring from a lost game, the sullen flyers milled around as though waiting for the coach to make things right. And the coach would try. Old LH-X's prop was still spinning down long after its pilot bolted the wing and roared off in his jeep. Glenn Duncan was hotter than his men had ever seen him.

In short order the Group Commander cleared with Wing Headquarters at Sawston Hall, Cambridge, for a grudge sweep to balance the score. Two hours later a fresh contingency of Slybirds, under Lieutenant Colonel Rimerman, would head for the hunting grounds east and south of Paris. Before their return, nine enemy aircraft would be dispatched, with three other probable kills. Slybird suffered no losses.

Debriefing was exceptionally quiet as the weary pilots made their unenthusiastic reports. With the group's eight losses, including three flight leaders and two element leaders, everyone was missing a friend.

Matt's lukewarm shower, a slight improvement over the more frequent cool or chilly ones, took the edge off a bit. He was glad to find the barracks quiet when he returned. Baker and Shilling were dead to the world, and only Herrington hurried about. "What's up, Captain?"

"Duncan got us a sweep in the area where you were bounced. Rimerman took the Group out and did a job on the Huns." Herrington watched Matt sluff across the room and sprawl on his bunk. The symptoms were all too clear to the veteran flyer. "Got pretty tight up there, didn't it, Tower?"

"Ever more! When I looked up, I swear it was raining 109s." Matt paused reflectively, his fingers slowly massaging an aching neck. "Captain?"

"Yeah."

"I came close to buying the farm over there this morning. This German got on my tail.... Well, there were two at first and somebody shot one off me. He wouldn't let go. I did everything I knew to do, everything, and I couldn't shake him. I mean... like I had my hand on the canopy release. You ever come that close?"

"Yeah."

"How did you feel about it?"

"Mad as crap!"

Matt leaned up on his elbows. "Mad? About what?"

"For letting my butt get in the mess to begin with." Herrington paused, then threw his jacket over a shoulder. "Tower, we all get scared. The difference is in what we do about it. If you give it a good home, it'll hang around and take up your time. I learned a long time ago to roll it over to anger. Now, if somebody shoots at me, I get real mad. And when I'm real mad, I shoot back real good!"

Matt dropped back on his bunk as Herrington walked over and stood beside it. "Look, Tower, you're a darn good pilot. Now, somebody jumped your tail and shot at you. I wouldn't rest until I got back over there and extracted my pound of flesh." He started for the door, paused, turned back and rested a hand on the door casing. "You've got three swastikas on your cowling. If you don't make ace before the end of the month, it'll floor me."

A couple of hours later Matt awoke to the snapping of checker discs. Barry Stockton and a pilot from the 351st Squadron were in a heated match at the end of the barracks. The nap left Matt with the blahs. When he shifted to a sitting position, he could identify every muscle that lived through the tense hours of that morning. Some dear saint had heated up a fresh pot of coffee, and the aroma was putting the ailing flyer's life back together.

"Who's winning?" Matt inquired passively as he stirred the dark liquid.

"Not me," Stockton replied with a laugh. "Tucker here is wiping up the board with me."

"I thought everybody in West Virginia played checkers on a bar-relhead in the general store when they weren't in a coal mine."

"Not this old boy," Stockton shot back. "I rode range on my Dad's ranch."

"Come on! You're telling me they've got cows in West Virginia?" Matt teased.

"Absolutely. The day I went off to war, we had a thousand black Angus ready for market." Barry could tell by Matt's expression he had educated the senior lieutenant. "By the way, I picked this up for you."

Matt reached for the letter with his free hand. "Thanks, and by the way, thanks for warning me about the Messerschmitts. I don't know where they came from, but I was dang well in a jam."

The handwriting was unfamiliar, but the British stamp should have been a strong hint. Matt sat on his bunk and opened the letter carefully. Yes, from Vivie. A small pressed flower fell in his lap as he unfolded the two pages.

*"My Dearest Sweetheart, I miss you dreadfully. Last weekend was the happiest for me in years. Before I forget I'm to remind you about the pheasant hunt. It will be a grand do at Lord Havely's estate. It seems the British and American high commands are organizing invasion celebrations all about the country, so they've had to set a date. A goodwill thing, you know. The weekend of July 22. It should be terribly exciting. I do so hope you can get away."*

Vivie was a vivacious writer, splashing thoughts and happenings excitedly across the pages, and Matt felt the need to catch his breath to keep up with her. His mind was plotting even then to arrange leave. Whatever it took, double missions, paperwork, he was willing. The "do" was enticing enough, but not so much as a weekend with Vivie.

The loss of so many flight and element leaders brought about the predictable personnel adjustments. Major Kenneth Gallup assumed command of the 350th Squadron. The handsome, dark-haired, 25-year-old New Mexico native with squadron level CO experience was quite popular with the men. If anyone could ease the transition after Dewey Newhart, Gallup was an excellent choice. And so it was, a day later, that Matt was called to his office.

"Tower, I've got to have the best possible men under my command. Whenever we have the losses and changes that the Group sustained yesterday, the job is not just leadership but morale as well." The major flipped open the file before him and studied its contents. "Captain Herrington is assuming command of 'A' Flight and will act as deputy squadron leader. I asked him for a recommendation for 'B' Flight leader and your name was first on the list. How do you feel about that?"

War dictates its own conditions, and Matt had painfully learned over the months that a soldier must think with his head, not his emotions. He relished the promotion and would accept it. How it would affect his availability for the "do" at the Havely estate was a real concern. So much was happening, from different quarters, and needing attention now.

"Can I ask who would take over my element, sir?"

"I think you ought to have some input on that, Tower. Who would you suggest?"

"I'd feel real comfortable with Chuck Shilling, sir. And I'd want Barry Stockton as my wingman if that's okay."

"What about Lieutenant Baker?"

Matt's hands went to his hips as he paced in front of Gallup's desk. "I'd like to keep him in the flight, but he's a line man. He just wants to fight. His instincts are more of the bulldog than the leader."

Gallup's grin widened into laughter as he pushed back his chair and stood up. "Stan's right! You're my man, Tower."

That was the tonic Matt needed, and he lost no time in seeking out Herrington, who was holding court at Auger Inn. Matt took a seat beside him at the bar, keeping his excitement in check as much as possible. "Major, I really appreciate your recommendation to Major Gallup."

Herrington straightened up on the stool and looked at Matt through glassy eyes. His hand rose slowly to the lieutenant's shoulder. "Don't put no mush on me, Tower. Just make me look good, okay?"

Though it was the major's nature to be abrupt, Matt was observing a side of the man seldom exposed. Herrington was down. When he had returned from the second sortie, he found that two of his pilots in the earlier mission were MIA. That night, S-2 confirmed they were lost in combat. The letters to their parents had been extremely difficult. It was a duty Matt's previous level of command had not yet required.

But the captain bars that went with the promotion did much to revive his spirits. He would indeed make Herrington look good.

# CHAPTER 14

# The Great Conspiracy

Fᴏʀ Mᴀᴛᴛ, ᴛʜᴇ command of a flight was an exhilarating responsibility. The paperwork did not excite him, so much so that he began to wonder if he possessed more bulldog than leader himself. But there was no question he would suffer through it patiently, for such opportunities were rare.

As the days passed, he grew anxious about the event at Lord Havely's. His increased responsibilities and the continuing demands for support of ground forces in France had the 353ʳᵈ Group flying every day without a break. Another emergency had come on June 13 when the first of a torrent of flying bombs crashed into the English town of Gravesend on the River Thames east of London.

Hitler's Rachewaffe, or vengeance weapon, had long been suspected, and many bombing missions were attempted to destroy the launch sites. They were extremely well-hidden, and weeks would go by before the bombers could make an impact. The fighter groups would be called upon to search out, at low level, possible locations. They were missions of intense danger due to anti-aircraft positions around such targets. Meantime, the eastern cities of England, especially in and around London, would feel the brunt of hundreds of the V-1 doodlebugs.

As Matt and Vivie exchanged letters and phone calls, she became more concerned that he was not going to get away for the event at Havely Estate. While he shared her disappointment, he had pulled all the strings he dared to. "I've even considered approaching Sergeant McDuff," he joked. "There seems little he can't come up with."

Because of Vivie, Matt's leave time had been exhausted. It was a resigned and dejected flyer who responded dutifully to Major Gallup's summons. The squadron leader rocked back in his chair as Matt stopped before his desk and saluted smartly. "You sent for me, sir?"

"As you were, Captain." Gallup's questioning eyes ran over the flyer before him, which compounded Matt's uneasiness. Momentarily the major leaned forward, his fingers tapping a communiqué on the desktop. "Do you know an RAF Air Commodore named Dennison?"

"No, sir."

"You never heard of him?"

"No, sir. I don't know what an Air Commodore is."

Gallup rubbed his forehead and pursed his lips suspiciously. "A ranking British officer. Does that help?"

"No, sir! May I ask what this is all about, Major?"

"This guy made a direct request to 8th Air Force Headquarters that you be assigned as a representative to some affair that the Allied High Command is hosting."

For Matt the picture came together instantly and a thousand butterflies spooked in his stomach. Without doubt, Major Moore was involved somehow. He shook his head slowly as the grin sneaked across his lips, for Vivie's resourcefulness never ceased to amaze him. *"I don't believe this is happening,"* he reasoned. But if it worked, he would darn well go along with it.

"What?" Gallup snapped, his suspicions still in bloom.

"Err... happy... that is I'd be happy to represent the 353$^{rd}$ Group if it's the major's pleasure."

"It's Headquarters' pleasure, Tower. I'm danged pressed to do without you. I just can't figure out why they would reach way down here to this forsaken little mud puddle of a fighter base and pick you out."

Matt played it cool, thinking out his reply carefully. "Well, you think about it, sir. With you, Colonel Bailey, Colonel Duncan, and the others, I would guess they just went to the least indispensable level on base."

The major stood up, bringing Matt to attention, and slid his hands in his back pockets. "That's good, Tower. That's pretty good. I'll bet you run for political office if you get back home." Finally, he had to give in to a half-smile himself. "I don't know how the Sam Hill you pulled this off, but I've got to hand it to you."

For the next five days Matt applied himself diligently to the business of flight leader. When Friday came around, he had managed a commendable mission record with nothing to endanger his special leave. Then, rendezvous agreed, he boarded the train to meet Vivie at Lord Havely's sprawling estate in the countryside between London and Colchester.

It had been a long rail ride from Ipswich to a small depot in rural Essex County southwest of Colchester. In the States, this platform with its small frame office would have been simply a whistle stop. Matt sat impatiently as the engineer took his time aligning the various cars with loading ramps. At the end of the platform stood a young woman, attired in smart riding habit, rocking on the toes of her boots to scan the slowly passing passenger windows.

Squinting through the late afternoon light, Matt recognized his

English love but did not call to her just yet. As his car eased into position, he used the time to appreciate the woman he had not seen in nearly three weeks. What her dresses had hinted at, the riding habit accentuated grandly. Hair done just so, black jacket, tan jodhpurs and puffy white ascot, he could have eaten her with a spoon. The prankster in him prevailed, however, and he ducked down until his window passed her.

Hurrying to the door, he slipped off the train while she was looking away. Then, placing his bags on the platform, he moved up behind her quietly and waited. The soft scent of perfume and her nearness required maximum effort on his part to remain still. Her arms crossed in frustration as she rocked repeatedly on her toes to search the cars again. "Oh, dear," she murmured. "He's not on the train?"

By now, when he wanted to, Matt could draw up a fair English accent. And so he did to complete his little game. "Just like a bloody Yank, ain't it, miss? They loves 'em and leaves 'em, you know."

She was plainly annoyed by the rude interruption but continued her faithful vigil. "No, that's not true. I'm certain something must have come…." Realizing suddenly that she owed no explanation to a stranger, she turned to face the bold intruder. She was set to give him what for until their eyes met. "Matt!" she squealed, her face glowing with pleasant surprise. "How did you get behind me?"

His roguish grin was quickly interrupted with the pressure of her lips and he responded instantly, folding her in his arms. "I've missed you so much!" she exclaimed as their lips parted. "I was so worried that you wouldn't be able to come."

He took her face in his hands and gently kissed her again. "You're something else, lady. Were you behind that Commodore Dennison business?"

"And what if I was?"

"I ought to bust your britches, that's what!" His scolding never dented her worshipping smile. Indeed, she stood there before him, hands clasped behind her back, ready to endure his worst harangue. "The squadron CO's ticked off at me, and the guys in the flight sent me off with a jealous cold shoulder, so I've got a mile of fences to mend when I get back."

But she would not be intimidated. "Are you quite done, Captain?"

"Evidently," he chuckled in surrender. "You adorable creature, you. I wouldn't have missed this for the world. Where's the lorry... car, whatever."

He retrieved his bags and followed Vivie to the end of the platform. Descending the steps, he searched right and left for a vehicle, but the only thing with wheels had a perfectly matched set of chestnut horses attached. Vivie motioned him in their direction. "Lord Havely would never consent to a guest arriving in a common vehicle," she chirped merrily. "Of course, a few do. The roads are fine, but he prefers to leave civilization behind when he's in the country."

As they approached the elegant Victoria carriage, its coachman, attired in white riding britches and thigh-length gray coat, tipped his black top hat in greeting and reached for Matt's luggage. "Evening, sir."

"This is Edward," Vivie explained. "He's Lord Havely's man about."

Edward, with the weathered face of old English peasant stock, easily could have sprung from a chapter of Dickens. It was quite a scene, and Vivie took great pleasure in Matt's amazement as he circled the harnessed team. "This is some kind of horse flesh!" he exclaimed. "What breed are they?"

"Oh, they be Hackney, sir." The older man seemed pleased at Matt's interest. He returned from the luggage rack and placed an affectionate pat on the neck of the nearest horse. "From his Lordship's own stock, they are, as were the sire and dam before them. This youngster here is Sirius and this fellow is Rigel."

"Strange names."

"Rightly so, sir," the coachman chuckled. "But his Lordship is quite the astronomer. They be two of the brightest stars in the heavens."

Matt ran his hand along the animal's powerful shoulder in obvious appreciation. "About 15 hands?" he questioned the coachman.

"That they are. You've a keen eye, sir."

"Must I whinny to share the attention?" Vivie interrupted.

"You know better than that," Matt replied as he reached for her hand. "Besides, you've got a much prettier mane."

"Good recovery, sir," Edward whispered as he moved away to the coachman's seat.

He kept the horses at a steady pace, granting his passengers a refreshing countryside drive. The well-sprung carriage negotiated road and lane with equal ease, gently rocking its occupants as it progressed. They were content to interlock arms and hold hands, sharing and enjoying the clop of hooves, gentle breeze, and scenic beauty slipping by. *"This has to be Heaven,"* Matt thought as his mind's eye compared it to the 353$^{rd}$'s base. *"What a break!"*

Within a couple of miles, the carriage passed through a gateway braced with tapering walls of grayish stone. In the distance, at the end of a century-old tree-lined drive, three-story Havely Hall with its twin turrets commanded the horizon.

Edward's seasoned hands reigned in the horses precisely at the front steps, where a footman assisted Vivie from the carriage. Matt followed her along a well-landscaped walk leading to the massive front door. "Where is everybody?"

"Preparing for dinner at this hour, no doubt," Vivie replied. "They make quite a thing of it. Besides, with the 'do' tomorrow, most won't arrive until then."

The marble foyer contained an exquisitely curved stairway to the upper floors. Guarding the archway to the great hall, two shiny suits of armor caught the glow from a massive chandelier. Matt struggled to suppress the gawk of a tourist, his manner suggesting previous experience with such surroundings. Only the butler, impeccably attired in formal tails, appeared to harbor any questions on that matter, though he treated the American flyer as nobly as the others. "May I take your hat, sir? His Lordship will receive you in the library, if you please."

Vivie, having visited the estate on other occasions, was at home among all the pomp and took great pleasure in watching Matt's reactions. "Come on, poppet, Lord Havely is quite charming."

The butler tapped politely on the library door then opened it to precede the young couple. "Captain Tower and Mrs. Davis, sir," he announced as though they might have been of some notoriety.

The uniformed officer Matt did not recognize. He knew Vivie's father well enough and had to assume the tall aristocrat in a smoking jacket to be Lord Havely. He was an imposing fellow indeed, with a prominent wide mustache, which matched his wavy white hair. He was so profoundly British in stature, with high cheeks and slightly recessed chin, that Matt could only think of a kindly old walrus. "Come in! Come in!" he ordered in a raspy baritone conditioned by age.

Matt took the extended hand and nodded politely. "It's my pleasure, your Lordship."

"I'm sure you know Major Moore, MI5's Suffolk coordinator, and this is Colonel Burgess, also with His Majesty's intelligence service." As handshakes and greetings went around, Matt was pleased to better understand the significance of Vivie's father's position. His modesty belied the responsibility and authority the man wielded.

"The women have retired to prepare for dinner," his Lordship advised. "We were to have a scotch before following the ladies. Would you care to join us, Captain?"

Suddenly it had become very much a man's world, and Vivie wished to change for the evening as well. She took Matt's hand and squeezed it inconspicuously. "Your Lordship, gentlemen, if you will excuse me, I still have a bit of unpacking." They nodded politely as she left the room.

Though Matt never saw an order given, the butler reappeared, balancing the drinks on a small silver tray. While the young flyer was not prone to liquor, he felt it propitious, in the company of his host, to at least hold the glass. Lord Havely, turning to the three men before him, raised his glass abruptly, "To England!" he exclaimed, to which a chorus of "Hear, hear!" responded, for two of these men had seen their country firsthand in its "finest hour." "To America!" obtained a like response as the Britishers looked to Matt. "To the early demise of the bloody Hun!" brought a hushed, almost reverent, "Hear, hear!" from the four of them as glasses touched lips.

"Well, young man, we've heard a bit about you," the nobleman said. "Fighter pilot, I understand."

"Yes, sir."

"Good show! Vivian tells us you've shot down three enemy fighters."

"Two fighters and a light bomber."

"We'll drink to that! Every little dent in Goering's Luftwaffe is a nail in the Hun's coffin." The nobleman ushered his guests to the chairs before the fire. "I met him once, you know. Lady Havely and I were touring Germany in the 1930s, before the war. Brown Shirts everywhere."

As Lord Havely paused to sip his drink there was little doubt he loved to tell a story. The larger the audience the more he seemed into it. "I served with Thomas Cubitt in the Great War." He laughed at the thought. "That's General Sir Thomas Astley Cubitt, if you please! In the last years of the war, I served as his adjutant in the 38th Welsh Guards. Grand fellow, Cubitt. Very much the warrior."

His Lordship cleared his throat and pressed on with the adventure. "This Goering was a rather charming fellow. We were guests at a British Embassy reception where he stood in for Hitler. Quite a large chap, but spry. Very much the Prussian gentleman. It was no surprise to me when they made a bloody fool of Chamberlain."

Colonel Arthur Burgess was at least 60, much more the peer of Vivie's father than the older Lord. Nursing his drink, he had held his peace during the nobleman's discourse, but now his competitive instinct surfaced. The three men had evidently known each other for some time and Matt could sense a certain satisfaction in their game of one-upmanship.

The colonel took advantage of the opening, "Yes, I remember the Brown Shirts quite well. Particularly in Stuttgart not long after Hindenburg died. We were on holiday and the streets were filled with people, banners everywhere. All across Germany they were reenacting the president's funeral procession. We jolly well made our desire known to take photographs and were promptly taken to an upper-story room. It commanded a grand view of the street, which was filled with Brown Shirts. They were rather civil at that point."

Robert Moore was every bit as congenial as the rest, but not so talkative. More studious by nature, he was subtly appraising the young American with whom his daughter was so taken. "I say, Captain, have you traveled abroad?"

Matt had felt the evaluation from the first day they met. His strategy in dealing with it had been one of good-natured patience. "Canada, sir. And of course, now England." He reflected for a moment and grinned. "I guess France and Germany from a 20,000-foot perspective."

They had yet to really talk together. The older man, while never hostile in his manner, had made no attempt to encourage familiarity. But the American flyer's influence on his daughter had become profound, and a standoff policy was no longer feasible for either. It was now that Robert Moore would make the initial overture. "You will be joining us for the shoot in the morning, I trust?"

"I'm looking forward to that, sir. Your Lordship, I very much appreciate the invitation," Matt added, turning to his host.

"Delighted, delighted, young man. Perhaps you'd care to choose your fowling piece. We'll go to the trophy room and see what fits you," the nobleman declared as he rose to lead the way.

The room, lined with rich paneling, was stocked with martial curiosities, assorted game trophies, and a five-foot gun cabinet exhibiting an assortment of sporting arms. Matt was impressed. "Good heavens, sir, you have quite a collection!"

"Thinned down a bit, I'm afraid. We all contributed pieces to the Home Guard at the beginning of the war. Rather discouraging to see a fine gun in the hands of some ruddy beggar mucking about in the dark." Lord Havely hefted a sample or two of the double bar-rels, sighting and bracing to his shoulder, then handed one to the admiring captain. "Try this one, old chap."

The balance of the weapon was excellent, lighter than Matt had handled before. An exquisite grain pattern showed through the smooth walnut stock. Gun buff that he was, Matt seldom had seen wood fitted to metal so painstakingly. "This is beautiful! What make is it, sir?"

"Make, indeed! You'll not find this piece in a village ironmongery, Captain. You're holding a Purdey & Son 12-gauge. And these two, a Churchill and a Rigby. Try them and decide which you prefer."

Lord Havely's attention was directed to the door where the butler stood attentively. "Yes, Wiggins?"

"Lady Havely requests dinner at half past, sir."

"Very good, very good," the nobleman agreed. "It's not cricket to keep dear Martha waiting, gentlemen. I suggest we repair to our rooms and dress for dinner."

Matt chuckled to himself. In his case, dressing for dinner was the simple act of freshening up, changing his shirt, and don-ning his pinks and green uniform. Hat would not be needed. He was delighted to see the same for Colonel Burgess. Vivie and her mother were waiting in the anteroom to the dining hall when Matt returned. His reunion with Etta, attired in a lovely black dinner gown, was warm and cordial.

As well, this was his first time to see Vivie in formal attire, and she smiled at his evident approval. A darker green, sleeveless dinner gown and short triple strand of pearls with matching earrings was a tasteful combination. Roedean had prepared these ladies well.

The formalities increased as Lord and Lady Havely arrived on the scene. Her bearing was that of noble birth, but graciously tempered. She must have been a tremendous asset to Lord Havely in the circles they frequented. A bit plump, gray hair styled in empire lift, she wore the tasseled powder-blue V-neck gown extremely well. A more interesting group for dinner Matt could not have envisioned.

The great table could accommodate up to 50 dinner guests plus their hosts. But tonight it had been shortened for a cozier setting with but two of its 10 grand candelabrums. There was never a boring moment in the conversation, what with Lord Havely's recollections of service in India, and the contributions of Lady Havely on the social and protocol whirl of government life compounded by war. Her Ladyship's curiosity about their American guest surfaced repeatedly, with Matt questioned suddenly on family matters of life in the States.

Under the table Vivie squeezed his hand reassuringly but he took it all well, using the opportunity to fill in his own gaps on British life. Especially the environment Vivie grew up in, for everything about her was of deepest interest to him. Though the evening and the company were delightful, he had grown impatient to have her to himself. Imagining how it might go if they were stuck in the drawing room, he fashioned a plan of escape. When the dinner party adjourned, he positioned himself near Lord Havely. "Vivie tells me you raise Hackneys, sir."

"Indeed. And thoroughbreds. We breed them for polo and racing, you know. Marvelous animal, the thoroughbred. Did you know that all thoroughbreds can be traced to three stallions?"

Matt realized quickly that the nobleman took his horses seriously and if he were not careful, he might be drawn into a rather lengthy equestrian discourse. "No, sir. I would have thought the lineage to be much broader."

"Oh, my, no! It all began in the late 1600s, you see, with Darley Arabian, Godolphin Barb, and Byerly Turk."

Lord Havely retrieved a box of custom-rolled cigars from the drawer of a huge, old glass-paned secretary and offered them to his male guests. Matt was now wrestling with two problems: how to avoid the cigar and tactfully exit Vivie and himself. "Vivie offered to show me the stables, sir. Would you mind if we went down to have a look?"

"Very little light left at this hour," the nobleman responded as he pushed the box of coronas at Matt. "I should think you would do better in the morning."

Vivie, glued to Matt's side, came to the rescue. "Tomorrow is such a busy day, your Lordship. What with the shoot and preparations for the evening, we felt this might be a better time."

The old Britisher seemed perplexed, for no specific duties of the morrow would incur to the guests of Havely Hall. But as he viewed the expressions of the young people before him, a bit like two children seeking permission of a parent, he quickly perceived that their interest in visiting the stables had only a bit to do with horses. "Humm. Perhaps you're right, my dear," he answered, smoothing his mustache to obscure a wry smile. "Indeed, indeed. I'll have Wiggins bring you a torch."

Lady Havely, attentive by nature to the happenings around her, saw the young couple leaving and turned to her husband. "Willie, where are they going? I was looking forward to some time with the captain."

"I'm sure you were, my dear, but they wanted to visit the stables."

"Oh? Does the captain have an interest in horses?"

Lord Willie paused to fire up the cigar, then smiled broadly at his wife. "Well, I should think one filly in particular."

At the foyer, Wiggins stood with a lantern lighted and ready, which he passed to a surprised Matt. "Thank you," Vivie smiled as she primped in the great mirror. "We were going to the stables."

"Very good, sir. May I suggest the north path at night."

"The north path," Matt repeated as he ushered Vivie through the door. "Wiggins, I think that deserves a cigar. Have one on me," he added, pressing the smoke into the hand of the astonished butler.

"Err…. err…. thank you, sir."

Taking Vivie's arm as they stepped to the walkway, Matt could suppress his curiosity no longer. "How the devil did he know to do that?"

"What?"

"To have that lantern ready. It's mysterious, you know that? He brought me a drink and nobody told him to. He ends up at the door with a lantern and nobody told him to."

"He's just a very good butler, that's all," she laughed. "What else mystifies you, my brave soldier?"

He pulled her to him playfully and wrapped an arm around her waist. "Oh… I'd say, why women spend time primping in a mirror when they're going out in the dark to see horses."

"We always primp for someone special. I've missed you, Matt Tower. Terribly!"

They had waited patiently for the seclusion of the path before stopping to face each other. The lamp's meager glow was just enough to chase the shadows from her tilted face and soft, round shoulders. "Poppet," she whispered.

It was the third time she had addressed him with that endearing term, and he found he could only respond with his eyes and arms, which was exactly what she wanted. Tenderly, he kissed her temples, brushing soft twists of hair with his lips, stirring little whiffs of delicate perfume. Her hands left his neck and eased their way to the sides of his face, gently steering his lips to hers. "Humm."

After a time, they began walking again. "I think we should see the stables," Vivie chuckled, her voice still in a whisper. "Lady Havely is an inquisitive one, you know. There's a new foal she's quite pleased with. I'm certain you'll be questioned."

"Okay, mommy," he whispered back. "Little Matt will behave. But must we keep whispering out here in the middle of nowhere?"

"No," she laughed. "Come on, here's the stable."

They were greeted with the curious stirring of animals as he eased the door open. "Here," Vivie motioned. "This stall. Isn't he lovely?"

Matt raised the lantern to reveal a perky bay colt, gangly legs as yet unsteady, nursing a late snack. The mare stood her ground dutifully, ears cocked forward, nostrils flared and blowing rapidly to test the intruders' intentions. Vivie's lilting baby talk seemed reassuring enough, and the mother horse settled down to her chore. "Now, what's this little fellow's name?" Matt asked as they leaned over the stall door.

"He hasn't one as yet. Edward says Lord Havely is still consulting the stars." She studied the face of the man beside her, reaching over to tuck a lock of his hair in place. He was still thinner than when they first met, and as the evening progressed she had grown increasingly aware of his moments of preoccupation. "You've deep thoughts just now, darling. Is it something you can share with me?"

He was reluctant to risk spoiling her evening with the combat losses, which still weighed on his mind. But the concern in her voice told him she would not be put off easily. "Oh, it's nothing really. I was just curious about your father. Lord Havely referred to him as a coordinator. What's that all about?"

"I'm sorry I couldn't talk about it before now, darling. It's all quite hush-hush. He's involved with Colonel Burgess in MI5 domestic intelligence work."

"I would never have dreamed that," Matt replied, his interest picking up. "I saw him as maybe a retired officer. How long's that been going on?"

"Before the war, when the fifth column was so active. You wouldn't believe how it was. There were Hitler Youth parading on London streets and some women were wearing swastika jewelry, if you can imagine that."

"You never cease to amaze me, dear lady. I wouldn't be surprised if you told me you were Mata Hari reincarnated."

"Oh, dear no!" she laughed. "Nothing as glamorous as that, I'm sure."

Matt nodded in amusement, a tiny smile teasing his lips. "That's how you were able to get me out here. And here I am trying to make time with a British intelligence officer's daughter. I'll probably be 'accidentally' shot in the field tomorrow."

"I certainly hope not! Dad may be a bit inquisitive, but he's really an old moggy at heart. Besides," she added, playfully smoothing the lapels of his jacket, "it appears you're doing a rather muzzy job of making time with me."

"Well, we can't have that now, can we?" he responded, his arms gathering her to him. He had to but look into those clear, loving, blue eyes to know he wanted to spend the rest of his life doing exactly that. She had fallen in love with him, he was certain now, but the time was not yet right to press her for commitment. "Do you have any idea what you mean to me?"

"Noooo," she smiled. "But I'm dying to hear!"

"I'll bet you are!" he chuckled. "I'd be smarter to keep you guessing. Women are terrible that way, once they think they have you in their pocket."

She loved his smile and the devilish twinkle in his eye when he teased. How reassuring his arms were: secure, comfortable, freeing her more and more over the weeks from the anxieties of earlier years. Her expressions of affection for him were much more candid now. "I had the distinct feeling that you rather liked my pockets, Lieutenant."

"Pockets," he whispered. "Sleeves... collar... buttons... bows... eyes... ears... lips and nose!"

Her arms encircled his neck as she rose on her toes until their lips touched. There were no doubts now that she loved him very much and that his and her happiness were more one and the same. He draped his jacket around her shoulders against the chill of night as they settled on a bale of hay by the feed room. There, in the suspended world of lovers, more intimate expressions of affection reflected a growing confidence one in the other.

Later, when discretion prevailed, he pulled her to her feet and adjusted the warming jacket. She had lost a shoe, which sent him fishing in the fluffy straw while she patted her hair in place. "You're falling apart, love," he jested.

"Is that why you're turning me in so soon?" she asked.

"I should think not, to use your favorite expression. It's nearly 10 and we've been gone a good while. Officer and gentleman that I am, it's time to see the lady safely home. Besides, I have to face your father tomorrow, and we don't want to fuel any suspicions, now do we?"

"I should think not!" she chuckled merrily as she squeezed him closer. It was an endearing quality, his caring, his respect for her, so refreshing from the usual Tommy seeking her favor.

Unfamiliar with the entrances to the old mansion, the front door seemed a logical choice to Matt. Was it appropriate to give the latch a try and slip in, he wondered, or announce themselves with a tap of the iron knocker? As a guest, etiquette suggested the latter. Predictably, Wiggins was in attendance and ushered them in. "Good evening, sir. Good evening, madam. Did you find your way?"

"Oh, yes," Matt replied as he retrieved his jacket. "Thanks for the suggestion."

Vivie, her manner quite content, moved with long, slow steps toward the arch to the great hall as Wiggins dutifully assisted Matt into his jacket. While the young flyer fastened the row of brass buttons, the butler leaned toward him. "May I make another suggestion, sir?"

"Sure, Wiggins. What's on your mind?"

"Would you and Mrs. Davis be joining the others or retiring for the evening?" he asked in a half whisper.

"We had planned to join them. Why?"

"Then may I offer an observation, sir?" Matt nodded attentively. "It appears that your lips have been rather chapped by the night air. It also appears that the wind has lodged bits of straw in Mrs. Davis' hair."

For a moment Matt could only stare at the butler, who never batted an eye. Then, shaking his head slowly, the young flyer had to smile. "Wiggins, I don't know what Lord Havely is paying you, but you're bloody well worth double it!"

For the first time, Matt saw the old servant's thin lips quiver against a half smile. "Very good, sir. Thank you, sir."

"Vivie!" Matt called, moving quickly to her side. "Wait a minute!"

# CHAPTER 15

# Competition at the Havely Estate

**T**HE COCK'S CROW, heralding a gray dawn, stirred Matt to consciousness. It was not that he was so easily awakened, but more the drill of innumerable early morning missions. After reassuring himself that no one would roust him from bed, he dared to indulge in a moment of reverie. Even that would be short lived, compliments of two competitive roosters somewhere on the grounds below.

The irony of the situation amused Matt as he considered his Lordship's guests, in the grandeur of Havely Hall, being treated to common barnyard cackle. It reminded him of his last week of leave at his father's home in Augusta's fashionable Hill section. With the war effort in full swing, palatial and humble home alike housed those crowing and egg-laying feathered friends, along with the proverbial victory garden vegetable patch.

An hour later the hunting party was treated to fresh golden eggs with toast and smoked herring. A jovial time it was as the Britishers baited each other into bets on the outcome of the shoot. Matt had no formal hunting gear but had made do rather well with flight boots and old summer uniform pants.

"I say, gentlemen!" Lord Havely declared over the clamor of his guests. "I know quite well the marksmanship, or lack of it, between my two old friends. I propose that Arthur and I take on Robert and the captain. The rest of you pair up as you wish." All seemed to agree so Matt nodded his approval, though he had no way of knowing any of their firearm capabilities.

"Now, I propose a wager or two between the teams," his Lordship said. "Let's say five quid for the first double and a quid per bird for the number shot between the teams."

The young flyer assumed the arrangement implied that Vivie's father and the Lord were the best shots, thus evening the teams. That is until Robert Moore patted him on the shoulder and remarked, "The old boy seems to put a bit of stock in you, Captain. I hope you're up to it."

Matt chuckled to himself as he realized that the Squire of Havely Hall was a slick one and had every intention of winning, even to stacking the deck among shooters. However, in Matt's case, it did place the courter in the cart with the father of the courted, a welcome and anticipated arrangement for both.

The Spaniels were beside themselves: anxious, straining on their leashes, eager for the scent of game. Edward and his son, Amon, a husky blond lad of 16, had their hands full bringing order among the six canines and readying the horse-drawn carts. Matt loved every minute of it as though he were home in the treasured fields of south Richmond County. Only there it would have been Pointers, or Henry Matthews' brace of fine Setters.

They rode for a good 20 minutes, chatting and swapping stories, as the three senior members of the party did all possible to unnerve each other. As the joshing went, Matt and Vivie's father seemed to be getting the worst of it since the young American did not feel privileged to raze his host.

Amon, driving the cart Matt was in, evidently took the kidding personally as though he had been left with the hind quarter of the hunting party. He slowed the horse a bit to gain some distance between the carts, then turned back to his passengers. "Never you mind, now," he grinned. "I ain't as dim as they thinks. I'm in these fields and I know where the newest growth of heather is."

"Yeah, but your dad does too, doesn't he?" Matt challenged.

"That he does, sir. But he goes where his Lordship wants him to go."

The two teammates grinned silently and nodded encouragement to each other. How satisfying it would be if the old nobleman's trickery should backfire on him. "Carry on then, young man," Robert prodded. "We'll rest easy in your capable hands."

As the hunting party entered the first field, the dogs were set free and bounded quickly into the lead. Edward controlled them well with a whistle and hand motions, dividing them into sectors across the field. Matt perceived that this was serious business. "Birds, sir!" Edward called out, gesturing to the edge of the field some 50 yards ahead.

What a sight greeted Matt as he stood in the cart. Three Spaniels backing each other, a sight to warm the heart of any bird hunter. He had had no opportunity to test-fire his shotgun, another convenient oversight of his host, but he had not expected an early turn anyway. To his surprise, Lord Havely motioned for his two opponents to take the first covey. "Let's go, sir, before he changes his mind," Matt urged with a wink at Vivie's father.

The two moved cautiously through the calf-high grass, peering intently at the lead dog. "You have a go at it first, Captain," Robert offered. "I'll back you up."

Matt felt a tingle run through his fingers, for it had been nearly two years since he had lifted a sporting arm. The pressure of several sets of eyes, wondering how the Yank would do, didn't help either. He sucked in a deep breath and released it slowly to settle himself, which summoned instinct to the rescue. "Hold boy... hold... boy," he called softly to the lead dog.

With gun stock under his arm Matt watched the Spaniel's head, for that would tell him the direction the birds were moving and their likely flight path. The dog's nose inched slowly to the left. He wondered if the signals in England were different from those back home. "Close, boy.... Easy... easy... close."

The sudden wing flutters of six birds pounding the air in as many directions delivered a rush of adrenaline to all near the flush. Experience prevailed, though, as Matt fought the urge to spray the quickly shrinking targets. Picking a bird straight out, he blocked it in his sights and fired. He had only time to see a few feathers fly before a stray from the right attempted to rejoin its group. It was a natural pickup in his field of fire, and Matt swung instinctively for lead. The double barrel spent its remaining shell with a second loud crack, and the plump Red Grouse locked its wings in a spiraling glide to the ground.

Things moved quickly, faster than quail back home, and Matt was uncertain of the results until Robert Moore moved to his side. "By Jove!" he gasped. "Two on the rise. I say!"

The Spaniels were well at the task of retrieving as Amon came running up to bag the game. "Whacko, sir!" he cried, a broad grin stretching the chunky cheeks to their limit. "That'll show 'em a thing or two!"

By then Matt was feeling pretty good about it himself and pleased with the performance of the gun. So smoothly balanced and light in his hands, he felt he had cheated. His two competitors stood motionless in their cart while Edward smiled smugly from the driver's seat. "Bloody good shooting, Captain," Colonel Burgess declared, willing to give the performance its due. Lord Havely, on the other hand, managed a polite, "Nice one," his body language signaling all too well that he had not expected such results.

"Okay, team," Matt whispered to his party. "Let's be good sports about it. There's a lot of morning left."

But nothing could wipe the smile from the faces of Robert Moore and the young Amon. It was justice served, the chickens coming home to roost all rolled into one. And Vivie's father, not the best of fowlers, was utterly delighted. "Well done, old chap!" he grinned as they mounted the cart.

Lord Havely made short order of separating the two hunting parties after that. He was five quid down with the first gunfire and quite determined to recoup his position in his favorite fields. So Amon was free to use his talents, and he turned the cart for the west hedgerow dividing the two huge fields.

"You've been shooting for a time, haven't you, Captain?" Robert Moore inquired as the cart rumbled along.

"Since I was 13, sir. My grandfather and my dad loved the outdoors and I started going with them."

"Well, I'm rather good with a rifle, but wing shots are another matter." He settled back, shifting to find what comfort was available on the wooden bench. There was team spirit now, which did much to break the ice between the older man and the American flyer. Robert felt comfortable directing the conversation to more personal matters. "Vivian tells me you're from an industrial family."

Matt grinned at the description of his parents' livelihood, tactfully employed to explore the depth of his family resources. "Actually, it's supplies, sir. Mill and industrial supplies. We have a lot of textile plants around Augusta."

"Can we speak candidly, Captain?"

"Certainly, sir," Matt replied, his stomach tightening a bit in anticipation.

"I'm rather direct at times, you see, a failing Mrs. Moore would no doubt attest to. But there are some things that concern me, and since you're involved, I think we should discuss them."

Matt sat attentively, figuring it best to leave the ball in the Major's court until he saw where the conversation was going. The older man adjusted his cap and leaned back on the side of the cart, his left arm running along the edge. "You see, Vivian has changed quite a bit in the last few months. I'm certain you know something of her earlier circumstances. Well, she never really regained her spirit as far as her mother and I could tell. Eventually, friends encouraged her to serve in the WVS. It became an outlet for her, something she could do to fight back at the things that had hurt her."

Robert Moore did not try to shield his own hurt, plainly written in his eyes and the set of his weathered face. It was a moment before he felt ready to continue. "The feeling of being needed again seemed to sustain her somewhat. But recently she's been much brighter, more alive than I and her mother have seen in a while. It seems to have something to do with you, Captain."

"Umm, I hope I haven't done anything wrong, sir," Matt replied cautiously.

The major shook his head reassuringly, his eyes searching the young flyer's face intently. "The fact is that she's quite taken with you. It's progressed to such a point that she could be terribly hurt if your intentions were not sincere."

The ball was suddenly in Matt's court and he was keenly aware of it. "I understand that, sir. I care about her very much."

"Mrs. Moore feels that you do. But I must be very honest with you, Lieutenant. I'm rather skeptical about the matter. Frankly, I had hoped that if she were attracted to another man, he would be British." Robert thought for a moment then leaned forward, a brief smile deepening the wrinkles at the edges of his eyes. "Nothing personal, young man. Just the desires of a father's heart."

"Third generation is the best I can do, sir," Matt responded, returning the smile.

Robert's face drained a little as he looked again to the passing meadow before speaking. "She's our only child. I held her the day she was born.... A tiny thing nestled in the blanket, pink and helpless, little eyes straining to focus on this ruddy conk," he added, touching a finger to his nose. "She held my finger on her first steps." He drew a breath and expelled it quickly. "Then it seemed no time at all that she was a gangly lass busy about school. Quite pretty by the time she left for Roedean. Oh, she had the attention of all the young men on the beach at Felixstowe when we were on holiday."

"I can tell that you and Mrs. Moore are proud of her and that you care deeply about her." It was a rather evident statement, but Matt felt a comment was needed, likely expected, at that point. And he meant it. "She's very fortunate to have that kind of love, sir."

"She's been a marvelous daughter, given us nothing but the greatest pleasure. It was quite painful to see her in such tragic circumstances, and I bloody well don't wish to see her hurt again."

The glint in the major's eyes as he spoke his piece assured Matt that the man could be a bear of an adversary if his cub was threatened. Strangely, the thought did not provoke the American flyer but gave him new respect for the father on the opposite bench who would tolerate even a Yank for the sake of his daughter. Matt wanted, indeed must have, the blessing and goodwill of Vivie's family in his courtship. As much as he loved and wanted her, a family row would be yet another painful episode in the life of a very special and brave young woman.

The discussion had left both men in a reflective and sober mood. The relationship between father and suitor would most assuredly be settled that morning. Candor demanded candor in Matt's mind. With a man like Vivie's father, credibility lay in honest response, and the suitor chose his words carefully. "Major Moore, I hold your daughter in the highest respect. From the first day I saw her I knew she was different. There was a certain quality there that I have never experienced in another woman. Yes, she's very pretty. But I saw *pretty* more as *lovely*, one of many qualities like character, bearing, intelligence. And since I've known her and something of her family, I understand how that's all come about."

It was difficult for the young American to tell if he had overstated his position, for the older man sat tight-lipped as they creaked along the country path. Eventually, he folded his arms and turned back to face Matt. "I must say you have a way with words, young man. You're quite the nobbler."

"My interest in Vivie is sincere, sir."

"There's a bit of war ahead, Captain," the Major said, seemingly oblivious to Matt's appeal. "When it's over, the world will never be quite the same. I've lived through one war, and there can be unforeseen consequences. Hopes and plans so clear just now, only to be dashed at the whim of fate."

Up to that point Matt had assumed the lightly veiled apprehension to be simply a father's concern when an unknown male enters his daughter's life. If that played a part at all, it was but the tip of a deeper troubling. A chilling uneasiness gripped the young lieutenant, for the major's evading eyes held premonitions so uncomfortable that his mind refused to verbalize them.

"Birds!" Amon called from his forward position.

The sudden change of subject brought relief to Robert's face as he turned to check the position of their three dogs. It was not that easy for Matt, who continued to wrestle with the remarks. There were personal implications, and he could not dismiss them as simply the philosophical lamenting of an old soldier.

"Tally ho, old chap!" Robert called to his hesitant American partner. "We'll lose the birds!"

Matt forced his thoughts back to the hunt and his first priority, that of gaining the confidence of Vivie's father. Gathering his gun, he smiled and slid out of the cart. "It's your go this time, Major," he encouraged.

"I suppose it is," Robert replied flatly, exhibiting the chagrin of one destined to let the team down. He stalked ahead hesitantly, carrying the shotgun close to his chest, as though wishing for a false alarm. He did extremely well with rifle and pistol, but his experience with scattershot at flying targets was spotty.

"Can I make a suggestion, sir?"

Robert Moore nodded affirmatively at his self-appointed tutor.

"Place the butt of the stock just under your armpit with the barrel well out in front." The major cast a half-believing glance in Matt's direction and obeyed reluctantly.

They were very close to the dogs now, and Matt let Robert take the lead. "We'll get a bird this time, too, Major. When you hear the covey flush, move the butt to your shoulder fast, black out the first bird you see going straight out, and fire."

"First bird straight out, and fire," Robert repeated.

"And pick one bird. Don't try for two." The comment extracted another questioning glance from the major.

The lead Spaniel's head was steady and the birds were cowering. They would scatter broadly on the break and tax the best efforts of a slow shooter. Matt was doubly glad he had instructed as he did. "You'll have plenty of time now," he reassured the intent gunman just in front of him.

The four-bird covey broke randomly and the major, still mumbling the instructions to himself, moved the gun to the challenge. From his rear position, Matt knew the bird was dead before the gun fired. The major had followed his drill to the letter. "By Jove, I think I hit him!"

"Nice shot, sir!" Matt exclaimed as he watched the dog fetch. The major's face was aglow with success, exactly the reward his instructor had wanted. "We'll work on a cross shot or a double next time. I think you're gonna have a good day, sir."

"Humm, we'll see, we'll see," Robert replied, still sporting traces of the smile and a kindling of confidence.

They both ignored the crack of gunfire a few hundred yards to the east, resisting any intimidation from the competition. The major grinned broadly as they climbed back in the cart. "You know, I wouldn't put it past that old geezer to spend a cartridge or two just to worry us."

As they seated themselves, Matt felt it best not to press the earlier subject right away. The mood was jovial, spirits high, and the conversation best kept spontaneous. Robert Moore examined his kill with the scrutiny of a diamond merchant over a precious stone, finally laying it to rest under the seat with the other two birds. "Well, Captain, as you said, there's a lot of morning left."

"I'm curious to know what I've been invited to, Major. Who's coming to the shindig tonight?"

"Shindig?" Robert chuckled. "Interesting word. I never cease to marvel at the American vernacular."

"Likewise, sir," Matt jested in lighthearted defense. "I thought I spoke the language until I came to England. I'm still wrestling with things like *wallah*, *airscrew*, and which is the first floor."

The major chuckled again. "Indeed, indeed." Far more at ease now, he liked the spirit of the young American's tit-for-tat. "Well, as to the event this evening, you'll see a number of your own officers and a like contingency of British. An assortment of government officials to spoil the fun, no doubt."

It seemed only minutes until Amon called "birds" again. The boy was true to his word; he knew the game haunts. The dogs' point was farther away than the last, and Matt used the time for another lesson with the major who, with recent success, had become a more willing student. Coached on cross shooting, he would try for a double this time.

Robert was a different man as he approached this covey. Alert, positioned, but still mumbling instructions to himself. This three-bird covey flushed almost in unison, and Matt held his breath as the gun butt sprang to his partner's shoulder. The first shot was another clean kill. Then the barrel wavered after a crossing bird. It was a good try; a few feathers fluttered in the breeze, but the bird escaped injury. "That's all right, Major! It was a good try. You just paused your swing. We'll fix that."

A rare clear day and plenty of birds kept the conversation light as the two men talked of their earlier years, of likes and dislikes, finding common areas of agreement and a few of disagreement. It accomplished the difficult ice breaking far better than formal inquisition, and by the time they rejoined Lord Havely's party, there was a fine cache of grouse as well.

Amid the yapping of Spaniels and the clop of horse hooves, the rivals reigned to a halt at the rear of the ancient mansion. Like smug poker players with a red grouse up their sleeves, they were eager to claim victory as the drivers began placing birds on the weathered hunt table.

The clamor attracted servants from the kitchen and roused the curiosity of the ladies who gathered on the mansion's broad patio. Lord Havely was in excellent spirits as he strode between the two tables, confidently observing the count. "How many is that, Edward?"

"Twenty so far, sir."

Robert Moore was not about to give quarter or massage the nobleman's ego and he strode just as confidently. "Amon, what's the count?"

"Eighteen with that one," the youth replied as he placed another bird on the table. He was smiling rather sheepishly and Matt could tell he was deliberately keeping the count behind that of his father.

As the score reached 29 to 26, the tension grew to delightful proportions as did the incessant joshing between the teams. At 36 to 30, with the bags hanging limper and limper, Lord Havely feigned the good sport. "I say now, the outcome is quite evident. I suggest that we cease the count here, settle up, and leave a bit of mystery in the bags."

Colonel Burgess stood smiling, puffing on his pipe, for he knew the nature of their opponents and doubted that his Lordship's appeal would prove popular with them. Robert Moore turned to his partner, his expression reflecting outwardly, for the first time, the question of limiting their loss on the wager. "Well, Captain, how does it strike you? Should we call it a good day's sport?"

"In the States we have a saying about a pig in a poke. I think we ought to see the last bird, myself."

If they lost, the money would be a minor point to Vivie's father. But to watch the old nobleman squirm through the count would be well worth it anyway. "We'll see the last bird, then," he grinned defiantly.

Edward placed his final, number 40, on the table and stepped back. All eyes went to Amon, who, alternately grinning and frowning, was still rummaging. "Thirty-seven, thirty-eight, thirty-nine...." and the sack was empty.

"Blimey!" the little guy exclaimed, shaking the limp cloth. "I counted them kills meself and they was more birds than that!"

"Well, there they are!" Lord Havely declared as he sported a winner's smirk. "Bloody close, but clearly a win!"

The losers had only their spunk for consolation. They had stood to the last and congratulated themselves accordingly. "Belt up, Willie!" Robert snapped in annoyance. "We had the first double and there's still your whack for that, you know."

In Lord Havely's eyes, that was a side bet and detracted nothing from the win, so he was puzzled at the sudden glow consuming the major's face. "The double!" Robert exclaimed as he turned to his American partner. "The first kills didn't go in the sack! Remember, we put them under the seat."

Like kids at a soccer meet, the two scrambled for the cart, much to the delight of the patio audience. In they dived, hands thrashing through the floorboard clutter until the three feathery treasures were uncovered. Robert Moore shot his hands into the air, each clutching a bird. Matt lifted the third. "See here!" the major shouted. "Forty! Forty-one! Forty-two!"

Spreading the wings of the birds, the new winners flew them triumphantly to the counting table. *Dumbfounded* most appropriately bespoke his Lordship's facial contortions. He might have digested a tie, but a clear two-bird win had never entered his mind. Colonel Burgess' rasping laugh split the silence. "By the gods, Willie, I believe they bloody well have us!"

Young Amon was beside himself as he danced a jig to keep from exploding. It was plain to see that Edward was quite satisfied with his son's performance, though he managed proper restraint for the sake of his employer. Robert Moore caught the youngster and threw an arm over his shoulder. "You're one fine gillie, young man. Well done!"

Shrewd as he had been in pairing the hunting partners, Lord Havely was now just as quick to join Colonel Burgess in honoring their wager. As the British money exchanged hands, Matt turned to his partner with a questioning smile. "Sir, I feel like we should split this pot three ways. We'd have been lost without Amon." Robert was quick to agree as he handed half his share to the elated lad.

Vivie came down from the patio to claim her hunter, her smile reflecting the satisfaction of seeing the two important men in her life together and in great spirits. For the afternoon she had chosen a soft white blouse with long billowy sleeves and tailored gray slacks, which fit quite well. "It seems you did splendidly!" she beamed as she looped a hand through her father's arm and the other through Matt's.

"Captain Tower is quite a shot," Robert replied as they strolled toward the mansion. "And we owe a bit to Amon. The lad knows his fields well."

"Come on, now," Matt joshed at his shooting partner. "Vivie, your father got a double out there towards the end." She squeezed their arms in hers to release the energetic joy. "Now, now, there'll be no favorites. You're both my heroes!"

# CHAPTER 16

# A Memorable Evening

I N SPITE OF the favorable prattle, it would be at tea in the parlor before Matt experienced the encouragement he desired so earnestly. Robert Moore, standing in a strategic position, casually guarded the chair next to Vivie until its reservation was obvious to her American suitor. Just as casually, Matt meandered through the assembled guests until he was situated to take advantage of it.

Several British civilian types had arrived with spouses or dates as the case might be—some of the boring bureaucracy Robert Moore had hinted at earlier—and Matt summoned all his diplomatic reserve in dealing with them. As each injected his opinion on the war's strategy, Matt began to feel sorry for Winston Churchill. He concluded that with these detached underlings, their brains apparently as stiff as the collars of their formal wear, the Prime Minister must surely have a greater problem at home than in Europe. Indeed, Colonel Burgess feared postwar England would face socialism, with its political and economic challenges proving disastrous for a weakened country. The Labour Party was pushing for that before war began and the postwar population, so used to regulations and shortages, might fall for it innocently.

This was the first time Matt had been irritated to any degree by a British subject. But the older bureaucrat in the group seemed predisposed to opposition with the Prime Minister and the Supreme Allied Commander. It was the verbal cannonade directed at General Eisenhower that fractured the American flyer's social decorum. "Frankly, Captain, I think history will show that without Montgomery's tenacity and Dempsey's experience, your general would be a weak fish."

Colonel Burgess, in earshot of the remark, was about to come to the American's aid. But seeing the crimson flush at Matt's neck, he held back to give the young officer first crack. "And you, sir," Matt began, in the firm measured tones of restrained anger, "are quite evidently descended from the Ictalurus punctatus!"

Having spoken his piece, Matt turned away to cool down before he embarrassed Vivie's friends. A small balcony beyond the French doors offered the seclusion he needed as well as a prime view of Havely Hall's rolling meadows. The tea was hot and comforting as he sipped, and he closed his eyes briefly and drew in the fresh evening air.

Colonel Burgess slipped through the door and joined Matt on the balcony. "Good show, Captain," he smiled encouragingly. "I think the old boy would challenge you to a duel if he could figure out the insult. What in blazes is an... ictaluuuu... something or other, anyway?"

Relieved that he had not offended all in the circle, Matt gave way to a grin. "That's Biology One-O-One, sir. Back home we call 'em *catfish*. It's a grubby-looking thing with barbels around its face. Known for a large mouth and a small brain."

Burgess threw his head back in husky laughter, his eyes twinkling with delight. "Bravo! That's Alex Howard, you know, of the Loyal Opposition in Commons. Considered something of a pompous arse around Downing Street."

The old warrior and fresh captain sipped and surveyed the estate's abundant fields. "You'd rather be up there, wouldn't you, Captain?" Burgess asked, pointing above the trees.

The hum of engines drew Matt's eyes skyward, fixing on a formation of P-38s headed for the channel. "That's probably the 55th Group out of Wormingford. And you're right, Colonel, I would like to be up there."

By eight that evening, a congenial crowd milled around Havely Hall's tables awaiting a turn in the serving line of a less formal post-hunt buffet. Parade-size flags of Great Britain and the United States held sway over a spirited orchestra of 12, whose enthusiastic rendition of English and American favorites won the audience early on.

With Vivie freshening up after tea, Matt was on his own for the moment. From his vantage point two steps above the main floor, he could see nothing under the rank of major and wondered if a simple line captain would fit in. Colonel Burgess resolved that as he nudged the American flyer into the throng. "Take courage, old chap. They were all lieutenants once."

They filled their plates with finger delights from the table and rubbed shoulders with their counterparts from every branch of service. Colonel Burgess spotted a number of familiar faces, British and American, whom he introduced readily to Matt. "Come over here, Captain. There's someone you should meet."

Burgess steered the American flyer toward an imposing bird colonel in animated conversation with two other officers. "Who am I meeting?" Matt asked, quite aware of the upper-level brass he was approaching.

"That's Buster Collins of General Doolittle's staff. Never hurts to know these people." The British officer caught the mood of the little group and moved right in. "Buster, old man, splendid seeing you here."

"Art Burgess!" the colonel declared. "I might have guessed the British would plant the room with intelligence types. How did you get an invitation, anyway?"

"I want you to meet one of your own. Buster, Captain Tower. He's with one of your fighter groups."

Collins extended a hand and greeted Matt warmly, bringing him into the circle. "You'll ruin your reputation hanging around with this fellow, Captain," the colonel jested, nodding at Burgess. "Let me introduce you to a better grade of officers. This is Colonel Lawrence Thomas, CO of the 453$^{rd}$ Bomber Group. And Major Al Parker is with me from Eighth Air Force Headquarters."

Matt knew of the dark-haired Colonel Thomas, whose fresh strategy had saved the Air Force's daylight bombing program from disaster. He seemed more the matter-of-fact business executive, eyes intent, with determined set of the mouth, every indication that he ran a tight command. The handshake was quick, firm and brief. "Captain," he acknowledged.

"Mind your manners, boys," Colonel Collins chuckled, cocking his head in the direction of an approaching officer. "There's a star on the horizon."

What a grand gathering of heavy brass for a Slybird captain to fall into, especially when a newly arrived brigadier general knew everyone except him by first name. But social presence had never been a short suite with the Towers, and Matt just smiled and acted like he was supposed to be there when Collins launched into introductions. "Captain Tower, I'd like you to meet Brigadier General Evan Coleman."

A touch of gray at the temples and a battery of ribbons under the lapel were sure signs the general had been around. His manner was easy, confident, and remarkably disarming. "It's a pleasure, Captain. What group are you with?"

"353rd Fighter, sir."

"Okay! One of Glenn Duncan's boys. Is he here tonight?" the general inquired expectantly, assuming the lieutenant to be an aide.

"I haven't seen him, sir." Matt flashed his best smile. "I guess somebody had to mind the shop," he added, trusting levity to see him through.

Fortunately, Coleman didn't seem curious. He just chuckled and sipped his drink, which was fine with Matt, who hoped to avoid questions about his presence that night. All he needed was for Vivie's string-pulling to leak out.

Colonel Thomas would preclude that, for no conversation could remain social for long with him around. Ninety percent business, he took headquarters brass captive when and where he found them. Matt would get a first-hand look at how the war was really run as the bomber commander tactfully presented his Christmas list.

It was evident the general had a lot of respect for Thomas, and equally evident that this was a familiar path for them both. When the persistent colonel paused for liquid refreshment, Coleman tactfully turned to Matt for relief. "What's your command, Captain?"

"Flight leader, sir."

"That's what I had hoped," the general replied. "You men see it right across the cowling. I don't doubt you're biting your tongue, Tower. How do you see things over at Raydon?"

One look at Thomas assured the junior officer his comments better be relevant. The bomber commander didn't appreciate losing his place. Matt struggled to get his mind in gear. "There are others in a better position than I am to comment on operations."

"I doubt that, Captain. Speak up."

"Well, sir, we're sitting right at the coast, in the main bomber traffic zones, and we can't escort any farther than Frankfurt or

Hanover." Out of the corner of his eye Matt saw Thomas stop fidgeting. The colonel had caught the words bomber and escort.

With Thomas neutralized and the general still listening, Matt folded his arms in the most authoritative stance possible. "It's the P-47s, sir. They just don't have the range. They're tough, faithful, but we have to stop short of some super targets. The war is moving inland, General. Eventually it'll be out of our range altogether."

"Don't worry about that," the general chuckled. "We'll be moving some groups onto the continent to be nearer the front."

"Nuts, Evan!" Thomas injected. "That could take months! I thought the plan called for complete conversion to Mustangs."

General Coleman slipped a hand into his pants pocket and took a swig from his glass, the casualness effectively replacing Thomas' lid for the moment. "Duncan briefed you before you came, didn't he?" the general grinned at Matt.

"No, sir. That's my own observation. All you have to do is read 'Impact' to see how the groups around us are doing. The 352$^{nd}$, 357$^{th}$, 361$^{st}$, and the 4$^{th}$ based at Debden, they all have Mustangs. General, three weeks ago over France, we were bounced by some hot new Messerschmitts. We lost eight of our group in that little fight, including four element leaders, a flight leader and my squadron leader."

Matt felt his breath coming harder, a slight flush to his neck, and he knew he was pressing it with the general. "Sir, the Thunderbolt is tough and faithful. But it dives better than it climbs, and it takes emergency power to get it hot again."

Colonel Collins sensed the young flyer's passion and decided the mood was a bit strained for the occasion. "I think you've made your point, Captain!" he snapped firmly in defense of his superior officer.

"It's all right, Buster," the general countered, showing but scant affront. "If you ask a question, you have to be ready for the answer." He turned again to the young flyer whose eyes retracted nothing from his comments. "You're dang near as good as Curtis LeMay, you know that?"

"I... I'm sorry, sir. I guess I got carried away."

The exchange dampened the conversation to the point that even LeMay was willing to retire, and the officers eased away on one excuse or another. It required more finesse at Matt's rank to disengage from a brigadier general, and he found himself last man out, with hands so large he couldn't find a convenient place for them.

Surprisingly, the general hung around, and from the sober expression on his face Matt anticipated a stern lecture. Some contrast, these two soldiers. One with stars, one with bars; one with strips of ribbon two inches deep on his chest, the other with a short one-liner. From appearances, the only thing they had in common was the uniform.

But Evan Coleman had sensed the hurt in the young lieutenant's eyes and voice and had been moved by the honest appeal so free of ulterior motive. It was the general who broke the silence as he placed his empty glass on a passing tray. "I take it your squadron leader was a pretty capable officer."

"Yes, sir, he was," Matt sighed as the tension eased across his shoulders.

A waiter paused with a fresh tray. Matt shook his head politely but the general, who had not passed up a tray since the evening began, retrieved a glass and motioned the lieutenant back to the table where tasty ham biscuits beckoned. "How'd it happen?"

"We were going into a dive when about 30 109s bounced us out of the sun. It was every man for himself with guys breaking all over the sky. We heard Major Newhart call for help, but none of us could locate him. He was out in front at the worst possible angle when they hit us," Matt added, indicating a shallow dive with his hand.

"I'm sorry, Tower. It's not an easy matter," the general replied, his eyes set in reflection. "In the last war I was in France flying with Billy

Mitchell. One morning my flight of DH-4s climbed out of a fog bank into the path of a Fokker pursuit squadron." Coleman paused long enough to nip from the ever-ready glass. "Three of us survived the attack. My observer spent the last shell keeping the Krauts off our tail then bled to death before I could get the de Havilland back to base."

Matt realized now that Slybird's losses had occupied him to the point of obscuring the tragedies of others. In 1917 the old flyer had nothing like the speed, firepower and protection of a modern fighter. "But here's the irony of it, Tower," the general said. "We knew the markings were von Richthofen's group."

"He'd been shot down earlier, you see. Who the devil do you think was leading the Baron's squadron? One Hermann Goering!"

"Goering?"

"Intelligence confirmed it. And the bozo ends up an ace before the end of the war!" Coleman chuckled cynically. "Let me tell you something, Tower. I've got a score to settle, you see, and they won't let me near a fighter. What do you think of that?" He paused a moment to bottom-up the glass, then gave way to a broad grin. "I guess the only consolation is they won't let him in one of 'em, either!"

So consumed was he, in his audience with the tanked-up general, Matt forgot to watch for Vivie. There at the stair rail of the great room she waited, scanning the maze of guests for him. The haunting beauty that captivated him so in the NAAFI canteen dimmed in the radiance of this woman born anew. Sky-blue satin adorned her with low, square neckline and puffed shoulders. Her light golden-brown hair folded back softly at the sides in a regal coiffure.

In recent weeks she had evolved like a butterfly, freed as it were, from the years of self-imposed denial. The general, facing the huge doorway, discovered her before Matt did. It broke his concentration abruptly. "What an ex... quisite woman!"

The sight of Vivie brought a smile to Matt's lips. While he appreciated the general's evaluation, influenced by drink or not, he moved quickly to prevent an embarrassing assumption. "I'd like for you to meet her, sir. Excuse me a moment."

Seeing that the general and the captain were getting along so well, Colonel Collins worked his way back to his superior's side. "What are you looking at, Evan?" he asked, his eyes following Coleman's line of vision. "Oh, I see! You old lecher, I thought the Army was your mistress."

The general had hoped she was unescorted. A trace of disappointment lingered on his face as Matt returned with the object of appreciation. "Well, who do we have here, Captain?"

Had the young flyer not been so mesmerized with her, he would have fumbled less with the introduction. "General Coleman, Colonel Collins, may I present my... my...." He paused, an embarrassed smile lighting his face. "A very special lady, Vivian Davis, Major Moore's daughter."

As the pleasantries were exchanged, Matt reflected on his awkward introduction. He had come close to presenting Vivie as his fiancé. But he caught himself in time since they had yet to reach that point.

A gracious converser, Vivie never let on that the introduction bothered her, but she read all sorts of things into Matt's innocent fumble. Was their relationship no more than dating? She wished they were alone. Except for the stables the night before, there had been no privacy since he arrived. Little chance now, for the general had begged a dance.

Matt lost count of the drinks the man had consumed, but Coleman managed to lead Vivie tolerably well into the opening strains of *I'll Never Smile Again*. She loved to dance and for a time, the general did rather well until drink finally took its toll. It was then she became increasingly aware that he was capable of other things less appropriate on the dance floor. Politely speaking, the general was a flirt and not very subtle about it.

It was remarkable how adept Vivie was at handling such

circumstances. Nonetheless, the Slybird flyer didn't take well to it. Colonel Collins, stuffing his face with finger sweets, just smiled and shook his head. "Well, Captain, you lost your P-51s and now your girl. I'd go out there and break on 'em," he teased, placing an encouraging hand on Matt's shoulder.

"That would be too obvious, Colonel. Maybe you could break on them. Then I could cut in."

Collins pulled his hand from Matt's shoulder and chuckled heartily. "I don't break on generals, son."

Vivie skillfully danced him out of the crowd to the edge of the floor, a clear sign to Matt that she wanted a tactful escape. The lieutenant adjusted his tie and started forward. "Then I'll dang well do it myself!"

Fortunately, Colonel Burgess had returned in time to evaluate the problem and he caught Matt's arm. "Allow me, Lieutenant. This is an intelligence matter, I think."

It did not become the issue they expected, for the general was past the point of resistance. Indeed, he was past all points, swaying slightly with hands in pockets as he watched Vivie and the British officer glide away.

"It was a pleasure, Colonel Collins," Matt lied through his teeth. He was civil for the sake of protocol, offering a thin smile. "We'll leave the general in your capable hands and the lady in mine. Have a good evening, sir."

Vivie avoided Matt's attempts to break, turning as she danced to prevent him from tapping Colonel Burgess. She continued a lively conversation, smiling in her most charming way. It had the intended effect on the American flyer who, like most males lacking the savvy to sense feminine displeasure, waded in blindly. After a few more turns, the colonel brought the matter to a head as he paused on the dance floor. "Mrs. Davis, you dance sublimely," he said with a shallow bow. "But this old man feels he must give way to the younger generation."

"Thank you, kind sir," Vivie responded with a brief curtsy. As she straightened, Matt quickly assumed Colonel Burgess' place, leaving her little choice but to follow his lead, which she did but at a stiff formal distance.

Her gaze went past his shoulders and she would not meet his eyes. Matt was like a lap puppy who, without explanation, had just been denied his favorite chair. They danced in silence for a time, Vivie indifferent except for the smile she afforded a couple they bumped, and Matt in sober reflection.

"Dear Vivie," he broke the ice as pleasantly as possible. "I haven't seen you like this before."

"Oh," she responded matter-of-factly. "And just how am I?"

"Well, you're certainly not happy about something,"

"You noticed!"

"Mind filling me in?"

Her eyes, a bit blurry with hurt, met his now. "Are you that interested, Lieutenant? You've certainly shown little interest this evening."

"Is it something I've done?"

"Not done," she sighed.

Matt sighed and looked away. *"Women were alike the world around,"* he thought to himself. "I'm sorry, dear, whatever it is. Honest!" She remained unmoved. The only defense he could draw on was charm, a quality that had served him well in the past. He waited for the melody to change, looked into her eyes and sang softly to her. *"I'll never smile... again, until I smile at you... I'll ne... ver laugh again... until I laugh with you..."*

His debonair approach was ill-timed for she dropped her arms, ending their dance abruptly. He had made the fatal mistake of underestimating her concerns. "Ohhh!" she growled, her lips settling in a tight line. "Just, ohhh!" She was halfway off the dance floor before Matt could react.

He followed as best he could, but she was well ahead of him, reaching the library door and vanishing with a slam. Crossing the floor under such circumstances required a certain amount of tact. The returning of smiles and nods slowed him down like running in a nightmare. It was their first serious argument, and he was in a cold sweat by the time he reached the door.

Etta Moore had witnessed the separation, and while it may have caused no speculation among those around the couple, she could read her daughter at any distance. From her position she was able to reach the library door before Matt. "Give me a moment, Matt. Please," she added, her lips curved in an understanding smile.

Having not the vaguest plan of action, he obeyed willingly, letting Mrs. Moore slip quietly into the adjacent room. If he only knew what he was guilty of, he could plan a defense. If he could get her to talk with him. "Stiff upper lip, Captain," Colonel Burgess' husky voice encouraged. "Here, I've fetched a glass for you."

"Thank you, sir," Matt managed, doing a poor job of concealing his frustration.

Arthur Burgess wasn't fooled. He had been as much a spectator as Vivie's mother, and it was disappointing to see the young couple wasting a gala evening in petty contention. As well, he had developed a liking for the American flyer, if for no other reason than the first blush of color he had seen on the cheeks of Robert Moore's daughter in years. "That bad, is it now?" the Britisher probed cautiously.

"She's upset about something," Matt sighed. "Danged if I know what it is."

Colonel Burgess smiled empathetically as one who had passed that way on occasion. "They don't usually tell you, you know. It's like a guessing game and if you can't guess, they're all the more infuriated."

Having retreated to the sanctuary of the richly paneled library,

Vivie collapsed in Lord Havely's favorite leather chair, burying her face in its plush high-back wing. Etta Moore closed the door softly, shutting out all but the muffled efforts of the orchestra and the intermittent crackle of burning logs in the huge old fireplace. Vivie looked up long enough to recognize her intruder, then sank back again engulfed in the deepest sobs.

Etta stood patiently at the hearth sipping her drink until her daughter had spent the last tear and grown still. She moved to the ottoman and seated herself in front of her daughter. "One might think we were losing the war," she sighed.

"Ohhh, Mum!" the younger woman whimpered. "It's all ruined."

"*All* is a rather comprehensive word, dear. Can you be a bit more specific?"

"Just everything!" Vivie moved to a sitting position and dabbed at her eyes with a tiny lace handkerchief. "I wanted this weekend to be so special. Why are men like that?"

"It's a mystery, darling. A mystery that's certainly safe with the Creator. Now, what exactly has your captain done or not done?"

"Ignored me!"

"That must have been when I wasn't around."

"Well, he has! He hasn't spent a minute with me the whole day. And you should have heard him introduce me to the American officers, like he wasn't quite sure who I was."

Etta smiled sympathetically as her hand covered Vivie's. "Dear, this has been a very busy day. Now, it was you who arranged the hunting trip, and after that it was a rush for everyone to make tea. The guests began arriving and everyone rushed to dress for the evening. That's hardly Matt's fault."

"Mum, he left me on the dance floor in the clutches of a drunken octopus and never lifted a finger! What would you think?"

The smile lingered as Etta's gaze dropped to the glass in her hand. '*What a cycle life is,*" she thought, for she had endured two courtships herself. "I think my daughter is very much in love. And I think that love is returned."

"I do love him, Mum." Her voice was calmer now, concern replacing anger as she dabbed at her eyes again. "That's why I went to such trouble to have him here. Since the invasion we've hardly seen each other. And he's been so preoccupied, almost distant."

Etta moved to the fireplace again, warming her hands as her heart pondered Vivie's concerns. What seemed so clear to her anguished frustration had clouded for the younger woman. "Have you looked at Matt's face?"

"Of course I have, silly!"

"No. I mean the lines, the eyes. Vivian, he is exhausted! Now, he hasn't told you this. I learned it from Colonel Burgess. Last week his unit lost eight pilots including the squadron leader. During the invasion, he flew every day. I should think he would be preoccupied!"

"Oh, dear, what have I done?" Vivie whispered mournfully, her face grimacing in grief. "Why didn't he tell me?"

"If you ask me, I think he's concerned that you'd be worried, that old memories would be provoked."

"Mum, I can't hide from such things any longer. Perhaps there'll be hard moments, but I love him and I must be there when he needs me. It's just that I haven't seen him like this before. Impatient, so tense."

"Dear, dear, Vivian. I came from a long line of military men. Your grandfather, your father, uncles, even Colonel Burgess. It can be very difficult for them to talk about. Someone they've marched with or flown with is gone suddenly. It bothers them terribly that they made it through when the others didn't."

"Then getting away, coming to the party, should have helped him, Mum."

"Not always. They have an urge to be with their comrades at such times, and a party like this can be agonizing. If you're to keep company with a military man, then you must be sensitive to these things."

"Then I've ruined everything, haven't I?" Vivie sighed as she cupped her hands over her face.

"I doubt that you've ruined everything, but I do think it caused Matt to wrestle with his priorities," Etta replied as she sat on the arm of Vivie's chair. "There's one consolation, Vivian. He did decide to be with you."

"I feel so terrible about it, Mum. What do I say to him?"

Vivie rose slowly and moved to the comforting warmth of the hearth. The music had faded some time before, giving ground to spirited orations from British and American officers. The two women half listened in silence, able to pick up only parts of the more enthusiastic toasts. Smiling assuringly, Etta squeezed her daughter's hand. "You may need to say nothing, dear. I'm sure he's quite concerned by now. Just tidy up and rejoin the party."

Concerned that Matt might still be just outside, Vivie opened the library door cautiously. All eyes were fixed on the bandstand, and Matt was watching with Colonel Burgess near the stairway. The hall erupted with cheers and whistles as the last toast was given and the band struck up the music for England's popular fighting song. The chatter and laughter melded readily into a glorious chorus of proud British voices. *"May this fair land we love so well... in dignity and freedom dwell..."*

Those airmen who had been on the Isle for any time knew most of the words, courtesy of singer Vera Lynn, and their voices joined in, to the delight of their hosts. The mood was contagious, and the years of tragedy and trial seemed to well up from English hearts into a mighty voice of newfound hope. It was irresistible, even to a troubled young woman, and Vivie's voice joined her mother's as they held hands before the library door. On the final verse, *"There'll always be an England... and England shall be free... if England means as much to you... as England means to me!"* A great shout echoed around the hall from a hundred English voices.

Matt, who had mimicked the words as best he could, saw unashamed tears on the cheeks of the seasoned old Brit officer beside him. The Slybird captain had walked in the rubble of English cities, had seen them from the cockpit. He knew firsthand the personal toll on England's people through the life of one he loved. His own eyes blurring, he fought the tightening lump in his throat.

Gradually the uproar subsided and as though of a single mind, all present paused for breath. Matt saw Vivie from the corner of his eye, but he was as perplexed as she about the next move. Suddenly, across the hall, out of the silence, the rich alto of a lone American rose into song. *"God Bless America.... land that I love...."*

Voice after voice responded across the hall, and as the band picked up the tune, even the Englishmen thereabouts tried to return the musical complement. *"...Stand beside her, and guide her, through the night with the light from above.... God bless America... my home sweet home...!"* The impact was profound as these Yanks, thousands of miles from home, sang their hearts out, and their pride and a little homesickness as well, in the words of Irving Berlin.

Matt felt cold fingers take his hand, gripping it ever tighter as the music swelled. She was beside him now, and goose bumps mushroomed around his neck. The combination of song and Vivie's reconciliation were more than he could handle, and blurry eyes leaked down his cheeks. *"From the mountains... to the prairies... to the ocean white with foam...."*

When their eyes finally met, Vivie did her best to mouth the unfamiliar words, her face pleading forgiveness. He was quick to oblige with a broad smile and pulled her close with an encircling arm. As he sang, she studied him lovingly, keenly aware now of the lines and weariness. *"God bless America, my own sweet home!"*

The cheers died away as soldiers handled the wetness around their eyes as inconspicuously as possible. Many, mellowed by thoughts of home, emptied the freshly stocked trays or lined the bar. Vivie reached up and took his tears away with her fingers. She was enough for Matt, and he determined that nothing else would separate them that evening. "That was beautiful!" she sighed. "What lovely thoughts."

"It's a prayer set to music, Hon. You should hear Kate Smith sing it," he replied, smiling with relief at her evident recovery.

"Poppet," she implored in her soft English accent. "Can we go out for a moment? I really need a breath of air."

On the balcony the chilly night kept them close together, a welcome retreat from the boisterous celebration inside. Vivie's heart was impatient. There were things serious to her that needed to be said. She took his hand in hers and pressed it to her lips. "I'm sorry I acted as I did in there."

"No, no, no," Matt whispered, returning the kiss to her delicate fingers.

"But I must. It was so thoughtless of me."

"Hey, we're all under a strain, dear."

"Well, I'm certain you are. Why didn't you tell me your squadron leader was lost?"

She was shivering, as much no doubt from the emotional evening as the weather. He unbuckled his jacket and draped it around her shoulders. "Darned if you're not in this thing more than I am!"

"Matt, don't keep things from me. I need to understand." He started to speak but she anticipated, placing a finger on his lips. "It's all right, my darling. You don't have to worry about hurting me. I'm much better now, and you're such a part of my life that I worry when I don't know. I'll be fine."

She sat on the small glider, pulling him down beside her and adjusting the coat so it partially covered him. "Please tell me what happened," she whispered.

He rested his head on the glider's high back, his chest giving way to a deep sigh. "It was the worst I've seen, I guess. A couple dozen of us having coffee and breakfast in the ready room, telling stupid jokes to ward off the tension. Old Dewey Newhart carrying on, boosting our courage. There wasn't one of us who wouldn't have flown slap into the face of the Fallen Angels with him! But that night, eight empty cots."

Vivie drew his head to her shoulder. "I'm so sorry, darling. Are you all right?"

"I'm angry, I know that! Herrington, he's a flight leader, told me it would happen. It's a strange feeling, Vivie, like you've lost all fear. Like I could take on the whole German air force. That's one reason I didn't turn down this party."

She snuggled against him, content at last that her plan had not been in vain.

Her nearness brought a peace that had eluded him in recent weeks. He wanted her more than anything, even flying. The question of marriage would have to be addressed soon, and his arms and lips sought to assure her of it.

# CHAPTER 17

# The Home Front

ELECTRIC FANS IN the business office of Tower Industrial & Mill Supply Company weaved lazily from side to side. Even with the windows open, it was a warm September day in Augusta. Behind the executive desk, Gerald Mattlowe Tower, Sr. sat in open vest, his sleeves rolled a turn or two as he studied the latest parts catalog. His black hair, always neatly combed, was lightly dusted with gray. An inch shorter than his five-eleven son, it was evident he took care of himself. He was a handsome man, still strong in spite of his 70 years, and carried himself erectly. Around the paneled walls hung several excellent waterfowl studies that transported him to the marshes of the Savannah River whenever he wearied under the workload.

Thirty-five years earlier, Gerald was selling mill supplies for his uncle and learning the family business. Enthusiastic, knowledge-able and gifted of speech, he cultivated a faithful clientele among the textile mills and area businesses. Most impressed was George R. Lombard, president of Lombard Iron Works & Supply Company. When Gerald's uncle fell ill and placed the company for sale, Lombard offered to back the young salesman so the business could continue.

From his office window Gerald Tower could view the culmination of his energies in the 12,000-square-foot warehouse with rail siding. Beneath him the showroom and sales office did a brisk business. When he had time, he still called on many of the accounts himself to see in person how his sales staff was performing.

No one could have convinced him he was pausing longer these days on the few steps to his office. As he completed his notes to the purchasing officer, the soft chime of an old Seth Thomas clock, perched on the shelf to his right, struck 12 noon.

In those early years he was often late leaving the office. Eleanor Tower had found the clock on one of her antique treks to Charleston, South Carolina, and had old Mr. Furman, the clocksmith and jeweler, put his magical fingers to it. But the effect on her husband's tardiness was marginal at best.

He leaned back in the swivel chair to await the inevitable whine of an air-raid siren. If the clock held fond memories of a pretty little bride wishing her husband home early, the drills were stark reminders of war and of his son and were now ingrained as a signal for silent prayer.

Just as reliable was Miss Margaret Little, 50-year-old spinster and self-appointed secretary to Tower Supply's president. Precisely at 12:01 he could expect her with the early mail. A 20-year veteran with the firm, she could probably run the business in a pinch. Right out of Miss Funk's Business School, she began as a file clerk in the purchasing office, where her incredible energy and preciseness moved her in time to the position of office manager.

She was always impeccably dressed in business skirt and jacket, and Gerald took pride in showing her off to visiting clients. Her black hair, in characteristic 1940s style, was just revealing some gray, and with the complementing black-rimmed glasses she was an authority second only to the president himself. Here was a fair figure and comely face of a woman whose interest lay more to the practical. A mystery prevailed that she had avoided marriage all those years.

Beaming with mail in hand, she crossed the office in that quick little stride that gave those walking beside her the sensation they were being passed. "There's one from the boy, Mr. Tower!"

Though a friend of the family by now, Margaret held to proper office protocol, always addressing Gerald as Mr. Tower. Indeed, she required that discipline of all who worked there according to their rank one to the other. The result was a tight ship, tighter than Gerald would have insisted, but it worked.

"Thank you, Margaret," he replied with a smile as he quickly found the special envelope. Only a few of Matt's letters turned up at the office, and when they did, something unusual was in the wind. Something Matt felt his mother might have difficulty dealing with.

"How's your afternoon, Mr. Tower? Councilman Davis wanted to come by before the 'Tribute to Our Troops' hoopla tomorrow, and the new purchasing agent from Dole Mills wants to meet you personally."

"Set them up sometime after 2:30, if you will. I think I'll run by The Augusta Country Club for a sandwich and then get my locks trimmed. Don't want to embarrass Mrs. Tower on the parade platform," he chuckled. "Anything else to mar the day?"

"Nothing that can't be fixed. Augusta Plating & Manufacturing needs a specialized drill for their work at the Augusta Arsenal. It's a new process and we are trying to locate one. Beyond that, it's a normal day of confusion."

"Okay. I'll be leaving in a minute as soon as I take a peek at this letter."

The senior Tower leaned back in the swivel rocker and slit the envelope open. "Hum!" he responded discovering three full pages, followed by a stronger "Humm!" as the photograph slid into his lap.

*"Dear Dad,*

*"Sorry I wasn't able to give you more hint about the invasion in my last letter, but the censors were really on us the whole month leading up to it. Yes, I was in it for 10 straight days. You're probably hearing more about the progress than we are, but it was some kind of sight over that Channel. I have three enemy planes in the air to my credit, and I've busted a few on the deck. I'm doing fine, just a little tired. The pace is about back to normal now.*

*"By now you're holding the photograph. Her name is Vivian Davis, and that's a Women's Voluntary Service uniform she's wearing. She's become very special in my life. I met her the month I arrived at base, but it took almost two more before I got her attention. If something should come of our relationship, I didn't want it to be a surprise to you and Mom.*

*"I don't want to spread my heart all over these pages, but she's not like anyone I've known before. Her folks own a really charming hotel in a town called Ipswich not far from my base, and another on the coast. They had three of them, but one near the docks caught a bomb and a stick of incendiaries early in the war. Vivie is very much a lady, and attended a finishing school named Roedean in southern England and college in London. I think Mom would like her a lot. Anyway, I will send a little more about her as I see how things progress....*"

Gerald Tower let the letter drop on the desk and held the photo up for better light. "Humm," he grunted again, a smile creeping across his face, "My son, my son, my son!"

His hand went to the telephone. "Polly, get Mrs. Tower on the line for me, will you?" He reached for a magnifying glass as he waited for the call to be completed, and gave the photo a going over. "Hello, El, how about meeting me for lunch at the Club?... Well, I know you are. But it won't take us long.... Yes, but in this case the USO ought to wait."

The Augusta Country Club was only 20 minutes from Gerald Tower's office, a familiar drive up Walton Way past the huge, white-stucco Bon Air resort hotel and into exclusive Summerville, with its quaint cottages and elegant mansions: opulent monuments of the city's westward expansion from the 1800s to escape the Savannah River valley's humid summers.

As Florida tamed its marshes and mosquito haunts in the 1930s, Augusta's winter-resort position had begun to decline. But for years it had played host to Vanderbilts, Astors, Whitneys, Bournes, President William H. Taft and a chain of other Eastern families enjoying the "bon air" of Summerville. They arrived by rail at the city's Union Depot and made their way in handsome carriage or motorcar to "The Hill."

It was this grand recognition of the city that gave impetus to the hotel, with its excellent stables, and The Club's two fine original golf courses. Later, a bigger and grander Forest Hills Hotel, with its own championship golf course, expanded the playland still farther west of the city.

Milledge Road was the ridge road of The Hill, and it was along its shaded length that one might see some of the finest homes, including those of Alfred Bourne (the Singer Sewing Machine tycoon) and famed novelist Edison Marshall. Here nestles The Augusta Country Club, social center of the city, with its manicured lawn and terraces surrounding the expansive clubhouse. Built in 1903, its second level sported an encircling veranda with great columns modeled after the private clubs of Cape Cod.

Here, Bobby Jones and Clifford Roberts played golf and first became interested in the adjoining Berckmans Nursery that they would later fashion into Augusta National Golf Club. They purchased the rolling lands in 1932 and two years later, Horton Smith would win the first Masters Tournament.

Gerald Tower loved the game and had coaxed his handicap below 12 on occasion. But today there was no time as his dark blue Chrysler, with its grill of shiny chrome, eased to a stop at the clubhouse entrance. Old Jasper the doorman in his red jacket stepped lively toward the car. "Good afternoon, Mr. Tower. "Are you playing today, sir? I'll git Tasau to round up a caddy."

"I'm afraid not today, Jasper. Have you seen Mrs. Tower come in?" Gerald inquired, handing the black man his keys.

"Yes, sir. I thinks she already in the dining room."

An ageless fixture at The Club was Mattie, a tall, Black woman whose broad gold-capped smile greeted all entering the lobby. She was quite impressive in her crisp white uniform and ever so discreet. A discreetness that ensured her job over the years, for she was frequently in a position to know who left drunk in the evening and with whose wife. Only the close observer detected her one real flaw, the patch of snuff wedged between her lip and front teeth.

Gerald nodded and returned her smile. "You're looking too happy today, Mattie. What have you been up to?"

It was the type of banter she liked, and her hands went to her face to muffle the amusing high-pitched laughter. "I been up to nothing, Mr. Tower." Gerald shook his head in exaggerated doubt as he crossed the lobby. "I don't know. Sounds like the giggle of a guilty woman to me!"

Mattie could hardly contain herself as she slapped her sides to suppress another snickering outburst. She had her favorites among the club members and Gerald Tower, who had been on the Board of Governors when she was hired, made the list early on. He exited the lobby before she could make a comeback and just as well, for she was in no condition to speak.

The first of the week was generally slow at The Club, and Eleanor Tower easily gained Gerald's preferred table overlooking the number one tee. He found it extremely encouraging to watch the muffed shots. Every foursome had its predictable diversity with one slicing to the right, another hooking to the left, a third dribbling out a few yards, and the lucky fourth putting a fair shot well down the fairway.

Eleanor dressed when she visited the club, and she was truly lovely in her white sleeveless sun dress sprinkled with tiny black polka dots. The matching broad-brimmed hat secured her silky black hair. She had grayed little until early that year when Matt was shipped overseas. Just the appropriate touch of makeup for her, for she didn't wish to appear the hussy. Gentle, quick to smile, adorably distracted at times, she drew friends easily. A product of Burke County's landed gentry with all the personal graces, she was a natural complement to Gerald, fitting them smoothly into Augusta's business and social life.

Gerald was beaming broadly as he took a chair beside his wife. "My, my, aren't we beautiful today!"

Cocking her head coyly she returned the smile. "Compliments, lunch out with my husband? The anticipation is frightful!"

"Frightful?" he chuckled.

"Well, it's certainly not an everyday occurrence."

Gerald's order was a foregone conclusion at lunch time: a Dagwood style club sandwich. The waitress passed a single menu to Eleanor Tower. She chose her dish and turned to her husband. "Now, darling, what astounding piece of news are you harboring?"

He lowered his head slightly, a prankish smirk twisting his lips. "Must I have an astounding piece of news to join my wife for lunch?"

"It's written all over you, Gerald Tower. Good or bad news?" In that moment her face sobered reflectively and her hands sought the edge of the table. "It's not about Matt, is it?"

"Nothing tragic," he smiled reassuringly. "Good or bad, I guess that depends on the hearer," he added, taking the letter from his jacket pocket. "It seems your son has an interest in a fair lass of the Royal Realm."

Expression drained from Eleanor's face as she rested her arms on the table. "What? What exactly are you telling me, Gerald? That Matt is involved with some English girl?"

"I don't know if *involved* is the right word or not, but her name is Vivian Davis and she is quite attractive."

"I cannot believe my ears! How long have you known about this? And how do you know she's attractive?"

Gerald unfolded the letter and reached for the picture. "It came this morning. Here, have a look for yourself."

Eleanor hesitated, her deep blue eyes intently searching Gerald's face as though seeing the picture might make the matter true. It seemed minutes passed before curiosity won out and she reached for the photograph. After a moment she lowered her hand and stared out the window. "Another pretty face," she sighed. "It was bad enough when he went off to school and we had to live through Virginia Ellison."

"Oh, come on, El. The boy's met a young lady to spend time with. He says in the letter he's not certain that anything would come of it."

"A political answer if I ever heard one!" she replied in exasperation. "Sounds exactly like your politician friends. 'I don't choose to run at this time.' And you know very well they invariably do!"

Her eyes drifted back to the photograph. "We don't know a thing about this girl or her family. Look, she's in the army!"

"I don't think that's the army. He says she's active in one of their volunteer groups. Besides, Dot Thomas' daughter joined the WACs and you didn't seem to mind that."

"Well, she's not my daughter! And besides, little Dottie has always been a tomboy." So intent was Eleanor on the debate that she did not notice the waitress' return until the plate was placed in front of her. "Oh, Miz Tower, that sho' is a pretty young lady there. She some of yo' kin?"

"I certainly hope not!" the concerned mother retorted. Realizing she had been rather abrupt in her reply, Eleanor forced a brief smile. "Just a friend of a family member."

"Well, she do look grand in that uniform!"

As the waitress moved away, Eleanor's eyes cast the full impact of her concerns on Gerald Tower. But he was seldom at a loss for words. "El, I think you're underestimating your son. He's not the impetuous type, you know. He says he's not going to surprise us and he'll write more later."

Gerald thought he saw a trace of reassurance on her face as he straightened the photograph on the table. "And you've got to admit, she looks grand in that uniform!"

"For heaven's sake!" she snapped, reaching for the letter. "What else has happened?" She read along for a moment, her eyes getting bigger by the second. "Gerald, he's shot another airplane!"

"Dang right!" her husband responded, a contented smile widening his lips as he settled back in the chair. "That's three, Momma. If your boy gets two more, he'll be an ace!"

"Or dead," she whispered through lips drawn in anxiety. One hand slowly placed the letter to one side as the other covered her eyes. "Have you no concern for your son's safety, Gerald Tower?"

Grimacing with regret over the callous remark, he quickly covered her hand with his. It was pride in the accomplishments of his son that spurred the comment, not a lack of solicitude. "Oh, El…

El, I'm sorry. God knows he's on my mind every hour of the day. It's just that we have to think positively about it. Take the good moments when they come. It's a good letter, Hon."

But it was too late, for her shoulders shook gently with muffled sobs. "I want him home, Gerald."

How often had he heard that? Not just from his Eleanor, but from relatives and friends caught in the same agonizing wait. His thoughts drifted to the soft sniffles that punctuated the weekly prayer meetings at church. There had been losses, and now more and more of the prayer time was going for the bereaved.

"El," he tapped her hand gently. "They want to clear the tables, Hon." He caught the questioning eye of the waiter and offered a quick explanation. "There's just something in her eye. She'll be fine."

"Well," Eleanor sighed as she rose from the chair. "I guess it's the powder room for me."

Gerald watched until she disappeared through the dining room door. She had retained her figure rather well for 66, and her lovely blue eyes never lost the sparkle that fired his heart to that day. He would have given a handsome sum if only he could soothe away the latent distress she struggled with daily.

Five-month-old Susan Anna probably accomplished the job as well as anything, for Eleanor was a doting grandmother. With all the uncertainty round about, Gerald marveled at the future promise in the dimpled smile of that tiny, pink baby. She was born only weeks after Matt shipped out, as though God had timed the fill-in.

The lush green fairways of his home golf course ministered to Gerald as well, for the game consumed his mind pleasantly. At night, when troublesome thoughts challenged sleep, he would mentally practice the shots that provoked his game. It was just such activity on the first tee that lured him to the great picture window. "Ha! Muffed it," he chuckled at the chubby driver's efforts. "Go on, go on! Scrabble your mulligan as well."

The muffled whine of Joe Pine's voice drifted across the dining room, and Gerald instinctively tried to blend with the window curtains. There was no animosity between the men. It was just that jovial Joe, well-mannered if sometimes boisterous, never seemed to know when a conversation was over. The short, portly, slightly balding 60-year-old used a cane to evoke sympathy from his peers. It effectively dragged out his lectures along Broad Street by slowing the escape of his audience.

Joe's livelihood consisted of income from real-estate holdings, vestiges of timely parental investments in the main business district. Thus, preservation and enhancement of Augusta's commercial centers, and its weakening economy, was a growing public concern. But with Pine, it was mild paranoia. Though annoyingly persistent at times, his arguments were a fair representation of the frustrations endured by a majority of Augusta's commercial community.

Augusta had emerged as an industrial community from the 1840s. Textiles, foundries, brick and tile plants, a railroad center, and an inland river port all generated new dollars for the local economy. But city leaders preferred the community grow no further because the present industries wished to protect their labor pool from new competition.

Attempts to grow were discouraged quietly at first. But as the economy stagnated from the 1910s to the 1940s, pressure mounted for reform, which intensified the resistance to ugly proportions. Corrupt politics, law enforcement and fire services—accompanied by public apathy—dulled the city's image and put the community at an economic disadvantage. Big business, banking and financial interests stymied development of new roads, bridges, public facilities, and utilities as well as attempts to expand the job market with new manufacturing and business. Augusta's economy was at a stalemate.

"Hello, brother Tower!" Tactful escape was impossible now. The line of vacating tables in Joe's path was a pitiful testimony to the well-meaning landlord. But he never seemed aware of his impact. "Mighty fine day we're having, yes sir!"

"That it is, brother Pine," Gerald replied as he extended his hand.

"What have you heard from young Mattlowe? That's a mighty fine boy you have there."

Gerald knew better than to sit down, for Joe Pine would take that as an invitation. "Just had a letter today, in fact. He shot down his third enemy plane. We're proud of him, but it keeps us concerned, seeing he's right in the middle of the war."

Pine nodded in sympathy, his lips drawing a frown. "Brother, he's in my prayers. We've got so many fine young men over there." They stood together for a moment, taking in the green expanse from the window, until Joe could contain himself no longer. "You know, brother, we got a war going right here, too."

It was a typical introduction for the little man's eternal topic, and with Eleanor delayed, Gerald had no choice but to play to his audience. Pine assumed his lecture posture, leaning with both hands on the curved head of the cane. "You didn't make the League meeting Monday night, did you?" Gerald shook his head reluctantly, hoping not to be scolded. "Well, we sure could have used you. Some folks just don't understand, brother. If we don't make some plans now, if we don't get to work, we'll be in big economic trouble when all the soldiers come back home. Broad Street's gonna dry up!"

"I thought that was the job of the Community Development League," Gerald said in defense of the city improvement association he had worked with.

"Well, you'd never know it, brother! You need to be at those meetings. I never saw such foot dragging in all my life! I'm telling you, those people are either flat-out stupid or they got something against the rest of us."

"That's pretty strong, Joe. Some fine people sit on that board, you know. I've served on the Historical Committee for years and never had any problems."

"Historical Committee?" Joe repeated, his questioning eyes searching for its relativity to his point. "Brother Tower, I know you'd do a fine job at anything you took on, but the committee that calls the shots is Commerce and Trade. I tell you, we can't get through to those folks!"

Gerald pushed his hands into his pockets and lowered his head skeptically, which only spurred Joe Pine on. "Mark my word, brother Tower, we're living off the troops at Camp Gordon and the war effort at the Augusta Arsenal. When the war's over, that's gonna slow way down."

As irritating as he found the portly alarmist, Gerald could not ignore so evident a prediction. Tower Supply enjoyed a good share of the business generated by both government facilities. Had he, like other area businessmen, been lulled by the synthetic economy? Was the pain of the Great Depression so lingering that men would foolishly suppress any thought of another economic adjustment?

"The problem is," Pine said, "folks like you are kind of insulated from it all, brother Tower."

"Insulated? Insulated from what, Joe?" Gerald's brow wrinkled as he lost his smile. He prided himself on being an honorable man, and any indication that another saw him in a questioning light was a matter of real concern.

"Now brother, I don't mean any offense." Pine shifted his weight nervously, an instinctive reflex when others became irritated with him. "If we had all Gerald Towers in high places, what a fine community this would be. What I mean is that you don't depend on the public the way most of us do." He waited a moment to see if Gerald was following him. "You don't need the same things the majority of us do, so you don't see all the hassles."

From the corner of his eye, Gerald saw Eleanor speaking with a friend across the room. Relief would be arriving shortly if he could just hold out. Joe never talked business around the ladies. "Do you see what I'm getting at, brother?"

"I'm trying to, Joe."

"I can tell you things that you wouldn't believe, brother Tower. I can take you to well-meaning folks who harbor serious fear." Glancing over his shoulder to ensure privacy, Joe inched closer to his listener. "See, nobody can exactly put their finger on it. A little guy in the street like me can't get any attention."

"Attention from who? What are you trying to say, Joe?"

The little man's face grew sober, his hand anxiously scratching the balding head in anticipation of a skeptical reception. "Well, I've studied this town's history, spent a lot of time in the library, brother Tower, talked to some folks who go way back. And I'm telling you there have been, and there are, some powerful forces at work here. I'm a religious man and I wouldn't say this to just anybody, but danged if I don't think this town's been hexed!"

Gerald stood with hands in pockets staring at the floor, for he was certain his expression would have ridiculed Joe Pine. "Little old quaint Augusta? Joe, ol' buddy…. I tell you what…." But Eleanor arrived and he thought it best not to continue.

"Afternoon, sister Eleanor," Joe greeted graciously, his face wide with smile as he nodded his head. "How lovely you are this fine day."

"It's nice to see you, Joe," she replied in polite but reserved tones. She despised his calling her *sister*, well-meaning as it might be, for she was neither his sister nor Catholic, nor anything else to him that suggested such a salutation. "How is Martha these days?" she inquired of his mother, for at this late date in life Joe had yet to entice a lady of the community to the altar.

"Doing very nicely just now, sister. You know, she'll be 85 this year, God willing."

"You give her my best," Eleanor added as she retrieved her purse and nudged Gerald toward the door. Joe Pine had emptied another table.

Jasper offered to bring their cars around, but the short walk to the parking lot would give them time to talk. Eleanor took Gerald's arm as they stepped from the curb. "What was on 'brother' Pine's mind?" she sighed. "You were really going at it when I came up."

"Oh, the same old story. He'll bend the ear of anybody who gets near him. He thinks the town's gonna dry up." Gerald opened the door of the light gray LaSalle and seated his wife behind the steering wheel. "I used to think it was just old worrisome Joe. But you remember John Parkman? Well, he's not like Joe, you know. He's got his head on straight. Remember when he offered for mayor and suddenly backed out? Well, he hinted at some things on the golf course a few weeks back that were downright disturbing."

"Gerald?" Eleanor interrupted. She was staring through the windshield, her thoughts drifting far from his.

"Yes?"

"What do you think we should do?"

His chest rose and fell in exasperation, a little frown setting in. "Well, I guess I could attend the League's board meeting this month."

"Gerald Tower!" she snapped, lashing him for not reading her mind. "This letter from your son!"

His head wagged slowly from side to side as he rested a hand on the car door. "I thought we were talking about Joe Pine."

She paused reflectively, biting her lower lip. "I'm sorry, love. It's just all so sudden and there's no one to give him advice over there. I don't know what to do!"

Gerald reached into the car and took her hand, his smile as reassuring as possible. "I've got to get back to the office, and you'll be late at the USO." He leaned down and kissed her. "We'll talk about it some more at home. Okay?"

She returned his smile and put the car in gear. His lips held their affectionate curl until Milledge Road traffic absorbed the LaSalle. He loved her and he was proud of her, for she had played a major role in bringing Augusta's USO up to what it was. Thousands of young men passed through Camp Gordon, all away from home, most for the first time. Eleanor Tower, like so many of Augusta's ladies, was a marvelous surrogate mother with broad and sympathetic shoulders to those in need.

Hardly a weekend passed that a dozen or more crew-cut privates were not around the Tower dining room table. Her compassion knew no bounds, for she understood what it was to have a son in service.

On a late September afternoon, Gerald got a call that they would have overnight guests. Eleanor had adopted a soldier and his new bride who were unable to find off-base housing. Not that Augusta families were indifferent to such needs, but so many homes were already taken. The girl, a wisp of a 19-year-old and homesick, swept into the bewildering rush of wartime marriage and became a special challenge for Gerald's wife. Overnight lasted for eight weeks, suitably so in Matt's own bedroom.

# CHAPTER 18

# Hell in Ipswich

A N ORNATE CATHEDRAL ceiling arched high above the polished wood casket. Etta Moore's older half-sister, Joan, had passed away after months of declining health. Until recent years the two shared little more than birth from the same womb because of the older sister's jealousy when her widowed mother remarried. The second marriage, to a prospering shipping merchant, produced Etta and gave her every cultural advantage.

At 21, Etta met and married a dashing army captain who had distinguished himself in His Majesty's intelligence service during World War I. Robert Albert Moore was five years her senior and conveyed all the qualities of officer and gentleman that appealed to a lady of breeding. Upon discharge from service, he would manage the family hotels in Ipswich and Felixstowe on the coast.

In recent years, when Etta and Joan became sole family survivors, their relationship began to warm. Etta traveled faithfully to

Hadleigh when her frail sister's health began to decline. It was on such a trip that she crossed paths with Matt Tower. How ironic that months later, he would share her sadness on the family pew of Ipswich's historic old Greystone Church. He had not anticipated spending a day's leave in such circumstances, but fate overruled.

Graciously, the Vicar was brief though sensitive with the service, for funerals in England were all too frequent in these war years. The thick overcast day certainly mirrored the mood of the mourners gathered in late morning to comfort each other and pay their respects to this loved one.

The concluding hymn, a favorite of the deceased, tested the deep, rich pipes of the organ, and there were no dry eyes in the sanctuary. Vivie sat between Matt and her parents and held his hand as they shared a hymnal. "Good heavens," she whispered. "Something must be wrong with the organ."

"Holding a pedal too long?" Matt whispered back. Others around them registered equal wonder. The Vicar cast a glance in the direction of the organ stall without result. They sang on, making the best of it to the last note. But the pulsating drone continued, growing in intensity. Several people attempted to stand but settled back in their seats at the bidding of the Vicar, who waved them down. Across the aisle a youngster clung to his mother with a frown of concern over the unfamiliar noise.

Heads tilted toward the ceiling and others bowed prayerfully, for the disturbance was not from within but from the sky. Matt felt Vivie's moist palms surround his hand, her blouse rising and falling in deep, long breaths. He had heard the sound before, though not this loud, just south of his base and watched an RAF Hawker Tempest in hot pursuit of a flying bomb. He was denied the outcome as the adversaries were quickly out of sight.

Robert Moore put his arm around Etta, his free hand covering hers reassuringly. He leaned toward Matt. "V-1s, Lieutenant.

Strung out like one following the other." Winged death was directly overhead, their chilling roars numbing the souls beneath them. Barely audible were the child's whimpers as he lay on his mother's shoulder. Matt's lips parted, his eyelids closing slowly. *"Dear God,"* he breathed to himself. *"Spare these people!"*

His prayer attracted Vivie's eye and she raised her head slightly. In spite of the imminent danger, she felt a great sense of peace from the American flyer beside her. She watched him privately, his head bowed slightly, the bright silver bar perched proudly on the shoulder of his dark-green jacket. Her eyes traced his profile, forehead, nose, the gentle lips. Lips that could suspend her thoughts with their touch. Lips that would be so welcome just then.

The wait was excruciating. Horrible thoughts racked the minds of the threatened congregation, for the bombs were timed to reach certain cities where their engines stopped and drop them indiscriminately on the helpless below. After the longest of times, Matt's experienced ear may have been first to detect the miracle. The things were passing them by.

He leaned forward slightly, looking beyond Vivie to her parents. "They're going away. I think they'll miss the city. They were lower than usual, Major, if 1,500 feet."

Robert Moore agreed. "Haven't heard two before, like one trailing the other."

The "Doodlebug" was a new terror to England, a single one capable of leveling much of a block. Those leaving the church first did so hesitantly, scanning the sky for lingering danger. Alarmed groups from nearby buildings were already gathered at the curbs to evaluate the near miss.

Little was said as the funeral party drove through the misty sunless streets, then up Cemetery Road where the undertaker's tent provided comforting shelter for the smaller number at graveside. Here, divorced from formal ecclesiastical setting, the Vicar's concluding remarks were thoughtfully warm and comforting to the family.

Matt noticed the little boy, still red-eyed and sniffling, clinging to his mother as she came to greet the Moores. Sorrow could not tether Etta's graciousness. "Oh, Ann, thank you for coming."

The family exchanged greetings and condolences with the child's mother, then Etta turned to Matt. "I'd like you to meet Captain Matt Tower, Vivian's friend. Captain, this is Ann Taylor, a dear friend of my sister in Hadleigh."

Matt responded politely then lent his attention to the small boy, offering to shake his hand. But the youngster was no more ready for strangers now than at the church and promptly buried his face in the collar of his mother's coat. "I'm sorry, Captain," she apologized, patting the child's back softly. "Davy's a bit put out by it all."

"That's all right," Matt chuckled. "He knows better than to trust a Yank!"

The pun encouraged a polite ripple of laughter among the adults but failed to affect the lad's mood. "Tell you what, Davy," the American flyer said. "Ten shillings says we can find a smile in there somewhere." Matt pulled the note from his wallet and stuck it in the boy's pants pocket. "You tell mom to stop by a toy shop before she leaves town, okay?"

The youngster understood the word *toy* well enough and his mood softened a bit. "Tell the captain thank you, darling." After a second the little fellow whispered the words timidly and showed his mother the currency. "Mommy, can I have a toy?"

"Thank you, Captain," the mother repeated. "It does seem to be making a difference."

There would be overnight family at Falcon's Rest, and Etta needed a few items from town. Vivie assumed the responsibility, knowing readily it would provide time alone with Matt, and she had promised to take him through the quaint shops and streets that interested him so.

Vivie knew just the spot to park. A side street, off Butter Market, accommodated the Morris sedan nicely and placed them in the center of the business district. To Matt, the city was out of a fairy tale. This hodgepodge of architectural styles might have been from a Disney movie set, and Vivie smiled at his evident pleasure. "How old is this city?" he inquired, pausing at the curb.

"Oh, dear," she sighed, tightening the coat belt around her waist. "There were settlements here from the stone age. In the first century, it was quite a large Anglo-Saxon community. We survived the Vikings, the Danes, and finally the Normans."

"How about the buildings?"

"A church or two and a few other buildings date to 1000 AD. Come on, we'll have time to see a few."

Matt was so enchanted that the subtle changes in the woman holding his arm went unnoticed. That morning in the church, when the bombs passed above them, Vivie surrendered to her heart. The thought of tragedy separating them before they had shared life together was suddenly unbearable to her. Inhibitions that had plagued her for so long were beginning to crumble.

They were at the corner of Butter Market and St. Stephens when Matt spied the bookshop. "Hey, can we stop here a minute?" She nodded her approval. "This looks like an oldy," he added, gesturing at the two-story structure.

"And quite the pride of Butter Market. It's called *Ancient House*. About 1560 or so. The Sparrow family was the last to use it as a home." She smiled broadly and laid her head playfully on Matt's shoulder. "In school we thought that quite humorous. We called it the bird house!"

"And the coat of arms there?"

"King Charles II. They were ardent royalists, you know. Legend is they hid the king in that great old attic after the Battle of Worcester. No one really knows."

The old house, with its remarkable woodwork and pargeting, was adorned with five engraved bay windows. Matt thought them exquisite. "What's that under the windows, that engraving?"

"I think I shall charge you for tour guiding," Vivie laughed. "Each one represented a continent of the world, See there, a camel's head for Asia, the crocodile for Africa, and for Europe, a scepter of authority. Look, that one is for your America. See the Indian and bow."

"And the one on the end? I don't get that one."

"That's Atlas holding up the world. It should have been Australia, but the builders had never heard of it."

His spirits were immune to the weather as they walked along, up to Corn Hill and Town Hall, then the majestic ancient Corn Exchange. They detoured at Tower Street so she could show him the beautiful St. Mary-le-Tower Church, its exquisite spire shading the courtyard, where the burgesses gathered to receive the charter of King John.

After a snack and beverage on Tavern Street, Vivie pointed to a distant building at the end of the block. "Have you read much of Dickens?"

"Slightly," Matt smiled. "I did two reports from his books in high school."

"Then you'll love the White Horse Hotel. He used its setting in *The Pickwick Papers*. It was there Mr. Pickwick found himself in the lady's bedroom."

They both smiled at the implication of her quote, though they knew quite well that was not Mr. Dickens' intention. Matt loved the twinkle in her eye whenever the subject bordered on the risqué, but he knew the limits of her taste and respected her enough not to exceed them.

Several times, he caught the hum of aircraft engines rising and falling across the outlying terrain. Not uncommon with England, a virtual aircraft carrier at that point. Vivie understood his expression all too well. She hugged his arm tighter, hoping to keep his mind on terra firma right down there beside her.

It seemed she was succeeding as they strolled down Upper Brooke, for he was pausing again to view the shops. She brushed at the spots on his uniform where drops of condensation had found their mark. "Oh, darling, I should have brought a brolly."

"You're talking British again," he chuckled, hugging her close with one arm. "What's that in English?"

"A brolly?" she repeated, as though volume would help him understand. "To put over your head, silly. Like this." She worked her hands to show him.

"Umbrella. Right!" he grinned. Even as he talked, his pace was slowing again, his clear hazel eyes fixed in the direction of the River Orwell. He was listening intently. "Sounds like they can't find the field. They're circling all over the place."

Vivie could barely hear the planes, much less determine their changes in flight. But Etta had said, "If you're to keep company with a military man...." She sighed softly, making the best of it and praying under her breath that the engines would soon fade away.

"Viv, I think we should head back to the car." The suggestion surprised her, but not so much as his insistent change of direction. It was not the thoughtful handling she had grown accustomed to.

"Have I tired you so soon, poppet?" she asked with a nervous laugh, trying to understand his decision.

He picked up their pace a bit, smiled, and patted the soft, dainty hand draped through his arm. Before he could reply, she directed his attention to the end of the block. With few braving the elements that day, those out and about attracted one's eye. There stood Ann Taylor and her son. Vivie smiled and waved a greeting.

In spite of the distance between them, Ann recognized the

waving couple, bent down, and brought the youngster's attention to her friends. The little fellow lifted his hand to show them the item he clutched so securely. "Ohhh!" Vivie cooed. "He's found a toy!"

Suddenly, sharp, pounding echoes rolled over the quiet city, three maybe four, just seconds apart. The young couple stopped abruptly and turned toward the river docks, where cracking machine-gun fire replaced the fading rumble of explosions. "Matt!" Vivie gasped. "Those were bombs!"

The whine of Nazi aircraft engines grew in intensity as two ghostly silhouettes appeared in the distance just under the overcast. They were fighters of some description, lining up on the street, the all-too-familiar orange flashes sparking their wings. For a second, the couple watched in disbelief as the rain of bullets slammed into the roadway, curbs, and building fronts, racing toward them in lightning eruptions.

Matt lifted Vivie in a bear hug, springing into the nearest doorway and covering her with his body. Through the glass storefront, she saw Ann and the boy, panic-driven to cross the street and reach Vivie. "Ann!" she screamed. "Get back!"

Her voice was drowned out in the crash of firepower from the first fighter as concrete, wood and glass splintered and shattered within inches of Matt's back. Ann froze in terror, fully exposed in the street with the boy. As the destruction reached them, she squatted down over the child. Mercifully, the projectiles ate up the roadway on either side of them, raising dust and rubble, but missing their target.

Ann saw the second fighter coming. She grabbed her son by the shoulders of his sweater and pulled him toward the dubious safety of the sidewalk. They had little chance, for the second spray of bullets was already churning past Matt and Vivie, the ricochets and flying matter knocking out windows on either side of the couple. Debris rained down over the American flyer's back and arms, muffling Vivie's cries.

As the firing passed them, the couple turned quickly to learn the fate of mother and child. They saw them reach the curb just as the sidewalk shattered in a hail of bullets. Whirling dust obscured little Davey, but they clearly saw Ann spin and fall to the ground. Vivie's hands rushed to her face, "Noooo!" she screamed, stumbling from the doorway.

Matt grabbed her arm, slowing her until he could check the sky. In the distance, beneath the clouds, the two fighters raced away, their guns popping intermittently at random targets. Vivie was sobbing, her lovely cheeks smeared and pale, as she stared at the fateful corner. When Matt was satisfied with their safety, he tugged her back to life and raced down the block.

Ann had raised herself on hands and knees by the time the couple reached her. She was a pathetic sight, dazed, with grit and dust plastered over her clothing and hair. Blood oozed from facial wounds and badly scraped hands. Whimpering and disoriented, she crawled in circles searching blindly. "Davey! Oh, God please.... My son!...Where's my little boy?"

Anxiety heightened as belated air-raid sirens came alive, lending their nerve-racking whines to the confusion. The American flyer paused for an instant to search the skies again lest more of the raiders lurked about. "Matt!" Vivie whimpered, her extended arms pleading for direction.

As the dust settled, he spotted the child sprawled on his back in the gutter. It was a sight that would have done mother nor Vivie any good. "Viv! Tend to her! Keep her still! I've got the boy."

Matt knelt beside the little body, brushing away dirt and dust as he searched cautiously for injuries. As distressful as the youngster appeared, unconscious and spotted with blood, it was the small twisted left leg that wrenched the American's heart. Crimson liquid pumped from a gaping wound at the calf where debris had ripped flesh and fractured the bone. He glanced back to see how Vivie was doing with Ann. "Get her feet up, Viv! Put your coat over her!"

With rapid, precise movements, Matt slipped off his jacket and tie, covered the little boy, then went to work on the leg. Trained, nimble fingers fashioned a tourniquet from his neckwear and secured it with a fountain pen. He could not know the extent of the youngster's injuries and preferred to move him as little as possible. Vivie was better now and able to apply her WVS training to good advantage with Ann. For the moment they had done all possible.

Matt dragged a sleeve across his dripping brow, tucked the jacket snugly around Davey, and stood up. "Vivie, I'll watch them. You go get the car. And hurry!"

She sprinted away, brushing past the gaping spectators assembling at the corner, thankful she had worn low heels. A whiskered warden, complete with helmet and pouch, limped over to Matt in an effort to help. "I'm here, Yank, if I can do some good."

"Tell 'em to turn off those blasted sirens!" the American snapped. "They're too bloody late!"

The older man stared at Matt, taken back by the terse response, but his eyes held no offense. He understood the frustration well. It had been his lot for the whole war to meet the sneak attacks, whether butterfly bomb, incendiary, or raiders like today. "It ain't the CD's fault, Lieutenant. Them fighters slips in low under the radar. The one I saw was that new Focke-Wulf 190, the 'D' model. Lot longer nose. They carry tanks under the wings. They can get here and back."

Matt thought about that before the anger reached his tongue. It was a perfect day for what had just happened. Dozens of his missions employed the same tactic, except they didn't strafe the villages along the way. He had but to look down at the injured child, and knots of rage gripped his stomach. "Hey, I'm sorry. Okay?" he sighed at the warden, his eyes searching the vacant horizon that had swallowed up the Germans. "There's got to be a special cage in hell for people like that!"

The old warden's pouch proved invaluable, with its store of first-aid supplies. "Bring me a newspaper and be quick about it!" he ordered a woman spectator. As she hurried into the corner pub, the warden set about stripping off lengths of tape and laid them out on the curb. "We best secure that leg before we move the lad."

The clatter of fire equipment echoed through the streets in response to a blaze on the next block. In spite of the sirens, curious souls dared the streets, surveying the damage and peering down the block at the group tending the injured woman and child. The rolled newspaper fashioned an adequate splint for the wounded youngster, and by the time Vivie arrived with the car, the two men had their patient ready to travel.

As Matt straightened up, Ann was standing beside him, haggard, trembling, and clutching Vivie's coat around her. "Is... is he...?"

Matt forced a smile, hoping to ease her distress as much as possible, for there was no way of knowing how badly the little fellow was hurt. "He's alive. A little dazed, but all I could find was a leg injury." She collapsed on the American's chest, burying her forehead in his shoulder. Matt led the sobbing woman to the car and placed her in the back seat, then turned to Vivie. "A hospital?" he questioned.

"East Suffolk. It's not far."

"You drive. I'll help Ann with little Davey." He returned to the boy, and with the warden's assistance, placed him next to his mother with his head in her lap.

Abruptly, the crowd began breaking up, stumbling and bumping each other, their attention riveted to the sky instead of their path. "Mother of God!" cried a fat, aproned woman as she crossed herself and ran past the car. "They're back! The Germans are back!"

Matt's lips frowned in concern as his eyes met the warden's. The car was a sitting duck, sure to be singled out by an attacker. His one thought was to remove the passengers and get them behind the corner building. As he reached for Davey, the warden's hand stopped him. "Half a mo', Yank! They're Spits!"

Skeptically, Matt's eyes scanned the overcast skies as he weighed the probabilities. The engines were closing rapidly, and there was no time for judgment error. His hand locked onto the warden's lapel, aligning the old man's face with his own. "Spitfires!" the Britisher blurted assuringly. "I'd know the sound anywhere! I'd say they're looking for those Huns."

Not until the wide, rounded fighter wings slid out of the overcast did Matt ease his grip on the warden. There was no disputing the RAF insignia as the twin pursuers roared by a few hundred feet overhead. His hand went apologetically to the warden's shoulder, enticing a forgiving smile from the wrinkled face. "Be off wit ya', Yank! The lad needs help!"

Vivie negotiated streets and turns with a native's hand as Matt, seated beside Ann, cradled Davey's legs in his lap. He loosened the tourniquet for a moment, watching the red stain spread along the paper splint. "He's bleeding, Lieutenant!" Ann sobbed, her hands rushing to cover her face.

"It's okay," Matt replied softly, his voice steady and calm. "We have to let some circulation through. You've got a strong young man here. I think he's gonna do just fine."

The child stirred slightly, the first encouragement since Matt reached him in the street. A mixed blessing at best, for the pain would be excruciating if he awoke. "How're we doing, Viv? I think Davey's coming around."

"Just a block. We're nearly there!"

Unfamiliar with the hospital, Matt carried Davey in the front door, where the sight of his small, limp body summoned nurses on the double. "I'm Nurse Croft," the first to greet them announced. "What happened to him?"

"Air raid. His leg," Matt panted, feeling the strain of the last few minutes. "He's bleeding a lot."

"Get Dr. Jefferies quickly!" Croft ordered a nearby aide. She turned and motioned to Davie's group. "Follow me."

Coming to the front of the hospital had placed them some distance from the treatment rooms, but the nurse made no comment on the error as she jogged ahead of them through the hallways. The medicinal smell grew stronger as they reached the emergency stations, where medical personnel had been notified of casualties at the docks. Davy became the center of attention as Matt gently laid him on one of the curtain-encircled tables. "You better loosen the tourniquet for a second," the American cautioned. "It's been a while."

Nurse Croft smiled sympathetically and checked the wound. "Never you mind, Lieutenant. He'll be in very good hands now with Dr. Jefferies."

It was unnecessary for the slender, graying man in flowing white duster to jog to the patient, for his long rapid stride would have done the job adequately. This doctor's attentive eyes and sure movements won Matt's confidence quickly. In seconds he had the makeshift splint off. His hands sought out the youngster's injuries from head to toe as Matt explained the events leading to the injuries.

Vivie's supporting arm prevented Ann's collapse. Such agony she had seldom seen on the face of a mother. A mother, smeared with blood, who had yet to treat her own wounds. Dr. Jefferies paused briefly and glanced at the anxious cluster around him. "Nurse, would you find some chairs in the hall for the ladies? You too, Captain. I'm certain they could use your support."

A nurse's aide ushered the trio to an alcove near the treatment room, where cushioned benches received their grateful bodies. The petite, brown-haired young woman returned in a moment with a basin and towel. She seated herself beside Ann and dampened the cloth with warm water. "This should make you feel much better. Let's just freshen up a bit and tend these nasty scrapes."

Ann pressed the damp cloth to her face, the first consideration she had given herself since the attack. "Tell me about my son, please. Is he badly hurt?"

"The doctor will know more about that shortly. They've given him a local so he'll have no pain. He's resting quietly now." She produced a small bottle and cotton swab. "This may sting a bit. But we don't want any infections, do we?"

It would be a long wait, impeded by the squeaking stretchers at the end of the hall. Casualties were arriving from the docks where bombs surprised workers on Eagle Wharf near the oil depot. To the layman, it might seem an unlikely day weatherwise for an attack, but Matt knew better.

Ann was calmer now, though her face was whiter than it should be. Shivers ran the length of her body every few minutes in spite of the warm water and the coat she still clutched. Their guardian angel reappeared, this time with steaming mugs of coffee. "I can make it Irish if you like," she chuckled.

"This will be fine, thank you," Vivie replied. "I would like to use the blower if I may. Matt, will you stay with Ann while I ring up Mum?" He nodded his willingness and slid over next to the anxious mother.

Ann's unsteady hands had difficulty with the coffee, and Matt placed his palm under the mug for support. She smiled her appreciation and sampled the warm, therapeutic liquid. "How can I thank you, Captain? If you had not been there...."

"Oh, someone would have," he replied with a modest grin, as he watched her lips draw from the rim of the mug. "What matters now is that Davy's in good hands."

"Pardon me, Captain. Might I have a word with you?" The voice was that of a thirtyish RAF officer who stood above them with cap and clipboard under arm. He leaned heavily on a black cane and his limp was quite noticeable. "Major Howard, here."

The American airman rose to greet the brown-eyed, dark-haired senior officer. "Matt Tower, sir."

"My apologies for interrupting. I'm with RAF Intelligence. We understand you were caught in the raid earlier."

"That's an understatement, sir," Matt replied soberly.

"Are you up to a question or two? These attacks have grown in intensity all along the eastern coast since the invasion. Anything you can tell us may be of help."

Matt glanced back at Ann, who nodded her approval. "I'm fine, Captain. Do what you must."

The British officer retrieved his clipboard and flipped a page or two. "Did you get a good look at the aircraft?"

"Focke-Wulf 190's. A pair of them."

"Markings?"

"A lot like the ones we see over Holland and Belgium." Matt took the pen and sketched the numbers and markings as best he could recall them. "I won't forget the leader. There was a bright yellow decal of some sort on his cowling, like a shield with a wide black stripe. They came from the south, the dock area, and went straight north out of sight."

"Luftflotte Three. That would be their sector, right enough," the British officer nodded. "Can you recall anything else that might be helpful?"

"No, unfortunately. It only lasted a minute and we had our heads down for most of it."

"Was anyone in your party injured?"

"Yes, her son," Matt confirmed, glancing at Ann.

I'm dreadfully sorry, madam. What's his condition?"

"We don't know as yet," Ann replied, dabbing at her eyes with a tiny lace handkerchief. "His leg is hurt and he's still groggy."

The major expressed his hopes for a speedy recovery and Matt accompanied him to the hallway. "What in blazes were they doing in the streets on a day like this?" he whispered to the American. "We've warned the town about these sneak attacks."

"Well, they're not from here," Matt countered in defense of the worried mother. "They were attending the funeral of a friend." The RAF officer seemed unimpressed as he hobbled away, mumbling to himself, in search of other witnesses.

Dr. Jefferies leaned against the wall, watching the activity in Davey's treatment room. Matt eased around the doorway so as not to draw Ann's attention and approached the physician. "How's the youngster doing?"

"He's had a concussion, Lieutenant. It appears quite mild, but those things are unpredictable, you know. We'll have to watch him closely for the next few hours." Dr. Jefferies raised the boy's leg and slid his pants up a few inches. "Nasty leg wound about here. Damaged the fibula, and there's a clear fracture of the tibia. Of course, we can set those and they should mend. The damaged flesh and veins are another matter. We're preparing for surgery now."

Ann was on her feet and heading for the hallway when Matt returned. He forced a smile. "Just checking on the little patient."

"How is he? I want to see him."

"He's holding up very well. They need to operate on the leg right away and you have to sign some papers."

"Oh… if his father were only here! David is so good at these things."

"Can we reach him?"

"No. He's in London. They arrived there this morning, and I'm not sure where he is staying yet."

A sigh of relief escaped Matt's lips as Vivie returned. She was closer to Ann, and he did not relish advising the distraught mother alone. "Mum and Dad are on the way. Is there any word on little Davey?"

Matt explained what was happening, and the two of them accompanied Ann to the treatment room. She bent over, kissed her son on the forehead, and smoothed his hair into place. Dr. Jefferies explained what they hoped to accomplish with the veins and muscle that were damaged. Bravely, she agreed and signed the forms.

The long, anxious vigil had begun as the three huddled together in the sterile white alcove. They talked and tried to laugh to ease the tension as the minutes slipped by. Then Etta was in the doorway. Burdened with her own sorrow, she had come to console another: a mother, away from home, frightened, and required to make serious decisions on her own.

Matt marveled at the effect Etta's presence had on Ann. Such inner strength and composure he had seen in few women. As the two embraced the younger woman poured out, in jerking sobs, what was left of her pent-up emotion. "Oh... Etta, Davey's been hurt!"

Mrs. Moore seated herself beside the teary young woman, her voice soothing and reassuring as they held hands. Within minutes order had returned, the conversation grew lighter, and Etta could, at last, give some attention to the couple sitting across from her. "I say, aren't you two a wretched sight!"

Matt shrugged as a helpless smile creased his lips. Vivie went for her purse and mirror, a move which seemed to amuse Ann. "It's quite a mystery to me," Etta said goodheartedly. "Every time you two go out to play, you come back in a horrid mess!"

It was just the levity needed. Ann chuckled spontaneously—a welcome, if short, reprieve for those who shared her season of trouble. Etta seemed pleased with the response. "Go on now, children, tend to yourselves. Mary Pearson is on the way and Major Moore is trying to get through to London."

# CHAPTER 19

# The Proposal

MATT DREW DEEPLY of the fresh air as he waited for Vivie on the hospital steps. The afternoon had tested the metal of everyone, and now the day was darkening to match the mood of the hour. The couple had taken advantage of the lavatory and cleaned themselves as much as possible. She came along shortly, carrying her coat and purse. She had done a fair job of repairing her makeup, but the dress and coat were still badly soiled.

"Oh, poppet," she mourned. "Your uniform is ruined!"

"Yep," he grinned as he took her hand. "Hanging out with you is pretty rough on a fellow's wardrobe."

She just smiled and looped her arm confidently around his. "It does seem I'm forever apologizing for the way your leave turns out, doesn't it?"

They found a bench in the garden area, and Matt brushed it off with his handkerchief. She sat close to him, her eyes soft and adoring. "You quite bowled Mrs. Pearson over, you know. Where did you get the flowers?"

He chuckled and stretched his arms behind his head. "One of the nurses knew a patient that had a lot of them. Cost me a buck... crown, whatever, but I owe that dear lady a heck of a lot. If it weren't for her..."

Vivie's gaze dropped to their joined hands. Her heart had been measuring him over the months, and the events of the day capped the examination for her. "Poppet, you were wonderful with Davey and Ann this morning. We were all in such a state! But you... you were like a rock." She lifted his hand and kissed it tenderly.

"353rd Fighter Group at your service, ma'am," he grinned, waving a casual salute. "You did a pretty commendable job yourself, dear." His fingers straightened her hair and rested on her soft, white cheek. "It's up to the folks inside now. I just hope that little fellow comes out okay." Matt's brow wrinkled slightly as he leaned back on the bench. "I didn't appreciate that RAF guy's attitude. He was danged abrupt to Ann. Is he dumb enough to think she wanted the kid to get hurt?"

"Of course not, sweetheart. But the children have been a concern for so long. When war came, they were evacuated from the coastal towns and larger cities. They came through by the hundreds, and your heart would go out to them. Little ones leaving their homes and families for camps and country estates."

Vivie shook her head slowly, her eyes dropping reflectively. "Some so very small, tagging behind an older sister or brother, their name tags in disarray. And of course, the inevitable gas masks bumping about their little sides."

"Gas masks?"

"Oh, we all carried them. No one knew what the Germans were capable of. The women formed brigades to meet the evacuation trains. We fed and comforted the children as best we could. Many stayed a night or two at Falcon's Rest, awaiting placement inland."

The thought of children in such defensive gear was repugnant to Matt. He stretched and rose to his feet in an attempt to break the sullen mood. Vivie's eyes followed him to the railing, where he stood for a moment watching evening settle over the city. "Poppet?" she questioned in concern.

"There's never enough time, that's all," Matt sighed. "I haven't spent two minutes with you, and the last service bus leaves in a couple of hours."

She moved to his side and took his arm. "Well, you shan't be on it, dear one. I shall personally deliver you to your Uncle Sam in the Morris sedan."

They returned to Falcon's Rest, where Vivie changed to her WVS uniform. Easier to pass the Home Guard checkpoints that way, she explained. Matt smiled as he watched her adjust the headlight hoods. The restricted beam resulted in a slower trip, which fit their needs nicely. It amused him when she flashed her credentials at the stops and explained authoritatively, "I'm returning an Allied flyer to his base."

"You get a kick out of that, don't you?" he chuckled.

"What?"

"Flashing your papers, putting it over on those old guys like that."

"Well, that's what I'm doing, isn't it?" A smug little smile bent her lips as she glanced at him in the semi-dark cab. "Perhaps the Allied flyer would prefer walking the last three miles."

Matt leaned over and offered a penitent kiss. She kept him suspended for a moment as punishment, then gave him a quick buss. The narrow turnoff to Great Wenham required a good driver at night, leaving little time for meaningful conversation. After the longest time, Matt spotted a landmark he recognized: the Walldons' lodge off to the right.

"You could stay the night there," he motioned, voicing his concern about her return alone to Ipswich.

"I'll be just fine. You don't have to worry about me. I've made the trip a hundred times."

Vivie proved her point as she steered smoothly through Great Wenham to Lodge Farm, which was in walking distance of Matt's barracks. She switched the engine off and leaned back in the car seat. "There now, satisfied?"

"I'm not worried that you'd get lost. I just don't want the buggers to get you."

"Love," she sighed, shifting to face him. "I'm not a little nipper, you know. I'm a big girl and I can be quite resourceful. Besides, dear Webley is always near on such trips."

"Webley? Who is Webley?"

She smiled broadly and reached under the car seat. "He's not a *who*, silly; he's an *it*!"

She retrieved an impressive revolver, handling it quite well. "Standard army 38 issue," she snapped proudly. "I'm not a fem-sissy about weapons. I'm quite at home with them."

Matt chuckled as he examined the weapon. "Neat. I'm impressed."

"From Dad; it was his. I'm never out alone without it." She sensed his skepticism as he hefted the firearm, and took it back from him. "Really, I'm quite good with it. Six holes in a 12-inch target at 30 feet. Double action, I might add." She paused to get his reaction.

"Just watching you wave it around would impress anybody!"

Vivie tucked the revolver under the seat and smiled up at Matt. "Now, don't you feel better about it?"

"That you put the thing away?"

"No, silly! That I should be quite safe going home." Her face glowed with confidence, the steady blue eyes and firm lips stating emphatically that she could take care of herself. That she would take care of herself, just for him.

Their eyes met, conversing in the special optical language of lovers, and her face began to soften. It was just such expressions of vulnerable surrender that made Vivie irresistible. They had come a long way in their courtship, well beyond the point of infatuation. The tragic events of the day confirmed that.

Vivie could still feel his arms around her, jerking her off the sidewalk into the safety of a doorway. He had placed his body over hers as they crouched inches from death.

They had worked as a team, overcoming a mother's hysteria, bringing life-saving order in the rescue of a young child. It was a little different this time as her head turned slightly to meet his advancing lips. When they kissed, they nestled together, savoring the warm nearness. How gracious fate had been.

Matt laid his cheek on the side of her face, loving the feel of her hair, the faint perfume. "Vivie?"

"Yes," she sighed, her breath softly brushing his ear.

"Will you marry me?"

She lay very still, her breathing suspended. In times past, when he had approached the question, she had discouraged him. Would he feel the tension mount in her body once again? Would she pull away and ask for more time?

Matt could not have prayed harder if he were on a sinking ship. "I love you, dear lady, and I can't picture the rest of my life without you."

She leaned back just a bit, but this time there was no tension. Her face was sober, the lovely eyes moist as they searched his. "Oh, poppet, there's nothing I want more."

He whistled softly as his hand brushed his brow. "You don't know how much I've worried about your answer. Anyway, it's the first hurdle," he beamed with relief. "Now I need to talk with your mom and dad. What kind of response do you think I'll get?"

"She returned his smile and cupped his face in her hands. "Well, you certainly have an ally in Mum! With Robert Moore, we'll just have to see."

She paused and turned away from Matt, her hands dropping to her lap. There was one reservation she must inject, and how he would react troubled her greatly. They read each other rather well, and he was concerned that she might have second thoughts on the matter of marriage. "Viv… what is it?"

After a moment, on the border of tears, she turned back to him. He took her hands reassuringly, patiently, and held his breath. "Matt, there is one thing I must ask. I don't want to set a date until the war is over."

Though his grimace was barely visible, the pressure of his fingers on hers testified to his deep disappointment, a letdown so strong she was quickly compelled to soften the impact. "At least, until it's clear the war is ending. Please. That's all I ask."

Matt slumped back against the car seat and stared through the windshield into the darkness outside. "Till the end of the war, Vivie? There's no telling how long that could be!" She remained silent, painfully resolved to this condition of engagement and praying to him with her eyes.

His sweaty fingers moved to ease the tension on his wrinkled brow before he could continue. "Do you realize what you are asking?"

"Yes," her voice pleaded softly. "It's horribly difficult for me as well. I've wanted you to ask the question for so long."

She made no effort to conceal her anxiety, for the stakes were the highest ever in her life. Matt's hands went to her face, where his thumbs smoothed away the moist streaks. "Sweetheart, I'm trying to understand, but with the war we have so little time. Anything could happen and we would never have been together, never really shared our lives. Don't you see?"

"Yes, I do see! I see an army bride waiting in the wings again with all the anxiety and entanglements. It frightens me, poppet."

It seemed a hundred years ago that she had sworn to protect herself from just such a dilemma. But she had made the mistake of confiding in flirtatious Ruth Hardy, who inflamed the romance. Then there was Mrs. Pearson, well-intended busy body, whose breach of confidence opened the door for all that had followed. Silently, she gave each of them a piece of her mind.

But in the Morris sedan's hushed darkness, overcharged emotions soon gave way to pensive reflection. In a final analysis, Vivie was forced to acknowledge the real culprit: her very own heart. Even now it told her there would be greater pain if she lost this man who so completed her life. If he continued to press for a wedding date, her resistance was sure to weaken.

"Now I know how Jacob felt," Matt sighed. "It took that poor guy 14 years to win Rachel's hand." Vivie was crying softly, and he could feel and hear her. "Well," he said, turning to her. "I'm just as stubborn as he and the prize is more than worth it."

She came into his arms eagerly, her head resting on his shoulder. "Please don't give up, darling. I love you so much!" He stroked her hair gently, holding her against him until she grew calmer. "It would never be 14 years," she sniffled.

"I should think not," he chuckled, mimicking her favorite expression. "But it's motivation enough to get this stinking war over with!"

The whine of a jeep engine filled the night air, bringing the couple to a sitting position. Two fine lines of light squealed to a stop in front of the Morris. Vivie hurried to freshen her face as Matt smoothed his hair. One of the MPs stood beside the jeep as the other approached, his flashlight illuminating the wagon's front seat. "Good evening, ma'am, Captain. May I see your pass, sir, and your papers, ma'am?"

Vivie rummaged through her purse as Matt retrieved the pass from his folded jacket in the back seat. "Is anything wrong, Sergeant?"

"Security patrol, sir," the MP replied as he looked over the papers. "Your car's been here a while. Just checking."

Vivie was compelled to assure him there was no threat in their presence. "I'm just returning one of your flyers to the base, Sergeant."

Glancing at Matt, who unknowingly sported a very evident pink smear across his lips, the soldier smiled and nodded at Vivie. "Yes, ma'am, and you're doing a darn fine job of it, too!"

The sergeant started to leave, then as on second thought, leaned back down. "Sir, have you been off base all day?"

"Yes, since about 0800. Why?"

"Well, I hate to be the one to tell you this, but Colonel Duncan was shot down this morning."

Vivie's hands rushed to her face, her eyes wide with concern, for she knew Matt's feelings about the base commander.

Disbelief consumed the American flyer. He had seen Duncan handle many a tight situation, and it was not easy to accept that much experience being shot out of the sky. "Do you know the details, Sergeant? How it happened, where he went down?"

"They were over Germany, sir, escorting B-17s. I heard it was flak that brought him down. That's as much as I know. There's a lot of change in command right now and the details haven't filtered down yet."

"Thanks, Sergeant. I appreciate your letting me know. I'll be coming in shortly."

"Oh, poppet!" Vivie wailed. "How horrible. I'm so sorry!"

"That just about wraps it up." Matt growled. "I get a day's leave, and that morning a funeral, the afternoon a hospital, the evening a rejected proposal. I park with my date and the MPs get me. And my CO is blown out of the air. What the heck is next, the invasion of England?"

Vivie, at a loss for something to say, rested her head on the steering wheel. The surge of the jeep engine broke the stillness as it drove away, leaving the couple alone with their web of problems. Matt had the greater of those problems, one of which was reassuring the woman he had proposed to. "Viv, I'm sorry. I didn't mean to blow off like that. It's nobody's fault."

She responded without hesitation, grateful that he had broken the mood. "But it is so unfair. I cherish every moment we have together." She turned to him and took his hands, smiling tenderly. "But you're wrong about one thing, my love. Your proposal wasn't rejected. It was accepted."

"I know it was, sweetheart. It's just that a guy wants to pop the question at a special time, and this didn't turn out to be it."

"You don't know much about women, do you?" she chuckled. "When that question comes, it is a special time and we build our own setting around it. Tonight is so very special for me, darling."

She kissed him and they clung to each other as though it were the first of the evening. As their lips parted, she ran her hands through his hair and rested them on his shoulders. "Now, I know you're concerned about your colonel, and I don't want you weaving in flight tomorrow from lack of rest. So you go home like a good little tyke, and when you come into town, we can talk about our plans."

"You are something else, dear lady," he smiled, reaching for his jacket. "How can a guy get so lucky!" He climbed out, closed the car door, and kissed her again through the window. "Let me know how Davey's doing as soon as you hear, okay? You and Webley have a safe trip. He's guarding precious cargo, you know."

As he crossed the base, Matt could hear machinery at work in the T-Hangar, where maintenance crews labored overtime on sick P-47s, a sure sign there was an early mission. He was anxious to know the story on Colonel Duncan, and it was irritating to find the barracks empty. After freshening up, the soiled coat was exchanged for a flight jacket against the chilly English night. He would find answers at the officers' club.

In spite of the beating the 353$^{rd}$ had taken in recent weeks, Auger Inn was in full swing. It was the only source on base for anesthesia against the painful realities of combat flying. The discomfort level that night was at an all-time high. John Smaragdis sat at a booth across from the bar, staring blankly at the empty bottles and glasses crowding the table. Matt eased through the crowd and made himself at home in the opposite seat. "What the devil happened to Duncan? Did you see it?"

Smaragdis sighed and slumped back in the booth. "Yeah, I saw it. I just never thought I'd see old Glenn Duncan go down."

"What happened?"

"We were flying cover for some 17s around Dummer Lake. On the way out, Duncan spotted a lot of aircraft on Wesendorf Airfield and took us down. We shot it up pretty good. He got an He 111 and pulled out, but a ton of flak at the end of the field caught him." Smaragdis drifted for a second, shaking his head, his mind rehashing the spectacle. "It had to be an oil line because he was trailing vapor."

"Did he go down right there?"

"No. He headed for the Dutch border, and the squadron followed for cover. Fifteen minutes later he had to belly in. We looked for a place to land, you know, to pick him up. It was just too wooded." Smaragdis grinned and rested his hands on the table. "What a character! He comes on the radio, says he's okay and he'll see us in three weeks. The next thing we see, *Dove of Peace* is going up in flames and Duncan is running for the woods."

Somebody primed the juke box, and Duke Ellington's *Take The A Train* wedged its way through the bar noise. Matt had been so wrapped up in Duncan's situation, he failed to notice the change on Smaragdis' collar. It was a good chance to lighten the mood. "Congratulations!"

"Yeah," John grunted.

"Double bars! You finally got them." Matt offered a casual salute with his smile of approval. "Captain John D. Smaragdis! The Luftwaffe better watch out now!"

Smaragdis mustered only a weak smile and returned the salute playfully. "I tell you this, Captain. I'd give 'em up in a minute if it would do Duncan any good." He leaned back again with a sigh. "So what have you been up to? Fallen in love yet?"

Matt, caught off guard, took the comment seriously. "What do you mean by that?"

"Hey, every time I get a pass off-base I end up falling in love."

Matt laughed heartily at the implication as he slid out of the booth. He wasn't about to take this motley crew into his confidence just yet. "I don't know, John. I guess it would help if I were Greek, right?"

# CHAPTER 20

# Matt's Supreme Test

JULY 1944 WAS a rough month for Adolph Hitler. Allied units were pushing their way successfully into France, and he narrowly escaped death at the hands of his own high command. For weeks thereafter the Fuhrer was obsessed with retaliation and insisted on attacking the will of the English people with all means available to him. Sneak attacks from the air, as Matt had experienced. Hundreds of vengeance bombs rained overhead, destroying and killing indiscriminately. For that month alone, 2,441 were killed and 7,107 injured, including little Davey Taylor.

Two "buzz bombs" hit Ipswich: one at the airfield and one at the west end of the city. These intensified Matt's concern for Vivie. The command changes and mission activity after the loss of Colonel Duncan made passes hard to come by. So she would frequent the Walldons', where he craftily arranged, with Chuck Shilling's help, to slip off-base to meet her.

Lieutenant Colonel Benjamin Rimerman took command of Slybird Group, which was not an unpopular move with the troops. This stocky, slightly balding warrior both complemented and contrasted the tall, wavy-haired Glenn Duncan. Where Duncan found success through a cunning and crafty engagement with the enemy, Rimerman balanced an impetuous tendency with the qualities of an excellent air leader. When Lieutenant Colonel William B. Bailey moved up to group executive officer, the stage was set for Glenn Duncan's revenge.

The weeks that followed were a fighter pilot's dream. There were often two missions a day as the bombers labored to destroy the Third Reich's ability to make war. On more than one occasion the targets could be spotted miles away by the columns of smoke from the previous day's attack. Enemy fighter response grew scarcer as the days dragged on, and Matt wondered what the Germans were saving them for, considering the pounding they were taking.

But the 353rd never came home with loaded guns. Rimerman turned the flight leaders loose to attack targets of chance and Matt reveled in it. They seemed the greatest days of his life, leading these four lethal fighters. Their specialty was railroads and marshaling yards, and if Matt could have counted the billowing steam from strafed engines, he would have been an ace twice over. He found immense satisfaction in destroying anything that shortened his engagement to Vivie.

September would be different. There were no missions on the 15th of that month because all 66th fighter group commanders were at wing headquarters in Sawston Hall, Cambridge. The results of that meeting fell on a hushed audience at the 353rd's next briefing. Operation Market Garden, a vast airborne invasion of the Netherlands, would begin early on the 17th when some 1,500 aircraft collected over southeast England. Douglas C-47 transports and British Short Stirling heavy bombers, converted for troop carrying, headed out with 478 gliders in tow.

The 353$^{rd}$ headed out also, 50 fighters strong, led by Matt's squadron leader, Lieutenant Colonel Ken Gallup, who had won his silver leaves the month before. The group's objective was to neutralize anti-aircraft installations around Arnhem that threatened the glider and paratrooper landings, a tricky business that cost the squadron one lost and eight damaged before the mission was over. But 31 flak positions were destroyed and 18 others heavily damaged. For three days Slybird stayed at it with about the same result on both sides.

The Luftwaffe must have been late learning about the events in Holland. The 353$^{rd}$, along with other fighter groups, did a thorough job on area ground targets. That is until the sixth day dawned clear and chilly over Raydon. Though it would be after lunch before the big heavily armed Jugs barreled down the runway, Matt had become restless. Waiting to get airborne was always a trying time for him. When he dropped into that bucket seat, he wanted forward motion. But today was the worst he could remember and the thought of flight fatigue sobered him up. The last thing he wanted was for some flight surgeon to ground him.

Meanwhile, he found it easy to talk with John Smaragdis. The Greek restaurateur had been with the group nearly a year when Matt arrived at the base. Since Stan Herrington had been promoted to major and was spending more time in operations, Smaragdis had assumed most of his responsibilities. Matt made his way to the coffee bar in the ready room and cornered the new captain. "Let me have some of that stuff before I blow a fuse."

Smaragdis looked up, his friendly brown eyes studying Matt intently. "Looks like you got the heebie-jeebies, boy. What's going on?"

"Danged if I know," Matt sighed. "I know I want to get on with this mission. You ever have a mission you got more anxious about than usual?"

"What kind of anxious? You feeling a little apprehensive or on the upside?"

"Kind of charged up, I guess. More anxious than most times."

Smaragdis responded with a grin as he took a sip of coffee. "Good! You'll probably have one heck of a day."

"Why do you say that?"

"Because I've had a day or two like that. Some of the best flying I've ever done. That head doctor, Thomas, says it's called *premonition*. But if it's the other way, like you're feeling kind of down, a compulsion to get your things in order, you better stay on the ground, my friend."

"Come on!"

"Say what you want, but a lot of old-timers swear by it. I know some pilots that aborted before they reached the coast because of it. You check with the guys over at maintenance. Planes will come back with rough engines, hydraulic problems, what have you, and those guys will spend all afternoon on it and find nothing."

Matt wasn't sure if Smaragdis was helping or not, but the coffee was doing a super job. The warmth settled over him and calmed him, enough that he couldn't restrain a smile. "I think somebody spiked the coffee, John."

Smaragdis chuckled and patted Matt on the back. "I wish! You haven't got anything to worry about, Tower. You got the best rubber neck in the squadron."

At 1400 hours, 46 P-47s lined the main east-west runway, the earth pulsing beneath their 92,000 rumbling horsepower. It was always an electric moment when, two by two, they pulled in line and slipped into the air. Seconds later, wheels were tucking neatly away as they veered off to take their positions in the formation. When Gallup was leading, the squadron always seemed to engage the enemy. The real hawks of the unit were not above bribery to be included on his missions.

Bristling with rockets and bombs, the 351st and 352nd squadrons had completed their first passes at flak installations around Arnhem while the 350th flew cover at 15,000 feet. Perhaps it was a flash of sunlight on distant cockpit glass that caused Matt's double take. He and Smaragdis probably had the sharpest eyes in the squadron, one reason their flight was on the point. "Seldom Red One to Seldom leader, we've got company at 10 o'clock!"

"Roger, Red One. I see 'em," Smaragdis responded. "What do you make of that? Two... three squadrons, maybe?"

"Count again. Look just above them to the rear!"

"Seldom leader to Slybird leader! Knock it off down there and grab some sky! We have bogies closing at *six zero*, approximately 18,000 feet!"

The enemy aircraft were just under the 350th Squadron's altitude as they approached. It appeared they were mesmerized by the attacking American fighters below and doing little rubbernecking. They ignored Matt's squadron and peeled off in hot pursuit. Gallup called to his pilots, "Drop tanks, get mad!"

The Luftwaffe had lost its earlier timidity. Most of Gallup's pilots were strung out from 2,000 to 5,000 feet, climbing their hearts out and no match for a first-wave assault from above. "All right, Seldom, let's break this thing up!" Smaragdis snapped to his squadron.

The 351st Squadron had made it to 10,000 feet by the time the first stack of Messerschmitt 109s closed in. Gallup turned the squadron straight into the Germans, which readjusted their formation. "Elements, stay together. Watch your tails!"

The Messerschmitts dived through without wounds and sat upon the 352nd Squadron below. In seconds, the airwaves were jammed with warnings and urgent commands. "Jockey Blue Four, break! Two on your tail!"

"Blue Leader, break! Dang it! They're like flies at a picnic!"

"I'm hit! I'm hit!... Get 'em off my back! Get 'em off my back! Somebody... somebody!"

"Slybird leader to Red leader, we're going back down to help Jockey Squadron! You keep that second gaggle off our necks!"

Under Smaragdis' hand, Seldom was already at work in a circling dive, staying on the up-sun side of the second gaggle. "Heads up, Seldom! That's a pack of Doras down there!"

Appropriately warned, the squadron peeled off to do battle with the sleek, nimble Focke-Wulf 190-Ds. Depending on the pilot, these FWs were every bit as capable as the P-47s. "Let's take 'em flight for flight, Seldom!" Smaragdis directed. "The first is mine. Red, take the one on the left. Green, the right. White, get the rear!"

So intent were the FWs on following the Messerschmitts that Seldom Squadron had closed to 500 yards before being noticed. "Fire when you're on target. Keep your elements together!" It was the last command Smaragdis would have time for in the clash that followed.

In Matt's target of FWs, tail-end Charlie spotted the American fighters and blurted the alarm. Matt could imagine the rubber-necking going on as they veered around trying to figure out which way to break. Smaragdis was the first to fire, getting strikes on one of the FWs, which scattered its flight like quail on the rise.

Matt was no longer a novice at this game of aerial combat, but the tingle was still in his hands as he turned into the fray. There were more than enough Germans to go around, for Slybird had chanced upon a major enemy fighter sweep that was itching for revenge. It would be a long, demanding dogfight with empty cots at the end for both sides.

A White Section P-47 zipped by, dark-brown smoke streaming from its cowling, its pilot struggling to outmaneuver a determined pursuer. Matt knew the feeling. He had felt hot German lead pelting his own fighter more than once. Straining against the controls, he manhandled his fighter aircraft into a tight turn, but there was no chance for rescue. The doomed fighter nosed up and stalled, its pilot rolling from the cockpit into the dreaded reality of being downed over enemy territory.

Matt's stomach muscles eased when the parachute finally opened, jerking the flyer upright. "All right, West Virginia," he sighed in helpless resignation. "We've got work to do!" *Paladin* turned back to the fight.

"Red One!… Matt!… He's shooting our man!" Barry Stockton's voice was shrill with disbelief. "That Kraut's back! He's strafing the guy in the parachute!"

Swaying vulnerably beneath the billowing silk, the distressed flyer clutched himself in pathetic defense as the Focke-Wulf bullets tore through his body. Numbing disbelief overwhelmed the Red Leader and his wingman as they stared at the lifeless form dangling in its harness. "He did it!" Stockton screamed. "He actually did it!"

The utter inhumanity of the act consumed Matt Tower. From the first mission he had flown against the enemy, there had never been an incident to equal this. A flush of rancorous anger boiled his blood. "Stick to me, Stockton!" he raged. "You keep my tail clear!"

"Yes, sir!" the reply shot back as the two avengers rolled into a power dive.

Coldly, systematically, the German went after another target, his preoccupation offering Matt the element of surprise. At just under 300 yards, *Paladin*'s tracers framed the enemy cockpit, causing the startled pilot to ram power and dive.

"Red One!" Stockton bellowed. "We got company! There's a Dora on my back!" He half expected a reply when he gave the alarm, but Matt Tower would not be distracted. When the German was close enough to wax Stockton, he white-knuckled the stick in self-defense and dropped like a rock.

Oblivious to escalating hostilities around him, Matt stuck with his target, barreling across the pale blue sky in hot pursuit. The German was good, zigzagging between the menacing wings of friend and foe alike, hoping to confuse his American pursuer. But the single-minded terror on his tail stuck like glue, unintimidated by the crossing tracers.

The chase broke them clear of the fighter swarm, and just as well, for the adversaries above were too engaged to give assistance to either pilot. Matt wanted none. This was his exclusive meat. His only regret was that the target lacked the big yellow decal on its cowling that had become an obsession for him over the weeks.

*Paladin*'s sights drifted across the FW, the eight 50-calibers chewing away at its right wing. Then a white flash and the wing sheared off, rolling lazily end-over-end toward the earth. The German struggled with the canopy, slapping his hands against the reluctant hatch.

"Juuuump, you devil, juuuump!" Matt growled harshly. As though following the sharp command, the Focke-Wulf rolled on its side, its single wing slicing through the air like a shark's fin, and dumped its human cargo.

"Red Leader," Smaragdis' voice crackled through the earphones. "Where the Sam Hill are you guys?" Down below, he spotted LH letters on a P-47 circling an obvious kill. "Red One? Is that you, Tower?" There was no reply.

Visibly shaken, Matt blotted the soaking sweat from the rim of his flight helmet as *Paladin* circled down with the enemy pilot. At just under 5,000 feet, the German's parachute strung out and popped open. Mechanically, the American flyer banked his fighter toward the German, circling closer with every pass.

"Matt!" John Smaragdis' sober voice rose above the combat chatter. "Matt, wait a minute!" There was no reply from Red One. Sensing the worst, the flight leader dived steeply to intercept *Paladin* and leveled off to its rear in wing position. "What are you doing, Tower?"

"Cold… blooded… killer!" came the garbled retort.

"Matt, don't do it!" Smaragdis couldn't gain an inch on the Red Leader or he would have cut him off. From experience, he knew that later on some men didn't handle well what Matt intended to do. But no amount of reasoning slowed the intent avenger.

"Tower!" Smaragdis roared in frustration. "Break... off!" He could see Matt's head set defiantly to the gunsight. The captain would risk court-martial, and in seconds he would be in range to fire. Smaragdis groped for words. "Matt," he called calmly. "In the name of our Lord... at least for your girl... the girl in Ipswich... Viv... something. She would hate this!"

Matt's finger rested on the trigger. He had stared so intently at the floating target his eyes ached, and for a moment he closed them. It was then he heard her name in the earphones. "Vivie.... She would hate this.... She would hate this!"

Sweat stung his eyes as he squinted to relocate his target, and in that watery blur another image began to form until it veiled the object of his pursuit. Her eyes so clear and the lips, with their unmistakable prim little smile that so commanded his heart. Muffled sobs constricted his throat as he struggled with the obsession to punish. But there was no way he could fire on his target now. As Vivie's image drifted slowly to the right, away from the German flyer, so did *Paladin*.

John Smaragdis veered left to miss the parachutist. The Hun's legs were tight together, his arms wrapped around his head, mouth gaping. He would never know his life had been spared by an English girl who owed nothing to the Luftwaffe.

Smaragdis resumed his position on Matt's wing and they flew along in silence for a minute. "You okay, Tower?"

A bland "No," came back. "But I'm functional."

*Paladin* was flying level, but its pilot had fallen back to silent mode. The flight leader waited with growing concern for a positive sign. "Hey, is anybody home over there?"

Matt's hand rose weakly in an acknowledging wave as Smaragdis eased forward to take the lead. "We're sitting ducks down here. You follow me around and let's grab some altitude."

As the two fighters rose in a climbing turn, Matt glanced to his right to clear their exposed side. Above them he saw an orange flash and a fighter spin out of control. Smoke and flame engulfed the spiraling hulk as it plummeted straight into Smaragdis' flight path. "Break, John! Break left!"

Smaragdis jerked the stick obediently, rolling his fighter away from the unseen danger. "Where? Where?" he bellowed.

Matt didn't need to answer. The flaming wreck passed a few feet off Smaragdis' right wing, spinning an ever-widening circle of smudge against the sky. "Crap!" Smaragdis gasped. "Where the devil did that come from?"

"Up there."

"I owe you one, Georgia boy! Was it one of ours or one of theirs?"

"Had a swastika on the tail." Matt's voice was still shaky from the earlier drama. "You don't owe me a thing, buddy. I owe you."

They watched the smoke trail as the German aircraft spun earth-ward. When it leveled out momentarily, Matt wondered if the pilot was still alive. Whatever the case, the result would forever be etched on the walls of his mind. Like a homing missile, the burning mass flat-spun straight into the parachute of the pilot he had just spared, snagging the cords and dragging him into a ghastly merry-go-round of flaming death.

"Man!" Smaragdis broke the stunned silence. "Did you see that, Tower?"

"Yeah, I saw it."

The tone of Matt's voice troubled Smaragdis, especially the long pause before his fellow flyer had replied.

"Man, that ought to make your day!"

"I think I would have shot him, John."

"Maybe, but you didn't!" Smaragdis knew what could happen

when pilots psyched out on a mission. "You didn't have to, Matt. 'To Me belongeth vengeance and recompense; their foot shall slide in due time. For the day of their calamity is at hand.' He handled it for you."

At such a juncture, the lucky might wander away and head for home. But then there were those others. The flight leader poured on the first aid. "Hey, look, I've been there. We'll talk about it over a couple of bitters, okay?"

Matt responded with another flip of the hand, and Smaragdis knew his tactics must change drastically. "All right, soldier, shape up! You gonna take it out on the machines up there where you're needed, or stay down here and sulk?"

Smaragdis' banking tactic surprised Matt profoundly, forcing him to take charge of his thoughts. "Okay, John!" he gasped. "I get the message!" He roughed his helmet back and forth to ease the tension as he watched his challenger slip away to rejoin the battle.

*Paladin* nosed up, and the firm, persistent lift of the bucket seat brought Matt's attention to the job at hand. Against the pale clear sky, brownish streaks of smoke and gray cloud puffs formed a macabre game of tic-tac-toe, where brave players—intent on scoring for their teams—wove through the residue of destruction.

Fuel gauges indicated precious little time to settle the score. And there were other lives at stake, men of Matt's flight separated at the onset of hostilities, particularly a young blond crew cut from West Virginia. "Red Leader to Seldom Red Two... where are you, Barry?" There was no reply. "Chuck? Roger?" But the combat chatter ran on uninterrupted.

Fighting was strung out from 10,000 feet to the quilted wreckage of the pocked earth below, and it found Matt immediately. To his right, a Messerschmitt finished its run on a P-47 and dived into cloud cover. Energized with latent anger, he positioned *Paladin* over the long white fluff and waited for the German, hoping to be at the right spot when the 109 reappeared.

For a moment Matt thought he had misjudged but suddenly, to his left and slightly below, the enemy aircraft slipped into the clear. By the time the German saw the big Jug, he was already in *Paladin*'s sights. A steady stream of armor-piercing 50-calibers ravaged the gray fuselage, ripping across the left wing and cowling. White smoke billowed out. Matt throttled back so as not to overshoot his prey and nosed down, a chase custom-made for the Thunderbolt. When the 109 made the inevitable turn, *Paladin*'s 50s ripped the enemy cowling apart. Multiple explosions blew the engine off, its flaming wreckage cartwheeling into space. There was no lack of satisfaction this time for the elated American flyer.

Just a voice or two in Matt's headphones now: element and flight leaders attempting to put their units back together. No time to search for his section; fuel gauges were at the limit and the guns were spewing straight tracers. *Paladin* was running out of everything that made him dangerous.

The pursuing dive brought Red One out at barely a thousand feet. Too demanding on fuel to climb, the run for home would be on the deck. A speck in the distance, weaving slowly from left to right, brought Matt up tight again. He fingered the gun safety, wondering if there were enough tracers left to bluff an enemy pilot. Senseless to try to evade; if it was a German, he might smell blood. Trusting in a posture of aggression, he headed straight for the boggy.

The speck proved harmless, actually pathetic. A Jockey Squadron Thunderbolt limped along, the front of its cockpit and portions of the dash shot away. The guy was without compass or radio, lost, and flying on dead reckoning. Matt came alongside him, and they exchanged thumbs up. The distressed pilot wiped his brow and smiled, gratefully taking wing position to *Paladin*.

Minutes before, the young Georgian had been unable to save another pilot. Now he was leading the blind home and the choppy gray North Sea had never looked so good.

# CHAPTER 21

# Finally, the Ring

ETTA MOORE STOOD in the family living room on Falcon's Rest's upper level, her hands working with the new curtains Mrs. Pearson had made for her. She liked things tidy and in place when the Graystone Church Auxiliary met for tea.

Vivie paused in the hall doorway and smiled at her mother's efforts. "They're lovely, Mum."

"Mary does splendid work, doesn't she?" Etta smoothed the floral fabric a final time and stepped back to assess the result. It was then she caught a glimpse of her daughter. "My, aren't we lovely this afternoon. Special occasion?"

"Awards day at the air base. Remember? Matt's to be decorated!"

"Oh, yes, you did tell me," Etta replied as she circled the younger woman inquisitively. "Vivian, are you putting on weight, or has that skirt shrunk?"

"Neither, I hope. I found it at Footman's. Quite the rage in London just now. Took the rest of my ration book."

"Humm!" Etta responded, unconvinced. "I like the jacket and gloves. And the hat will do nicely, but if you insist on that skirt, no one will be watching the parade!"

"Mum! You're simply awful. It's a complete set. I haven't another to go with the jacket."

Etta sighed hopelessly, a knowing smile stretching her lips. "You love him very much, don't you?"

Their eyes met in that mystical communion so common to mothers and daughters, which penetrates far deeper than words. "Mum, what do you think of him, really?"

"Well, he seems a fine young man." Etta sensed her daughter expected a more extensive evaluation, and with mixed emotions she took a chair near the window that framed the patio garden below. Vivie ran her hand along the seam of the new curtains as she gazed at the first hints of fall in distant Christ's Church Park. She could barely see the thicket that hid the old gazebo where she had taken Matt to escape the rain on their first outing and, soggy wet, they had slipped and sprawled on the messy floor.

He was making subtle dents in her armor even then. But now, she tingled all over thinking about it. "Mum, he's asked me to marry him."

Etta bit her lower lip thoughtfully and motioned for Vivie to sit across from her. "I expected as much by now. I just pray that you've thought it out well, all the consequences of a relationship like this. He is a Yank, you know, and you've known him only a few months."

"Mum, you can't imagine how I've wrestled with it. I never thought I could feel this way about another man. He's made my life... so... so complete." She paused for a moment, the soft blue eyes transfixed, intent on feelings she had yet to share with anyone.

"It's different, Mum. A bit eerie, as though he's always been there… waiting."

Etta smiled, nodding her head in understanding. Unlike her husband, she saw the young couple growing more intimate, like children at play, exchanging their secrets with a smile, eating out of each other's hand, a disposition long lacking in her daughter. What he was doing in Vivie's life she could not ignore, for the depression had been long and painful.

RAF Flight Lieutenant John Davis had lacked nothing as a son-in-law. Their families were acquainted, and the two young people made a handsome couple. After Dunkirk, it seemed that England held no other like him as far as Vivie was concerned. How strange that the qualities Etta hoped to see in the next man in her daughter's life should appear in this Yank captain, who could have turned her own head 40-plus years ago.

"My darling Vivian," she said, taking her daughter's hands in hers. "How could I not be happy for you?"

"What do you think Dad will say?"

"Oh, probably over-paid, over-sexed and over here," came the chuckling reply. Then Etta's face sobered. "He loves you so much, dear. You're the only child we could have, and to him there will never be a man quite adequate."

"I couldn't bear to hurt him, Mum. When I was in the hospital he would sit by the hour. Once, when he thought I was asleep, he cried, softly, all bent over with his hands on his head." Vivie touched a glove to the corner of her eye. "I never want him to be that unhappy again because of me."

"Well, if it makes you feel any better, he's actually slipped up a time or two and said something nice about your captain. He was boasting to the Mayor, no less, about the hunt at Lord Havely's."

"I do hope so," Vivie sighed. "He insists on speaking with Dad about it soon."

"What are your plans, Vivian? With the war and his duty, is this a good time?"

"We've talked about that. It's our greatest concern, the war." Vivie fingered the watch on her left wrist, her brow wrinkling nervously. "Oh, dear! I must beetle off."

"Go on, go on," Etta smiled. "We can talk later."

Vivie paused in the doorway, arms by her side. "I do need to talk, Mum. My head's spinning a bit from it all. I know I'll be late getting back, but tomorrow we could do something together if you have time."

"I have time, daughter. Mothers always have time. Besides, I haven't had you to myself in quite a while."

The ride to Raydon Wood was filled with daydreams, and Vivie found herself steering instinctively. She and Matt had been apart for over a week. Her heart raced at the thought of being with him for the rest of the day. She had grown to like his friend, Chuck, who risked trouble on more than one occasion so they could be together. The stocky Alabama crop duster was another matter. Roger's rough edges limited her admiration to his reputed qualities as an aviator and the fact that Matt trusted him explicitly in combat.

The formation was assembling by the time she arrived. Vivie moved quickly through the maze of uniforms and visitors to gain a seat as near the front as possible. Sunbeams poked through the high overcast, painting a silvery sheen on the damp concrete below. Vivie prayed the beams would persevere as she searched diligently for Matt's unit. A small military band began its overture, heightening her concern lest she miss any portion concerning him.

In her excitement she stood for a better view, brushing the major seated on the front row and dumping his hat in his lap. "Oh dear, I'm terribly sorry!" she exclaimed, attempting to retrieve the headgear.

He rose slightly, turned and smiled, his square jaw set in support of a smoking pipe. "No harm done. If I had more hair, it would stay on better." Adjusting his officer's hat, he observed Vivie for a moment with evident appreciation. "Lucky guy, whoever he is. What's his name?"

"Tower, Captain Tower. Would you know him?"

"Matt Tower?"

"Yes! Then you do know him!"

"Well, that explains a lot of things," the major smiled prankishly. "Terrible company you're keeping there. I think he's up for court-martial today."

Vivie's face dropped, her blue eyes darting, searching for the truth. In no way had the major anticipated so literal an interpretation of his jest. "No, no!" he grinned broadly. "I'm Stan Herrington. I was his flight leader for a while."

"Oh, yes.... Matt spoke of you. It's such a pleasure Mister... err..." The slip of title blushed Vivie's cheeks and her palms rushed to hide them. "I'm terribly sorry, it's Major, isn't it?"

"How about Stan?" his smile encouraged. "I like that better."

"I'm Vivian Davis, Stan. This is just so exciting. I'm afraid I'm a bit taken by it all. Matt and I are, well, we're quite good friends, you see."

"Quite, quite, I'd say. Tell you what, why don't you step over and take a seat on the front row here beside me. You can see much better."

"It says *reserved*. Should I?"

"Certainly!" Herrington replied as he reached for her hand. "I run this air base."

Thrilled to have a better view, Vivie leaned on Herrington's arm for support, planted a dainty foot on the seat of the front bench and stepped over. "Dumb lucky stiff!" he chuckled softly.

"I'm sorry?" she offered as her feet settled on the pavement. "I was trying not to fall."

"It was nothing," he sighed. "I'm just a little stiff. All this flying, you know."

A dark-complexioned, well-built officer took the seat on Vivie's left. Rather reserved, he smiled nonetheless, and nodded at Stan Herrington, who offered the introductions. "Miss Davis, this is Lieutenant Colonel Bailey, our executive officer. Sir, Miss Davis is a friend of Captain Tower in the 350th Squadron."

"My pleasure, Miss Davis. We're delighted to have you with us. I'm sure Captain Tower appreciates your coming."

"Thank you, Colonel. I was concerned about sitting in the reserved area," Vivie smiled. "But Major Herrington assured me that because he ran the base, it would be quite all right."

Bailey's questioning glance pushed the major deep into his seat. The senior officer cleared his throat and shifted to give Herrington the full brunt of his retort. "Well, he does fill in occasionally, when Sergeant McDuff is on leave."

Vivie sensed the dig and turned to Herrington in question. "Did I say something wrong?" she whispered.

"Oh, no," Herrington replied from his slump. "No, no, not at all. I did!" He sat up slightly and pointed to a group of airmen assembled to their left. "Matt's over there, near the end."

She found him quickly, standing tall and splendid in his dark-green jacket and light trousers, with officer's hat properly affixed. Herrington patted her hand and smiled. "Down girl, down." She sat back then, returning his smile, satisfied her view would be fine.

At a sudden roll of the drums, all seated rose to their feet. The uniformed men snapped smart salutes as the civilians placed hands over their hearts. The strains of America's national anthem, *The Star-Spangled Banner*, echoed across the field, taking Vivie by surprise. She had given no thought to a proper response for a British subject. Her lovely blue eyes searched quickly to take note from

RAF officers at hand and a few English women seated behind her. "Just stand," Herrington whispered assuringly. "That will be fine."

She knew some of the words and tried to place them in her mind as the music swelled. *"How ironic,"* she thought. *"This is all about their independence from us!"* The emotion of the hour was inescapable as these men, so many of whom risked their lives daily, stood in respect of their country. Even Old Glory, which had been limp in the moist air, responded to a gentle English breeze.

For the first time Vivie thought about her own citizenship and the consequences of marriage. *God Save The King* and the Union Jack wrested equal emotions from her as did this music and flag for the men gathered there. She had seen her country, to quote the Prime Minister, in its "finest hour". She looked at Matt, proud and erect. Surely, he would not want her to give up her British citizenship.

Vivie shivered under her goose bumps as the crash of cymbals heralded the American national anthem's final notes. Salutes ended as smartly as they began, but no one moved. Across the field came the sound of engines, many engines, and she could feel the vibration through her feet. Just above the runway, strung out in line astern, a squadron of P-47s began their flyby. One by one, the gleaming fighters streaked the length of the runway and lifted skyward in a thunderous acrobatic finish.

As the ovation subsided, Lieutenant Colonel Rimerman welcomed guests and dignitaries on hand for the awards. General Murray Woodbury, from Fighter Wing Command, and Colonel Bolling of Wing Headquarters commended the 353rd Fighter Group for its impressive performance in support of Operation Market Garden over Holland. They announced that the Group was to receive the coveted Distinguished Unit Citation, which set off another ovation.

A reverent hush settled over the formation as General Woodbury approached those singled out for meritorious service. He stood before the airmen one by one, stating the award and pinning the appropriate medal. Vivie sat erectly as Matt's turn came, straining to hear the general's words.

"Captain Gerald Mattlowe Tower, Jr., for distinguished service to your country, in the face of a hostile enemy and at the risk of life, it is my pleasure to award you the Distinguished Flying Cross. General orders of 15 September provide for two Oak Leaf Clusters to your Air Medal as well. Congratulations, Lieutenant."

But the general was not through. He lifted another medal from the tray and turned again to Matt.

"Captain Tower, for exceptional service and bravery before a hostile enemy, from which you suffered significant injury and threat to life, your country hereby awards you its highest honor for those occasions: the Purple Heart."

Vivie's eyes danced as she watched the general and her captain exchange salutes. She knew the medals were justly deserved, for he would perform in the air every bit as well as in the streets of Ipswich. She wanted to hug him, to tell him how proud she was, but another frustrating 45 minutes would pass with medals to others and the pass in review before the magic word, "Dismissed!"

Matt made his way to the reviewing stand, dutifully saluting Bailey and Herrington, his smile more for Vivie than the events of the afternoon. "Oh, Matt! I'm so happy for you!" she squealed, catching both of his hands while struggling to retain a proper decorum.

Colonel Bailey adjusted his hat, enjoying the anticipation of the couple beside him. "Go on, woman, kiss him before you explode all over us," he chuckled. "I'd keep a dang close eye on her tonight, Tower, if she was my date."

"Thank you, sir. I don't plan to let her out of my sight!"

Vivie kissed Matt, a brief discreet peck, considerably less than her heart directed. "Carry on, carry on," the colonel sighed as he turned to leave.

"How in the world did you end up on the reserved row?" Matt inquired with some amusement.

"Oh, Major Herrington invited me. He's every bit as nice as you described him."

Herrington shrugged with a smile, firing up the dormant pipe. "Lot better than sitting next to a stuffy oak-leaf colonel. But it will cost you a dance with this lovely lady."

"You got it," Matt grinned. "And you'll find something else to do right after that, right?"

Herrington's wheezy windup of a laugh amused Vivie. "No promises, Captain. Miss Davis, it was a pleasure finally meeting you. I trust you'll enjoy the evening in spite of the escort service."

"Oh, I will, Major, very much because of the escort service!" As Herrington left, Vivie turned back to Matt. "He's a nice sort, isn't he?"

"Quite a guy. If it wasn't for him, I'd still be flying tail-end-Charlie somewhere. I owe Herrington a lot."

Vivie slipped her hand under the new medals. The Distinguished Flying Cross, with crossed propellers and blue ribbon, and the Purple Heart gleamed against her white glove. "I'm so thrilled for you, darling! You're growing quite a patch of ribbons there."

"Ah, but I don't have the big prize yet. You! And we're going to see about that shortly. Colonel Rimerman is meeting with us at 1700. It takes a while for permission to go through."

Vivie's smile relaxed as she patted the medal back in place. "You're certain you still want to go through with this?"

"Well, it would have helped a little if you had wings and a propeller," he grinned. "Of course I want to go through with this!"

Her smile returned as abruptly as it had subsided. "Me, too! And we must meet with the Vicar. The marriage banns should be posted for the parish."

Their audience with the base CO was cordial, and Rimerman

agreed to process their request pending a second conference with the couple. The Air Corps cared about its own and took precautions to prevent ill-advised or hasty marriages among homesick airmen.

Then it was heavy *hors d'oeuvres* at the officers' club where Matt, with five destroyed German fighters in the air, was inducted into the Ace's Club along with two pilots from the 351st Squadron. In time, those inclined and still functional hung around for the night's stomp. Vivie, minus hat and gloves, was passed around among Matt's friends, and she delighted in the attention and opportunity to meet those he flew with.

She was the loveliest girl on the dance floor, and in time, the green-eyed monster moved him to retrieve her from his own wingman. "All right, West Virginia, I hear your momma calling," Matt kidded as he tapped Barry Stockton's shoulder.

"Is that an order, sir?" the second lieutenant grinned sheepishly.

"Whatever it takes to get your paws off my girl. I've been at this shindig over an hour and haven't danced with my own date yet!

"It's wartime, sir. You're supposed to share," Stockton grumbled good-naturedly as he stepped aside.

"Do you hear this guy?" Matt chuckled as he put his arm around Vivie. "Let 'em get a little success and it goes to their head. This guy has just been credited with destroying his first German fighter!"

"Good for you, Barry Stockton!" Vivie exclaimed. "That's quite an accomplishment in my opinion."

"But you don't know the half of it, dear lady," Matt said. "Most of us shoot 'em down while facing the enemy. Not my wingman! While I'm going after this 190, another one gets on his tail. Barry pulls away in a dive to save his backside. I didn't see this. They told me about it when we got back to the base. Anyway, the German chased him all over the sky and suddenly, flame pours out of the 190's cowling. Then a flash and it comes apart in the air!"

Stockton, arms folded, nodded his verification, a satisfied grin plastering his delighted face. "Well, I was the only fighter near him!"

"And the only guy in the 8th Air Force to down an enemy fighter with prop wash. And you've had the honor of dancing with him, my love." Matt added as he led Vivie back to the music.

It was his favorite, *Stars Fell on Alabama*, and as he snuggled Vivie close to him while they waltzed slowly beneath the club's decorative vaulted ceiling, she could feel the tension easing in his body. With her he was home, safe, away from the grueling pace of war. She loved those moments. A couple of flyers attempted to break on the couple, but Matt never felt the taps. She was his for the rest of the night. They were still dancing in a world of their own when the band eased into Glenn Miller's *Don't Sit Under the Apple Tree*. They were hardly aware of the clicking heels around them until a squadron buddy passed nearby. "Hey, you two! Wake up over there. It's jitterbug time!"

But this couple was far beyond the one-night camp blowouts, and as though of a single mind, they walked away from the noise and stomping feet into a rare moonlit English night. "Oh, Matt! Can you believe this?" Vivie sighed.

Back home in Augusta it would be harvest moon right now. Coming up big and orange over the pines, searching for its coat of silver. "Hmm," he mourned softly. "There's hardly a cloud up there."

She took it as her job to ward off the melancholy and lifted her lips to kiss his cheek. It worked and he bent down to place his lips on hers. "All the better to show you a couple of surprises," he teased.

"What?"

"You'll see!"

They rounded the hangar, where the silhouettes of four aircraft rested on the circular dispersal pad. "What do you think of these babies?" Matt asked as he ran his hand along the shiny wing of the nearest.

Vivie touched the cold metal, her eyes taking in the sleek image from propeller to tail. "They're quite like Spitfires, aren't they?"

"P-5ls. We're changing over. By the first of the month, we'll all have them."

"Is that good?"

"It's the hottest thing I've ever been in! Maneuvers like a hawk." Matt ran his hand over the long-nosed cowling, letting it rest just short of the wing. "Right there goes '*Paladin II!*'"

"What a name!" Vivie chuckled, pointing to the next fighter. "*Willit Run?*"

"That's Major LeFebre's pride and joy. He's with the 351st Squadron. The top brass taste the goodies first, you know."

"Matt, where is *Paladin?*"

"You've never seen him up close, have you?" He headed her back across the long hangar apron to the dispersal pads in the distance. She stayed close to him, their arms locked around each other.

"You talk as if they're human, poppet."

"To a pilot, dear love, an airplane takes on a soul of its own. Old *Paladin*'s caught a few licks, but he's waddled home for me every time."

The officers' club was far behind them now and Vivie's arms took advantage of the privacy that had eluded them all day. "I think Mum's on our side. She really seems to like you."

"She's quite a gal in my book. There was something about her, even on the train. I think I liked her then." He drew Vivie a little closer as they walked. "The first time I came to Falcon's Rest I was all thumbs. They processed us so fast and piled the training on, and I had just met you in the canteen. A pretty uptight guy, huh? She sat with me and talked. I felt like I could have spilled the story of my life. I guess mothers are mothers all over—the good ones, that is."

"We've grown to be best friends. I can share with her. She has such a shoulder."

"So now it's up to Matt and the major, I guess. He sure loves you. I like him for that. You're a close family. I thank God for my own."

*Paladin* stood poised at the ready, his cowling and body massive compared to the 51's, but every bit as menacing. "Hello, *Paladin*," Vivie whispered as she touched the wing.

"Want to see my office?" Matt grinned, pointing to the cockpit.

"Should we?"

"It's my airplane!"

"Like this was Major Herrington's base?" she quipped, stifling a smile. "You men are all such peacocks!" But she did want to see where he spent the dangerous hours. Perhaps to ease her mind on *Paladin*'s worthiness and certainly to wipe the disappointment from her captain's face. "Oh, dear," she sighed, following him around the wing. "I shall need a lift."

"One lift deserves another," he smiled.

She patted his cheek playfully, "You're sweet, you know that?"

He lifted her easily and perched her on the broad wing, then climbed up beside her. Vivie leaned unsteadily to peer into the compact opening. "It's rather small, isn't it?"

"Climb in and try it. Come on, I'll boost you over."

"Matt, I'm in a skirt, silly!"

"I won't look. Go on, put a leg over."

"Oh, dear." Vivie's voice wavered as she gripped the windshield framing. She placed one foot in Matt's clasped hands and stretched the other into the cockpit. Up came the skirt, exposing two well-turned thighs. "Matt Tower! You're looking! That's what you've been waiting for, isn't it?"

Matt was chuckling innocently, straining to support the climbing adventuress. "Vivie," he panted. "If you don't hurry up and get in there, we're gonna be in trouble here!"

The second foot went in and she was standing in the bucket seat. "How do I sit down, smarty?"

"Grip the sides and just let yourself down. Let your feet slide to the front." He pointed to the space under the control panel. "See, right there."

She hesitated, turning her head from side to side as she weighed the matter of settling into the seat. "This is fine. I can see well enough as it is."

Matt squatted on the wing, his arm resting on the edge of the cockpit. "But I can't show you the other surprise until you're seated, sweetheart."

She dropped to her knees, still hesitant, and turned to him. "Listen, I've no intention of flying in this thing."

"Trust me, lady. Go on, sit down."

Vivie squirmed and twisted until she was able to drop onto the seat, her head rising just above the sides. "Oh, my! What is this I'm sitting on? How can you see where you're going?"

"That's the parachute pack you're on. We'd raise the seat for you, tiny thing."

"Well, I've done my part, but it's rather uncomfortable in here. What's the other surprise?"

Matt retrieved a small package from his jacket pocket and placed it in her hand. "Open."

Dainty fingers eagerly peeled away the paper, exposing a tiny oval box. She lifted the top carefully, hardly breathing, until the contents gleamed in the moonlight. "Oh, Matt!" she whispered. "Matt!"

She was pleased, and he smiled until his cheeks hurt. "I hope it fits. Try it on."

The ring slid freely onto her finger, maybe an eighth-size large, but quite exquisite. Matt reached in, turned the map light on to release the hidden sparkle of the diamonds. The larger stone was tastefully mounted between two smaller ones in an antique silver setting. Vivie was speechless, her right hand covering her gaping lips. Matt kissed her ring finger. "Now you can tell your grandchildren you became engaged in the cockpit of a P-47 Thunderbolt fighter. Not many women will be able to say that."

"Matt…" Vivie was crying softly. She reached up for him to lift her, and her arms went around his neck. "It's so beautiful! I love it. Where in the world did you find such a ring?"

Matt kissed her cheeks, her ear lobes, her lips again. "I used the 353rd special-purchases system, run by a sergeant named McDuff. I'm going to have it checked to be sure it's what he claims it is."

She looked into his eyes, her soft lips in the prim little smile he adored. "I'll have your children, Matt Tower, and we'll have grandchildren, and I'll tell them it all started in the seat of a fighter plane with their wonderful grandfather who chased me until I caught him!"

They clung in an embrace of celebration, their lips melting passionately together until the awkwardness of the cockpit forced them to part. "Oh, Captain!" she breathed, her heart still thumping. "I think you better help me out of here." She paused and looked back at him. "But I'm not lifting this skirt again."

"It's probably best that you don't right now," he chuckled. "Just turn your back to me and I'll lift you out, okay?"

She seated herself on the edge of the cockpit as his encircling arms secured her. Gently, he lifted and drew her over the side. It was then that the bubble of romance burst, for he lost his footing, falling backwards onto the wing, dragging Vivie with him as her lungs filled the still night air with a resounding exclamation of shock.

Still clutching her, he could find nothing to grab as the two began sliding down the wing. The sudden free fall off its lower edge only prompted the female of the sailing pair to top her earlier vocal exertions. Fortunately, his feet hit first but the angle pitched them backward, and he landed on his rear with Vivie in his lap.

Silence returned as abruptly as it had been broken, leaving the dazed couple hesitant to move lest some essential component of their anatomy be endangered. Recovering from the shock, Vivie became aware of a new presence. Shadowed against the moonlit sky stood the tallest human she had ever seen. The faint beam from his hooded flashlight crawled over the pavement until it illuminated the sprawled pair.

Vivie quickly tugged her skirt into place and turned to Matt, who rested uneasily on his elbows. "Milt?" he enquired of the waiting figure.

"Captain, sir?" came the twangy reply. "Y'all lose something down there?"

"Severely damaged dignity," Matt sighed as he began checking Vivie. "You okay, hon?"

Embarrassment tied her tongue, leaving only a nod of the head to confirm a safe landing. Milt moved closer and extended his arm. "Let me give ya' a hand, ma'am. That ain't no place for no lady."

Hesitantly, she took the outstretched palm and pulled herself up, managing a discreet "Thank you, Sergeant." Her concern turned to Matt, still sitting where he had landed. Milt's lanky arms lifted the downed flyer and helped him balance against *Paladin*'s fuselage. "Good gravy, Captain. What in the world happened?"

"Landing gear collapsed," he groaned. "Boy, that was a wallop!"

"You're hurt, poppet!" Vivie exclaimed as she moved to his side.

Matt reached over and brushed a lock of her hair back in place. "Superficial damage, that's all." Steadying himself with one hand to ease the discomfort, he flashed a smile of reassurance for her. "Just a good charley horse."

Sensing the crew chief's lingering concern, Vivie quickly reflected Matt's smile. "We really are fine, Sergeant." She had recovered sufficiently to tend to her tousled hair and allow the humor of the impromptu descent to set in. "A bit more exciting than the great slide at Felixstowe Park!"

Milt threw back his head in a raspy chuckle. "Dang if you ain't a spunky one, ma'am! Of course, we're kind of used to it around here. The lieutenant's a heap more dangerous fooling around this here plane than he is in it." Milt checked to see how his boss would take the ribbing and was pleased to find the smile still in place.

"Milt, you're looking at an engaged man. Meet my fiancée, Vivian Davis. Viv, this is Milton J. Foxx, the best crew chief in the 66th Fighter Wing!"

Vivie knew what stock Matt placed in this man who groomed the fighter he flew, and she expressed her feelings in a warm smile and extended hand. "I'm pleased to meet you, Milt."

The crew chief looked down at the beauty before him, a big Tennessee grin stretching his bony face. "So, this here's Vivie! Well, the captain has gone and did his self proud!"

Vivie turned to Matt, her half-smile seeking interpretation. He pulled her to him with his free arm and gave a reassuring hug. "That's hillbilly for 'he thinks you're wonderful.'"

The evening quiet was broken again with the sound of a half-dozen feet hitting the pavement at double time. Four helmeted soldiers with carbines at the ready flanked out in combat approach. Milt turned slowly to face them, his hands edging into the air. "We give up, Corporal!"

"Begging your pardon, sir," the intent soldier replied, nodding at Matt. "We have to know what's going on here. There was a lot of noise and screams."

Matt rose up to his full rank and faced the inquirer. "Just inspecting the aircraft, Corporal."

"With a civilian, sir?" came the insistent response.

Tired of the game and growing impatient with the line of questioning, Milt dropped his arms. "We're having a celebration here, boy! The captain's got en-gaged! Don't y'all know a cry of joy when y'all hear one?"

The guard digested that for a moment, then firmed up his jaw to 'do his duty.' Milt stopped him dead with a menacing stare. "Corporal, we could have blowed this here plane slap up if we'd had a mind to! Where the devil y'all been? I clocked that response time at 3.5 minutes. Right poor showing, I'd say. Who's your training officer?"

"Well... you see, we couldn't exactly figure out where the screams came from at first." The corporal was on the defensive now, wetting his lips, thinking it out. "But..."

"But?" Milt interrupted angrily. "Yo' butt! That's what! If y'all couldn't figure out whur it come from, maybe this ain't whur y'all spose to be!" The crew chief let that soak in for effect, then pulled his last bluff. "You see them stripes?" he demanded, pointing to his sleeve. "That's three mo' than you got. Now, y'all secure this here area and we'll go on 'bout our business."

Milt maintained the initiative, ushering the flustered guards back in the direction of their station. Matt, getting around with much less discomfort now, began chuckling. "You've got a set of lungs, woman! My ear's still ringing."

The snickers were creeping up on Vivie as well as she replayed the last few minutes in her mind. "You should have seen your face, Matt Tower. Such discomposure!" Her lilting laughter only served to excite his own. "Like your pants were on the flagpole, as you Yanks say."

"No, Viv." So deep were his guffaws now that he could hardly speak. "Not on the pole! Your pants run up the pole, hon!"

On his return, Milt found them both collapsed in stitches against *Paladin*. The ground crewman had not been blessed with much of a laugh, and his best effort made it appear the thing was caught in his throat. "I think we've seen the last of them fellows, Captain. I'm sorry 'bout that, ma'am, but they ain't our kind, you see. They's just regular Army."

"Oh, Milt," Vivie sighed in her recovery. "You were splendid! I shall never forget this evening: a poor maiden at the mercy of two bloody idiots."

As composure returned to the three, Milt ambled over to the fighter, still chuckling. "I'll take care of the dents in the wing, and y'all go on back to the dance."

"Won't you come with us?" Vivie entreated.

"No, ma'am. You ain't seen the sight of seven foot of lanky bone messing 'round on no dance floor. Shoot, I'm so tall I've stepped slap over my partner without knowing it."

"Well, I would be delighted to dance with you, Milt, if you change your mind." Vivie's heart went out to the good-natured sergeant and the spirit in which he tried to make light of an embarrassing dilemma.

Milt patted the fighter's wing as he looked back at Vivie. "The captain might have named her *Paladin*, but this here's my gal." The great grin resurfaced. "She don't talk back, she spends ever' night with me and don't holler when I put my hands all over her." Milt choked up a couple of laughs. "But she don't hold a candle to you, ma'am. That dinky little picture he's got in the cockpit don't do you no justice."

The couple covered most of the return walk in silence, each enjoying the embrace of the other and the special moment just shared. It wasn't long until Vivie's heart ran over. "Do you really have my picture in your cockpit?"

"Yep. You fly on every mission with me. If things get a little rough, I've got an extra incentive to get back. That picture, a couple of days ago... probably kept me from...."

"From what, poppet?"

He didn't reply right away and she knew better than to press. Whatever the matter, she could tell he was still dealing with it, and the last thing she wanted was to put a damper on the evening.

The sound of music helped as they neared the club. She could tell by his change of expression that his train of thought had been mercifully broken. "You know," he sighed. "We better dance and make merry while we can. I still have your father to convince."

"Let's!" she giggled, pulling him into the brighter atmosphere of the jiving officers' club.

# CHAPTER 22

# Serious Family Business

THE COLDER DAYS of November 1944 brought many changes for Slybird Group. Lieutenant Colonel Gallup, with nine enemy aircraft destroyed in the air and two on the ground, ended his tour. Major Wayne Blickenstaff, already an ace, returned from the States for a second go-round and signed on as squadron CO. Other than the regret of Gallup's departure, not a ripple formed among the men of the 350[th.] They had simply exchanged one dynamic leader for another.

Against increasingly brittle weather, the portly coke stoves were fired to capacity around the clock. A third stove had been installed in Matt's barracks, raising the habitability of the Nissen hut to bare-minimum standards. Only the stout-hearted attempted to bathe, because frostbite in the shower was only slightly less probable there than at 20,000 feet.

While Vivie was his first reason for visiting Falcon's Rest, that long tub of hot water ran a close second, with bars of Avon soap enhancing the luxury. The single exception this day, as he emerged warm and refreshed, was the pending meeting with her father. In his anxiety he saw little difference between that conference and a mission briefing.

Etta Moore was waiting for him at the lobby desk. "You look so much the better, Captain. A bit of color in the cheeks."

"It's worth going AWOL, Mrs. Moore. A bath, per chance a hot one, my kingdom for a bath!" he grinned in Shakespearean pun.

"Well, I have a surprise for you. There's someone you must see." Etta led him across the lobby to the drawing room where Ann Taylor sat with her son. Unhindered by his bulky leg cast, the little guy stiff-legged it from chair to chair around the room.

Smiling broadly, Ann rose to meet the American flyer. "Oh, Captain, I've waited so long for this moment!" Her arms quickly encircled him, lavishing the gratitude of a young mother's heart. "We're so terribly grateful!"

As her bear hug eased, so did Matt's blush. "Boy, does he look great! He's been on my mind. What does the doctor say about the leg?"

"He'll... he'll be walking again," she replied, her voice losing out to the emotion of the moment. "I'm afraid only time will tell about the scar. How can we ever thank you enough, Captain?"

"Listen," he chuckled. "Just seeing this little fellow up and around is a gracious plenty for me." He walked over and dropped to a knee beside the four-year-old. "How's it going, Davey?"

Just the trace of a scrape or two remained, and the youngster seemed to be taking the cast with typical childish tolerance. Shy at the sudden attention, his gaze dropped to the floor. "Toy broke," he said softly.

Amused by such simple concern in light of what had happened,

Matt exchanged an assuring smile with the two women. "You know, Davey, I never did see your toy. What was it?"

"A boat. But it's gone."

"I'm afraid it was lost in the attack," Ann volunteered. "He doesn't seem to recall all that happened."

"He's luckier than the rest of us," Matt sighed. "Davey, do you think Mum could find you another boat if I gave you the money?"

A smile crept across the youngster's face as he nodded in agreement. Spontaneously, two small arms reached out to gather all they could of the American flyer, and Matt quickly returned the gesture. "You're welcome, Davey, you're welcome."

Mother and son were in town for a doctor's visit when, hopefully, the cast would come off. So, they said their goodbyes to the man who played such a part in their lives and whom they very likely would not see again. Etta closed the front door behind them and walked back to the lobby desk. "You've quite a way with children, Captain. An admirable quality."

Matt smiled to himself, wondering if the admirable quality would endure for his meeting with the resident Major of British Intelligence. Through the office door he could see Vivie's father working at his desk. "Good morning, sir."

Hands busy with an evidently tedious task, the major peered over his glasses and nodded for Matt to enter. "Have a chair, Captain. I'm at a rather crucial point here." With resolute patience, skillful hands separated a stamp from its envelope. "There now," he smiled, holding up the trophy. "A Victory Eagle from your own country, no less."

Matt seated himself near a desk cluttered with assorted pages of postage. "That's quite a collection, sir. How long have you been at it?"

"Twice as many years as you've lived, very likely." The major proudly displayed his rarer specimens, eager to share for appreciative eyes the efforts of some 40-plus years. Then easing the pages to one side, he settled back into the high-back leather chair. "There now. All quite interesting, I'm sure. But I perceive there are more important matters on your mind, young man."

"Yes, sir. Important enough to seek your counsel." Matt was careful with his words, understanding the major's protective instincts toward his daughter. "I've been seeing Vivie for a good while now and... well, she's become very special in my life."

"And you want my blessings on your marriage," the major interrupted, his eyes intently scrutinizing the young flyer seated before him.

The directness caught Matt off guard. He had wanted to set a better stage for the question. "Well sir, I guess that's what it comes down to. We were hoping you and Mrs. Moore would be agreeable."

Silence, like the pause between thunderclaps, hung heavy, forcing Matt's gaze to the floor and Robert Moore's wearily to the ceiling. The older man's chest rose and fell in a deep sigh as he pushed himself to his feet and opened the squeaky cabinet door behind his desk. "Brandy?"

"No, thank you, sir." Matt waited until Robert filled the small snifter and closed the cabinet. "Neither Vivie nor I would feel right unless it was a family affair."

"I'll be quite frank, Captain. My hopes for Vivian did not include betrothal to a Yank." Robert sipped the brandy slowly, then placed the glass precisely in front of him on the desk. "Nothing personal, you understand. I daresay it's the concern of most English fathers. Having you chaps over here is a mixed blessing at best."

"I can understand that."

"How could you possibly understand that?" the major challenged as he retrieved the glass for another sip. "Do you have a daughter?"

"No, sir, but I have an older sister. I can remember when she was dating, some of the characters who wanted to take her out."

"Indeed! It's more your father who would understand, in my opinion." Robert rested his arms on the desk, his eyes fixed on the back of his hands. "At your age, you've no experience in such things. I'm older than most fathers, Captain. For years we thought no children would come. Do you know what it is to want a child and not be able? No, of course not, of course not."

The gray head bowed for a moment. "October 1920. I remember the date quite well. I was in Felixstowe at the time sparing my father a few days from our inn there. Etta took the train so she would be with me when she broke the news that she was with child."

Matt sat quietly, hands clasped over a crossed knee, his expression respectful, attentive. The major sipped the brandy again and settled deeper into his chair. "I was on leave from Germany when Vivian was born. We were still settling matters with the bloody Huns. She was on the honor list most of her college years. She's bright, resourceful, well bred, if I say so myself, with her whole life before her." Robert Moore leaned toward the young flyer before him. "What are you going to do with her, Captain?"

Matt gripped the chair arms, his eyes reflecting a concern equal to the older man's. "That's precisely the way I feel about her, sir. And, if I don't marry her, some 'ruddy bloke' will come along and work his way into her life, and neither of us could stand to see that, could we? Would it help some if you knew more about me?"

Stillness, except for the ancient wall clock whose vigilant face presided over the contest. Grueling seconds ticked away without denting the older man's armor or Matt's concern. The major retrieved a paper from his jacket pocket. "Gerald Mattlowe Tower, Jr. Born January 10, 1919. Youngest of two children. Educated, University of Georgia. Sister, Elizabeth, married to attorney Leslie Carter. Enlisted in Army Air Force 1943. Father, Gerald M., president of industrial supply company. Mother, Eleanor M., homemaker.

Family respected in community, considered upper middle class by American standards."

Matt had a choice: to be offended and snap back at the major, or to view the matter empathically through the eyes of one who had loved Vivie longer than he. "Sounds pretty good, doesn't it, sir?" he grinned.

"I've heard worse," Robert replied, evidently moved by the young flyer's composure. "Did I omit any essentials?"

"Yes, sir, you did. Number one: Matt Tower is very much in love with Vivian Moore Davis, born October 3, 1920, only child, educated at Roedean, and college at London. Married 1940 to John Davis, law apprentice and RAF KIA. Enlisted in Women's Voluntary Service 1942. Father, Robert A., owner of better hotels in Ipswich and Felixstowe, and rank of major in His Majesty's intelligence service. Mother, Etta L., wife and husband's business partner. Family respected in the community, considered upper middle class by British standards."

The trace of a smile twitched Robert Moore's lips as he rocked slowly in his chair. "You've got the metal, young man. I'll give you that. Frankly, you won your case with Mrs. Moore early on. I will admit that Vivian is quite a different woman now, and all for the better. The credit seems to accrue to you."

"I'd like to have your confidence in all this, Major Moore."

"My confidence is in Vivian. She's level-headed, not prone to snap decisions. It's her interest in you that influences me. I do think you love her. If I didn't, you'd find me a dangerous adversary, Captain."

"Can I take that to mean we would have your blessings?" Matt pressed tactfully, suppressing a smile against the mounting optimism.

"What are your plans?"

"Vivie wants to see how the war goes. She keeps talking about after the first of the year."

"Short of three months," the major nodded. He leaned on his elbows and studied Matt with a distinct concern. "We should be well into Europe by then. I would be far more comfortable if you did wait."

"Comfortable about the war?"

"The war is certainly a part of it, in more ways than I care to speculate." Silence again, of the awkward kind when neither party is certain where the conversation should go from there.

The major had his brandy snifter for a crutch, but Matt was left with hands the size of baseball gloves.

"I shan't oppose your courtship, Lieutenant," Robert said, relieving the tension a bit. "It would serve little purpose but to put the lot of us in a flaming argy-bargy. But there are reservations, which have little to do with you, and only time alone can resolve them."

They talked, then, on less controversial matters: about the war, how Matt saw it from the air, and his recent decorations, which seemed to impress the major rather profoundly.

Aware of the change in atmosphere from her vantage point at the lobby desk, Etta tapped on the open office door. "I should think you two would have enormous appetites by now. Cook has roast beef and Yorkshire pudding. Won't you join us, Captain? I'm certain it would be more enjoyable if Vivian were here, but you're most welcome."

"Thank you," Matt grinned as he politely rose to his feet. "I couldn't turn down linen napkins, a dining room, and gracious hosts. Only don't tell her she just might not be missed."

Conversation flowed smoothly between Matt and Vivie's parents now that the couple's plans were in the open. Characteristically, the wife was far ahead of the husband in anticipation of nuptial details. "Have you considered where you will live, Cap.... Oh, dear. I can't continue to call you *captain* now, can I? It must be Matt. Yes, Matt.

I rather like that." She turned, smiling for his approval. "You don't mind, do you?"

"No, ma'am, not at all." He had long anticipated the sound of his name from her lips and all that it implied.

But her residence question wouldn't be answered just then. One of the clerks from the lobby, a slender blonde in her crisp Falcon's Rest black and white, moved briskly to the dining table. "Major Moore, sir," she panted. "It's on BBC! The British have liberated Athens and the Germans are withdrawing from Belgrade!"

"Smashing!" the major interrupted, slapping the table so smartly as to make Etta start. "Now, if they'd turn this bloody war over to the likes of your General Patton, and our Montgomery, we'd see a thing or two!"

The clerk remained by the table rubbing her hands together, hardly restraining her excitement. "There's more, sir."

"What?"

"Rommel is dead."

"Rommel!" the major echoed with a perplexed cock of the head. "There's a story there!"

Such panoramas of war news were exhilarating to those in Matt's position who, regularly transgressing political and military high-level boundaries, had less a sense of the war's progress than ground forces. He knew the bomber escorts were deeper into enemy territory than ever before but attributed that mainly to the increased range of Slybird's new P-51 Mustangs.

He was aware of Etta's hand resting on his arm and faced her with a smile. She seemed so happy for him. "How does all that make you feel, Matt?"

"Great!" came the beaming response. He looked from Etta to the major, his face sobering slightly. "Truthfully, I can't wait to get back in the cockpit. We've got to bring this war to an end."

Through the eyes of experience, the old soldier looked across the table at the eager young warrior and the spreading patch of ribbons on his chest. He had known others with similar intentions and feelings in earlier conflicts and in far too many cases, the tragic consequences.

"Keep your perspective, young chap, and your guard up. The nearer his den the Hun retreats, the more desperate his efforts to defend it."

Indeed, Matt had witnessed that desperation in the streets of Ipswich and beneath a parachute over eastern France.

# CHAPTER 23

# Pandemonium on Wheels

ICE-CRUSTED MUD, FLEDGLING snow flurries, and thick over-cast skies brought the air offensive to a halt, grounding Slybird for the next four days. Restless boredom set in at Raydon. The movies were two weeks old, and what excitement existed centered around the dozens of perpetual poker games. To most, even the attempt to bring off a Thanksgiving celebration fared poorly, simply fanning nostalgic aches and pains among homesick airmen.

The English were no help because they lacked any inherent appreciation of the tradition. The Americans had seemed just as baffled a few weeks earlier when the youngsters of the area, drag-ging around a tattered scarecrow effigy, pestered them with cries of "A penny for the guy, Yank!"

"Guy Fawkes Night," Vivie laughed at Matt's inquiry. "The rotter tried to blow up Parliament in 1605, but they caught him. There were great barn fires before the blackouts, and they burned him in effigy," she explained.

Finally, a break in the weather let the P-51 Mustangs out of the barn. Bomber escort to Hanover to pepper Hitler's aircraft plants was a sweet tonic indeed. The approach would take the attackers straight across Holland, a route Matt looked forward to in his quest for the German pilot who brought havoc to the streets of Ipswich.

Outside the briefing hut, cold, damp blackness brought out flight helmets and gloves, the latter indispensable against the frigid metal of a ferrying truck. A dozen bodies flung themselves aboard, eager to move out. "Hey, Tower," shouted a 351$^{st}$ Fighter Squadron flyer. "You still got that reward out?"

"Yep, a month's pay!"

"A month's pay? What do you gotta do for that?" chimed in a three-mission newcomer.

"Tower's looking for a 190 with some kind of yellow picture on the cowling. He's been worrying the crap out of us about it for the past month."

"That'd be a hard call to pass up," the newcomer chuckled. "I've been out three times and never fired my guns. He must have ruffled your feathers real good. I'd give a month's pay just to hit one of them."

"I want that one," Matt injected tersely. "You just let me know if you see it. Understood?"

"It might have been a unit marking. There could be dozens of them out there."

"Oh no, his wingman didn't have it. That's his own little trademark."

Forty-five minutes later, 50 of Slybird's finest were chasing the bomber contrails to rendezvous 25,000 feet above the Dutch coast. An AB-Flight pilot, getting the first glimpse of a squadron of P-47s moving to top cover, broke the silence. "Look at the Jugs, guys! You know, I wouldn't mind having mine back."

"You gonna let your 51 hear you say that, Spears, and you sitting way up here in its lap?"

"Knock it off!" Colonel Bailey interrupted. "This ain't a public phone system, gentlemen. You better roll those necks. There'll be company today and they'll be itchier than you are."

Strapped into oxygen masks 3,000 feet above the bombers, Matt's squadron settled into the exasperating routine of top cover, which could go on for miles until the Luftwaffe made its move. To relieve the boredom of scanning the enemy sky, he attempted to count the B-17s below but managed to peg only 50 or so in the confusing streams of contrail vapor.

What deceptively easy targets the broad-winged slowpokes appeared to be. Matt tried to imagine a German pilot coming upon the scene and forgetting for the moment that each B-17 bristled with a dozen 50-calibers capable of spitting dozens of rounds per second. Conversely, the chance to attack German bombers had eluded him to that point. That remained the choice domain of the RAF.

For a good 10 minutes the bombers endured a sea of black and gray explosions, which had caused them to open ranks slightly, for if one took a direct hit in the bomb bay, the debris could take out another. That's when the enemy fighters liked to do their bit, before the collective fire power of the Fortresses resumed a tight defensive box.

"Wolfpack leader! We've got bogeys at 12 o'clock!" The unfamiliar voice jolted Matt back to reality. Regardless of the fighter group giving the alarm in a joint mission, all participants took a shot of adrenaline.

"Steady, Slybirds, steady," Colonel Bailey countered. "They'll handle that piece of business."

"Coming straight in, Wolfpack Red One!"

"To the right, Blue One!"

"Four! I see four! Break Blue Two, now!"

It was distant and unreal, the combat chatter and rattle of machine guns in Matt's ears, like a radio dramatization, for he could not see the action yet.

"Did you get a hit, Blue Two?"

"Are you kidding? What the devil was that?"

"Greased lightening!"

"They're jobs, those jets we told you about. They were all over us on the Berlin raid."

"I got this thing wound flat out. I can't get near him!"

"190s, two o'clock!" Smaragdis was right on the money as usual.

A half-dozen Focke-Wulfs circled cautiously to the group's right, their charcoal gray hulks enticing, inviting attack. Bailey was wise to the bait. "John, you see anything else out there?"

"Not yet. Ain't this enough?"

"Drop tanks!" Bailey barked. "Seldom, Lawyer, follow me down! Jockey, get the decoys and cover us!"

By the time Slybird was spotted, their 50s were in action. The first pass netted Smaragdis his eighth victory and broke up the German's run on the bombers. Matt closed quickly on the next target, but the chase aborted in a hail of tracers from a trigger-happy B-17 tail gunner. The error cost Matt a minor wing pelting and his chances at the enemy fighter.

Stockton was close behind. "Watch that jerk tail gunner, West Virginia! He's popping anything with one lung!"

The 17s were on their bombing run now, gliding through the damnable bursts of black death all around them. Till his dying day, Matt Tower would never forget the sight or the dedication of the bomber crews who, mission after mission, endured the nerve-wracking, stomach-churning pass over ground zero.

The fighter groups could do no more. Their Big Friends must go it alone until withdraw support arrived, if it arrived, and found them on time. A trying moment for the escort pilot, hating to look back lest he see a wounded Fortress slipping from the formation's protection to face returning enemy fighters alone. Fortunately, everything was P-51 and P-38 now and the lack of fighter cover would be but minutes before relief showed up.

As usual, the dogfight scattered the squadrons, leaving their elements to reassemble as best they could. On the run for home, Matt and his wingman found themselves in the company of two red-nosed P-5ls of the 356th Fighter Group out of Martlesham Heath. The visitors took the third and fourth positions off *Paladin's* wing.

"Mind if we hitch a ride, checkerboard? Names are Nelson and Clark."

"Delighted!" Matt encouraged. "Tower and Stockton over here." Two hundred miles into enemy territory, there was comfort in numbers. "How's your fuel, Red Nose?

"Adequate for the trip. Why?"

"We like to moonlight after hours. Bust up a train or something on the way back. You game?"

"Count us in! We're three times new at this, checkerboard. We can use the experience."

The makeshift fighter flight made a wide sweep to the south before heading for the North Sea coast. Villages, hedgerows, and rail lines were thinly defined against a German countryside blanketed in a light fresh snow. The Christmas card beauty camouflaged many familiar landmarks, testing Matt's navigational skills.

A thickening overcast deprived the Mustangs of their shadow as they chased the rail lines along a winding river. The Germans had a habit of hiding side-track depots in the forest beyond their major rail centers. Usually lightly defended they made juicy targets. But these rails were running south and if something didn't show up shortly, the four winged hunters would have to break for the

Dutch coast. "Checkerboard One, target at three o'clock! Looks like a freight train! She's rounding the hill there!"

"Good sighting, Nelson. Now we're getting somewhere!" Matt studied the chain of rail cars and worked the flight of P-51s in closer. "I count six boxcars and a Pullman on the end. You don't see them running inland like that very often. Most stuff moves toward the front. What do you make of it, West Virginia?"

"Must be some valuable stuff. She's pouring it on. Look at her go!"

"All right, let's work on the engine and stop her if we can. Then we'll take care of the cars," Matt directed.

Clearly silhouetted against the white hills, the train had no chance of covering the couple of miles to a forest thicket. *Paladin*'s left wing dropped to lead the first run on the locomotive. The 45-degree chase was a testy one requiring a well-timed deflection shot. Matt watched his first burst rip up the snow in a trail straight across the black hulk of the engine.

By the time all four fighters had crossed the target, it was covered in billowing steam. The eager pilots lined up for a second run only to see the engine roll off track, its bulk mushing up a tidal wave of cascading snow and derailing half of its cars. "Right in the bull's butt!" Nelson roared. "Now let's cut it up into steaks!"

"We better see if there's any flak down there," Matt cautioned, remembering his first experience with fake boxcars when an arsenal of 20mm cannon had introduced him to ground fire. "We'll take them at an angle, low and fast!"

"What the heck is that coming out of the first two cars?" Stockton mused.

"Cows?" Nelson chuckled. "Dang if we've shot up a cattle train."

Matt led the Mustangs on a cautious pass over the smoldering engine for a closer look. Nothing could have prepared him for the sight. It wasn't cattle. "Heaven help them!" he gasped. "They're people! Stockton, those are people down there!"

There was little distinction to the figures draped in shades of gray and black. A scene of pathetic confusion, some huddling around those injured in the wreck, the more militant racing to the bolted doors of other cars. A few, crazed with hope, sloshed across the white fields, trading the horror of boxcars for the uncertainty of a winter wilderness.

Matt's hands and arms tingled, his throat dry as the desert as he watched the drama below. Finally breaking the stunned silence, Clark of the red-nosed P-5ls forced the dreaded question. "Do you... do you think we hit any of them?"

"Come on, Clark!" Nelson fired back at his wingman. "Don't start with that crap! We were after a train, a German train!" But his voice reflected the same grave concern.

Either the hoards on the ground recognized the American planes or had surrendered to fate, for none appeared to raise a hand or even look up. Their lot worsened when the first squad of helmeted troops poured from the Pullman and began firing at the wanderers in the fields.

"What have we done?" Stockton cried.

"All right, all right!" Matt countered. "That's enough! At least we can even the odds. Red Nose, you take the troops on the right, and we'll get 'em on this side!"

Matt looked back to see bodies dropping in the snow. It seemed forever, like the slow motion of a bad dream, before he could bring the fighter into position. The first two squads made the mistake of grouping for firepower, and that's where the P-5ls caught them. Geysers of white erupted over the ground, cutting through the assembled uniforms, throwing them left and right.

Matt finished his run with the Pullman in his sights, exploding its windows and catching more dismounting troops. Those who survived the first pass rolled under the rail car, returning fire with their rifles. The precious minutes of shock and confusion benefited the militants from the boxcars, who pounced on the weapons of fallen soldiers.

Nelson's Mustangs extracted similar results on their side of the engagement, leaving the German survivors to face a new battle front on the ground. Twice the fighters returned, their sleek silver bodies racing a dozen feet above the ground, firing eyeball to eyeball at the troops under the Pullman car.

"I'm all tracers!" Stockton exclaimed.

"Save it!" Matt ordered. "That's all we can do. Save your fuel."

Now the people were waving, the militants thrusting their newly acquired weapons into the air. Matt's last image of the tragedy below was of the ragged militia probing beneath the Pullman for Germans still alive. He dipped *Paladin*'s wing in salute before leading his foursome west over the trees.

Buster Clark, Nelson's wingman, was out of fuel 15 minutes over the North Sea, ditching into its murky gray waters after an extended glide. The others could only radio his position, for circling would ensure that they joined him. Nelson broke off to the right as they sighted the English coast, hoping to reach Martlesham Heath. His last words were a dry preoccupied, "I'll catch you at the pub in Ipswich." The day had been too much.

"Crap!" Stockton broke the silence. "My engine's cutting out!"

"Throttle back. Let's get some glide. You can make it!" Matt encouraged.

"It's dead, sir! She's nose heavy!"

"All right, trim it up." *Paladin*'s fuel gauge lay well into the reserve line, and Matt struggled to conceal his own concerns. "You've been wanting to go to the beach, haven't you, West Virginia?"

"Not like this, I haven't!"

"Come on, it's a piece of cake! Watch the whitecaps. The wind's to the southwest. Turn to starboard and line up on that stretch of open beach. Watch your airspeed, drop your gear. I'll stick with you."

"Get out of here, Matt, while your engine's running. There might not be room for two of us down there."

Matt watched his wingman growing smaller against the water below, struggling to reach the narrow strip of sand along the coast. "Nose down, watch your speed. Don't stall it." The troubled fighter touched down and rolled on the beach for a moment, then turned and nosed up. "Stockton! Stockton! Are you okay?"

Matt sighed, his lips tight in anxiety. After an eternity, his earphones crackled and a voice responded in familiar West Virginia twang. "Piece of cake, huh?"

Shaking his head, Matt smiled in relief. "You sound kind of funny. You catch cold in the cockpit draft?"

"Broke my stupid nose, you jerk! I've got a handful of slop here. Tell them to bring me a handkerchief. A big one, okay?"

In seconds Matt had reported the crash position, demanding an immediate response. He knew Stockton would play it cool and might lie about his condition. It would be late that night before he learned that his wingman had cracked a rib and broken two fingers in addition to the nose job.

Minutes later *Paladin*'s engine quit, beginning a perilous three-mile glide to make Raydon's main runway. "Seldom Red One to Control, clear me for a dead stick to runway twenty-seven!"

The wind prevailed, dropping the P-51 on the dirt road just short of the runway in an explosion of flying snow and slush. *Paladin* recoiled from the impact, springing the height of a man into the air. The third bounce, lifted by a guardian angel, cleared the berm on the road shoulder and planted the Mustang's gangly legs in a snowy field beside the runway.

Awesome sudden silence ensued. Matt's ears ached from the

hours of intense radio chatter and the constant hum of *Paladin*'s 12-cylinder Rolls Royce engine. Sighing deeply, he slumped into the bucket seat, his legs suddenly gone to rubber. Tension drained his mind of thought for the moment.

Crash trucks slid and slogged across the field, chasing a jeep to the downed fighter. In spite of the circumstances, the absurdity of the approaching conglomeration wrested a fleeting grin from the exhausted flyer. "Keystone Cops," he moaned, pulling himself to a standing position.

Smaragdis was on the Mustang's wing in a single bound. "What the devil happened, Matt?"

"Did they reach Stockton yet?"

"Yeah, but what happened to you guys?"

Matt was the flight leader, and his concern for one under his command was every bit as great as Smaragdis'. "What's his condition?"

"I don't know, but he's alive."

"Chuck and Roger?"

"Shilling put it down at Boxted, Essex, out of fuel. I don't know how he ended up over there because Roger's drinking it off at the officers' club."

The captain held his questions on the ride back to briefing, giving Matt time to collect his thoughts. Some of Red Section's radio transmissions had reached the tower, and Intelligence was in a frenzy to get at *Paladin*'s pilot. Stan Herrington arrived in the middle of it, taking his position as silent observer in a corner chair.

The intensity of the questions grew to the point that Matt's answers, sprinkled with increasing corrections and clarifications, were taking longer and longer. Herrington leaned forward, his eyes drifting from the flyer's drawn face to his trembling right hand on the table map. "Okay, gentlemen, that will do for now."

The chief Intelligence officer turned abruptly, surprised at the interruption. "Major, we're at a critical point here!"

"We certainly are, Lieutenant, and we're going to take a break."

"Sir, it's imperative that we fix these coordinates! This is the first verification of the trains in that area. We have earlier reports of people being transported inland out of those areas."

Herrington rose slowly, dominating the hushed room. He puffed for a moment on the pipe, pulled it from his lips and pointed the slim stem at the four seated inquisitors. "Let me phrase it another way, gentlemen. Get the devil out of here!"

The shuffle of paper and drag of chair legs testified to the clarity of the order, and the room emptied quickly. On a nod from Herrington, John Smaragdis escorted the last man out.

Blessed silence prevailed again. Herrington walked to the coffee bar and poured two cups. "Black or muddy?"

"Muddy," Matt sighed. "I'm sorry, sir."

"They have a job to do. We rely on them just as much as they rely on us. But I'd like to see some of these young crew cuts on the point 20,000 feet over Krautville one time."

Matt pulled his helmet off, closed his eyes, and let the coffee do its work. Herrington stoked the pipe until an acceptable stream of blue smoke wiggled its way from the bowl. "There's a P-51 at the bottom of the North Sea, one tailed up on the beach, another over at Boxted, and you landed short of the runway. Where were you guys?"

Matt stared at the table, the coffee cup steadied between his hands. "After we left the bombers, we were pretty spread out. Two fighters from the 356th Group joined up with Stockton and me for the run home. There was a train near the Dutch border, and we shot up the engine, derailed it."

"And?"

"It was full of people, Major! They... they came out of the cars, wandering around! I don't know if we hit any of them or not." Matt paused, his face twisted in reflection as he tried to recall every burst of his guns. "There was a troop car full of soldiers, and they started shooting at the people! Just shooting them in the snow!"

Herrington's hands slipped into his pockets as he rose slowly from the chair. "What did you do then?"

"We strafed the troops until we ran out of ammunition." The stillness hung heavy, broken only by an occasional pop from a chunk of coke settling in the heater stove. "How could anybody know?"

"What kind of markings did the train have?"

"What do you mean, markings?"

"Decals, printing, markings."

Matt ran his fingers through his hair and leaned back in the chair, his brow wrinkled in thought. "There were flags on the engine. Red flags. The troop car had a long spread-eagle on the side under the windows. It was holding a circle or ring with a swastika in it."

"And the freight cars?"

"Just old wooden cars, same as I've seen a hundred times. Had large numbers on them, but nothing unusual. Major, how were we to know? Where were they taking those people?"

"I don't know, Tower. Lot of stories are coming out of there now. I hear some things over at Wing."

"What the heck's going on? I mean, we're out there going after the Hun and...."

"You didn't do anything wrong, soldier. You did exactly what you were supposed to do. I trust your judgment, Tower. If I didn't, you wouldn't run one of my flights. Huh, there's not a one of us that hasn't shot up something we weren't expecting."

Herrington wasn't about to lose a seasoned pilot to the pits of remorse. "All right, Tower, here's the plan. One, you high-tail it over to sick bay and see Doc Hughes. Tell him I want an evaluation on my desk by 1300. Two, when you leave Doc you head straight for Chaplain Wheeler's office, and I don't care what the hour is, you wait until he can see you. Three, I want you in my office at 1600 sharp."

Herrington's emphatic directions coaxed a fleeting grin from the young lieutenant. "Major, I'll get it together."

"Dang right you will! But you're going to do it my way: Steps One, Two, and Three. And that ain't fatherly advice, soldier. It's an order!"

# CHAPTER 24

# Blessed Consolation

**M**ATT'S OPPORTUNITIES TO see Vivie grew scarcer as
December progressed. Backs to their border, the Germans mounted a series of counterattacks to break the
Allied offensive. In the face of a severe winter, surprise was complete, resulting in the worst fighting of the war. More than a month
would pass before the Allies would stem the drive and return the
lines to pre-Battle of the Bulge positions. Slybird was in the middle
of it when weather permitted, which wasn't often enough.

The visits Matt managed to Ipswich and Falcon's Rest were godsent.
He wrestled less now with the train incident, thanks to the excellent
ministry of Chaplain Stirling Wheeler and a blessed act on Vivie's part
in introducing him to Frau Hanna Minska.

Frau Minska and her sister had escaped Germany in June 1941 at
the insistence of her husband and only son, who intended to follow
later. A farm family near Hamburg had given them sanctuary, but

as persecution of Jews increased, savings were spent on escape for the women through Holland. The last communication they received from those left behind came in August 1941 by the hands of another escapee.

Hanna and her husband were teachers until declared unfit to instruct the children of the Third Reich, a warning they followed wisely. The bleak, agonizing wait for word of her loved ones accented Hanna's threescore years. But beneath her hollow eyes and drooping shoulders, Matt saw the countenance of a gracious and lovely woman.

Seated now in her modest apartment, lips frozen in a deep frown, she listened intently to the American flyer's encounter with the train. "Deportation," she responded in heavy accent, for much of her English had come in the last four years. "Perhaps to Buchenwald, oder Flossenburg. Likely zay ver Dutch, Captain. It vood not be goot for zem."

"We didn't know," Matt sighed, his eyes avoiding hers. "Some of those people were hurt. I saw some shot."

"Nein, nein," she mourned, leaning closer to her American guest. "You dit nothing vong, Captain Tower." Firmly and deliberately her hands folded over his, her steady brown eyes confirming her point. "Ze vons zat fell in ze fields, zay ver ze fortunate vons. Zuch grauen!" she paused, her gaze drifting away, lips firmer than ever. "Von day.... ze vorld vill know.... ja, von day!"

She spoke freely then of her experiences of Nazi-instigated intimidation. "Ze children... it vas so sad. Zay could not understand, zare little vorlds crumbling... so frightened." She patted his hand and attempted a smile. "Nein, you fight ze Nazi, Captain! You shoot zem."

Contrary to body, there was nothing frail about Hanna's spirit. She had been tested severely. Matt sat in awe of this daughter of Israel, who gradually changed their conversation from tragic to more pleasant reflections of her youth in Hamburg. Vivie sat quietly as the older woman and young flyer warmed to each other. She had hoped their meeting would further reassure Matt.

"We had a Hamburg near my hometown," Matt injected. "In the early days, the Charleston Railroad sent a fellow named Schultz to their rail ending across the Savannah River from Augusta. He named his new community *Hamburg* after his hometown in Germany. Then to draw business into South Carolina, he built a toll bridge and began to capture his fortune.

Hanna's eyes sparkled at the prospect. "He dit goot zen. Ja?"

"For a while, until Augusta put up a free bridge. It went downhill from then on. He was a pretty bitter guy when he died. In a final gesture of defiance, he was buried in the hills above the river, standing up, with his back to Augusta. It's still known today as *Schultz Hill*."

"And vut of Hamburg?" Hanna inquired hopefully.

"Just a few ruins now. But Schultz has his place in history all the same."

Hanna's eyes drifted across the room, locked into scenes Matt and Vivie could never know. "Zat vill be my Hamburg, too," she sighed. "All in ruins."

Hanna could only speculate, and Matt did not respond, for he had flown over the city and knew its fate all too well. She walked the young couple to the snowy courtyard of her building. She clasped Matt's hands again, nudging them in a gesture of encouragement. "May God bless you, Captain, und keep you from all harm!"

Fighting the lump in his throat, he responded with the warmest and deepest sentiments of his heart. "Merry Christmas, Frau Minska!" She accepted the spirit of the young American's wishes and smiled knowingly at Vivie, whereupon Matt caught his spontaneous error. "I'm sorry," he winced. "That's Happy Hanukkah to you, isn't it?"

"Vell," she smiled again. "Let it be 'Gut Yom Tov' to everyone!"

Hanna stood in the courtyard with sweater pulled tightly around her until the young couple were out of sight. They crossed Henley Road, arm in arm—she in a long black coat with fur collar hooded over her ears and he in a trench coat—into the great white expanse that was Christ Church Park in the winter. It was still their special retreat, rich in memories and hope for the future.

Only an occasional snowflake fell now as the couple walked silently along familiar paths on this late December Sunday, an evening filled with holiday magic and destined to provide the citizenry of Ipswich a gracious reward for their long suffering. A reward Vivie was quick to grasp as they reached the lower end of the park. "Look, poppet!" she squealed, her eyes dancing with excitement. "The lights are still on!"

He followed her gaze to the great old church a half block away, each of its tall windows a kaleidoscope of color against the darkened walls. Spectacle that it was, he was more taken with Vivie's reaction. "Beautiful," he managed, his tone questioning the extent of her fervor.

"Matt, don't you see? She spun to him, her hands gripping his lapels. "Maybe they are going to lift the blackout altogether."

Intellectually he understood, but a few months of war experience could not approach an Englander's last six years. Slowly, expectantly, they turned in a circle. Other windows were aglow along Fonnereau Road and down into the city. Vivie drank it all in like a child at the gate to a circus. When their eyes met again, her slightly parted lips wept silently as tiny crystal streams streaked her soft white cheeks.

His arms enfolded her, absorbing the muffled sobs until she rested quietly against him. "Merry Christmas, England," he whispered softly.

"I'm sorry," she laughed weakly, dabbing at her eyes. "I came quite apart, didn't I? It's just that England has been dark for so very long."

He lifted her collar back in place, carefully tucking in each lock of stray hair. She rested her cheek against his hand as it paused and smiled up at him. "We must be winning, sweetheart. We are, aren't we?"

"It's a good sign," came the cautious reply. How difficult to conceal what he knew about the war without bursting her bubble. Hitler had slowed the Allied advance at Germany's border, and Intelligence determined early on that the Fuhrer was unlikely to surrender—conditional or otherwise. The end would not be quick in coming.

They stood watching the stragglers hurrying up the church steps, the younger exchanging greetings amid the joy of the lights as the older wearily pulled themselves up the rail. Vivie tugged her handsome flyer's arm. "Let's go in, poppet! It's Christmas Eve vespers. We've a bit to be thankful for, I'd say."

Matt nodded agreement. He had not been in a real church since the funeral for Etta Moore's sister. How grand this one was, with its vaulted ceiling and ornate furnishings, compared to the services in Station Chapel on the base. The organ's rich tones were exhilarating as voices of choir and parishioner joined to make a joyful noise unto their Lord. Matt closed his eyes, picturing for a fleeting moment the simpler but elegant sanctuary of his own Trinity Presbyterian Church in Augusta. There he had so often sang this same ancient English carol, *The First Noel*.

"I'm impressed!" Vivie whispered as they sat down. "You've a lovely voice, Captain."

"I'm likewise impressed," Matt grinned back. "But the lovely extends well beyond the voice in your case," whereupon he encircled her shoulders with his arm.

Vivie patted his hand and tactfully lifted it away. "This is the house of the Lord, Casanova, after all!"

"Love thy neighbor," he replied playfully.

"Keep thy hands to thyself, lest thou provoke a painful incident!"

His intention was innocent affection and she knew that, but in this hour she wished nothing to distract from the reverence and thanksgiving that filled her heart. For so many years she had longed for brighter days, for a time of optimism, for peace in her soul, and this was as near as she had come.

Based on the 107th Psalm, the Vicar's homily beautifully entwined the advent of God's redemptive grace and thanksgiving for new hope brought about in the partial lifting of the blackout.

*"O' give thanks unto the Lord, for he is good; for his mercy endureth forever. Let the redeemed of the Lord say so, whom he hath redeemed from the hand of the enemy; and gathered them out of the lands from the east and from the west, from the north and from the south. They wandered in the wilderness in a solitary way; they found no city to dwell in. Hungry and thirsty, their soul fainted in them. Then they cried unto the Lord in their trouble, and He delivered them out of their distress."*

How easily Matt could relate those verses to the solitary struggle of every soldier, to the return of those on foreign soil with no city to dwell in. He believed in his heart of hearts that God would finally save Europe and England from the enemy. But the price was steep and his prayers were for those who braved the skies of Europe and those from his own Group whose fate was still unknown. The names of Dewey Newhart, Glenn Duncan, and Don Morris were among many he breathed silently.

Vivie read his lips and took his hand in hers. She had her own names: friends like Mrs. Pearson's son, young Bobby Brooks' father, little Davy, a relative or two dispatched in His Majesty's service. Then unexpectedly, when her emotions were deepest, it happened. John Davis' image filled the screen of her mind. Handsome in his RAF uniform, his playful crooked grin just as she last saw it on the station platform nearly five years earlier. *"Hooo...!"* she mourned to herself, conflicting emotions running rampant. *"Why... why now?"* Spontaneously, she had included his name in prayer.

As the Vicar prayed on, Matt sensed the change in Vivie. Head bowed, he eased a lid open in time to see the deep wrinkle on her brow and the handkerchief cover her eyes. At first, he thought it deep prayer, but moments later he knew better. Her anguish was far too intense and his concern grew. She allowed his arm to encircle hers without response.

Not until the Vicar's call to benediction did she regain some composure and stand with the aid of Matt's arm. "Now unto Him who is able to do exceeding abundantly above all that we ask or think, according to the power that worketh in us, unto Him be glory in the church by Christ Jesus throughout all ages, world without end, amen."

Moving along the aisle, they were a somber couple compared to the joyous worshipers still basking in the beauty of the service. She nodded and smiled, as need be, to the pleasant greetings directed their way. But she clung tightly to Matt's arm, praying they would see no one she knew.

The night was crisp, cold, and very still as they reached the curb. Pilot's instinct drew Matt's eyes skyward in time to glimpse a break in the clouds where a lone star flickered dimly. Nineteen hundred years earlier its distant cousin heralded peace on earth, but on this Christmas Eve the herald seemed only to assure combat missions by dawn's early light.

Vivie was shivering and he surmised it had as much to do with her upset in church as the weather. In either case, the walk back would be uncomfortable for her, and he decided to hail a taxi. The streets could be clear of vehicles for blocks in each direction until a mass exiting from a public building. Mysteriously, the cabbies always seemed to know. Relief plainly marked Vivie's face as she ducked into the automobile. "Falcon's Rest on Henley, please," Matt ordered.

The young couple sat silently as the taxi slipped away, rocking them gently with each change of the gears. There was just enough light for him to observe her, head lifted slightly in the British tradition of stiff upper lip, struggling yet to settle her emotions. He knew it was not the time for direct questions. "You okay, sweetheart?"

She nodded and reached for his hand but made no effort to close the distance between them. Her mood had changed little as minutes later she quickly mounted the steps to Falcon's Rest, where even the dim, cozy warmth of the deserted lobby failed to work its usual magic. She went busily about, placing her things away behind the desk, vaguely acknowledging the greeting from the clerk in the office just beyond.

When she could occupy herself no longer, Vivie turned to her patiently waiting captain at the end of the lobby desk. She had not asked for his coat, and that bothered him a lot. Even her smile seemed an effort. "There's time for a cup if you like."

He slipped his coat off and folded it over his shoulder as they walked to the kitchen. Strained as things were, his heart went out to the woman preceding him. So great was her need to be busy that she had the cups in place before he had a chance to offer a hand. "Sugar?"

"Darling!" he snapped, hoping to lighten the mood.

"In your coffee," she countered, only mildly amused.

"Just your little finger," he tried again. She paused, head down, resting her hands on the back of a chair. "I'm sorry," she said softly. "I didn't mean to ruin such a lovely evening."

He was quick to console, moving to her side, taking her gently in his arms, grateful the ice was thawing. "You had me going, sweetheart. Is it something you can talk about?"

She settled in a chair and took a sip from the cup. Their eyes met as he joined her. "It was silly," she began, attempting to make light of it. "Just memories I'm still learning to deal with." She reached for his hand. "Must you go back to base tonight, on Christmas Eve?"

"War is like time and tide," he breathed deeply. "It waits for no man. But I promise, the minute debriefing is over, I'll find a way. Just pray it's a morning mission."

She folded her hands over his, pulling them closer to her. "Matt, I love you so much. You've been such a patient dear through all this. I've been thinking we really should set a date now."

He leaned across the corner of the table and kissed her lips. "Tonight!" he grinned. "We could get that Vicar at the church to do it. He's probably still there."

"Matt," she smiled back. "Be serious. That wouldn't be fair to your parents. I do so want them to approve. I want to write them, to have a chance to talk with them even if by mail. Have you sent any pictures?"

"A couple. Mom would be crazy about you. You'd be best buddies in no time." Matt slipped a photo from his wallet and placed it on the table.

"You have her eyes," she smiled. They are such a handsome couple. There's such strength in his face, the chin, the set of his jaw. He would be gracious and kind, wouldn't he?"

"A Southern gentleman of the old school, as we call them. A man of his word and he expects you to be the same. He wasn't beyond applying correction to your rear end," Matt chuckled, "when it wasn't absorbed at the front end."

"I feel very strongly about your mother," Vivie said as she picked up the photo. "I must write her. If I give you a letter, it would go through military mail more quickly, wouldn't it?"

"That's what they tell us. If you have a picture of your folks and one of Falcon's Rest, it would be great."

"I'll have them for you tomorrow. Would it be possible to ring them up? After they have the letter, I'd love to talk with them." Vivie's eyes drifted in thought. "We could have two ceremonies, you know, if they can't be here."

"Two! Boy, you want to tie that knot tight, don't you?"

"Silly!" she snapped, slapping his hand playfully. "I'm quite serious. You're the only son, and they've family and friends. Don't deny them."

"Lady, you'll have my mother eating out of your hand."

Vivie's brow wrinkled prankishly as she punched his chest with her finger. "She's not the one I want eating out of my hand, darling. But I do want our families to be close."

"All right, I'm sold," Matt grinned as he pressed her fingers to his lips. "When does the first ceremony take place?"

"Oh, dear," Vivie sighed, her face suddenly aglow with expectation. "A million things one must do, you know. I'll talk with Mum in the morning. She's marvelous at these things. Perhaps we can announce our plans Christmas evening."

The great old clock in Falcon's Rest's lobby pealed out the eighth hour, its melodious bong sobering the faces of the enchanted couple. The anxiety of war added unspoken dread to their every parting, and there seemed always more to say than time allowed. Reluctantly, Matt rose to his feet and helped clear the table. "If I don't get out of here, I'll be walking back to Raydon. Besides, Santa won't come until all the good boys and girls are fast asleep."

She walked him to the lobby door and kissed him with a passion that blurred his earlier concerns at the church. "Fly safely, poppet," she begged as their fingers slipped apart.

# CHAPTER 25

# Christmas at Falcon's Rest

**D**ECEMBER 25, 1944, Raydon, England. Amid slush and snow, many homesick American airmen experienced their first Christmas away from home. The officers club was done up fairly well to host the holiday bash, but it could never do justice to family and home. At Youngstown, the 350th Squadron's barracks, the mood was no different.

Of all days, the weather had cleared sufficiently for the heavies to bomb Ahrweiler, and Slybird took to the skies in escort. The Luftwaffe didn't sleep late either, but backed off after a short encounter, leaving one of their kind splattered in the snow below.

It was after lunch before the Americans returned to base, pressing Matt's schedule to the limit. He tried to grab some shuteye, but the tension of the mission and expectations in Ipswich left him as miserable on the cot as he was on his feet. Ipswich won out.

Chuck Shilling, equally exhausted, rolled over to see what the bustle was about. "Wh... what are you doing, Tower?"

Matt jumped around on one foot trying to get the other shoe on. "Chuck, have you ever been a best man?"

"At what?"

"Best man. You know, like at a wedding."

"Hey," Shilling sighed, rising to rest on his elbows. "That's pretty serious stuff, pal. You and Vivie finally gonna do it?"

"Keep it down, will you? I don't want these lugheads getting wind of it," Matt grinned, spreading his hands in question. "Well, what do you think?"

"I've seen some lucky stiffs, but you take the cake," Shilling chuckled as he rose laboriously to his feet and planted a congratulatory hand on Matt's shoulder. "There ain't a man on this base who wouldn't follow her off a cliff. I'll be your best man. I wouldn't miss it for the world! When are my services needed?"

"I'll know tonight. We're setting the date. Now keep it under your hat, okay? I don't want a lot of razzing."

"I gotcha, old buddy," Chuck nodded, glancing at his watch. "But if you miss the shuttle to town, you'll find out what razzing really is."

Matt was nodding within minutes of settling into the cushioned minibus seat. The driver was an old gal, clinging to the wheel and wearing a uniform much like Vivie's. But there the similarity ended. She did a fair job, however, of keeping it in the road, considering the winter conditions. Lulled by the engine's muffled growl and murmurings of fellow passengers, Matt dozed and dreamed.

*"How strange,"* he grinned to himself. *"It's just now Christmas morning back home."* In his mind, Matt could see the spacious parlor in his father's house. Eleanor Tower would have the largest cedar available, weighted to the limit with years of decorations. Fresh green garland, secured with exquisite red bows, would deck

the white spindled banisters of the foyer staircase. The memory was so vivid he could taste it.

*"Mattlowe Tower!"* was the threat on his mother's third call. Elly would have already gone to the breakfast table. Sisters were annoying that way, especially older ones. Elly obediently selected a toy from under the tree, taking it to her chair. He never understood why they got so excited over some stiff-limbed, round-eyed similitude of a human infant. Now, a shiny new Red Rider BB gun was a different matter.

Though he would have been up for three hours by then, it was sheer torture to leave the marvelous disorder of the parlor on Christmas morning. But with the help of Zip, the blond fluff of a cocker spaniel seated beside his chair, Matt would finish breakfast in record time.

"Ipswich it is, Yanks!" the little English lady chirped from the driver's seat, and Matt shook his head to clear away the most painful lump ever lodged in his throat. "God love ya, everyone!" she smiled as each passed through the doorway.

How quaint and inviting, this English village in winter's glow. Surely Dickens was inspired by these very streets, where fluffy white camouflage now hid the scars of war. But Vivie wasn't hidden. Matt would know her from any angle, even with the collar of her black coat raised around her ears. She waved as he stepped to the curb and hurried to meet him.

"What are you doing here?" Matt grinned in surprise.

"I came to save you from the snow dragon!" she laughed. "Aren't you happy to see me?"

"Happy?" He lifted her and kissed her full on the mouth. "I didn't expect you. How did you know?"

"There were only two shuttles today; this is the second." She led him to the car at the corner. "What's in the duffel bag?"

"Duffels," he grinned. "Don't ask so many questions."

"Come on then," she giggled, slipping into the driver's seat. "We'll be late for tea."

Currier and Ives would have loved it: Falcon's Rest beckoning nostalgically beneath its snowy cap as holiday candles twinkled merrily in each window. Longstanding tradition opened the great lobby to friends new and old on Christmas Day, when high tea expanded to buffet proportions. Here Etta Moore, the natural hostess, was at her best. "Matt!" she smiled, kissing him on the cheek. "Merry Christmas, dear!"

There was barely time to tuck the duffel bag behind the huge lobby tree before Etta had him in tow. All who had not, as yet, met Vivie's fiancée would do so now. One thing he had learned, the Moores kept company with the most interesting people. A London professor kept pressing Matt for information on Harvard University and its English endower and namesake, John Harvard. Colonel Burgess' guest, an Indian captain complete with turban, related in broken English fascinating excerpts of battle with the Vichy French in Middle Eastern deserts.

For nearly an hour Etta escorted the patient American flyer until dreamy-eyed Ruth Hardy tactfully separated them. Ruth's dark-green dress had one too many buttons undone, a trademark of the black-haired charmer. "Well, Captain, it's been a while," she cooed seductively, her fingers nimbly retrieving a cigarette.

Matt patted his pockets courteously and smiled. "Sorry, I don't carry a lighter."

"Humm, I remember now. You're the one without any vices," she replied, dropping the cigarette back in her purse. "Such a pity. You'd be quite a challenge, you know."

"You'd be bored to death," he chuckled. "What have you been up to, anyway?"

"Boosting troop morale," she smiled, casually easing her arm under his. "Come on, I'll boost yours. We can have a friendly drink, can't we? Don't worry; it's only egg flip."

Ruth's actions always seemed to catch him off guard and he

found himself being steered across the room. "Two," he managed to the fair young thing pouring as he attempted to gain control of the situation again. Conversation with the impetuous brunette was less than comfortable for Matt, usually leaving a flush of pink around his neck.

Her arm still encircling his, she sipped the creamy holiday brew. "So, we've a wedding in the making, I hear. Whatever do you see in her that you don't see in me, Matt Tower?"

"Hey, that's not a fair question. Besides, we're only allowed one wife at a time."

"Ha!" she smiled, snuggling against him. "Then you do like me!" He looked away, mentally whipping himself for not thinking out his words around her. How much was sheer flirtation puzzled him, for she seemed just as forward around Vivie. Such coquetry carried a certain allure all right, but he had yet to picture her as the mother of his children.

"I can't help it if Vivie asked me first," he grinned. "But I'll tell you one thing, you'd make some guy a heck of a wife."

"Indeed, I would," she giggled, snuggling him all the more, her long black eyelashes batting away.

"Let's not tire the guests, darling," Vivie intruded, easing herself between Matt and the vamp. "Besides, I'm certain Lady Ruth has an escort waiting somewhere."

"How pleasant to see you again, Captain Tower." Ruth extended her hand politely, overplaying the disinterest role.

"Is it safe to have you as my maid of honor or not?" Vivie sighed, cocking her head at the trim brunette. "And you!" she scolded Matt playfully. "I thought I left you safely in Mum's hands!"

"All right," Ruth chirped merrily. "I'll leave you two love birds to drool over each other. But if it hadn't been for me, we'd never have gotten it this far, would we?"

Matt wisely slipped an arm around Vivie as the vamp made a tactful retreat. "Without her?" he questioned.

"Well, I must admit she was one of your strongest supporters early on, and a wonderful shoulder when things weren't so clear." Vivie turned in response to joyous goodbyes across the room. "Come on, poppet; people are beginning to leave. We should see them out."

Matt was happy to see the guests departing and quiet prevail again. It was rare that he did not get a couple of hours of sleep after a mission, but the excitement of Christmas at Falcon's Rest had driven him on. Eagerly, he settled into a cushioned chair near the huge lobby tree where a few brightly wrapped packages remained. Unnoticed, he slipped those from the duffel bag in beside them.

His thoughts drifted to home again as he watched Vivie helping her mother tidy up the lobby, not unlike his own mother and sister putting the parlor back in order after Christmas dinner. England opened its doors to untold numbers of homesick Yanks that day, and many from Matt's base found welcome in the manor houses of Great Wenham, Raydon, Holton St. Mary, Layham, and Shelley.

"What's Christmas like at home, Captain?" Robert Moore inquired as he settled in a chair across from Matt.

"A lot like this, sir, but on a smaller scale. Most of our friends dropped by, or we visited them the day before. It was mostly family on Christmas Day. When I was younger, my grandparents stayed over sometimes to enjoy the confusion of Christmas morning." Matt nodded his head in reflection. "I guess England has a long-awaited gift that the war is winding down, the end of hostilities and a return to normality."

Major Moore's brow wrinkled slightly, not the reaction Matt expected. "Captain, that would be quite nice, but all those in the know have serious doubts."

"I would think everyone would be happy."

"You're not privy to England's political situation, Captain. We have a serious danger lurking in the shadows. The war interrupted efforts by the Labour Party to mount a drive into socialism. England is stretched to the limit economically, and it will take much effort and time to address the problems. If our meager resources are confiscated and placed in the hands of bureaucrats, and a welfare state develops, England will not get well. Economic depression will, in many ways, equal that resulting from the war."

"Uh, I didn't know. People not getting the message from the likes of Russia and other socialist countries?"

"They don't have a clue. So used to war regulations that 'pie in the sky' blinds them to reality. If you read the Labour Party agenda, personal taxes will creep to 50 percent. That will put a clot in the artery! They plan to discourage personal homes and force people into rental facilities. Run by bureaucrats, of course."

Etta, having heard much of the exchange between her husband and Matt, sought to lighten the mood. She brought them cups of tea and seated herself on the arm of Matt's chair. "Did you sleep well last night, dear? You seem perished today."

"It's been a long one," Matt replied, suppressing a yawn. "We were up at 0500, then a four-hour mission. But I'm holding up okay."

"I know it was nearly 10 o'clock when you left last night," Etta said, her brow showing concern. "Vivian, he should be in bed early this evening," she insisted.

Robert Moore scratched the back of his head nervously and cleared his throat. "I say, Etta, the Captain is a grown man."

"And grown men require sleep," she insisted.

"Very well, Mum," Vivie intervened. "I shall see that he gets a proper 40 winks." She dropped to her knees, all smiles. "Who shall play Father Christmas, then?"

"I thought those were for Boxing Day," the major injected, leaning over for a better look at the packages.

"Not all of them," Vivie replied gleefully, shifting them around. "For this one has your name on it."

"By Jove!" the older man gasped as she plopped the package on his lap.

"And... well, one for Mum, and let's see, two for Matt."

"And two for Vivie," Matt interrupted, sliding the gifts toward her.

"Why, Matt!" Etta breathed in surprise. "You didn't need to do this, dear!"

"It's not much," he grinned. "I haven't had time to shop and there's nothing much on base."

The rustle of paper replaced conversation as the little group opened the gifts. Robert Moore, well ahead of the others, withdrew a bulging envelope with stamps from his package. "Smashing!" he roared.

"They're from all over, sir. I think there's one from Hawaii. It took a while, but the guys on base were good about letting me have them." Robert started to put the box down. "Oh, there's something else in there."

The major rooted around and withdrew another item. "It's an Air Force survival knife," Matt said. "There's storage in the handle. Makes a fine hunting knife."

Etta carefully undid her package to reveal two exquisitely decorated miniature vases. "They are lovely!" she exclaimed. "How thoughtful, Matt!"

"I don't know a lot about porcelain," he confessed. "But Vivie told me you collect it."

Etta turned them over to read the markings. "They have the Royal Seal of Belgium. You may wish one day that you had kept them."

Vivie was all thumbs as she slid the first box from its wrapping. On the blue felt liner rested an elegant, three-strand necklace of pearls, their silver clips sparkling like diamonds. "Oh... Matt!" she sighed. "What have you done?"

She struggled to hold back tears as he placed them around her neck. Etta leaned forward, lips parted in awe. "They are breathtaking, aren't they? Where, pray tell, did you ever find such a setting?"

"A very exclusive source," he smiled, recalling his dealings with Sergeant McDuff. The NCO was a walking mail-order catalog that, allowed sufficient time, seemed able to materialize the impossible.

Vivie kissed him discreetly on the cheek due to present company and whispered, "Thank you, my love."

Excitedly, she pulled a long, slender box from beneath the tree and laid it on his lap. "This is from the three of us, poppet. I do hope you like it."

He worked quickly with the wrapping and lifted the box top away. Nothing could have prepared him for its contents, for there lay Lord Havely's Happoldt masterpiece, its sleek blued barrels and red mahogany stock perfectly preserved.

For the first time in his life, Matt Tower was short on words, but the expression on his face made Vivie's eyes dance with delight. "Major, Mrs. Moore, I mean... this is too much!" he stammered.

There were few occasions when Vivie's father lost his poker face, and this was one of them as he connected empathically with the young flyer. "She's a beaut, isn't she? Don't be concerned about accepting it, Captain. I struck a rather good deal with His Lordship, especially when he found out why we wanted it. You made a fair impression on the old boy. First time he's been outgunned in a while." Robert Moore leaned back contentedly, knife and stamps prominently on his lap. "A rather satisfying experience for me, I might add."

As the hour grew late, the Moores retired to the pleasures of their gifts: Etta eager to try the vases on her living room display shelves and Robert irresistibly drawn to his stamp albums.

Vivie rested her arms on Matt's knees as she knelt beside him, watching him handle the shotgun. "The competition is unbearable!" her pouting lips pined. "To suffer the flirtations of a buxom seductress, who is supposed to be one's very best friend, is quite enough. But to find oneself competing with a fowling piece, well!"

Matt looked down at her, so bright-eyed and lovely, the pearls in splendid array against her dark-green sweater. He put the gun to one side and lifted her onto his lap. "Nothing could upstage you, my dear little English princess." He pulled her against him and kissed her as he had been wanting to all evening.

She made up for the earlier peck on his cheek as they nestled beneath the flickering shadows of the great fireplace. How warm and comfortable she felt against him, his mind perfectly at peace, utterly content, until she stirred and sat up. "We are in the lobby," she whispered. "Not everyone has retired, you know."

"Nuts!" he whispered back.

"Oh," she giggled, sliding off his lap, "I have one special little gift just from me. I almost forgot it!"

In a second she was at the back of the tree on hands and knees, fishing out a brightly wrapped square box. "This, my darling, has a very special purpose."

"And so does this," he laughed, retrieving an additional package from the duffel bag.

They paused, looking into each other's eyes, delighted as small children to play the game. Matt, faster at removing the wrapping, held up a handsome royal-blue pullover sweater, its soft wool texture folding smoothly at his touch. One quick examination and he knew she had seriously dented her ration book. "I love it! But you didn't need to do that, sweetheart. The gun was more than I ever dreamed."

"But I wanted you to have something just from me, poppet, something a bit personal. Then when I'm not around, it can snuggle you tightly for me."

"Poor substitute," Matt grinned, spreading the sweater across his chest.

Vivie lost no time in slipping the paper off her box, her fingers gently lifting the sheer fabric folded inside. "Oh, Matt! These stockings are silk! Where did you find them?" Collecting herself with a sigh, she turned to him. "How can I thank you, darling?"

A mischievous wrinkle creased his brow. "Let me watch you put them on!"

"I should think not, you naughty boy," her prim little smile reprimanded. "You'll be bored with that soon enough."

"Oh, I should think not!" he teased, blurting her favorite exclamation.

She bent over and kissed him, her hands lingering on his face for a moment. "You are tired, aren't you, darling? Why don't you put your things in the room, and I'll stir up a nightcap."

The thought of getting out of his jacket and tie was incentive enough, and he headed for number G001, arms bulging with Christmas. Vivie folded the torn wrapping paper and ribbon and deposited it in the kitchen trash can. "Oh, Mum, I didn't see you."

"Just taking your father some warm milk. He's terribly restless tonight."

"Too much holiday, no doubt."

"I don't know, dear. He was talking with Colonel Burgess not long after he arrived. They seemed rather serious to me, but he would only say it was Intelligence business. Whatever it was quite unnerved him."

"Perhaps the fifth column is at it again," Vivie questioned. "What with the war going our way for a change."

"Whatever it is, this should help," Etta replied, placing the cup of warm liquid on a saucer. "And you take care of your man. Don't keep him up until the wee hours. He'll be right here in the morning."

Vivie smiled at her mother and waved her out of the kitchen.

Looking forward to the relative privacy of Matt's' room, she fixed a small tray with tea and snacks and flipped out the light. Falcon's Rest had fallen asleep at last, clearing her way across the darkened lobby. She tapped at the door, which was slightly ajar, but without response. "Hello," she cooed in hushed tones. "Is Captain Tower in quarters?"

The stillness of a classic winter's night was her response as she eased the door open. He was there, at least in body, laid out full length on the single bed. How like a little boy he appeared: one leg dangling over the edge, Christmas gifts in disarray at his side. She smiled tenderly as she placed the tray on the dresser and stood beside him.

"Poppet," she whispered softly. But the shallow rise and fall of his chest told the story, and she had not the heart to wake him. Carefully, she undid the tie and eased it from his neck, slipped off his shoes, and placed the dangling leg on the bed. Then she finished her tea, legs curled in the big rocker, and watched her adored as he slept.

# CHAPTER 26

# The Dead Returns

B Y THE FIRST of the year, Matt had added another swastika to *Paladin*'s cowling, his sixth destroyed in the air. Herrington moved him to acting flight leader in Smaragdis' absence, adding to the excitement and giving him an earlier crack at enemy fighters. He was bursting with the news when he next visited Falcon's Rest. Vivie was her usual loving self, showering him with praise, then preaching caution lest he become too cocky in his successes.

It was Etta who puzzled him. He had grown accustomed to her attentiveness, but that afternoon she seemed preoccupied, acknowledging his feat rather matter-of-factly, her smile brief and synthetic. Robert Moore had left that morning for London with Colonel Burgess. Neither would elaborate, only attributing the hurried trip to Intelligence matters. Vivie tried to make light of it, but Matt could tell she was just as mystified as he.

The turn of 1945 found Slybird busier than ever, forcing the courtship to endure by telephone when Vivie couldn't make it to the Walldon lodge. With the exception of one patrol, all missions were for bomber escort with the heavies plastering some 15 assorted German cities in rapid succession. Though it shortened his time with Vivie, it was assuring a shorter war, which was to both their liking.

Certain of those targets, the Luftwaffe defended with a vengeance. But there were noticeably fewer aircraft in their attacks in recent weeks. The tide had turned on the Axis, placing the advantage of experience on the side of the Allies. Now, on a cold, gray February day, Matt grinned at his crew chief from *Paladin's* cockpit.

"I think Shilling got his ace today."

"It's about time! What'd he git?"

"He was after a Focke-Wulf the last time I saw him. We got separated west of Stuttgart."

Matt jumped from his fighter as Chuck circled his aircraft, *Snake In The Grass*, into the dispersal pad, the menacing fangs of a huge rattler flashing from the P-5l's cowling. A questioning thumbs-up to the deplaning pilot brought a puzzled shrug. "I think I burned him, Matt. He was smoking on his back when we went through the clouds."

"Did you see him hit?"

"No, but Roger saw him smoking, too. I came out of the clouds looking for him and went down to the deck, but I couldn't find him. Man, I ran both sides of the River Somme for 20 miles, but I never saw any wreckage."

"Well, hang tough, buddy. There were a lot of us up there today. Somebody's gonna confirm it."

All through debriefing Shilling questioned pilot after pilot without success. His growing disappointment burdened Matt as well, for they had become good friends over the months in England.

So much so that when Matt took over for Smaragdis, Chuck asked to be his wingman rather than take a flight himself. They proved to be a devastating team, flying with twin-like precision and wondering why they had not tried it in the beginning.

But the day would close without confirmation of a kill. Back at the barracks, the two sat over their mission maps noting every location detail and scribbling a page full of notes. Perhaps the gun-camera film would tell the story, but that would be a painful wait.

"Mail call!" the corporal bellowed as he banged the barracks door. "Captain Tower, sir, these two memos were on the OD's desk from yesterday, but I brought them anyway."

"Thanks, Bennie." Matt smiled at the youthful face, remembering McDuff's pledge to take care of him. No one had the heart to question his age to the upper brass, because it was evident the youngster felt very much a part of the group. He was certainly in no danger running errands for the sergeant.

Exasperation creased Matt's brow as he unfolded the wrinkled paper. Two separate calls from Falcon's Rest, one the afternoon before and one this morning, had not been forwarded to him. "I have to make a call, Chuck. Some Officer of the Day has been sitting on these for two mail calls. Bennie, is there an extra seat in that jeep?"

"Yes, sir. I can drop you off."

The Walldons were great about Matt using their telephone, but the angered flyer thought better of covering the mile and a half to their lodge on foot in the thick of winter. He would wrangle a phone on base. After all, it was headquarters' fault. The Women's Auxiliary Army Corps volunteer at the switchboard was sympathetic but apprehensive about giving him a line. "We're supposed to have clearance, sir."

"Clearance?" Matt grumbled. "For what? We're winning the war! Besides, there's no one in here right now." How could he make her understand? "Look, how would you feel if your boyfriend didn't return your call?"

"I wish!"

"Okay, Okay," Matt sighed, pacing in short circles. "Suppose, just suppose, the switchboard lit up from the phone in that office back there. What would you think?"

"Well, I suppose I would think that Colonel Bailey was requesting an outside line."

"Thank you!" With the WAAC on lookout, the eager young flyer placed his call and endured the eternal wait for a clear line. "May I speak with Vivian Davis, please?"

"Is this Captain Tower?" the soft English voice inquired. "Yes. Can I speak to Vivie?" "Mrs. Davis is not in just now, sir, but Mrs. Moore wishes to speak with you. Will you wait for a moment?"

Puzzled by the strange reception, Matt tapped the desk anxiously. At last Etta's voice broke the silence. "Matt?"

"Yes?"

"When can you come in?"

He didn't like the sound of that. Her voice was strained and unsteady. "Is anything wrong with Vivie? Where is she?"

"No, there's nothing wrong with her. It's not that. She's in London. She left with her father early this morning. We tried to reach you."

"I've been flying for a solid week. I think I can get a pass in the morning." His palms began to sweat. "What's wrong, Mrs. Moore?"

"Well...." She was weighing her reply, collecting her thoughts, which heightened his anxiety all the more. "It has to do with an illness in the family, Matt. I just can't say any more until you arrive. I have a train reservation for noon. Can you be here before then?"

"I think so. I'll get there! Don't leave, okay?"

In spite of Mrs. Moore's explanation, Matt still feared something had happened to Vivie. If she had just been up front with it, it would have been easier to handle. He hid his frustration as best he could from the questioning eyes of the WAAC. "Can you find out who was OD yesterday?"

"I'll try, Lieutenant. Were you able to patch things up?"

"Patch up?... patch up what?" Matt stammered in distraction.

"Your girlfriend. Are things better now?"

"Oh... that. I'm not sure right now. Look, here's my barracks number. Just see if you can find out who was on duty yesterday, please."

"Yes, sir. I'll try. Boy, she must really be something," the WAAC grinned as she waved him out of the office.

The night proved exhausting for the troubled flyer, his sleep interrupted repeatedly with the most fitful of dreams. Though his name wasn't called at 5 a.m. for the day's mission, he was on his feet anyway, plotting for a pass and transportation into Ipswich. There were no shuttles before noon, and by 8 a.m. he was desperate, desperate enough to seek out even Sergeant McDuff.

The mustached noncom listened with all the respect due a commissioned officer as Matt took him into his personal life considerably deeper than he wanted to. "Sir, what you're asking could end my military career right here. It would be a lot easier to check out a fighter to you than a vehicle."

"Sergeant, I can't land a P-51 in Ipswich. Look, do you want to buy back those nylon stockings? Or better still, how about the diamond ring?"

"No sir," McDuff sighed, his fingers massaging the tingle in his scalp. "I wouldn't want to do that. Now, where there's a will, there's a way, right? You sit there, sir, and let old Mac see what aces he can call in."

The sergeant's efficiency improved noticeably as he placed the phone to his ear. "Put me through to motor pool, and ring 'em off the hook if you have to." He turned reassuringly to Matt, giving the *okay* sign. "Rallo?... McDuff here. What have you got over there that needs a checkout?... No, I'm trying to solve a serious problem for a silver bar. You got maybe a jeep or something?... Don't start that crap, Rallo. The records show something gets checked out nearly every day... uh huh, and the same guy checks 'em out, and he goes just about the same number of miles every time."

The pause suggested the sergeant had attained Rallo's attention. "I knew you were a reasonable man. What have you got... a beep?" McDuff groaned, shrugging his shoulders.

"Motorcycle! Whatever!" Matt injected, rolling his hand in a hurry-up sign.

McDuff placed the receiver back on its hook. "A 4x4 truck, Captain. There wasn't anything else available. It's on the way."

Matt checked his watch and rested his head on the back of the chair. "I'm sorry, Sergeant," he sighed. "This thing's got me a little uptight, I guess. I really appreciate your help."

"Oh, that's all right, sir. The Army looks after its own. Besides, I kind of feel like I'm part of this thing, you know, supplying the ring and all."

The lumbering truck wasn't known for its speed, but the private first class at the wheel handled it well enough that they should arrive in time. Judging from the road condition, Matt speculated there might be no shuttle at all that day, so Falcon's Rest was a welcome sight indeed.

Etta stood at the lobby desk, her face sober and unsmiling as she completed instructions to the clerk. When she turned to meet the American flyer, a handkerchief filled her hand. "Matt, let me have your coat, dear. I've made tea. You're probably chilled to the bone."

They sat in the family parlor over a coffee table, where she poured the steaming brew. She was dressed for travel, smartly as always, a gray suit and white blouse, not unlike the first time he saw her on the train. "Matt, we tried to reach you before she left. I offered to stay behind and explain what has happened." Etta dabbed at her eyes with the handkerchief. "There's just no easy way to begin."

"I hope she hasn't changed her mind about the wedding."

Etta reached over and took his hand, her eyes brimming to capacity. "They've found John. We don't know the whole story. That's why she's in London. He's in a hospital there. Oh, Matt..." she sobbed, covering her eyes with the tiny white cloth.

For a moment he felt nothing, as though her words were intended for another, until the hot flush of reality stabbed his chest. It seemed forever that they sat there, her hand still on his, their eyes unable to meet. Weakness invaded his arms and he could barely form a fist. "Are... are they sure?" he managed through the numbness.

"Yes. Colonel Burgess got wind of it awhile back and took Robert in to be certain. They feared what the shock would do to Vivie, to all of us, if it were true."

Matt rose slowly from the cushioned sofa and walked to the window, his mouth so dry that it hurt. Etta could only stand, arms limp at her side, confused as to her role under the circumstances. Her concerns as mother-in-law were no more intense than those toward the stunned captain. "Matt... I don't know what to say. I'm just so terribly sorry."

His eyes bored into the grayness beyond the glass as though searching for an escape that was impossible. "How... how did Vivie handle it?"

"She fainted, Matt. Robert made her sit down before we told her. We were up quite late that night until Dr. Compton gave her something so she could sleep. This morning was not much better, I'm afraid."

He could imagine. She would be so broken, so devastated, and he had let her down by not being there. If only he could hold her and try to take the hurt away. He pictured her even then in bleak white hospital corridors struggling for composure. He turned to Etta. "I'll go with you. Let me call the base."

She crossed the room, her eyes still liquid and puffy, and took his hands in hers. "I know you love her, Matt. The pain has to be unbearable. But it would be too much for her just now. Please give her some time. We should be back Sunday. I'll call you and you can come in then."

It was a restriction hard to accept. He had held and comforted Vivie for the better of a year. They were engaged. It never entered his mind that she might still be the wife of another man. *"God, please,"* he whispered through clenched teeth. *"Why is this happening now?"*

Etta read his lips, though they were half hidden between the palms of his hands. "Oh, Matt dear, if we say that, it's like wishing John dead. You must understand, we prayed so long for his safety, for his return, for the anxiety Vivian went through."

Etta took the initiative, part motherly instinct, part recognition of his role in her daughter's life, and put her arms around him. There was no one else to do that. She could feel the tension, but he eagerly returned the gesture. As their embrace relaxed, her hands settled on his arms and she attempted a smile. "Matt, we shall always be friends, very special friends, whatever happens now."

"I love her, Mrs. Moore. I'd like to have both."

"I know, I know," she sighed softly. The half-hour chime from the lobby quickened her pace. "Come, dear, we must finish our tea."

Matt fidgeted with the cup, more concerned with putting the events in perspective than the transient comfort of warm liquid. "How did they find him after all this time?"

"After the crash, Resistance forces found him and hid him. From what the report said, he was badly injured and quite confused. The confusion increased as time passed. His identification was removed in the event of capture and evidently lost as they moved him about.

He was much too ill to escape through Underground channels. They turned him over to our troops when they reached Belgium."

Matt carried her suitcase to the lobby and helped with her coat. "Do you have a ride to the station?"

"Yes," she nodded in the direction of the approaching soldier. "Colonel Burgess arranged a car."

He had wanted to accompany Etta as far as possible, but her driver snapped a sharp salute and reached for her luggage. "Good day, sir."

"Sergeant," Matt acknowledged, then turned back to Etta. "Please," he implored. "When you get back...."

"I will call," she assured him, placing her fingers gently on his lips.

The chilly air captured his breath momentarily as he held the door. Etta moved quickly to the waiting car without looking back, leaving Falcon's Rest in the hands of hirelings. He could not remember being there when some member of the family was not present, and the void only deepened his despair.

The beep driver, vaguely aware of his passenger's dilemma, waited patiently before the great fireplace, content to spend as much time in his heavenly surroundings as occasion would permit. But for Matt Tower, it seemed the doors of Heaven had closed in his face. Reluctantly he gathered his hat and bulky trench coat, cast a last longing glance around the lobby and nodded to the driver. "Let's move out, Private," he sighed.

CHAPTER 27

# Waiting it Out

"*THIS IS BBC news of the hour. The 21ˢᵗ Army Group, British and Canadian, has reached Goch, which was captured by the 51ˢᵗ Highland Infantry Division. In other reports, as of 26 February, Canadian units have driven well into Holland. The American Third Army, under General George Patton, continues to carry the battle to the Hun on a rapid and broad front through central Europe. Wireless updates from Pacific operations bring good news as well. Military reports say American forces now control most of Manila, and the fall of Corregidor is imminent. All are reminded to remain tuned at half after the hour for the Prime Minister's address to Parliament. This evening's special presentation at 8 o'clock features the humorous Charles Penrose and the lovely voice of Miss Vera Lynn.*"

Without opening his eyes, Matt reached up from the bunk and switched the radio off, his arm falling across his forehead. The tension headache was persistent. He could feel it through to the back of his neck, and two aspirin had accomplished little.

"It's cold as a well digger's knee in here!" Chuck bellowed over the scraping barracks door. He tossed a chunk or two of coke into the stoves before noticing Matt's lack of response. "You missed a good one today. Roger got his eighth destroyed on the ground. That crop duster can handle strafing dang well!"

Chuck nudged the bunk with his knee. "Hey! Are you in there, buddy?" Matt's eyes blinked open. "I saw the gun camera footage. I hit that Focke-Wulf pretty good. You can make out every detail, but they still won't confirm it."

Matt pushed the blanket down and forced himself to a sitting position. "I... I'm sorry," he mumbled, running his fingers through matted hair.

Chuck got a good look at him then. "What the heck hit you?" He sat on the end of the bunk and pulled his cap off. "I know you don't drink, so it's gotta be the flu."

"I wish it was. I'd settle for a hangover in a minute."

"Hangover? This can't be the shining boy of the 350$^{th}$ Squadron. Have you been grounded or something?"

"You could say that. They found John Davis. Chuck, he's turned up."

"John Davis? What squadron's he in?"

"Her husband, Chuck. Vivie's husband."

"You're pulling my leg, right? I thought you said he augered in over Dunkirk."

"I did. The RAF had him listed as killed in action. Now the guy shows up in a London hospital, and she's gone down there to see him."

Shilling stared at the floor, his head wagging like a dog's tail. "When did you find out?"

"This morning." Matt forced his body to a standing position and ambled to the coffee pot. His olive drab shorts and T-shirt, wilted in wrinkles, gave testimony to a restless nap.

"Just like that?" Chuck pressed as he spun a chair into position across the small wooden table from his distressed friend. "Nothing in the wind? No indication?"

Steadying the cup with both hands, Matt rested his elbows on the table and closed his eyes against the rising steam as he sipped the hot brew. "Something was really eating her dad last week. He must have gotten wind of it."

Over the rim of his cup, Chuck searched the haggard face before him. He was more than aware of Matt's feelings, and it pained him that he had no solution to offer his friend. "What are you going to do?"

"What can I do? I mean, you can't wish a guy dead. He was out there just like you and me." Matt shook his head slowly, his eyes closing again. "She has to care about him. I wish I'd never met her, Chuck."

Chuck leaned over and put his hand on Matt's arm. "Look, I'm sorry as crap about this. I wish I could do something to help. I'd arm wrestle you for that girl any day of the week."

They sipped coffee in silence, Matt lost in painful thought and Chuck growing more concerned about him by the minute. "Look, it's not good to sit around here. You need some diversion. What do you say we run a couple of games at the club?"

"I don't want this to get out, Chuck. It's nobody's dang business."

In the following days, Chuck stuck to Matt like glue, taking every opportunity to keep his flight leader occupied and buffered from the curious. The first day was the worst, when the exhausted captain reluctantly gave in to sick call. A move orchestrated by Providence, no doubt, due to Chaplain Wheeler's practice of seeking out all who were under the weather.

Over the next few days, a merciful Providence also arranged withdrawal support missions, which did not require deep fighter penetration. With the chaplain's positive counsel and Chuck on his wing, Matt functioned, though he seldom was free of anxious thoughts about Vivie. He could no longer fly with her photo in its sacred place above *Paladin's* instrument panel. For now, it rested safely in the map pouch under his seat.

But he functioned efficiently. In the days since he left Etta at Falcon's Rest, his dislike for the enemy had intensified. He blamed them for the circumstances that led him to Vivie, and any engagement against them became an outlet for his frustrations.

On March 2, 1945, near Hanover, Germany, Slybird dutifully intercepted homebound B-17s of the 447th Bomber Group. Matt spotted the inevitable straggler below their ragged formation, its trailing smoke guiding in the Messerschmitts of Luftflotte 3's northernmost patrols.

"Little Friends, we've got a brother in trouble back there!" the bomber group leader pleaded over the radio. "Give him a hand, will you?"

Matt's flight drew tail-end position with the bombers, placing it up sun of the troubled B-17. Four silver Mustangs peeled off for the Messerschmitts buzzing the distressed aircraft. Faithfully, Chuck tended his leader's wing, though lately the drill had taken on hair-raising qualities.

"All right!" Matt barked at his pilots. "Don't waste the trip! There's enough for everybody!"

The Germans were true to recent strategy: do unto the bombers as long as possible, then clear out when the cavalry appeared. But experience had taught Matt to watch for the 11th-hour hero impressing his peers with a last defiant pass at a mangled bomber.

As the flight scattered after the Messerschmitts, Matt rolled *Paladin* toward the wounded B-17. "Off his starboard wing, Red Two, 10 o'clock!"

The Messerschmitt's pass took it beneath and to the rear of the tail-end Fortress. Anticipating the move, Matt pushed stick and throttle forward, careful to angle his fighter to arrive low and behind the enemy. He could see the bomber's belly guns hanging straight down—out of ammo or gunner dead. He knew not which.

The German's dive took him confidently inland, away from the last sighting of approaching cavalry. *Paladin's* first burst spooked the Hun, who snap-rolled away from the stream of 50-caliber tracers. Conscious of little else, Matt pressed the attack, sky and clouds a swirling maze through the cockpit glass as the fighters dropped in chase at 50 feet per second. Matt relished these moments that purged his depression so thoroughly.

Fruit would be picked that morning, for this Luftwaffe pilot unwisely traded the expanse of sky for a run to the deck, where his pullout collected the impact of *Paladin's* full complement of armor. Minus a wing, the smoking hulk plummeted into the forest below, netting a seventh swastika for *Paladin's* fuselage.

Matt pulled back on the stick, the G's pressing him against the bucket seat, and raced upward with the hope of a second engagement. His earphones crackled wildly. A major fight was in progress, but where? He called every name in his flight with no result. Frustrated, he picked up the smoke trail and escorted the crippled Fortress as far as the North Sea.

*Paladin* was the first to touch down, a good 30-plus minutes before his cousins. Matt waited out their return on the control tower roof listening to the end of the Group's radio drama. His eyes joined those around him, fixing on the eastern horizon until the urgent transmissions began to subside.

"You ought to be happy, Tower. I heard you got one."

Matt turned to see Stan Herrington lighting his pipe. "Bittersweet, Major. I came off the deck and couldn't find the fight. Ended up nursing a damaged Fortress to the Dutch coast."

"They say seven's a lucky number."

Matt chuckled. "You've got a cool 10, sir."

"Ten's an even number, kind of a roundoff. The Germans aren't coming up like they used to. I don't know if this war's going to last long enough for the new guys to score."

The field was uncommonly quiet as the two officers surveyed it from their elevated advantage. Ground crews materialized, ambling out to the hard stands to hold vigil for their pilots. Matt understood. It was their hands that readied and armed the aircraft. His mind drifted back to the first time he brought *Sweet Pea* home from a real fight. Milt had been livid, whining over the 32 bullet holes splotched over rudder and elevator. *"What about my tail!"* Matt barked at his crew chief. He never did get an answer.

"What are you grinning about, Tower?"

"That Tennessee string bean that's married to my fighter."

The first happy warriors began appearing, their thin line circling into the landing pattern. The bright trail of a signal flair spouted from the last Mustang angling into final approach, its left wheel refusing to drop. Ambulance and fire truck jockeyed for position to chase the P-51 along the runway. Matt shielded his eyes as he searched intently for markings, "LH!" he exclaimed. "He's Seldom Squadron!"

Impulsively, Matt whisked the binoculars from Herrington as the Mustang's single wheel touched the runway. On the cowling loomed *Snake In The Grass*' menacing coiled rattler. "It's Chuck!" he blurted to anyone listening. "Come on, baby! Hold it up! Hold it up!"

The stricken aircraft, balancing on one wheel, raced past its helpless observers on the control tower. Chuck struggled to keep the Mustang level as long as possible. But within seconds the tail settled, dropping the left wing to the runway in a trail of sparks and billowing dust. The impact collapsed the extended wheel and turned the fighter into a dirt plow in the field beside the runway.

Matt bolted down the tower steps and struck out across the field, flight jacket flapping wildly in his wake. The logic of sprinting such a distance paled before his concerns for his wingman, and at the halfway point he was sucking wind in earnest.

"Tower! Get in!" Herrington shouted as he braked the jeep to keep pace. Matt grabbed the windshield brace and swung aboard gratefully.

Within the circle of emergency vehicles and personnel, crewmen struggled frantically with the fighter's stubborn canopy. At the moment of freedom, a burst of billowing flame from the engine cowling engulfed the cockpit and blew the rescuers off the wing. Matt's heart sank as he watched them scramble to their feet and wait precious seconds for fire control to subdue the blaze. Again, with selfless determination, the crewmen applied their trade, cheating death as they wrenched the pilot free.

By the time Matt pushed his way through the security ring, Shilling was secured on a stretcher. He dropped to his knee beside his wingman, grimacing at the matted blood on the side of Chuck's soot-smeared face. The golden pompadour that so occupied Chuck's pocket comb had been reduced to singed crust above his blistered forehead. As the medics ministered and IVs were attached, Chuck grinned weakly into the face above him. "That bad, huh, buddy?"

It was enough to reassure Matt that the worst had been avoided, and his shoulders sagged in relief. "Well, you could be a night fighter without makeup. You scared the crap out of me. What happened?"

"Aw, I hit a little turbulence. Nothing to it."

They both knew better than that, and judging from the pain on Chuck's face as the stretcher was lifted to the ambulance, there would be no running the pool table at the club that night.

As the meat wagon pulled away, Matt caught up with the attending medic. "What's it look like, Doc? Is it bad?"

"Nasty gash on his head and some burns. X-ray will give us the whole story."

Herrington rested his hand reassuringly on Matt's shoulder.

"Come on, I need to stop by Operations a minute. Then we'll check on him."

Once assured that Chuck was stabilized, Matt returned to his barracks. The day's drama confirmed one thing: his bond of brotherhood with the banker's son from Decatur. They had shared and confided in ways casual friends could not, and a tragic separation was unthinkable to either.

The small bundle of mail on Matt's cot offered reprieve from the day's harshness. Allowing anticipation to build, he fixed hot coffee first and then stacked his pillow for comfort. The light blue envelope would be his mother's, the square one from his sister. The folded note was unexpected, racing his heart, for it could be from only one source.

*"Captain Tower, 350th Squadron, 2 March 1945. Call Mrs. Etta Moore in London, Gerrard 48-9, between 1800 and 1900 today. O.T. Smith, Sergeant, OD"*

In the first few days, the waiting had seemed unbearable. Now, when he had finally adjusted to the suspense, this single sheet of paper completely undid him. The inevitable meeting must surely be on. Matt glanced at his watch. There were but 45 minutes to get a call through.

# CHAPTER 28

# The Hospital

**M**AKESHIFT HOSPITALS RINGED the safer perimeters of London to compensate for the steady stream of wounded from the Continent. It was to such a facility northeast of the city that John Davis had been transferred. They were anything but havens for the squeamish who would be confronted with the most grotesque results of war. While such settings were not unfamiliar to Vivie in her WVS capacity, she had yet to see her husband, and the parade of affliction passing along the halls only heightened her anxiety.

For three days Robert Moore had dutifully waited with his daughter on the hard, unfriendly benches of the hospital lobby. And just as regularly their hunger had sent him in search of food. She dozed restlessly in his absence, her head propped on his folded greatcoat.

"Mrs. Davis?"

She did not recognize the voice and blinked against the glare of late-hour ceiling lights, "Yes," she managed wearily. The form addressing her approached more closely, shielding her eyes from the brightness. "I'm Dr. Burton, Mrs. Davis."

The long white lab coat was heavily wrinkled as was the kindly slender face above its collar. It seemed that all the doctors left in England were gray and weary of gate, truly unsung heroes of the wartime home front. "I'm terribly sorry you've been forced to wait so long."

"How is he? How is John?"

"Resting presently. He's had a rather difficult day. Dr. Tanner completed the hip operation this morning. Are you feeling well enough to discuss his condition just now?"

"Oh, yes. Very much so," she responded, tugging her skirt discreetly over her knees and patting her hair in place. "When will I be able to see him?"

"Shortly. However, there are things you should know about his case before you do." Dr. Burton pulled up a chair and sat facing Vivie. "Your husband received some rather severe injuries, Mrs. Davis. As you might imagine, initial treatment was, by our standards, rather inferior. It's a bit early for a clear long-range rehabilitation prognosis."

From dark-ringed hollows, Vivie's tearless blue eyes stared back at Dr. Burton. "What kind of injuries?" Her lips were so dry. "What happened to him, Doctor?"

"Well, there were symptoms of concussion. Laceration of the skull is evident. A few fractures over the skeletal frame, both simple and compound, the most serious of which was the left hip. We are evaluating how much we can do for him. The hip needed the earliest attention."

"I see," Vivie sighed deeply. "May I see him now?"

Dr. Burton reached over and took Vivie's hand, offering a brief smile of sympathy. "Mrs. Davis, your husband may not recognize you. He is quite underweight and very confused by all that's taken place. As far as we can tell, he recalls little before the crash."

Vivie nodded her understanding and rose to her feet as Robert Moore returned with a neatly rolled bag of eats. Dr. Burton extended his hand in greeting; they had met on Robert's earlier visit with Colonel Burgess. "You've a very courageous young woman here, Major. I've briefed her as best I could, and we were just going in to see her husband."

Robert Moore placed the bag on an end table and returned to his daughter's side. "Do you want me to go with you, Hon?"

"No. The first time I would like to be alone, if you don't mind." She followed Dr. Burton to the hallway, then stopped and turned back to the stoop-shouldered hulk of her father. She read his thoughts so easily, that he wanted to take her in his arms as he had done when she was a child, and make it all right again. For the first time in two days, her lips formed a little smile. "I'll be fine, Dad. I know you're right here."

Standing in the doorway of the dimly lit room, Vivie could hear the patient's weak response to the nurse hovering around the medical paraphernalia. Shortly she came to the door in whispered greeting. "Mrs. Davis?" Vivie nodded, returning the warm smile. "He's still a bit drowsy, I'm afraid, but coming around nicely. I'll be just outside if you need me."

Vivie felt as though she were balancing on a tightrope as she neared the white metal-framed bed. She stood quietly, staring at the face that barely resembled the smiling aviator she kissed goodbye on a late May afternoon in 1940. On that tragic day, his squadron repeatedly took to the skies in support of British and French troops retreating to the beaches of Dunkirk. King Leopold III's surrender of Belgium to Hitler had removed the last strand of barbed wire before the advancing German army.

John Davis' eyes were closed and she hesitated, wanting him

to rouse, yet fearing that he would. "John," she touched his hand gently. "John, it's me... Vivie."

His lips parted slightly as though to collect his thoughts. Every move seemed such an effort to him. "Another... bloody injection?" he breathed feebly.

Vivie's lips tightened. Was her voice that unfamiliar to him? She bent a little closer. "No, John, I'm not the nurse. It's me... Vivie," she pleaded softly.

Slowly his head inched in her direction, his eyes but questioning slits. "Not the nurse... not the nurse."

She yearned so for even a tinge of recognition, but she feared pressing him too early. He grew quiet again, drifting off, his chest rising and falling in long shallow breaths. Her eyes followed the outline of his body along the covers. How little space he appeared to occupy, this frail body before her, so unlike the robust man who shared her bed for over a year.

"Oh, John," she whimpered softly. "What have they done to you?" As she moved to blot the tears, she realized his hand had clasped hers. Now, in sleep it fell away loosely. Sobs welled in her chest, and she hurried for the door so that the patient would not fall victim to her emotions.

In the hallway, Etta's arms collected her daughter and buried the younger woman's tears on her shoulder. As the sobs subsided, she stepped back and gently lifted Vivie's chin. "How is he? What did the doctor say?"

"Oh, Mum. He didn't know me. He looked at me and he didn't know me."

Etta smoothed her daughter's hair, letting her hand rest on the side of her cheek for a second. "I think it's a bit early, dear. He's been through an awful lot, you know." Etta steered Vivie toward the lobby, holding her close with an arm for support. "He's in good hands, and tomorrow may give us an altogether different story. The doctor is talking with your father now, and I'd like to hear what he has to say. The Davises are on their way from Bury St. Edmunds, and tomorrow will be rather involved, to say the least. You must have some rest to hold up under all this."

Vivie's concentration was succumbing rapidly to the pressures of the day. The conversation between Dr. Burton and her parents left her staring blankly into space. Etta noticed and extended a hand of concern. "Vivian.... What is it, dear?"

She turned to her mother, seeking privacy from the conversing men. "Did you see Matt?"

"Yes. We had a rather long talk. I explained everything."

"Poor, dear Matt," Vivie sighed. "How did he take it?"

"Not very well, I fear. He was quite distraught. I wish there had been more time to spend with him. He really wanted to see you."

"Mum, whatever am I to do?"

"Whatever it is, 10 o'clock at night in a hospital waiting room is not the time, dear. First, you must care for yourself, and that means a good night's sleep or you won't be of help to either of them."

Vivie's eyes, wet with despair, questioned her mother's intently. "I do love Matt, Mum. He's filled my life so. I don't know that I can bear to be without him." She paused to dab at the corner of her eyes. "Now that I've seen John, stood by his bed, touched him...."

Etta gave her daughter a hug and rose to her feet. "Robert, I'm taking Vivian to the hotel. She's had quite enough for the day."

"Very well, dear. I won't be long. I'll check the train schedule for John's parents and join you straight away."

The next two days were all that Etta cautioned they might be. Restless sleep, sandwiched between long hospital hours and mutual family consolation, left Vivie drained. By the third day, John Davis' condition improved to the point that he grew increasingly curious about the visitors frequenting his room. Dr. Burton had delayed their identity to allow his patient to stabilize emotionally.

The disclosure was painfully difficult for the young British officer and heart wrenching to relatives so desirous of reconciliation. What began as a politely tolerant family conference soon overwhelmed the frail, frustrated patient. Being ordered from the room by her own son was especially difficult for Edith Davis, who collapsed in her own pit of despair.

Hesitating at the door, Vivie stood with her back to her husband. "Out! All of you!" John repeated angrily. Still, she waited. "Nurse! Get her out of here!"

Dr. Burton's hand restrained the nurse before she could move. "Wait a moment, Miss Britt," he whispered. "Let's see where this is going."

Vivie adjusted the purse strap on her shoulder, then turned and walked resolutely to the hospital bed. John's daggered eyes followed every step. "What the bloody hey is wrong with you?" he snapped.

"You!" she snapped back, summoning every ounce of restraint left in her exhausted body. "You're what the bloody hey's wrong with me, John Davis!" He started to reply, but she raised a threatening hand. "Granted, all this seems a ruddy cod's head to you, and it's none the easier for us. But you needn't be such a stroppy shower about it!"

He had been so babied since his return that Vivie's redressing caused him to cower back into the fluff of supporting pillows, tension and anger momentarily draining from his face. "I'm... sorry. You can't imagine how bewildering this is for me."

"Oh, yes I can! Recollection or not, we are still your family. Our hearts went down with your aircraft nearly five years ago, John! It's every bit as bewildering to us."

Avoiding her eyes, he stared at the foot of the bed, his thoughts wrestling over his options under the circumstances. They were all showing such concern over him even though he could not share or return their feelings. Silently, he reasoned that he was flesh and blood and therefore had parents, and it was altogether possible that he had married. Curiosity alone demanded inquiry, and the process might as well begin with these people. He might well be this John Davis, though the idea was highly uncomfortable to him.

"It won't be easy for either of us," he sighed. "You know that, don't you?"

"Yes," Vivie replied softly, taking advantage of the thaw in the ice to sit on the edge of his bed. "But we're like a book without a last chapter, John, and that's all the more unbearable."

His eyes came up to meet hers. They were clear and steady, though lacking emotion. "Suppose you don't like the ending?"

She acknowledged the possibility with a nod, her back and shoulders straightening against the reality. "But we still must write it, John. We still must write it."

His eyes lowered again, and it was evident the evening had wearied him. Vivie patted his hand gently. "I'll come back tomorrow when you're rested and we'll write a bit."

Already sleep was settling in, and he could but nod in silent agreement as Vivie rose and backed away from the bed.

# CHAPTER 29

# Facing Reality

MATT ARRIVED AT Primrose Hill Station to the northeast of London. Small, out of the way, lightly scarred during the air attacks, it was nearest the hospital treating John Davis. Etta, well dressed as always, waved her gloved hand to get his attention.

He dropped his single bag as she approached. An embrace would have been awkward, the clasping of hands seeming more suitable. "You look none the worse, Matt. Was it a long trip?"

He could not yet match her greeting smile. "Fine... fine until we neared London. Then a dozen whistle stops."

"We've taken rooms at Camden House. Vivie is waiting to see you."

They walked in the direction of the inn, each pressed for words, but he needed to know what he was facing. "How is she?"

"Better now, but very difficult at first. The doctor placed her on a mild sedative for a few days. I waited to call until she was more collected." Etta stopped and faced him. "Matt, please don't press her. This will take time to resolve."

"I know," he nodded. "It's the toughest thing I've ever done in my life."

He went through the motions of registering and left his bag with the aged clerk. "Here's a crown if you'll see it to my room."

The old man stared at Matt for a second, then lowered his eyes to the roster. "The likes of me can't get it up them stairs, governor."

"Then watch it a crown's worth and I'll get it later." He turned back to Etta for directions.

"First floor," she nodded toward the stairs. "Number four, at the end of the corridor. I'll wait in the pub. Godspeed, Matt."

The anticipation was terrible, his weak legs requiring conscious effort to mount the stairs and cover the distance to the appointed door. He knocked softly and heard her unmistakable voice. "Yes?"

"It's me, Vivie. Can I come in?"

In a moment the door opened. She had stepped well back, her hand still on the knob. "Matt."

He hesitated, adjusting to the sight of her after so long a time. The light golden-brown locks he adored lay in turned-under roll on the shoulders of her navy V-neck suit. A white blouse, its collar spread neatly on the lapels, provided the tasteful, crisp accent that was her trademark. Except for pearl earrings and a watch, she wore no jewelry. Had it not been for her pained blue eyes, she would have camouflaged her distress remarkably well.

It was so natural for them to desire each other's embrace. But unsure of the rules just yet, they suppressed the urge. "Hi..." seemed the best he could do.

"I have tea, if you like," she offered, closing the door behind him. He forced a quick smile. "Fine, I'd like that."

She busied herself in the efficiency kitchen of the modest suite, her movements more to keep occupied than to prepare the brew.

Matt closed the distance between them as much as he dared and leaned on the counter, where a dainty handkerchief lay stiff and wrinkled from a hundred wrenchings. "How is John?"

"Stabilized, whatever the doctors mean by that. Sophisticated way of saying he survived, no doubt. He has little recollection of things before his plane went down."

"And what about Vivie?" Matt explored, turning the more to face her.

"What about Matt?" her voice quivered, her sympathetic blue eyes meeting his fully for the first time.

The rise and fall of his uniformed chest answered better than words, and she could no longer restrain the crystal drops staining her cheeks. The imposed wall of restraint quickly crumbled, each unable to forego the comfort of the other's arms any longer. He quickly gathered her to his heart, his face nestling hers, burying into the soft fragrant tresses of her hair as he so loved to do.

Thus they stood, swaying gently as she wept away the weeks of frustration. When she grew still, he gently traced her cheek until his lips found hers, open so slightly, freely offered, both claiming the moment as just compensation for the interruption in their lives.

But all too soon reality would nudge and slacken their embrace, until only their hands were touching. They were painfully aware of the implication when their fingers finally slipped apart.

The whistling kettle filled the awkward silence, and she whispered a prayer of thanks for its timing. Matt seated himself at the table and watched her movements as she placed the cup before him. For just that second, with the ceiling light haloing her head, he saw again the angelic beauty that had captivated him so in another time and another place. His eyes dropped to the tea as she sat across from him.

"When must you return to base?"

"Tomorrow morning. We're flying much deeper into Germany now," he added, following her lead to lighten the conversation. "The sky over the cities is full of smoke. The billows are like beacons to the bombers."

"Will it ever end, Matt?" She reached over and placed her hand on his cheek. "Look how thin you are."

"I don't know," he sighed, taking her hand in his. His eyes grew distant, drifting past her somewhere into the room. "It does crazy things to you after a while. In the beginning we were going to beat up on these bullies. Now I think we fight just to end it. But at the same time, we thrive on the routine. We crave taking to the sky, more alive on the hunt than anywhere else…. except when I was with you."

She squeezed his hand and pressed it to her cheek, no more ready than he to relinquish their roles as mutual comforters. "I know," she replied barely above a whisper as her hands withdrew to the cup. She could think more clearly when she did not touch him, certainly in light of what must finally be said. "We have no choice, Matt."

He nodded his understanding. Though he had lied to himself in moments of desperation, he knew her character, and in his heart of hearts had expected no other decision. *"But God!"* he prayed. *"I wish there was some way."*

"I've anguished over this for so long, Matt. But I can't desert John. I can't ignore my vows."

Not wanting to see the answer in Vivie's eyes, he stared into the cup clasped tightly between his palms. "Are we going to see each other again? Or do we just break it off?"

"I don't know what to do, Matt. You're such a part of my life, I can't stand the thought of being without you." She looked away, her lips tightening against the throbbing emotion.

She was asking for his help, and he needed to come down to earth and carry his share of the burden. "I'm not going to be that far away, you know. I'd like to call sometime, just to see how you're doing."

"I'd like that very much," she whispered softly, her hands covering teary eyes. "I do so want to know what you're doing, how you are."

He watched patiently as she composed herself, marveling at her beauty even in such distraught circumstances. He would try for her sake, but it seemed impossible that she could ever be completely out of his life. Even now he could read her mood, the set of her chin that meant unfinished business. "Hey, little lady, what's going on in there?"

She reached into her purse and fumbled with its contents. "Matt, this is ever so difficult for me. I simply don't know how…. I'm so afraid I'll hurt you." Avoiding his eyes, she laid the small ring box on the table. "The necklace is at Falcon's Rest. I'll get it to you somehow."

"Look, I understand about the ring. But I really want you to have the necklace. Please," he implored, his fingers gently lifting her chin. "Even if you won't wear it, just keep it tucked away. I want you to have something from me."

They talked for a time then, more in the language of very old friends, their conversation ranging from the war to their families and to the future. It was merciful therapy for the young couple. The lighter memories refreshed their hearts, enticing a chuckle or two, sealing their feelings for each other until the shadows of late afternoon sneaked across the table to steal away the precious moments.

He helped her clear the table reluctantly, knowing it speeded their parting. This was not the last memory he wanted. "How do you feel about granting a dying man his last wish?"

"I should think it would depend on the wish," she smiled, folding the drying cloth away neatly.

"He's granted a last meal. Could we have dinner together this evening? Maybe the Piccadilly Hotel."

She turned slowly to face him, her hands clasped behind her back. "Are you suggesting, Captain, that a proper English wife…" She paused with a cock of her head.

"Be seen gallivanting on the town with a foreign officer?" he finished hopefully.

"Precisely!"

"Precisely?" his waning hope echoed.

"Precisely.... at half after seven. 1930 hours to you, sir."

# CHAPTER 30

# Running Down the Lost

THE LINE OF sleek 350<sup>th</sup> Squadron Mustangs rumbled along the taxiway, turning off one at a time onto their hardstands. Intelligence reports would show mission 443 to be a group record. One hundred thirty-one enemy aircraft destroyed on the ground and 53 damaged seriously. Those destroyed in the air might never be known because many, appearing only damaged, would go down later. But the count was high in recorded numbers and many pilots made ace, or double and triple ace. Even Matt Tower, who had been quiet and reclusive since his visit to London, could not suppress a grin as fellow pilots let off steam with a war dance around their squadron leader.

Chuck Shilling had come down to welcome their return. Still limping on a crutch and very much the bald eagle, he joined in anyway, awkwardly dancing the circle with his fellow pilots until he reached Matt's side. "I wish I'd been there."

"It was awesome!" Matt shook his head reflectively. "I could have used you, buddy. I had three 110s right in a row. They must have been loaded with fuel. Come here, look at this. Look at this!"

Matt ran his hand along the leading edge of *Paladin's* right wing, which was dotted with dents the size of softballs. What had been the wing tip dangled in shredded metal. "It all came at once: smoke, flame, stuff flying everywhere. Scared the crap out of me!"

"How far off the deck?"

"Maybe 500 feet."

"Matt, how dang far off the deck were you?"

"The altimeter wasn't reading. How the heck should I know?"

Chuck turned away, scratching his head in disapproval. "You... dumb... I should have been there. I should have been there!"

Matt used Shilling's wince to change the subject. "Does it still hurt?"

"Only when I use it. I'm glad to see you puffed up for a change."

They began walking to a waiting jeep, the last ride left. "Matt, I want you to look at my gun footage. I'm not getting anywhere with the bums at Operations. I know that Hun went down. I need somebody on my side to look at it."

"Boy, you are obsessed with it, aren't you?"

Chuck labored to seat himself in the jeep, his bandaged leg jutting over the side rail. "Look at me, Matt. You think I'm gonna get another chance? It would be my fifth kill!"

In his own confusion over the past few weeks, Matt had missed the significance of his friend's concern. Thoughtlessness was not his nature, and he rested an apologetic hand on Chuck's shoulder. "Let me get debriefing out of the way and we'll roll some film, okay?" Shilling threw up his hands in exaggerated victory and collapsed into the jeep's bucket seat.

An hour later, the two had the training room to themselves

except for the projectionist, who seemed to be very familiar with Shilling. "Number 65 again, Lieutenant?"

"One more time, Carter. And hey, thanks for hanging in with me all this time."

"I don't mind, sir," the sergeant replied as he flipped the lights off. "You've pretty near made me a believer."

The screen lit up with flickering scenes of enemy aircraft and swirling Mustangs. Chuck sat upright, his eyes glued to the action. "It takes a minute. Just keep watching."

Abruptly, the scene smoothed out, framing a large, fluffy cumulous cloud against clear open sky, into which repeated bursts of streaking tracers disappeared. Matt watched for what seemed endless seconds as the scene banked slowly around the target. "You trying to shoot down that cloud?" he snickered annoyingly.

"I don't want to talk about it, okay?" Chuck shot back in irritated bluntness. "Now shut up. It's coming up right here."

The distinct silhouettes of two Focke-Wulf 190s moved into view, low in the camera angle maybe 300 yards out. "The one on the left, the element leader, that's him!" Chuck blurted. "On the first spurt, the wingman breaks off. I think he got into it with another Mustang."

The scene progressed as described, and the element leader banked in a defensive dive, with Chuck's fighter closing rapidly. At 150 yards, strikes clearly flashed across the 190's rear fuselage. But this was no novice in the cockpit. His evasion, quick and clever, dropped him out of view.

But the pursuer had the advantage of a dive from superior altitude, and the German was framed again quickly in the camera.

"Good recovery, buddy," Matt injected as the engagement quickened his pulse.

"Watch this, Matt. I think I got something on the first couple of bursts. No pilot in his right mind would keep kicking left rudder like that."

As their turn tightens, the Hun's left side was fully open for a classic deflection shot. Matt roared to life. "Look at that! Do you see that?"

"I know, I know!" Shilling shot back defensively. "But he pulls one on me right here. See, he noses straight down and spins in the opposite direction. A perfect 180! I couldn't slow down enough to follow him. When I did make the turn, I couldn't see a dadgum thing!"

"No, no, not that! Didn't you see the marking on the cowling? Carter, can you back that up, back to the turn?"

Slowly, the projector went into reverse, the German aircraft comically backing up from its dive to a two-thirds side view. "There! Stop it! Freeze that shot!" Matt commanded. In a single move he was on his feet, cupping his eyes against the glare. "See that crest? That's it! See, yellow with that dark center." He moved closer to the screen, squinting to the point of pain. "It's a knight's helmet. And there, the bar I saw, that's a Roman broadsword."

"Boy, you are obsessed with it, aren't you?" Chuck teased with Matt's own words.

"Every mission I looked for that plane. That's the devil who shot up the street in Ipswich, Chuck. I saw the pavement explode around a 4-year-old kid and his mother." Matt returned to his chair, his right fist grinding into the palm of his left hand. "Okay, buddy, you've got my full attention now."

Over and over, the two pilots replayed the engagement between Chuck and the German in slow motion, a frame at a time. "Watch his prop rotation, Matt. He's losing RPM."

"That's not exhaust, either. I'd say he's throwing oil. If that's the case, he didn't get far."

"Yeah, he went lower but I climbed out. That's why I couldn't find him when I turned."

"Right there, when he dives, how far are you off the deck?"

"Five hundred feet, maybe."

Look at the ground, Chuck. There's that little church with the damaged bell tower, the one we cross all the time. If he went down, then he's in that area somewhere."

"That's one giant long shot, Matt. He could have crashed and exploded or lucked up and made it back to his base."

"Well, he's too low to bail. He's got little or no power. I say he rode it in."

Matt spread a map of France across the table, pressing its stubborn creases into submission. "Okay, that church is along here just east of Rouen. When the Focke-Wulf made the dive the bell tower was on the left, so you were heading more or less northwest, maybe 340 degrees. It makes a 180 to the southeast, and I think he wasted much glide with a lot of turns. What's the glide rate of a Focke-Wulf, anyway?"

"It couldn't be much more than a P-47," Chuck guessed.

"He'd be under a thousand, and with little or no power, maybe one-and-a-half to three miles."

"What's all this leading up to, Matt? All I wanted was your opinion on my getting that 190."

"I think you got him; I just don't know how good. But we've got to find out for both our sakes. Does Herrington owe you any favors?"

Within the hour the two had corralled the unsuspecting major in his office. Seeing both grinning pilots descending on him at the same time, he fired up his trusty pipe and stuck it between frowning lips. "I don't like the looks of this," he grunted, waving them off with a flick of his hand. "Whatever it is, the answer is no!"

"Sir, all we ask is that you reserve judgment until you hear what we have to say," Matt began.

Herrington leaned back in the swivel chair and clasped his hands behind his head. "As long as you understand that I sit through this out of sheer curiosity."

"Thank you, sir." Matt reasoned that overt honesty might be the best course in the case of hair-brained schemes. He proceeded from the beginning: the strafing at Ipswich. By the time he explained Shilling's film, Herrington's elbows were on the desk, his head resting between his palms.

Assuming his superior's silence a license to continue, Matt spread the French map on the desk. "We've calculated about where the Focke-Wulf would have gone down. If we could get a pass for just a couple of days, we think we can find it."

Herrington's hands now rested on the chair arms, his blank eyes staring over the top of the desk. Shilling surmised it was now or never and decided to put what he considered the icing on the cake. "It would be great PR, sir, and another kill for the group. What do you say, sir?"

The major scanned the map briefly, stared up at the two lieutenants before him, and rose to his feet. Turning away, he rested a hand on the back of the swivel chair and the other on his hip. "I'm trying to run a fighter base here in the middle of a war. Two of my most capable pilots, whose judgment and integrity I've had rare occasion to question, suddenly put cold chills up my back. Shilling, do you have any idea how many flyers, on a given day, want to verify some kill they were cheated out of? We wouldn't have a squadron at full strength for a single mission."

Herrington turned back to the stooped shoulders hanging on his every word. "On top of that, you'd want to use group aircraft for unauthorized activities. And as for the PR, Uncle Sam forbid if anyone ever found out about such a venture. You understand my position, soldiers?"

"Yes, sir," Matt cleared his throat nervously. "I think we can see your point, sir."

"Good. Was there anything else, gentlemen?"

"No, sir," Shilling sighed. "I'm sorry if we were out of line."

The junior officers snapped their salutes to leave, which Herrington appeared not to notice. "However, in my desk drawer is a directive from Pine Tree, the last sentence of which says, 'Suggested locations will follow.' But in three weeks, nothing has followed." Herrington took a moment to put fire to the pipe, then continued. "A good soldier should use some initiative, don't you agree?"

Though missing the connection, the two flyers nodded their agreement. "I guess so, sir," Matt responded, unable to fully conceal his disappointment.

"You guess so, uh?" From a stack of papers on his desk, Herrington retrieved a single official page, which he proceeded to read. "Due to Allied advances in Europe, additional groups will be relocated to the Continent. COs will compile a list of airfields suitable to their operations in the event their group is so relocated, etc., etc., etc."

The major touched the stem of his pipe to a wall map of France and motioned the two lieutenants closer. "There are two old German bomber fields just south of Rouen. I need a couple of volunteers to check them out, see if the buildings can be used, if the runways are worth repairing, etc. Two... three days at the most. Do I have any takers?"

The two airmen restrained their euphoria at the turn of events, considering themselves well ahead of the game. Discretion demanded they play by the rules with no hint of presumption. "Yes, sir," Matt confirmed quickly. "We know the fields. We've strafed them."

"Very well," Herrington confirmed, suppressing a grin with evident difficulty. "But get this straight: it better be a darn good report. Map coordinates, at least four pages of commentary on each field, and snapshots. I'll clear the use of a hack for you. And Shilling, I want a medical clearance on you or no go."

A hundred feet from the Operations Building, exhilaration erupted. "Bingo!" Shilling whooped to the bewilderment of passing personnel.

"You know something?" Matt grinned, shaking his head in disbelief. "We've gotta do something special for that guy on Father's Day."

# CHAPTER 31

# Quest to France

O N A COOL, clear morning at 0800, a twin seat P-51 LH-L rose from Raydon's main runway under Matt Tower's steady hands. Within minutes the gray, choppy North Sea spread out below, and the Mustang took a familiar heading south toward Dieppe, a fishing village on the French coast.

Near Calais, where pilots instinctively grow cautious, Chuck's voice broke the silence. "This thing doesn't have any guns. You know that, don't you?"

"If you whisper, maybe they won't hear us. Just keep your eye out for Le Havre so we can sit this thing down."

A converted German fighter base east of the French coastal city served as an Allied air crossroads, its hard stands bristling with aircraft of every description. After settling neatly on the runway, LH-L followed the yellow-and-black checkered jeep along the taxi way, parading in review as it were, before a line of snooty B-25s that seemed to know the Mustang had no guns.

It took a good hour for the Slybird pilots to clear their orders and get a little cooperation. The indifferent young lieutenant they were saddled with took his royal time in processing their requests. "You guys are lucky. Engineers have motor pool priority," he yawned.

"Engineers?" Matt blinked "Is that what it says?"

"Flat out, in big letters." The more the first lieutenant thought about it, the more inquisitive he became. "Hey, you are engineers, aren't you?"

"Does a cat have fur?" Matt shot back authoritatively.

"Yeah, what kind of engineers?"

"Air Force," came the unwavering bluff.

The lieutenant's brow wrinkled as he struggled with the plausibility of their claim. His eyes searched the two flyers cautiously for any sign of weakness, finally coming to rest on Chuck's multiple bandages. "Yeah, how does an engineer get in that kind of shape?" he smarted off.

Having come this far, Shilling was not of a mind to give an inch of ground. "Occupational hazard. Rat attack."

"Rat attack?"

"Yeah," Chuck charged on. "Pine Tree sent us to a base to investigate complaints about big rats. Now I'm talking big rats. These little mothers were the size of a young pig."

Unable to keep a straight face, Matt turned away momentarily as Shilling measured out the rat's length with his hands. "They were about... so long. Pretty near took over the base. They'd holed up in a giant refuge dump during the day and came out at night to ravage the place."

Matt's throat and stomach were in knotted pain as he fought for control. And Chuck, Chuck never missed a beat, moving ever closer to the apprehensive lieutenant. "We had to design these huge double-snap traps to catch 'em with. I think they saw me doing it, because when I went out to check the traps one night a herd of 'em bounced me!"

"The rats bounced you?"

"Oh, yeah. It was awesome! Me, the garbage dump, and about 20 big rats. But I took four of 'em down with me before my partner here beat the others off with a discarded machine-gun barrel and pulled me to safety."

Matt had no choice but to move for the door. His face was red, restrained laughter whimpering through his lips, and his bladder was on the verge of letting him down. As the door closed behind him, he could still hear Chuck in full bloom.

"Don't come any closer to me!" the flustered lieutenant insisted as he stamped and processed the papers rapidly. "You guys are nuts, you know that?"

Motor pool was a different story. There, they were in the hands of another Sergeant McDuff, equally eager to enhance his position among commissioned officers. The jeep at their disposal, though of vintage service, easily accommodated the equipment and supplies required for the mission. Chuck sat in the passenger seat with map spread over his knees as Matt tended the wheel. "What's the name of the road there in case we see any markers?"

"Err... let's see here. There's some writing running along this line, says, 'Salete route,' whatever that means."

"Salete? Salete? That's a heck of a lot of help. We've got to watch the odometer, Chuck. It's about 25 miles to the Rouen turnoff."

Though hillier, the countryside was not unlike Raydon. Along the way, the two Americans passed the grotesque monuments of recent conflicts. Charred, rusting armor of ally and foe alike dotted the countryside, their impotent hulls surrendered to the vines and greenery of early spring. Did the children playing in the cockpit of a crashed German Stuka dive bomber have any concept of its earlier threat?

Men had died at the controls of these assorted vehicles, as had those trudging on foot beside them. In time, the shear vastness of it drew a web of solemnity over the two flyers. Preoccupied with the sight of an entire field of disabled war machines, Matt had slowed the jeep to a crawl. "Chuck, look at it! Could any of this be stuff we hit?"

"If you believe in the law of averages, yeah. It's mostly German." Chuck stood, braced against the windshield for a better look. "This is awesome, buddy, seeing it from down here."

They endured nearly an hour of the jeep before a probable intersection appeared. Unlike the map, it offered a third possible fork, and if one believed the sign, Le Havre, their point of departure, was straight ahead. Chuckling, Matt slapped Shilling playfully with his cap. "Another fine mess you've gotten us in, Stanley!"

Busy with the map, they paid scant attention to the shadow inching across their laps until it took human form. It was three feet to the carbine in the back seat. Matt's panicked efforts to retrieve the weapon must have been truly absurd to the old Frenchman watching them from atop the road embankment.

He proved to be quite harmless as the airmen came to their wits. Had he been what they feared, the carbine would never have made it into position. His clothing showed considerable wear, though its cut and style was that of a country gentleman. The black hat, with its wide brim curled up on one side, lent an old country dignity to the smiling white-bearded face. His hand rose slowly in a rigid French salute. "*Americain!*" he called excitedly. "*Bonjour, bonjour!*"

As the old man shuffled unsteadily down the bank, Chuck's hand retreated from his 45's holster, and Matt returned the rifle to the rear seat. "*Bonjour, monsieur,*" Matt responded, comfortable in the language at elementary level.

The response flattered the Frenchman, whetting his excitement as he kissed Chuck on both cheeks, then scurried around to repeat the greeting with Matt. "*Que dieu benisse L'America!*"

When the old man calmed a bit, standing with hat in hand and smiling down on his prize find, Matt motioned for help with the roads. *"Qui est la route de Rouen?"* he tried in what he knew must be pig French to the smiling native.

*"Oui, Rouen,"* he obliged tolerantly, pointing to the right fork. The torrent of enthusiastic French that followed passed Matt's ability at the speed of light.

"What the heck's he saying?" Chuck shrugged.

"I don't have the slightest idea. All I could get was something about a blue house, or blue something." Matt held up his hands to slow the Frenchman down. *"Merci, merci, nous devons continuer."*

With a nod of his head, the old man acknowledged their need to depart but continued to smile as his finger traced the brim of the hat in his hand.

*"Pardon, s'il vous plait. As-tu du chocolat pour mes enfants?"*

The Frenchman was overjoyed with his package of sweets, as were the Americans to escape their congenial captor. "I was impressed," Chuck conceded as the jeep gained speed. "You talked pretty good back there."

"Ha! It's evident you don't have a drop of French blood in your body. That was my language: French 101, 102 and 103 at the University of Georgia."

The blue something turned out to be a modest rooming house— the part that was still usable, that is. Rouen had its share of war damage, and the initiative of the populous to rebuild had but recently bloomed with the retreat of the hated Germans. Matt crossed his fingers as he approached the older woman busily wiping the desktop. In a town this size, surely someone would speak English.

*"Parlez-vous Anglais?"* he tried.

She looked up, but her hand continued to work. *"Non."* There was no change in expression and she did not try to communicate further, forcing Matt to try again.

*"Pouvez-vous obtenir un interprete?"*

She viewed the two airmen from head to toe, as though deciding on her degree of cooperation. There was a hardness in her eyes, and her muscular forearms, protruding from the casually rolled sleeves of a white blouse, suggested a lifetime of servitude. Matt smiled his warmest and said, *"S'il vous plait, merci."*

Reluctantly, she shuffled to the doorway of the café that adjoined the rooming house and motioned to one of the older spectacled men sitting at a small table. "Maurice!"

He took a moment to stack in neat order the three books he had been viewing and press the cork back into the wine bottle beside them. A warm smile spread the graying mustache under rosy weathered cheeks as he approached the Americans. He retained, in his senior years, sufficient evidence of a suave and courtly continental, much to the delight of character student Matt Tower. *"Bonsoir,* Captain, Lieutenant! I am Maurice Ravel. How may I help you?"

Equally delighted to find someone so versed in their language, the airmen explained their mission and the need for lodging that evening. Maurice, they learned, had for years been a school master in Rouen and had studied in the colleges at London. Lodging would be a simple matter because he now owned the rooming house, having purchased it from the previous owner at the height of German occupation.

The mission of the American airmen intrigued this Frenchman, who they found had risked his life against the invaders on more than one occasion. Among his assets was a fair command of the German language, which he made available to the French Underground on a regular basis. "I was too old to fight well," he chuckled. "But my ears were very good."

He would help them. After dinner the maps were spread out, with enlarged photos of the suspected crash area placed before Maurice. He quickly identified the small church, *"Qui, est le chapelle de Notre Dame.* Not so far away," he assured, tracing the road east from Rouen. "It was very lovely at one time, but the war, it brought much damage."

"Would you go with us, *Monsieur* Ravel?" Chuck inquired, knowing the value of a native guide. "We would pay you for your time, of course."

A smile wrinkled the exquisite mustache as Maurice rested his elbows on the table. "Please, it is just 'Maurice' to you, lieutenants." The more he studied the maps, the more his eyes twinkled. "That would be quite an adventure. Perhaps such a challenge would be good for an old man. But if I should go, I could accept no payment from you. There is much *Americain* blood in the soil of my country."

It was agreed, then. Maurice would accompany the flyers on their quest. The expectant trio, alternately swallowing and talking, savored the last of the bread, cheese, and wine as they planned the coming day's activities. It was an occasion that prompted excited, if not always welcomed, input from curious locals. Only the woman at the desk kept her distance through it all, her dark-brown eyes darting disdainfully at the gathering whenever voices rose in excitement.

Only when Maurice engaged her in conversation did her disposition mellow. Matt feared they had offended the woman in some way, perhaps with his pig French. "She seems unhappy about something, Maurice. Is it anything we've done or said?"

"No... no!" he assured apologetically. "Lillie? No, no. The war has taken its toll on all of us, Captain, some more than others. It cost her her husband."

Matt's troubled eyes shifted to the floor. "I... I didn't realize. I'm sorry. How did it happen?"

"The Boche, they killed him," Maurice sighed. "And two others."

"Why?"

"Come, I will show you. It is no secret now."

The Frenchman led his guests through the café's small kitchen to a narrow winding stairwell, its steps disappearing into the darkness below. "Take these candles," he directed. "The wiring is broken. There is no light down here."

The air grew cooler as they descended the creaky wooden steps to the cellar's dirt floor. Dim candlelight exposed some 20 or more feet of rustic plank walls, their length fitted with shelves and wine racks. A faint, sweet aroma lingered where one would expect the stuffy pungent odor of sunless earthen enclosure.

Maurice noted their amusement. "It has always smelled this way. Maybe it is the soil. Who knows?"

Matt surveyed the stored debris, his eyes coming to rest on an alcove door. "Where does that lead?"

"To the jardin patio. It was lovely before the war, but now it is blocked with rubble from the shelling. There were great hedges all around, an excellent way of escape."

"Escape?" Chuck's attention revived.

"*Oui.*" Maurice fit his candle into the crude holder on the wall and grabbed the end of a section of shelf. With his second tug it swung slowly out into the room, groaning under the pressure of ungreased hinging. "Come, bring your candles."

A small room, barely long enough for its two rough-hewn double-decker bunks, had been fashioned under the kitchen. There was no ceiling, only timbers supporting the kitchen floor from which a single wired bulb dangled. In the quiet of their discovery the Americans could hear muffled steps and voices from above. "Lillie's husband hid many Allied airmen here."

Reverently, the flyers stepped into the room, their candlelight becoming more brilliant in the confined quarters. Matt ran his hand over the bunk railings, finding them dotted with dozens of inscriptions beneath the dusty surfaces. "Look at this, Chuck. Names…. Dates. They're on the headboards, too."

Chuck moved in closer, tracing the lines with his finger. "*Robert Dalton, 452 Bm Group, 5 Jun. 44. George M. Ready, 447 Bm*

*Group, 7 Apr. 44. Tobby McLeod, 11 Group, 616 Squadron, RAF, 8 Mar. 1944. Tony Ramiro, gunner, 388 Bm Group, 28 Nov. 1943. Jack Parker, RAF, 17 Dec. 43."* The list went on, but Chuck reverently withdrew his hand.

The search for a 353rd Fighter Group name ended minutes later in a dry run. "I knew some of them," Maurice confided. "But their *escadrilles*, or how you say, squadrons... they run together in this old head. I am sorry. I do not remember if any were from yours."

After a time, the three men stepped out of the secret room and joined hands to push the shelving back in place. Maurice sighed as he dusted off his jacket. "The night Louis was killed, he took three of your airmen through that door to meet the Underground. They would go to Amiens, then down the *Somme Fleuve* to the coast. Fishermen would help get them to British patrol boats. Sometimes it did not work so well." Maurice lowered his head. "For that night it was the Gestapo, not the French Resistance, that met him."

# CHAPTER 32

# Hunting Expedition

**M**ONTHS AFTER THE D-Day invasion, American soldiers and equipment still provoked the curiosity of French locals. The Slybird airmen drew the inevitable crowd as they waited for Maurice outside the damaged chapel a few miles east of Rouen. He had done his best to disperse the gathering. But they returned, a few at a time, testing Matt's French as the children chanted, *"chocolat, chocolat!"*

Maurice returned as the crowd was reaching saturation level again. A lanky mid-teen lad, complete with beret, black vest over white shirt and brown knickers, strode along in the Frenchman's shadow. "Captain, Lieutenant, this is Emile, Emile Monet. He was one of my best students until he was needed to work the farm."

Emile shook hands awkwardly, a bit overwhelmed at his first encounter with American flyers. The youngster, they learned, was an aircraft enthusiast and spent leisure hours searching out crash sites in the countryside. He eagerly reviewed the map and photos spread on the hood of the jeep. Maurice translated that Emile knew well the possible crash area but did not recognize the Focke-Wulf markings. Many exploded, or burned and blistered their cowlings after crashing, he added.

Nonetheless, the young Frenchman relished the prospect of riding in an American jeep and becoming a willing member of the expanding search team. So began a grueling journey over narrow rutted roads and dirt paths as Maurice and Emile balanced atop duffle bags and boxed supplies in the rear seat.

*"Gauche, ici,"* the young guide directed. Matt anticipated the translation, edging the jeep into the meadow on their left, with a swastika tail visible above a thicket of stunted saplings. Within seconds the flyers knew they had the tail section of a bomber, utterly useless in their quest for a German fighter.

"Combatant," Matt smiled at the eager-to-please youngster. *"Un moteur."* Emile nodded that he understood now. They were only interested in fighters.

Within a quarter mile he was pointing again. "Combatant!"

This time the charred frame was that of an American P-47. The razorback cockpit and striped fuselage pegged it as a D-Day participant, but the group markings were illegible. Though another dry run, the airmen lingered a moment, soberly poking around every pilot's nightmare.

They must narrow the hunt for any prospect of success. "Emile," Matt said in growing urgency. *"Seulement Boche, un moteur, Boche."* He didn't want to discourage the boy, but they must stick to German aircraft.

There were good prospects between the jeep and the river, Emile assured the Americans, and rewarded them with 10 likely crashes within an hour. Many, ripped apart at impact, wasted additional time on scrap evaluation. Equally frustrating were area farmers, prone to remove parts and metal sheeting for projects around their farms.

Enthusiasm mellowed considerably by the time the foursome broke for lunch beneath the shade of a century-old tree. A postcard view of the river beyond the meadow did little to mend their spirits, except for Maurice, who graciously supplemented the GI rations with good French bread and wine.

From the stillness, an energetic songbird trilled a territorial warning to the diners picnicking below his towering perch. His claim was challenged periodically by feathered competitors in the distance, but he stood his ground well. Matt gazed at the pale blue sky blotched with billows of white cumulus clouds. Had he really been up there, bent on destruction, fighting perhaps above this very spot? Shaking his head at the contrast, he would bet on it.

"Chew, chew, swallow, guys," Chuck intervened. "If we're going to have a shot at this, we've got to stay busy."

Amid sighs and speculative comments, the search party loaded up and began its final sweep of the designated crash area. They had covered the east-to-west leg of the trip. Now, the return would take them parallel to the River Somme. It would be their last hope, for outside the specific map coordinates lay the whole of Normandy and the rest of Northern France.

At the edge of a small forest lay a pleasant surprise, the bellied-in fuselage of a Focke-Wulf 190, its wings ripped between the trees—otherwise intact except for pilfering. Its markings were exactly as those in Chuck's photographs. Adrenalin pumped the Americans around the crash like kids in a candy store as they called letters and numbers to each other.

Maurice and Emile watched the examination expectantly, but no amount of polishing would reveal the special crest on the fighter's cowling. "It's just not there!" Chuck snapped in disgust, his fist pounding frustration into the metal hulk.

"Maybe not," Matt replied, retrieving his camera. "But we're getting pictures of this one. I'd bet anything this is our guy's wingman. Remember when they split on you, somebody went after the other one. We can ask around. At least our coordinates were right." He patted the young guide's back encouragingly, *"Parfait, Emile! Focke-Wulfs, non-Messerschmitts, très bien?"*

So the afternoon went, zigzagging from one crash to another, using up the few hours remaining to them. Tomorrow the airfields must be inspected for Major Herrington, with little chance of renewing the Focke-Wulf quest. Feeding their anxiety further, the bridge, marking the search area's east boundary, beckoned a couple of miles ahead.

Then the sheep, a good 200 at least, ambling across the meadow to the river. Had the hill, which hid them from the driver, not slowed the jeep, there surely would have been mutton for dinner. The sudden braking catapulted the rear passengers to standing positions, wherein Maurice lost his hat while tumbling onto Chuck in the front seat. Young Emile, lighter of the two, slid smoothly over Matt, across the hood and into the herd. The sheep never looked up.

A squeaky jeep horn was a pitiful outlet for the trauma, but Matt applied it liberally. It accomplished nothing, except to attract the attending shepherds who, thinking it an enthusiastic greeting, waved gleefully. Emile, nursing deep lacerations to his dignity, pulled himself to standing position and rested his shaking body against the jeep. Matt recognized none of the emphatic verbiage streaking from the boy's lips but got the drift of it in Maurice's stern reproof.

The shepherds were hardly older than Emile but every bit as taken by the American men and machine. Matt tried to explain that they were in a hurry. *"Vite, mouvez les mouton!"* he barked, waving his arms, only to discover that dispersing a bonded herd of sheep was no simple task.

Maurice patted Matt on the shoulder, motioning for him to sit down. *"Captain, si vous plait,* perhaps they could be of assistance. Let me inquire about the crashes."

Maurice's explanation quickly won the youthful shepherds to the cause. They looked at the photographs intently, the youngest of their group tracing the outline of the subject fighter with his finger. The others could offer nothing of help, but the youngest revealed something they were not aware of.

"He says there is a plane in the river," Maurice interpreted. "When it is low, the tail can be seen." Doubt quickly arose, however, as the older boys made light of it, suggesting the youngest liked to hear himself talk.

Maurice spoke patiently with the lad and learned that his three companions were cousins recently come to help work the sheep. They knew little of the area. "It is true," Maurice continued to interrupt. "I saw it there," the boy insisted. His eyes dropped as he hesitated for a moment. "Monsieur Proust, he lives across the river. He saw the pilot swim ashore."

The two Americans stared at each other. They could continue to search the last unpromising leg of the trip or spend what was left of their time checking the claim of this youthful stranger. Something about his eyes, almost a pleading to be believed, finally convinced the flyers. "What the heck," Chuck quipped with a shrug. "It's a goose chase any way you cut it."

"More like a sheep chase from where I sit!" Matt laughed. "What's the kid's name, Maurice?"

"His name is Louis, Louis DuMont."

It took some time to get the herd on its way under charge of the cousins. They would return to assist as quickly as possible, hopefully with Louis' father and uncle. At the boy's direction, Matt turned the jeep toward the river, and the scavengers were at it again.

Louis indicated a spot about 500 feet upstream from the bridge. They walked along the River Somme bank, necks craning for any evidence of the aircraft. "When did he see it last?" Chuck inquired of the older Frenchman, since he spoke the native tongue better and faster.

"Several times. Again last month. Out from where we stand now."

Markings on the bank showed a river drop of at least two to three feet. "Enough," Louis said, "to show the tail." An occasional floating log or branch kept the searchers squinting and attentive as they walked the river's edge, but without result. Louis waded knee deep into the water, consumed in boyish disappointment. *"Nous devons avoir un bateau!"*

Chuck had been studying the expanse of water from further upstream and returned to the group with an unsettling disclosure. "Matt, this isn't the main body of the river. That's an island, not the other bank we're looking at. Is the plane in here or out in the main body of the river? If there's a plane at all."

Maurice questioned Louis intently, being certain the lad was sure of his sighting. "He is quite certain, lieutenants. This is the very place. There's a small *bateau* under the willows there. He will take you out to where it is."

There was little choice for the Americans but to board the flat-bottom boat with their eager guide and play out the plan. With Maurice and Emile on the bank as a point of reference, the boat made ever-widening circles as its passengers probed the water with their poles. Chuck lifted his for the others to see. "It's not five feet deep here, Matt. If it's down there we should have hit it by now."

Word spread in the countryside of strange goings-on at the river. Spectators perched on the bridge and a dozen or so along the bank. Among them, a rugged six-footer in his senior years marched through the gathering and confronted Maurice. Dark eyes, squinting below bushy white brows, reinforced the threat of the healthy walking stick he carried. *"Mon bateau!"* he demanded in boisterous French. "What are they doing with my *bateau*?"

Maurice secured his hat with one hand to look up at the

weathered face addressing him. A coarse dark-blue shirt and worn gray vest marked him as an area farmer. "They are searching for a German aircraft, *monsieur*. They are *Americain* airmen; they meant no harm."

The farmer turned to the three still circling on the water. "They are *Americains*? They fight the Boche?"

"*Qui!*" Maurice explained the flyers' mission, why they were searching and for what. "It would be a great help, *monsieur*, if they might continue to use your *bateau*."

The farmer moved to river's edge and circled the stick above his head. "*Americain!*" he shouted. "Come, you are wasting your time!"

It took little prompting for the despairing makeshift sailors to dock. Louis' eyes lit up as they drew near the shore. "*Bonsoir, Monsieur Proust*. See my *Americain* friends?"

Proust was polite, but only Louis at his side softened the farmer's face. "He is much like my son at that age. The Boche!" he paused to spit at the word. "They killed him on the beach at Dunkirk."

In the awkward silence that followed, Matt turned to Maurice. "Please, tell him we are sorry, that his son was a very brave man."

Proust acknowledged the condolences with a stern nod. "How many Boche have you killed, Captain?"

Matt was not ready for such a question, but the farmer's persistent eyes stared him down for an answer. Images of strafing runs and bursting locomotives crept from the closets of his mind. Flak towers, strikes on rows of hangars and enemy aircraft, columns of armor erupting before his guns joined the parade. "I don't know... exactly how many."

Chuck felt the pressure building and wrenched the conversation away from the farmer. "He's got seven confirmed in the air, fellow. And that could be my fifth," he added, pointing to the photographs on the jeep hood. "How many have you killed?"

Such rapid-fire translations taxed Maurice to the limit as he turned back to Proust for reply. *"Trois!"* the farmer growled, thrusting three fingers in Chuck's face. "We kill that pilot from the River Somme also!"

"You killed the pilot? How?"

"My friends see the German crash into the river. They come quickly surround him. Jacque so mad he put pitchfork into the German. The others did, too. I kept his Luger."

"So we've all killed Germans!" Shilling said, throwing his hands in the air. "But nobody wants to kill the rest of the day bragging about it. You called us off the river, right? We were wasting our time. Will you help us or not?"

For a tense moment the farmer looked from one flyer to the other, then turned to the jeep. *"Oui,* because you fight the Boche, Marcel will help." He held the photographs close to his eyes, then pointed to a distant hill near his home. "That day I saw many planes. The empty shells, they fell like rain. The Boche came from there, over the bridge. There was much smoke, but I could not hear the engine. In the river it drifted but a moment, then sank."

"Why can't we find it, then?" Shilling shrugged. "That's exactly where we looked."

"It is no longer there. A dam was built to repair the bridge. When it was removed, a great surge of water came through, and the plane was carried away. Come, I will show you."

Every move the Americans made drew a colorful trail of curious Frenchmen. Mothers, chatting socially, scolded rowdy children to keep them in check, vaguely aware of what brought them there in the first place. The men, a bit more enthralled, jockeyed for position as gamblers might at a cockfight. Such was the parade that followed the official party a few hundred feet to the bridge. There Marcel pointed to the protruding tail of an aircraft, its angled black swastika still discernible.

The River Somme's murky waters obscured the fighter's bulk, which had lodged against the bridge pilings. Chuck stared long and hopefully. "That's a Focke-Wulf tail, Matt."

A river recovery was unanticipated, throwing the original search party into great deliberation. Further complicating matters, it seemed every Frenchman in attendance possessed an "engineering degree." Tactfully weeding out the over-imaginative, they settled on roping the fighter's tail and pulling it with the jeep.

Competition then erupted among the farmers as to whose rope would be used. A plentiful supply of this rural necessity would be required, which appeased a large number of those offering it. It was fast becoming a community project, and within a short time coils of rope materialized on the site.

While the "engineers" fished from the bridge for the fighter, those on the bank worried how much pressure the tail could withstand. But that became a minor concern as repeated attempts to loop the aircraft failed. "The *bateau*," Maurice interpreted for young Emile, "we must row out to the fighter and put the rope on."

Due to his wounds Chuck would sit out the venture, leaving the work to Matt, Maurice, and Emile. The water was still too cold for comfortable swimming, and the three took every precaution to keep the boat steady. Maurice's pole anchored them at the site as the other two worked to attach the rope. It took some doing and a few chilly dips, but at last they had it well-secured.

With murmurings of encouragement, the ensemble watched intently as the jeep, with Matt at the wheel, took the slack out of the rope. Flexing with the growing pressure, it cut a straight line between the two war machines. The first foot or two brought a chorus of pre-mature shouts, but that was as much as the jeep could accomplish. When Matt let off the gas to apply the brake, the aircraft settled against the pilings, slowly dragging the jeep to its starting position.

Matt wiped his brow. "We've gotta have more manpower, Chuck. Tell them to get another rope on the tail, a long one."

Emile had the rope business down pretty well. So he, Maurice, and Louis the shepherd attached the second line. Like mind-readers, the onlookers took up positions along the additional rope and set themselves for the long pull. With three of the heavier men on the jeep hood for counterweight, the great effort was set.

"Wait a minute!" Chuck yelled, grabbing the camera. "We've got to get a shot of this, whether it works or not." The photo session pleased the volunteers immensely, their faces contorting into expressions of great effort.

The joint pull gained significant ground this time, but the pace was slow and grueling for those on the rope. Matt called for a break. This time the aircraft stayed in place. "Glad the gear's up on that thing. But it feels like a prop blade is digging in."

"If it's going to be three feet at a time, we'll kill these people, Matt," Chuck sighed.

Maurice approached, beaming broadly. "Lieutenants, look what has come! Someone has brought horses!"

Wedging through the crowd a lanky, grinning farmer presented a fine set of chestnut Belgians, in harness, to the floored Americans. "He says they are for the flyers who kill the Boche," Maurice reported.

Applause and cheers fanned a new enthusiasm through the throng as the stocky Belgians took their position at the end of the rope. Such selfless effort the flyers would never forget as they scanned the preposterous assemblage of men, women, and beasts awaiting the signal.

"*Tirer!*" Matt shouted, waving his arm. The plane was moving, its bulk displacing a shallow swell against the current. Men slipped in the mud, and those near the jeep were coated with spew from its churning tires. But the effort was sufficient. Ten minutes of determined struggle saw the great gray whale sufficiently beached.

Beneath a pasty coat of silt rested the unmistakable hulk of a Focke-Wulf 190. Matt left the jeep and ran, joining Chuck as he frantically wiped the fighter's cowling. The volunteers converged quietly, almost reverently, awaiting the verdict. Lower and lower

Chuck's rag cleared the cowling, until the ridge of a bright gold shield gleamed into view. "Bingo! Bingo!" Matt screamed, leaping into the air.

A startled first row of spectators stumbled back into the crowd, disrupting their ranks in gleeful laughter. "Bingo! Bingo!" they mimicked the strange term in a hilarious French accent. Close inspection revealed a perfect match of shield to photo, and as washing proceeded, other letters and markings eliminated all doubt.

Sweaty, caked in mud, chuckling like kids, the two Americans faced each other in victory. Matt shook his wingman's shoulder. "The best part, buddy, is now you're an ace!"

"Oh, no, buddy. The best part's you owe me three months' pay!" Matt froze in mid-gesture, his eyebrows rising a good inch. "Uh, huh," Chuck grinned. "Forgot about that one, didn't you? You made the deal in the officers club in front of the Lord and everybody."

It amused the Americans how every significant event led to a wine toast, a liquid that materialized as mysteriously as the rope. Celebration held sway, and it took another sheep herding miracle to assemble Maurice, the two lads, and the dozens of volunteers around the Focke-Wulf for a photo session.

Matt signaled for quiet and asked Maurice to interpret. "There is no way we could have accomplished this without your help. Many times we flew over this very spot. You were here, we were there, but with a common desire. Some memories we prefer to leave behind, but this show of friendship is not one of them. A simple thank-you seems totally inadequate, but we trust you will accept it. *Vive la France!*"

Lengthening shadows soon put a damper on the festivities, calling the Frenchmen home and to other responsibilities. Matt motioned to the *bateau* owner. *"Monsieur Proust, puis-je demander une question?"* The old Frenchman paused. *"Qui."*

Matt asked Maurice to help him because the conversation would likely be extended. *"Monsieur,* you said you kept the German's Luger. Would you consider selling it?"

The Frenchman shrugged. *"Pourquol voudriez-vous la Luger?"*

"Tell him that because it meant so much to Lieutenant Shilling to verify a kill that made him an ace, I would like to surprise him with a memento of the event."

Proust's head dropped slightly, but without change of expression. The unexpected request was clearly being weighed. *"Monsieur,* the German is gone. There's no other way to obtain a souvenir. It's our only chance."

*"Combien payeriez-vous?"* Matt picked that up pretty well and he thought hard for the best reply. "Since it's your property, *monsieur,* you should set the price."

It was a good choice of words, and it reflected in Proust's expression. "He says $50 in your currency," Maurice relayed.

"That's close to a half-month's pay. What about $25?"

Proust shook his head. Matt tried again. "Thirty-five dollars?"

"Forty," the Frenchman countered. Matt agreed. He knew the gun owner would go no lower. "Will you accept American?"

*"Oui. Papier!"*

As Proust left to get the pistol, Matt went quickly to his wallet. In his rush to negotiate, his memory of its contents was vague. Thirty-seven dollars stretched along the leather pouch. His heart sank, mind racing for an alternative.

The Frenchman returned with the trophy. The holster was intact with an extra clip, a really fine specimen. Matt dared not miss out on it. Holding his breath, he showed his wallet to Proust. *"Je n'ai que $37 avec moi. Auriez-vous confiance en moi pour obtenir les $3 restants?"*

The Frenchman's disappointment was evident. *"Non, je dois avoir de la valeur."*

Matt floundered. "Maurice, help me. I'm a sinking ship." Maurice approached Proust, and the two were rather engaged for several minutes. "Now, Captain, I have done all I can. Proust will accept your watch for the difference and keep the bullets in the pistol as his memento."

That was fine with Matt. He gladly would give up his GI watch for the cause. He emptied the pistol clip and handed the bullets to Proust. Since the Frenchman said nothing about those in the second clip, neither did Matt. *"Merci beaucoup, Monsieur Proust. Vous avez fait une grande gentillesse."* It took Matt but seconds to push the trophy deep into his duffle bag.

The soiled, scraggly American flyers spent as much time as possible bidding farewell before loading the jeep for Rouen. None of the Frenchmen would accept a gift or money for their labors. Being part of the day's quest appeared quite sufficient.

When morning came, bidding farewell to Maurice was far more difficult. In their two days and nights together, the old Frenchman had been a mainstay and something of a surrogate father to the young airmen. His knowledge of the area and empathy with the cause were indispensable.

They lingered with him until excuses for delay ran out. "Remember, you send Maurice copies of the photography. *Oui?*" He watched them to the turn at the end of the street, then headed back for the café. For some time to come, he would be the envy of his peers, with repetitive stories of the adventure. A contented smile curled beneath the bushy mustache.

# CHAPTER 33

# Late Victory

H ERRINGTON HAD STUCK his neck out for the Tower-Shilling adventure in France, and he was waiting expectantly as they climbed down from the twin-seat Mustang. "This better be good, gentlemen!"

"You've been living right, Major," Matt grinned. "The 350<sup>th</sup> has a brand-new ace! Wait till you see the pictures."

"Come on! I don't need any crap, Captain. I need one dang good airfield report."

"Well, you got both, sir," Chuck injected, determined to have his victory acknowledged. "There's no question we found the right aircraft."

Herrington shook his head in amazement. His keen discerning eyes failed to break the flyers down. "Shilling, you're one lucky son of a gun, you know that? That's two goodies in the same day. I hope my system can handle it."

"Try three. We found a second with the same unit markings. Hopefully, the guy who got that one is from our squadron. You'd have three, then. We are checking it out."

"Try this on for size. Wing says base relocations are on hold. The war's winding down, guys."

Their eyes met briefly, pensively. Though the idea had been joked around base, the sudden official acknowledgment churned up a strange dichotomy of butterflies and melancholy in the airmen. "Bittersweet, ain't it?" a grinning Herrington surmised. "But this will top it, flyboys. The old man's coming home."

Matt's hands settled on his hips. "You mean Colonel Duncan?"

"None other! Old Slybird evaded. He's been with the Dutch Underground."

Three days later, an AT-17 buzzed Raydon's main runway, circled, and deposited a beaming Glenn Duncan into one wild reunion with old comrades and young legend worshipers. No more fitting conclusion could have been devised for the testy little group's efforts in the war.

Euphoria reigned over the war-weary fighter base, with the main reception for Duncan sparking a rash of squadron celebrations. Shilling's ace and his remarkable adventure with Matt were no small part of the 350th's merriment. It would take 72 hours for composure to return.

Then on April 25, 1945, the 353rd Fighter Group sent its last offensive sortie of 47 Mustangs over the crumbling Nazi empire. As a fitting last gesture, they shepherded a contingency of RAF and American bombers to Hitler's once-fabled Berchtesgaden retreat. In the days that followed, inactivity—broken only by routine prescribed hours in the air—wore hard on base personnel. The camaraderie of warring men gradually gave way to speculation on the Group's future role in the war. The furlough list, favoring the longest tours of service, lengthened daily with Matt, Chuck, and Roger near the top.

"Camp Kilmer, New Jersey," Roger scoffed as he thumped the list. "Wonder if they still got those stinking tarpaper barracks."

"Anything that smells like the good old 48 is fine with me," Chuck sighed. "It seems like it's been five years." He watched Matt pacing, hands in pockets, eyes scanning the horizon reflectively. This last day would be especially difficult for his friend. "Come on, Matt, I'll go with you. I want to pick up a few souvenirs anyway. My mom collects those Wedgwood whatnots. Hope I can find some."

Roger stretched and shook his head. "Count me out, boys. There are three major-league poker games running around here, and I've gotta bankroll my law degree. Got the first three quarters knocked right here," he grinned, flashing a roll of bills for Chuck's benefit.

Chuck followed Matt to the service shuttle truck and climbed aboard. "Baker better be grateful his head's as hard as it is because somebody's gonna bash him for that wad."

For obvious reasons, Colchester had been Matt's recent choice for sojourns to town, so the changes in Ipswich over those few weeks amazed him. Imminent victory was firing up the populous to restore their city. People moved with a brisker gait, barricades and debris were greatly diminished, fresh paint adorned the trim of numerous buildings, and the streets were more crowded than he remembered.

Matt peered like a tourist through the taxi window at the quaint town bathed in rare bright sunshine. It was all very familiar, those roads leading to Falcon's Rest. It was funny, the feeling he had as he and Chuck left the taxi: all the apprehension of a first date. They asked the driver to wait, for in any case the visit would not be long.

Chuck followed Matt into the deserted lobby. "If she's here, buddy, I'll wait in the tearoom for you. Okay?"

Matt nodded and rang the bell on the registration desk. A familiar female face stepped briskly from the office. "Captain Tower, how nice to see you, sir!"

"It's nice to see you again too, Ann. Would Mrs. Davis be in by chance?"

"Oh, I'm sorry, sir, she's in London just now. Her mum and dad as well, I fear."

Relief mixed with disappointment as Matt didn't know which he actually preferred. "I just took the chance to come by. Do you have any word on Lieutenant Davis, how he's doing?"

"He's a bit better. They've upgraded his condition, but the doctors say it will be some time before they can really tell."

"Well, I'm leaving for the States in the morning and I wanted her to know. Would you have some stationery? I'd like to leave her a note."

Matt positioned the paper on the writing desk and studied it thoughtfully before his pen began forming words. For her sake he refrained from pouring his heart out, but he did not hide his affection. The rest was light, wishing her and her family well. He was compelled to leave his address and phone number back home, to what purpose he was not sure, for she certainly had them early on in their relationship. Anyway, it satisfied him somehow and more easily concluded the matter.

The three Americans had arrived at their duty station in Raydon by rail, and their departure was by like transportation. English punctuality was severely tested with the increased flow of troop trains, as was the patience of the three Americans crowded like cattle. But the direction of their train—the docks at Southampton—made it all quite bearable.

Beneath increasingly overcast skies, the tide dictated a late afternoon departure for the ship's passengers. Matt was soon stretching his last glimpse of England along the deck rail, for in a few hours they would be well into the Atlantic. He was still unsettled by the swiftness with which things had ground to a halt. The feeling of unfinished business haunted him, not just about Vivie, but the war itself. One became so geared to the frequent missions, the work at hand, it seemed odd that it had concluded so abruptly.

As night erased all vestiges of the British Isles, Matt was certain of one thing: he had been away from home long enough.

The pressure of Chuck's hand on his shoulder turned him away from the sea. "Hey, Matt. I hear you loud and clear, old buddy." They stood facing each other for the longest time as Chuck waited out his friend. "This old tub has a duckpin bowling alley and a pool table. What say we go hustle some guys, huh?"

# Epilogue

AFTER THE ALLIES defeated Nazi Germany in 1945, elements of the 353$^{rd}$ Fighter Group began preparation for a role in the Pacific war. The atomic attacks on Japan relieved the Group from that assignment and it returned to the United States to await any future mission. The 353$^{rd}$ received numerous unit citations, its airmen among those highly decorated in the U.S. Army's Mighty 8$^{th}$ Air Force.

## Notable Characters

**Bailey,** Lieutenant Colonel William B. – Deputy commanding officer, 353$^{rd}$ Fighter Group.

**Baker,** Lieutenant Roger – Matt Tower's 350$^{th}$ Fighter Squadron rough-edged pilot friend.

**Blickenstaff,** Lieutenant Colonel Wayne – A 350$^{th}$ Fighter Squadron leader.

**Brooks,** Bobby – English youngster working at Falcon's Rest.

**Burgess,** Colonel Arthur – Intelligence officer with MI5, the British security service.

**Carter,** Elizabeth "Elly" Tower – Matt Tower's older sister and Susan Anna Carter's mother.

**Carter,** Leslie (Captain) – Attorney, Elly's husband, Matt's brother-in-law.

**Carter,** Susan Anna – Elly's young daughter and Matt's niece.

**Cobbs,** Flight Lieutenant William – Royal Air Force training officer.

**Coleman,** Brigadier General Evan – Attended Lord Havely's Allied High Command gathering.

**Davis,** Flight Lieutenant John – Vivian Moore Davis' RAF pilot husband.

**Davis,** Vivian "Vivie" Moore – Matt Tower's English love interest.

**Dumont,** Louis – French boy who helps locate the downed German fighter in France.

**Duncan,** Colonel Glenn E. – 353$^{rd}$ Fighter Group's commanding officer.

**Ellison,** Dorothy "Dottie" – Ginger's mother.

**Ellison,** Virginia "Ginger" – Matt's college sweetheart.

**Ellison,** Randolph – Ginger's father, an Augusta attorney.

**Foxx,** Technical Sergeant Milton J. "Milt-the-Stilt" – Matt's fighter crew chief.

**Gallup,** Major Kenneth W. – 350$^{th}$ Fighter Squadron leader.

**Hardy,** Ruth – Vivian Davis' frisky friend, known to Matt as "the vamp."

**Havely,** Lord William "Willie" – Host of the Allied High Command party and outdoor hunt at his country estate.

**Havely,** Lady Martha – Lord Havely's patient wife.

**Haw-Haw,** Lord – British traitor who taunts Allied airmen on the radio from Germany.

**Herrington,** Major Stanley "Stan" – Matt's tolerant deputy squadron leader.

**Little,** Margaret – Office manager, Tower Industrial & Mill Supply Company.

**McDuff,** Master Sergeant Edward "Eddie" – Raydon base gold-bricker who works logistical miracles.

**Minska,** Hanna – German Jewish Holocaust escapee living in Ipswich.

**Monet,** Emile – French teen who helps locate the downed German fighter in France.

**Moore,** Major Robert – Vivie's father, owner of Falcon's Rest, and undercover officer with MI5, Britain's counter-espionage service.

**Moore,** Etta – Vivie's mother, who co-owns and serves as hostess at Falcon's Rest.

**Newhart,** Major Dewey – squadron leader lost in action on June 12, 1944.

**Pearson,** Mary – RAF canteen manager, friend of the Moores.

**Pine,** Joe – Augusta community character who warns of the Georgia city's deepening political corruption and methodical economic suppression.

**Proust,** Marcel – Lends boat for downed German fighter search in the French River Somme.

**Ravel,** Maurice – Frenchman who assists Matt and Chuck as guide and translator during hunt for downed German fighter.

**Rimerman,** Lieutenant Colonel Ben – Operations officer and alternate base commander.

**Shilling,** First Lieutenant Charles "Chuck" – Fellow pilot and Matt's best friend.

**Smaragdis,** Captain John – Matt's good friend and alternate flight leader.

**Stockton,** Lieutenant Barry – Roger Baker's wingman.

**Taylor,** Ann – Davy Taylor's mother, friend of the Moores, attends funeral for Etta Moore's half-sister.

**Taylor,** Davey – Ann Taylor's 4-year-old son, injured in German fighter attack in Ipswich.

**Thomas,** Colonel Lawrence M., Commanding Officer, 453$^{rd}$ Bomber Group. Attends Havely party.

**Tower,** Eleanor M. – Matt's mother.

**Tower** Jr., Captain Gerald Mattlowe "Matt" – War hero from Augusta, Georgia, and the novel's leading character.

**Tower** Sr., Gerald Mattlowe – Matt's father and president of Tower Industrial & Mill Supply in Augusta.

**Walldon,** David – Cecil and Katherine Walldon's prankster son.

**Walldon,** Katherine – Vivie's godmother and Cecil's wife.

**Walldon,** Cecil – Katherine's husband and cousin to Vivie's mother.

**Wheeler,** Reverend Captain Stirling F. – Raydon base chaplain.

**Woodbury,** Brigadier General Murray – 8$^{th}$ Air Force fighter wing commander.

# ABOUT THE AUTHOR

A S A YOUNGSTER, author Charles W. Bowen III of Augusta, Georgia, spent much of his free time tuned to developing news from the front lines of World War II. He listened by the radio when newscasts covered the war. He read Augusta's daily newspapers, regularly questioning his parents and people involved in the city's Civil Defense. Bowen recalls vividly the air-raid drills, gun emplacements around airfields and public facilities, and bombing practice over the city at night with searchlights scanning the sky. It was Augusta's two pilot training airfields that fueled the author's love for aviation and led him to obtain a pilot's license. Mental and written notes of the era serve him to this day.

Bowen is a frequent writer and speaker on events of World War II, the Civil War, and Augusta's 1940s-1970s struggles to escape decades of political and law-enforcement corruption. He attended public schools in Richmond County and graduated from Academy of Richmond County as an ROTC first lieutenant. University of Georgia studies contributed to a bachelor's degree in economics with a minor in journalism from Augusta College.

After college, Bowen joined the family retail and wholesale business, serving in various management areas over the years. He expanded into real estate and commercial investments in partnership with George Bowen, his brother and best friend.

A family man since he married high school sweetheart Barbara Pruitt in 1958, the author has lived in Augusta his entire life. His extended family includes a daughter, son, three granddaughters, a great-grandson and two great-granddaughters—all in the Augusta area.

*Paladin: The Story of Augusta's Fighter Ace—The Wars of Matt Tower Book 1* is the author's first novel and required significant historical research over many years. Bowen is nearing completion of a second novel in the Matt Tower series, *Thorns in the Garden City,* about political, law enforcement, and economic corruption in post-World War II Augusta. It extends and concludes the story begun in *Paladin.* His third novel, also in the works, takes a closer look at the efforts of men and women who did what the times required in wartime Germany and England.